THE WEA

"I'm putting together d
Kryx said.

"We all have dossiers on them," Barthol said. "If you figure out how to have *them* instead of their dossiers, let me know." As a commander of the Eubian Space Command, Barthol was always looking for ways to acquire a Ruby. Unfortunately, they were prodigiously well protected.

"Look at this one." Kryx flicked his thumb through the holo of a man with red curls streaked by gold. A full holo appeared, two handspans high, of the man standing with his thumbs hooked into his belt. He had on a sleeveless black shirt, black leather pants with silver studs, and a chain belt. His hair spilled down his neck, unruly and luxuriant.

"Who is that?" Barthol asked. "Some thug out of a porn holovid?"

Kryx smiled ever so slightly. "That, my dear Uncle, is the Ruby Dynasty's greatest weakness."

"What, their association with surly youths of questionable character?" Barthol gave a deliberately crude laugh. "And here I thought Kelric Skolia preferred women."

"You know this fellow." Kryx's mouth quirked upward, which from a Highton was an expression of immense glee. "He's a Ruby prince. Also something called a 'holo-rock singer.' "

"Holo-what?"

"Holo-rock," Kryx said. "He makes noise and calls it singing."

"What makes you consider this one in particular?" Barthol asked.

"He's the renegade." A glint came into Kryx's eyes. "And renegades are always a weakness."

BAEN BOOKS by CATHERINE ASARO

Sunrise Alley
Alpha

THE SAGA OF THE SKOLIAN EMPIRE
The Ruby Dice
Diamond Star
Carnelians

Carnelians

CATHERINE ASARO

CARNELIANS

This is a work of fiction. All the characters and events portrayed in this book are fictional, and any resemblance to real people or incidents is purely coincidental.

A Baen Books Original

Baen Publishing Enterprises
P.O. Box 1403
Riverdale, NY 10471
www.baen.com

ISBN: 978-1-4516-3849-3

Cover art by David Mattingly

First Baen paperback printing, November 2012

Library of Congress Control Number: 2011026706

Distributed by Simon & Schuster
1230 Avenue of the Americas
New York, NY 10020

Pages by Joy Freeman (www.pagesbyjoy.com)
Printed in the United States of America

To Kate Dolan

For her calm insights,

For helping me keep my head on straight,

And for her friendship

Acknowledgements

My thanks to the following people for their invaluable input: for their great (and fast!) comments on the full manuscript: Aly Parsons and Kate Dolan. To Aly's Writing Group for their insightful critique of scenes: Aly Parsons, with Al Carroll, Bob Chase, Charles Gannon, John Hemry, J. G. Huckenpöhler, Simcha Kuritzky, Michael LaViolette, Ed Lerner, Bud Sparhawk, and Connie Warner. I've been fortunate to work with a great group of people at Baen Books (Simon & Schuster): to my publisher and editor, Toni Weisskopf; to Laura Haywood-Cory, Hank Davis, Marla Anspan, Jim Minz, Danielle Turner, Alethea Kontis, Joy Freeman, Becky Catchings, and all the other fine people who did such a fine job making this book possible. My thanks to my excellent agent, Eleanor Wood, of Spectrum Literary Agency; and my publicist Binnie Braunstein for her enthusiasm and hard work on my behalf.

I would like to thank the musicians who collaborated with me to turn the book *Diamond Star* into a rock opera, including my song "Carnelians Finale" that also appears in this book. On the CD by the rock band Point Valid and myself, the song is sung by Michael Belinkie, arranged by David Dalrymple, with Dave Nachodsky on bass, Joe Rinaolo on guitar, and Adam Leve on drums. My thanks to Janis Ian for her advice on the album, and to my vocal coach Becky Ocampo for her work with me.

A heartfelt thanks to the shining lights in my life, my husband John Cannizzo and our daughter Cathy, for their love and support.

Author's note: The song "Carnelians Finale" is available on the CD *Diamond Star,* which can be downloaded from iTunes, CD Baby at www.cdbaby.com/cd/pointvalidca, at most other online vendors who sell music selections, and also from

Starflight Music
PO Box 4
Simpsonville, MD 21150

Prologue

It was one of the most effective weapons known.

It didn't explode. It shot no projectiles. It didn't spread chemical, biological, or physical poison. It created no flames or shrapnel.

It could bring down empires.

It was . . .

A song.

You dehumanize us
Your critics, they all died
You answered defiance
With massive genocide
—From "Carnelians Finale"

I

The Lost Time

"I'm already the most hated man in the universe," Jaibriol said. "Tell me something new."

"Damn it, Jaibriol," Corbal said. He considered himself a man of great patience, but he was close to his limit. He and Jaibriol were standing on a balcony of the emperor's winter palace overlooking the mountains. Mist blurred the forest that carpeted the soaring peaks.

"Be serious," Corbal told him.

"I am serious." Jaibriol rested his hands on the railing and gazed at the fog-draped landscape. A breeze blew back the glittering black hair from his profile, accenting his straight nose and high cheekbones. He had been born with phenomenal good looks, but Corbal had no doubt the young man had also enhanced his appearance. Anything to survive. As Emperor of the Eubian Concord, Jaibriol had made himself what everyone expected to see. At twenty-eight, he was still the youngest emperor in the empire's history, and he had already been on the throne for eleven years. How Jaibriol had survived would make a fascinating study on the strategic choices of a brilliant but painfully naïve youth. One of his wisest decisions, of course, had been to turn to his elderly cousin Corbal as an advisor. Smart boy.

Of course there was also the empress, the gods take her forsaken soul. Perhaps Jaibriol's savviest decision had been to marry the most powerful—and ruthless—woman among the Eubian Aristos. He had given her a reason to protect his handsome hide instead of tearing it to metaphorical shreds in her political maneuvering.

"You could enslave a trillion Skolians, and the Aristos would praise you," Corbal said. "But now that you've signed a peace treaty, everyone hates you." At least, Jaibriol's own people hated him for that reason. The Skolians hated him because he ruled the empire that wanted to conquer their enticingly lucrative civilization.

"It's done, Corbal. We're going to have peace." Jaibriol glanced at him. "Whether the Aristos want it or not."

"No one wants it but you."

"Imperator Skolia does."

"Like hell." Corbal didn't believe for one moment that the military dictator of the Skolian Imperialate had any desire for peace. "Gods only know his motives. No, I take that back. His motives are obvious. He knows we'll subjugate his little Imperialate. That's the only reason he signed the treaty."

"*Little?*" Jaibriol gave him an incredulous look. "One trillion people is 'little'?"

"Compared to us." They weren't really arguing

about the Imperialate. No, this debate was a distraction from the real battle.

Imperator Skolia was Jaibriol's uncle.

Of course Jaibriol could never speak the truth, that his mother came from the dynasty that ruled their enemies. He would forever give lip service to the pretty lie that his mother had been a Eubian empress hidden away with her son to protect them against assassins. If the truth ever became known—that Jaibriol was also an heir to the throne of their enemies—the Aristos would turn on him with a vengeance.

Corbal had no wish to use that secret against Jaibriol. The emperor knew about too many of Corbal's hidden skeletons. Nor did Corbal want the throne. Jaibriol's wife had yet to produce an heir, which meant that as Jaibriol's closest kin, Corbal was next in line. However, he preferred to wield his influence from the shadows. Staying off the throne kept him from becoming a target, especially now with Jaibriol's infernal peace treaty, which had to be the most unpopular "success" Corbal had ever seen. So many people wanted the emperor destroyed, Corbal wondered how the boy slept at all. Then again, Jaibriol had the courage to sleep with his gorgeous barracuda of a wife. Gods only knew how he survived that trauma.

"It doesn't matter what the rest of the universe thinks," Jaibriol told him. "We're going to trade goods with the Skolians instead of bombs."

"And when I'm on the throne, after some assassin puts you out of your misery," Corbal said sourly, "I'm sure Imperator Skolia will be just as pleased to deal with me as with you." After all, the Imperator had no idea he was Jaibriol's uncle.

"I'm going to survive." Jaibriol regarded him steadily. "I may go down in history as the most despised man ever to live, but I'll be damned if I'll die just to further the rest of humanity's desire to wipe itself out in warfare."

"Very noble," Corbal said. "Very dramatic. Very stupid. I thought you had outgrown this dream of yours to save humanity from itself."

"The day I outgrow my dream for peace," Jaibriol said, "will be the day I stop living."

"I know," Corbal said softly. Jaibriol had made up his damn mind long ago. Perhaps in a hidden recess of Corbal's subconscious, he even shared the dream. But this peace would never succeed. In the end, it would tear apart both empires, from within and without.

Aliana Miller Azina's happy world existed only in her mind. Reality was the fist of her stepfather Caul, the snarl of his mouth, the red stare of his too-small eyes. He looked like an Aristo, but he had never come close to that life. If his father was an Aristo, that exalted being had never deigned to acknowledge his illegitimate son; like everyone else Aliana knew, Caul wore the collar and wrist guards of a taskmaker slave. But those Aristo red eyes gave Caul an authority among the rest of the vermin here in the techmech slums, a reminder that Caul descended from a deity rather than crawling out from under a rock like everyone else.

Today Caul was yelling. Again. Fury turned his alcohol-swollen face even redder. Aliana stood pressed against the wall of the module where they lived. For most of the sixteen years of her life, she had tried to melt away when he screamed. It never helped. He would stop yelling when he started hitting. She hated the way his mouth moved, big and ugly, hated his crooked teeth, hated every scar and crease on his face. His black hair stuck up, glinting in the light coming through the window behind him, that window up so high.

Except today she was looking *over* his head. Today, she could see out of the window.

"You're a stupid girl," Caul shouted at her. "I told you never to be late."

I wasn't late, she thought. She said nothing. It would only make it worse.

"You can't do anything right," he said. "I work, work, work, and you take advantage of me, like your slut of a mother, who couldn't even give me my own child. No, I have to be happy with stupid you, the child of who knows what jack-ass idiot." He was shouting so loud, every one of their neighbors in the crammed module yard could probably hear. Not that they hadn't heard it before. "Don't ever claim I'm your father," he went on. "I'll deny it."

I'd rather die than have you as my father, she thought.

Caul stepped toward her, his fists balling at his sides. "You make me do this."

Aliana was gritting her teeth so hard, it felt like they would break. It hadn't been this bad while her mother had lived. Sweet and gentle, she had done her best to protect Aliana. But that meant she had taken the full brunt of Caul's anger. He had beaten her so many times that Aliana's mother had finally given up and died when Aliana was five years old.

He came closer, shouting, incomprehensible, as if he were going in slow motion. His mouth opened and closed, and her ears rang with the noise. The air seemed too thick, like invisible syrup. He raised his fist, slow, slow, slow. Then it began to descend.

Something snapped in Aliana, something pulled too far, for too many years. It broke. Released. Today she did the forbidden. Her arm came up as his came down, and she caught his wrist. Her fingers, which had once been so small, now closed all the way around him. Her arm stiffened as she resisted the force of his swing, her muscles hardened by the years she had worked in the mesh factory, doing heavy labor the broken robots could no longer perform.

His fist stopped coming down.

Time snapped back to normal. In this unreal moment, she didn't even feel the effort as she shoved him. He flew away from her, his face a mask of shock as he crashed to the floor. Her breathing rasped in the cold air as she strode toward him. He scrambled to his feet, his features so contorted with rage, she wondered that his heart didn't explode in his chest.

"You *bitch!*" he screamed, swinging at her. "You'll pay—"

He broke off as she ducked the blow and rammed her fist into his stomach. She had trouble aiming her blows, but even with her sloppy fighting, she hardly had to work. She slammed him into the opposite wall and pinned him there, holding him in place when he tried to throw her off. She looked down, *down at him,* and pounded her fist into his stomach, as he had done to her a thousand times, again and again and—

And she stopped.

Aliana drew in a deep breath, her fist poised in the air, her arm shaking with her drive to strike. She held it there, held it still, breathing hard.

"I'm not you." She forced herself to lower her arm. "I don't hit unless I need to."

He stared at her, his fury replaced by an emotion she had never before seen from him, not toward her.

Fear.

"I'm going to leave," she said. "Know this, you slime-slug bastard. You won't try to stop me, you won't come after me, and you won't *ever* hit me again. If you try, I'll kill you. Do you understand?"

He stared at her, his mouth open. "You've gone crazy."

"Answer me." She never once raised her voice. He had done enough of that for both of them. For a lifetime. "Now."

"Why would I come after you?" he snarled. "You're an ugly moron of a girl. No one wants you. *No one.* Not me, and not your pitiful excuse of a mother who wanted to *die* rather than raise you."

She shoved him away from her. "Fuck you."

Then Aliana left the dilapidated module that had been her home for sixteen years. Rage filled her, bitterness, and a deep-stabbing hurt she would never show. But today she felt a new emotion.

Triumph.

II

The Players

Kelric Skolia, Imperator of Skolia, looked like the military dictator so many people believed him to be. Almost seven feet tall, with a massive physique and close-cropped hair, he seemed to fill the room. His size, his metallic appearance, his silences, all of it frightened everyone—except his doctor, who wasn't the least intimidated, which was a damn inconvenience, because right now he had a raging headache, and his diminutive, sweet-faced tormenter wasn't helping.

"I prescribe sleep," Doctor Kai Sashia told him. "You may have heard of the practice? Many people do it. Several trillion, in fact."

Kelric scowled at her. She persisted in looking innocuous, with her large brown eyes.

"Rest," she told him firmly. "Or you'll kill yourself."

"I'm fine. I just need some nanomeds for my head." There had to be some chemical concoction she could inject him with that would conquer whatever was making his head hurt.

"For your brain?" she asked sweetly. "To help you remember what sleep means?"

"Enough!" He crossed his massive arms.

"Don't give me that 'I'm an implacable monolith' stare," she said. "It may freeze everyone else, but not me. I mean it, Imperator Skolia. You have to stop pushing yourself, or you'll end up with a lot worse than a sore head."

He stood up, towering over her. "I'll go see Colonel Drayson in the infirmary."

"Oh, sit down." Sashia waved her small hand at him. "Stop being cranky." She went to a counter along the wall and touched a holoscreen there.

Exasperated, Kelric sat down.

"I'll update the nanomeds in your body and reset their picowebs." She brought up a display of holos above the screen. They showed brightly colored macromolecules rotating in space: red, blue, white, green, yellow. Reading whatever had appeared on the screen below them, she added, "You're past due for having the system checked. When was your last physical?"

"I don't know." Colonel Drayson, his other doctor, always insisted on doing his routine physicals. Another damn time sink, but the government allowed the military to order even their highest commander to have such exams to ensure he stayed functional. Though he supposed he should think "healthy," rather than "functional." Despite what people believed, he wasn't a mechanical man.

"Ask Drayson," he said.

"I will," she said, intent on her displays. "Here we are." She tapped the counter, and a shallow drawer slid out from under the screen. After removing a medgun from it, she turned to him, weapon in hand. "You have to lie down."

Kelric stayed sitting. "That better not have some sleep potion in it."

"Oh, honestly." She sighed, her rosy face framed by curls. How anyone so infernal could persist in looking so harmless, he had no idea. "It contains the updated species for your outdated meds. Now lie down, Imperator Skolia. That way, they can disperse more evenly through your body."

Kelric lay down, wishing he was somewhere else. He didn't like feeling vulnerable this way. Yes, it was ludicrous. She was half his weight and two feet smaller than him. But gods knew, she could have fended off a Balzarian volcanic-devil.

"Well look at that," Sashia said. "Is that actually a smile?"

"Just inject me," he growled.

She set the gun's muzzle against his neck. "You don't fool me. You're nowhere near as nefarious as you'd like people to think."

"When did I ever say I wanted people to think I was nefarious?"

Sashia pressed a thumb-pad on the gun, and the device hissed. "There. All done."

"You didn't answer my question." It bothered him that she thought he wanted to hide his better qualities from people.

"You don't know you want them to think it."

"And you do?" Lowering his mental barriers, he probed at her mind as she turned and stowed the gun back in its drawer. Her mood felt calm. She didn't seem perturbed by his presence. If anything, she enjoyed it.

He picked up more from her surface thoughts than he usually gathered from someone who wasn't a psion. She believed he used his intimidating presence as a shield against his grief over the devastation that his family and his people had suffered at the hands of the Eubian Traders. He hid his gentleness because he felt he could show no weakness in protecting the Skolian Imperialate.

Kelric sat up, rubbing his stiff neck. Maybe he should go to Drayson more in the future; the colonel was nowhere near as perceptive. Then again, maybe that was why he always seemed to end up here. Sashia could treat the intangible injuries within him that had no physical presence.

His head was aching even more, though, from his mental probe. He raised his mental barriers, and his sense of her mind retreated to manageable proportions.

"Anything else?" he asked.

She turned back to him. "Not for now."

He regarded her warily. "Why for now?"

"Because if you don't rest, you'll be back." She waved her hand at him. "Now go."

With relief, he slid off the bed. "Thanks."

"Remember what I said." She waggled her finger at him. "Sleep."

He nodded and headed for the door, his steps long in the two-thirds gravity of the space station. He liked the lower gravity, not only because of his massive size, but also because it was easier on his limp. He had broken his legs when he crashed on the planet Coba decades ago. His doctors had repaired the damage, but last year an assassination attempt had shattered his right leg anew. He had more biomech in the limb now than real bone, but at least he could walk.

He paused at the doorway and looked back at Sashia. "Have you finished analyzing the results from your examination of my wife and my children?"

Her smile faded. "Yes. All three of them."

"Are they all right?"

"Your wife and daughter are fine." She spoke carefully. "Your son has lived his entire life on Coba, right? It's a world where much of the food and water is toxic to him."

He didn't want to hear what he knew was coming. "But he's so healthy."

"Now, yes."

"His mother's DNA is from the colonists who settled the world Coba." Kelric fought back his fear. "It adapts them to deal with the biosphere."

"That helps," Sashia said. "And he told me that he follows the same precautions you took when you lived there: boiling his water, keeping a special diet. But it's still a strain for his body."

"My daughter lives there, too. And she's fine."

"Their genetic make-up is different. Her physiology is better suited to the planet." Sashia came over to him. "I wish I had better news. But your son has lived twenty-eight years on a world that can poison his body. It nearly killed you, and you were only there eighteen years."

"He seems to be doing so well." Kelric couldn't believe how calm he sounded. He wanted to shout, as if that could make this go away. His son would never willingly leave Coba.

"Yes, he is," Sashia said. "I don't know how long that will last."

"He doesn't like it here." Kelric forced out the words. "He was glad to go back home."

"He doesn't have to live here," Sashia said. "Many places exist where his health wouldn't be jeopardized."

Kelric almost never spoke to anyone about the eighteen years he had spent imprisoned on Coba. But for his son's sake, he would do anything. "You have to understand. He's lived his entire life in seclusion. He never sees or speaks to anyone except the queen who rules his estate and the few men in his Quis circle." He floundered with the words. How did he explain the dice game of Quis that dominated his son's existence? He didn't know if someone who had lived a normal life could understand what it meant to play a game that defined a civilization. Every woman, man, and child on Coba played Quis every day of their lives. It created the entire political, social, intellectual, economic, and cultural structure of the colony there. Those who controlled the Quis, controlled the civilization. His son Jimorla was a master at the game. Someday, he would be a legend.

If he survived.

"Jimorla has appeared in public only once," Kelric said. "When I presented him as my son to the Imperialate last year. He can't operate in normal society. He doesn't *want* to. It would kill him to leave Coba."

Sashia's gaze never wavered. "It will kill him to stay there."

"Surely you can do something. Give him nanomeds to help his body deal with the toxins."

"I've given him a specialized replicating species," she said. "They'll help. But you had those, too. If the meds started to mutate within your body, they will with him, too."

"I was injured when I crashed on Coba," Kelric

said. "No one there knew our medicine. They didn't even believe I had meds in my body. I certainly didn't have a doctor who could monitor and update them." He lifted his hands, then let them drop. "Sashia, surely you can do something. If my daughter can deal with Coba, it must be possible for my son."

She spoke carefully. "They don't have the same mother, do they?"

Well, that was a minefield. "No, they don't."

"The DNA your daughter inherited from her mother helps counteract the problems better."

Kelric knew Sashia wanted to know more. He couldn't talk about it, beyond what she needed to help his children. He had been married against his will to his son's mother, a desert queen on Coba, then forced by political upheavals to leave her before his son's birth. His daughter's mother had died in childbirth, drowning him in grief, and her political foes had taken his daughter. He had fallen in love with his current wife, Ixpar Karn, the highest ruler on Coba—and it had started a war.

It all came from Quis.

The "game" had fascinated him from the day he first played it. His ability had evolved until he achieved a level higher than any other player in Coban history. The Cobans had held him against his will for eighteen years, and in the end, their peaceful culture had exploded into war because his anger had saturated their dice game. Coba had recovered in the decade since, in a large part due to Ixpar's rule, but she was needed there and couldn't stay with him. He had hoped his daughter would attend school here, but that hadn't worked out; although his children had visited him, they had already gone home, and Ixpar would soon follow. He had no wish to talk about his history there. It was too private.

He said only, "If you know why my daughter is all right, can't you apply that to my son?"

"It's not that simple." Sashia pushed her hand through her hair. "I'll see what I can do. But I'll have to see him regularly, at least two or three times a year, to monitor his health."

"It can be arranged," Kelric said quickly, before she came up with more protests.

Her gaze turned steely. "I'm assuming he's more cooperative than his father."

Kelric smiled. "I can't make any guarantees."

"Oh, go." She tried to look stern, but she smiled instead. "Go talk to him."

"All right. I will." With no more fuss, he left her office.

His head had stopped aching.

"What we need," Kryx Iquar said, "is to assassinate the whole lot of them."

Barthol Iquar, General of the Eubian Army, relaxed in his lush recliner. He enjoyed his time with his nephew Kryx, who was young enough that he never did something as stupid as challenging Barthol's superiority. They were kin, so they didn't need to speak in the oblique language of Aristos. As much as Barthol approved of such discourse, which further set Aristos above the rest of humanity, he tired of the inconvenience.

Barthol regarded his nephew indolently from over his crystal goblet. "Assassination is too kind a word. The Ruby Dynasty ought to be exterminated."

Kryx grimaced as if he had smelled a dead animal. "Starting with Kelric Skolia."

"But keep his mother." Barthol swirled his red wine, and light glinted on the exquisitely cut edges of his glass. "That woman is surreally beautiful. Never ages. She looks like an unbelievably golden girl."

Kryx shrugged. "I've plenty of pretty providers. I don't need another. Especially not one who thinks she's a queen."

"You miss the point." Barthol felt an edge in his thoughts that no spirits, alcoholic or otherwise, could soothe. Nothing would ease it except the transcendent screams of a provider. "The higher they believe their station, the more satisfying it is to see them humiliated."

Kryx inclined his head to Barthol. "I have to admit, the prospect of Roca Skolia naked and on her knees has a certain appeal."

"Indeed."

"But gods, her son. Where did he get the arrogance to believe he could be an 'Imperator'?" Kryx's perfect Aristo face, normally so like a marble statue, creased with annoyance. "If I live to see the rise and fall of galaxies, I will never understand what possessed our dear emperor, may the gods petition his exalted, etcetera, etcetera soul, to sign that deranged peace treaty."

Barthol gritted his teeth. "Deranged" indeed. It was an abomination. What he hated far more than the treaty itself was his signature on the document. His aunt, Tarquine Iquar, matriarch of the Iquar line and Empress of Eube, had outmaneuvered him. She had named him as her heir, granting him the title of Iquar Line; when she died, he would become the head of their noble house in place of her firstborn child.

The title should have been his to start with, given his innate superiority, but she had demanded an abhorrent price for it, his signature on that godforsaken treaty. For that, he would never forgive her.

Barthol said only, "The emperor claims that by opening trade relations with the Skolians, the treaty will make us wealthy beyond imagining."

Kryx snorted. "We're already wealthy beyond imagining."

"Not that I would object to more," Barthol said. "But nothing is worth trading with Skolians. Better we buy and sell *them.*" The idea of treating them as equals greatly troubled him. Skolians showed their inferiority in everything they did, from their inept attempts at warfare to their sloppy "democratic" government that shared the rule of Skolia with the royal family. Hell, the fools couldn't even figure out if they lived in a democracy or a dynastic empire.

Kryx tapped the ivory table that separated them. A display of holicons came up, tiny holo menus, in this case a mosaic of gold and green squares floating above the table. He flicked one, and it morphed into an image about one handspan high showing a man with a massive physique and metallic skin, eyes, and hair.

"Kelric Garlin Valdoria Skolia," the mesh-table said. "Imperator of Skolia."

Barthol raised his eyebrow at Kryx. "Does your table always announce people?"

Kryx smiled slightly. "I'm training it to anticipate my wishes."

A worthy goal. Barthol studied the Imperator. Kelric's hair had greyed at the temples. Barthol loathed flawed people. If they didn't make their appearance to his liking, he had no desire to acknowledge their existence. That he had to do so anyway with Kelric Skolia grated.

"Show the rest of the Ruby Dynasty," Kryx told the table.

The mosaic morphed into a collection of extraordinarily pretty people. That irritated Barthol even more than the grey in Kelric's hair, that even with all their flaws, the Ruby Dynasty were more beautiful than they deserved. They looked like expensive sex slaves, not interstellar potentates. Supposedly they were descended from a Eubian experiment designed to create gorgeous slaves who were also powerful psions, but of course that couldn't be true, because if they had been created in a Eubian lab, they never could have escaped and set up their own empire.

"What's that for?" Barthol asked irritably.

"I'm putting together dossiers on the Ruby Dynasty," Kryx said.

"We all have dossiers on them," Barthol said. "If you figure out how to have *them* instead of their dossiers, let me know." As a commander of ESComm, or Eubian Space Command, Barthol was always looking for ways to acquire a Ruby. Unfortunately, they were prodigiously well protected.

"Look at this one." Kryx flicked his thumb through the holo of a man with red curls streaked by gold. A full holo appeared, two handspans high, of the man standing with his thumbs hooked into his belt. He had on a sleeveless black shirt, black leather pants with silver studs, and a chain belt. His hair spilled down his neck, unruly and luxuriant. He had large eyes and a sneer, giving him an intensely sexualized look. That was certainly his most commercial asset, a blatant eroticism that could bring a high price on the pleasure slave markets.

"Who is that?" Barthol asked. "Some thug out of a porn holovid?"

Kryx smiled ever so slightly. "That, my dear Uncle, is the Ruby Dynasty's greatest weakness."

"What, their association with surly youths of questionable character?" Barthol gave a deliberately crude laugh. "And here I thought Kelric Skolia preferred women."

"You know this fellow." Kryx's mouth quirked upward, which from a Highton was an expression of immense glee. "He's a Ruby prince. Also something called a 'holo-rock singer.' "

"Holo-what?" Honestly, what absurdity would the Ruby Dynasty come up with next? Someone ought to put them in slave restraints and save their people from their misery.

"Holo-rock," Kryx said. "He makes noise and calls it singing. An embarrassment to the dynasty, I'm sure. He's one of the top-earning artists in the genre."

"Never heard of it."

"Yes, well, His Thugliness lives on Earth."

"Oh, that one." Barthol had put him out of his mind long ago. "He was there when our last war with the Skolians ended. His family didn't want him back. Hell, it's been eleven years." This all spoke to Barthol's conviction that human civilization was decaying. "I'll tell you, Kryx, this claim the Earthers make that they were neutral in the war—it's fucking bullcrap. If they were neutral, why were they protecting the Ruby Dynasty? I didn't see them offering to protect us."

Kryx cocked his eyebrow. "Would you have wanted their protection?"

"Of course not. That isn't the point. They didn't offer." Barthol had little interest in the singer. This Ruby princeling would be as well protected on Earth as anywhere else. Hell, if he was making some conglomerate wealthy, they would go out of their way to ensure nothing happened to him.

Then again, maybe he should take another look. Who knew what the boy was up to out there on Earth? If any vulnerability existed in the web of security surrounding the Ruby Dynasty, it just might be for this loud singer on Earth.

"What makes you consider this one in particular?" Barthol asked.

"He's the renegade." A glint came into Kryx's eyes. "And renegades are always a weakness."

III
Gem Child

"You want a job?" Harindor looked Aliana up and down, his dark eyes assessing. "I dunno, sweets. Some men like their sugar tall, I guess."

"I'm not interested in being one of your sugar girls," Aliana told him shortly.

Harindor shifted his bulk on his overstuffed recliner. The light from the orb spinning in a corner of the red-curtained booth gave his face a reddish cast. "Well, you won't be getting no jobs as a diplomat."

"I can be a bouncer in one of your bars," Aliana said.

He gave a snort of laughter. "Since when do I need underage girls as bouncers?"

As nervous as Aliana felt, behind her false bravado, she was still sure she could manage the job. Since that life-changing moment ten days ago when she'd fought her stepfather, she had begun to realize what she could do. She had grown tall, and all those years of heavy labor had given her plenty of muscles. Her unknown father may have left her in this cesspool of a life, but he had also given her an incredible strength.

"Put me on a shift at one of your bars," she said. "You'll see. I can do it."

Harindor laughed rudely. "You'll make more trouble than you stop. I'll need another bouncer just to take care of the bastards who come on to you."

"I can take care of myself."

"Tell you what." He leaned back in his chair, his smile oozing across his puffy face. "I'll give you that shift. If you fail, sweets, you give me a sweet-shift."

"I won't whore for you, Harin."

"Whatever." Reaching forward, he took a holofile from the battered table he used as a desk.

"Fine." Aliana had to make a conscious effort not to grit her teeth. "If I get knocked out on my shift working as your bouncer, I'll give you a sweet-shift."

He looked up, smirking. "Lot easier work, you know. You jus' lie on your back—"

"Shut the hell up," she said.

"Not good to talk to me like that." Harin looked more amused than offended. "Go on. Git. Sak outside will set you up for a shift at Capjack's Bar."

"Good." Aliana turned and headed for the door. Over her shoulder, she said, "I won't be seeing you again, not unless you come to Capjack's."

He laughed behind her. "At least not for a day."

Just wait, she thought. She'd start as a bouncer for his bar. Someday she'd own the damn place. She didn't know how, but she was going to be more than this.

Jaibriol Qox, Emperor of Eube, had a headache. He rubbed his temples, trying to ease the pain so he could concentrate on the jeweled Quis dice on his glossy black desk. The pressure from the minds of the Aristos he encountered every day, all day, were an unseen but never-ending weight on his empath's mind. Retreating to play Quis calmed him.

His Ruby Dynasty uncle had given him the dice. With Quis, Kelric had offered Jaibriol a gift of unimaginable proportions, a way to survive this life when he thought his mind would crack under the immense powers coursing through it. His greatest enemy was also his savior.

"You need to stop working," a silken voice said behind him.

He lifted his head and stared straight ahead at his apparently empty office. The hint of a smile touched his face. "And do what instead?"

His wife Tarquine came around his chair and leaned against his desk, facing him. Her hair fell in a black curtain around her face, and she watched him with her upslanted eyes. "Not sleep," she murmured.

Jaibriol leaned back in his chair, outwardly cool, resisting the urge to throw his empress across that huge desk of his and do something more entertaining than a dice game. "You want me to stop working in exchange for what?"

She arched a dark eyebrow in her perfectly sculpted face. "I need ulterior motives to enjoy my husband's presence?"

He reached out and traced his finger across the back of her hand, barely touching her. "You always have ulterior motives."

"There is one small thing." Her voice was like dark

whiskey. "You remember my nephew Barthol? Your Joint Commander. General of your army."

Unfortunately. "Of course."

"Perhaps you recall how I convinced him to sign your ill-conceived peace treaty. I gave up a little something."

A "little" something. What she had done could change empires. He had known she would bring this to him, eventually. She had named Barthol as the Iquar Heir. If she and Jaibriol ever had children, their firstborn would be heir to the Carnelian Throne, but not to the Iquar title; Tarquine's legacy would pass to her nephew instead. She had given up her title to the most powerful Highton Line after the Qox dynasty, doing it for Jaibriol's deluded and probably hopeless attempt to make peace with their enemies.

"Our son will still be the Carnelian Emperor," Jaibriol said. "He will rule the largest empire in human history."

"At the moment, it's all moot." Her words were smooth but unrelenting. "The Minister of Trade spoke to me today. Yet another member of our benighted Highton caste bringing to my attention, ever so subtly, that I have yet to produce an heir."

He had no answer, none that either of them could accept. Tarquine was a full Aristo. So was he, supposedly, though she knew the truth, that he was only one-eighth. But that was enough. Aristo genes were dominant. Any child he and Tarquine created together would be an Aristo. That child would grow up like every other Aristo, a predator who hungered for the pain of psions, a sadist who believed it was his exalted right to brutalize empaths and telepaths. It was already agonizing for Jaibriol to hide his nature every day of his life, every moment. How could he bear it with his own heir, knowing the child he loved would be driven, if he ever discovered the truth, to see his own father enslaved and tortured? He couldn't, and so he had kept himself from siring his own heir.

However, Tarquine no longer ruled the Iquar Line. Unless she bore a child to Jaibriol, her legacy would die with her. Nor did Jaibriol want to leave his throne to Corbal or his descendants.

He stood up and extended his hand to her. "Come. Let us give our empire the Highton Heir it so desperately wants."

She took his hand. "Never regret it, Jaibriol." Her gaze smoldered. "Our son will be an emperor like none other that humanity has ever seen."

Kelric didn't know how to say goodbye. He stood in the docking bay with his wife and struggled with the words trapped inside of him. He couldn't say what he felt, that without her, he would starve in loneliness. He didn't know how to give voice to such intense emotions.

Ixpar stood at nearly his height, her red hair falling in a thick braid down her back, her long, long legs sheathed in knee boots, her russet tunic fitted snugly to her leanly curved body. She had the face of a queen, elegant and keen-eyed, but with the ferocity of her warrior ancestors simmering below her civilized exterior.

Her leaving made him acutely aware of his age. In his youth, he had felt as if he would live forever, that time always existed to do tomorrow what he had to miss today. No longer. Every day they spent apart made him aware of his time with her trickling away. Even with nanomeds that delayed his aging, making him look thirty years younger, he felt every one of his seventy years as if he had lived them twice.

"I wish you could stay," he said.

"I too." Her deep voice flowed over him.

"I'll miss you." Inside, he thought, *Don't go. I don't want to be without you.*

Ixpar cupped her hand around his cheek, her skin smooth against his face. "And I you, Kelric." As she lowered her arm, she smiled, but the expression seemed more sad than anything else. "This summit for the peace treaty will keep you busy, though."

He took her hand. "I swear, sometimes I think no one in the universe wants the treaty to happen but Jaibriol Qox and me."

"Are you sure *you* do?" she asked. "After all they've done?"

"I'm sure." Gods knew, he had little reason for his certainty. The Traders enslaved trillions of people and wiped out any who resisted. They wanted nothing more than to conquer Skolia and destroy his family. For five centuries his people had battled them in crushing, bitter wars.

"We have to stop fighting," Kelric said. "Or we'll wipe out the human race."

"I don't trust this emperor of theirs."

"I doubt most any Skolian does." Kelric pulled her into his arms and held her close, unable to say anything more. He couldn't tell her that he trusted Jaibriol because the Eubian emperor was his own nephew. His family was always at risk for capture by the Trader Aristos, and methods of interrogation existed that could pry information from anyone, no matter how well protected their minds. For all that he would miss Ixpar and his children, he was glad they would be on Coba, which was better protected than most any other world in the Imperialate. The family he loved was safer there than with him.

So he would live alone with this secret that could destroy two empires.

Aliana stood at her post by the entrance to Capjack's Bar, her arms crossed while life-sized holos of near-naked women gyrated around the doorway. Leave it to Harindor to make her a bouncer at this noxious place. Apparently she looked older than her age, though; no one seemed to realize the bar's bouncer was half the age of the bar's younger patrons.

"Hey, love." A group of men sauntered up to the bar. "You a present to invite us in?"

"Yeah, right," she said. "I'll bounce you right through the door."

They chuckled and went on into the bar, more interested in the real "presents," the dancing girls who undulated in that laser-lit hell, their skin glowing with digitally-enhanced swirls of body paint.

"Enough!" a mechanical voice said from inside. A robot bouncer appeared, holding the arm of a burly man. "The girls are for watching," the robot told the man. "Not touching." It shoved him toward Aliana. "He's leaving." Then it disappeared back inside, its metal body reflecting the garish holos around the door.

"Hey." Aliana took the drunk's arm. She didn't know why Harindor bothered with a human bouncer. The robots were perfectly effective and he didn't have to pay them. He seemed to think having humans added class to his establishments.

The drunk peered up at her. "You going to dance for me?"

"You don't want to see me dance," Aliana told him. "It'd give you a stomach ache." She led him over to the magrail stop on the street that ran in front of the bar. "You go on home and sleep it off, eh?"

"Sleep-what?" His voice slurred.

"Here you are." She eased him onto a bench with glowing purple lights around its edges. To the bench, she said, "Keep watch over him until the mag train arrives, okay?"

"I guess I could do that," the bench said.

"You leaving me here?" the guy asked, squinting at her. "It's cold. Why don't you sit with me? Pretty girl like you shouldn't be alone."

Pretty. Sure. Her stepfather had never let her develop any delusions about that. She knew she was ugly. With all this fellow had drunk, she was surprised he could even tell she was female.

"I'll be fine," she assured him. "You take care of yourself, okay?"

"You's too," he mumbled, swaying.

After waiting a moment to make sure he wouldn't fall over if she left him on his own, Aliana went back to the bar and leaned against the doorjamb, watching the street. Gods, this was boring.

"You're new," someone said.

Aliana turned with a start. She hadn't heard anyone approach, not a good sign, because most people weren't that quiet unless they were trying to sneak up on you.

A man stood a few paces away, with dark eyes and bristly dark hair. He was taller than anyone she knew, with muscled shoulders and biceps bulging under his jacket. Gods. He was *big*.

He came closer. "You work here?"

"Bouncer," she said, watching his hands. He kept them in the pockets of his leather-and-mesh jacket. Not good. He could have a weapon in there.

"You're a bouncer?" His laugh rumbled. "Right."

"You going in?" Aliana asked, irritated.

"Maybe I'll stay here with you."

"I'm busy."

He stepped closer. "I'm Tidewater."

"I'm not interested, Tide."

"Right." He put his hand on her arm.

She jerked her arm, throwing off his hand. "Blast off."

Tide regarded her with curiosity. "You're tough, you think?" He moved fast, shoving her up against the wall. "Or maybe not, hmm?"

"Oh, grow up," Aliana muttered. She twisted and clumsily threw him off. She still wasn't used to the strength of her dense muscles.

She hoped he'd decide she was too much trouble and go inside. He didn't seem hostile. But he came at her again, and in that instant she flashed on all the times Caul had beaten her. Fury roiled over her, a rage that had spent sixteen years in the making. When Tide tried to toss her off balance, she whirled away and kicked as hard as she could, stabbing with the heel of her boot. It should have caught him in the stomach, but when her foot reached him, he was gone.

They really fought then, hard and intense, not a tussle like she'd had with a few other patrons. She was so angry, she didn't care that the damn robots didn't show up to help like they were supposed to. Tide kept evading her blows. This guy was *trained.* It made no sense. Pros didn't pick fights with girls outside piss-cheap bars. If she hadn't been able to sense his intent with her mind an instant ahead of his strikes, he would have knocked her out within seconds. Even with that, their bout only lasted a few minutes before he pinned her on the ground. Staring up at him, she wondered if he intended another kind of assault. It would be stupid, especially in front of the crowd that had gathered. Guys like this earned their pay by doing their boss's dirty business quick and quiet, nothing public. He wouldn't trash his reputation just to take out a kid. That was stupid—

Unless someone had hired him to do it.

She scowled at him. "Tell Harindor he's an asshole, sending his strong man to beat up his new bouncer."

To her unmitigated surprise, Tide *laughed.* "Yeah, well, his bouncer got in a few cracks of her own." He jumped up and stood there, offering his hand to help her up.

Aliana ignored his hand as she climbed to her feet. "He trying to prove a point or what?"

Tide shrugged. "I was supposed to bring you to the sweet house after I knocked you out."

Great. Just great. "So why didn't you knock me out?"

"Girl, you throw a fist like a Balzarian she-devil. Your training is crap, though."

"Don't got no training."

"You should." He pulled his jacket back into place, his huge biceps flexing. "Is this really what you want, to be a bouncer?"

She crossed her arms, making her far less impressive biceps bulge, too. "I wouldn't be here if it wasn't." In other words, it was better than the alternatives.

He glanced at the motley crowd, which was dispersing now that they realized no one was about to die. Then he turned back to Aliana. "Are you a provider?"

Heh. Strange question. Providers were small and pretty, neither of which came close to describing her, besides which, if she was a provider, she sure as blazes wouldn't be here. "Why would you ask something like that?"

"Your hair, eyes, skin. The coloring is exotic, like a provider."

"If I was a provider, Tide sweetheart, I wouldn't be chewing the air with you."

He smiled as if she was funny. "I'll talk to Harindor, see if I can get you some training."

"Yeah, sure." She didn't believe he'd do chug-chits for her, but he didn't seem so bad now that he'd quit trying to toss her around. As for her "exotic coloring," well, that was nuts.

So what if she had metallic skin, eyes, and hair, all gold? It meant nothing.

You hunt us as your prey
You assault and enslave
You force us bound to stay
For pleasures that you crave
—From "Carnelians Finale"

IV

Direct Words

Seen from outside, the Orbiter space station was a giant dark orb stark against the backdrop of interstellar space. Inside, the hollow sphere was a wonderland.

The interior consisted of two hemispheres. In the morning of the station's thirty-hour day, its Sky hemisphere glowed in a coral-hued dawn as the Sun Lamp appeared on the horizon. The great yellow light traveled across Sky on its disguised track until it reached the opposite horizon and Sky blazed with a fiery sunset. The horizon separated the Ground and Sky hemispheres, with grass on one side and a dimpled blue surface on the other. You could cross from land to sky in one step.

With a diameter of four kilometers, the Orbiter rotated once every ninety seconds, creating "gravity" for anyone on its inner surface. Its rotation axis pierced its north and south poles, both of which lay on the horizon. The pull of the gravity was at right angles to that axis, so the ground was flat at the equator, but walking toward either pole was like climbing a slope that became steeper and steeper. The gravity decreased as the slope increased. Bio-architects had landscaped Ground into hills that matched the incline, until at the poles, they became vertical cliffs with zero gravity. If you were moving, a Coriolis force pushed you sideways; the faster you moved, the greater the push, nothing too serious, but enough to make those unfamiliar with the effect dizzy.

Airborne robots patrolled the lower gravity areas, where a misplaced step could cause a fall. Hikers who fell onto Sky from the steeper mountains could slide with ever increasing weight down a slope of several kilometers. If you were careful, though, you could easily walk on either hemisphere. Sometimes the Sky filled with people relaxing or playing sports.

Parkland covered the flatter regions of Ground, meadows of cloud grass that rippled in the soft breezes of the always perfect climate. The spires of City rose in their center, a place of ethereal buildings and graceful arches in blue, rose, and lavender. Partway from City to the north pole, the mountains hid a valley. The Orbiter's best security guarded that peaceful dell, and the best security known to the Skolian Imperialate guarded the Orbiter, which traveled through space on a deliberately randomized trajectory. Those many layers of security made the simple valley one of the best protected areas within three empires.

That idyll sheltered the homes of the Ruby Dynasty.

Roca was drowning in pain, kneeling on a cold surface, her arms bound behind her back, her ankles tied. The ragged remains of her nightgown covered her, and her hair had fallen around her face. The Luminex floor provided the only light in the room; shadows dimmed the walls and shrouded the ceiling.

"Awake, I see," a woman said behind her. She spoke in Highton, the language of Aristos.

Roca looked around. A tall woman in black clothes stood there, her face lit from below by the floor. Her black hair glittered and her eyes glinted red.

"It is exquisite, the suffering of a Ruby psion," the woman said. "In providing me with transcendence, you exalt yourself."

Roca gritted her teeth. Pain blazed in her arms, legs, torso, everywhere. That was what the Aristos meant by transcendence, the brutally heightened pleasure they derived from the pain of a psion. The more powerful the empath or telepath, the more the Aristo transcended.

They craved Ruby psions.

An octagonal entrance appeared in the wall behind the woman. A man stood in the opening, tall and powerfully built, in a black military uniform, his glittering black hair cut short.

"My brother," the woman told Roca. "Raziquon."

Raziquon walked forward and nodded to his sister.

"She is yours for now," the woman told him. "Do as you please. Just remember that ESComm wants her alive."

And he did as he pleased, while Roca screamed and screamed and screamed...

Roca sat up in bed with a gasp, her heart pounding so hard she could barely breathe. It took several moments before she comprehended that she *wasn't* a prisoner, she was here, home, on the Orbiter, the space station that served as a governmental center for the Skolian Imperialate.

Roca leaned forward, her arms wrapped around her stomach, and rocked back and forth, tears running down her face. Her pulse gradually settled, until she could breathe normally.

"Sonata?" Roca whispered.

A soothing voice answered, the Evolving Intelligence, or EI, that ran her home. "What can I do for you?"

"Could you see if Kelric is available?"

"Right away."

Roca lay down and curled into a fetal position.

A few moments later, a chime came from the console by her bed.

"Receive," she said in a low voice.

Kelric's deep voice rose out of the console. "Mother, is that you? Sonata paged me."

"My greetings," she said, subdued.

"Are you all right?" he asked.

"I'm fine," she lied. "Why do you ask?"

"It's the middle of the night."

"Oh."

After a moment, he said, "Did you want to talk to me?"

"I just wondered if all the usual protections were in place for the Orbiter."

"Well, yes." He sounded puzzled. "Of course."

"Good." She stared into the darkness. It had been many, many years since she had escaped from Raziquon, but she had never felt safe since then. She could still see that glazed, drugged look on his face while she screamed in agony.

"I can send you more bodyguards," Kelric asked.

"No, that's all right. I already have two," she said. They were stationed in this house.

"What is it?" he asked gently. "You sound terrified."

"I—I had a nightmare."

"About what?"

Her voice cracked. "Raziquon."

"Someday I will find him." His voice hardened. "And he'll die. Slowly. In pain."

"Kelric, don't. You've worked too hard to make the treaty happen. Don't destroy it over your mother's bad dreams. Just—" She stopped, uncertain what to say.

"Yes?" he asked.

"Just stay alive," she whispered. "I couldn't bear to lose anyone else." She had outlived three of her children: her daughter Soz, who had been Imperator before Kelric; her son Kurj, who had been Imperator before Soz; and her son Althor, who had been Kurj's heir. The war had left Kelric crippled, deaf, and blind; only biomechanical augmentation allowed him to move, hear, and see. The Aristos had tortured her son Eldrin, devastated her son Del-Kurj, and shattered her husband, leaving him scarred for life, until he died.

Kelric spoke with the abiding gentleness that he so rarely allowed to show, except to his family. "I plan on living a long, long time."

She smiled shakily in the darkness. "Good. Bedevil me in my old age."

His laugh was soft. "That I will."

"I'm sorry I woke you up."

"You didn't. I was working."

"You need to take better care of yourself. Get some rest."

"I'll be fine." After a moment, he added, "Ixpar left today."

"I'm sorry." She knew how much he would miss his wife.

"She and the children are safer on Coba. Away from assassins."

"Do you still think someone in ISC ordered the attempt on your life?" She found it hard to believe one of his own commanders in Imperial Space Command, or ISC, might have been involved in the assassination attempt. It had taken place during his trip to Earth only months ago, when he and the Trader emperor had finished the peace treaty. What haven could exist anywhere if their own protectors turned against them?

"I don't know." His voice was guarded. Too guarded. He knew more than he planned to tell her. Well, so, it had been that way for many years. The little boy she had carried on her hip was a massive warlord now. He no longer confided his fears in his mother.

"Just be careful," she said.

"Don't worry."

"I will, you know."

His fond laugh soothed her frayed mood. "I know."

"Goodnight, honey."

"Goodnight." His voice rumbled.

After they cut their link, Roca tried to sleep, but too many specters haunted her dreams, night horrors born of the Traders they were so hopelessly trying to change with this treaty.

Kryx Iquar almost missed the platinum mine.

He was scrolling through his dossiers on the Skolians, searching for something to exploit, anything that would help him undermine the treaty. As an Iquar, he had access to the network of information accumulated by the combined brilliance of his kin, which included the Empress Tarquine herself and General Barthol Iquar, the top man in Eubian Space Command.

He had hoped the loud singer on Earth, Prince Del-Kurj, would be involved in scandals of some sort: bizarre sex, drugs, VR addiction, anything that might discredit him and by extension, his family, the Ruby Dynasty. Unfortunately, the blasted rock star behaved himself, or if he didn't, his handlers kept his indiscretions private.

Kryx was about to give up when he stumbled across a hidden file. He wouldn't have found it if his uncle Barthol hadn't granted him full security access to the military files kept by ESComm.

Eleven years ago, the emperor and ESComm had gone to great efforts to hide this file. Nor had it only been them. The governments of the Skolian Imperialate and the Allied Worlds of Earth had helped. What the file contained had been thoroughly wiped from the public record. It was nothing deadly, no terrible secret, nothing more than...

A song.

Barthol Iquar never relaxed no matter how comfortable his chair, how good the food, or how sumptuous the setting. Only his triumphs gave him relief from the constant edge of his life. Destroying those who mistakenly believed themselves to be powerful was one of the few things that offered him surcease. His greatest frustration was that two of the people he most wanted to destroy—Tarquine and the emperor—were his kin.

Untouchable. He settled back in the upholstered smartchair in his spacious office where black crystal shelves lined one wall and gorgeous holos of star cruisers glowed on the walls, but he felt no more relaxed here than if he were on one of those mighty warships.

His nephew Kryx was reclining on the black couch, his trousers perfectly creased, his leather-shod feet up on a chromed table in front of him. "You might remember the concert," he was saying. "It took place nine years ago on Earth during a 'Forth of Juli' celebration, some festival about, I don't know, a woman named Juli who was forthcoming with her charms. Or something. What matters is that the concert was in Washington, D.C., a major governmental center. So they broadcast it throughout the Allied Worlds of Earth. Our entertainment conglomerates and the Skolians both picked it up. It was one of the few music events the Skolians let us use their Kyle net for."

"*Let* us?" Barthol drummed his fingers on his desk. He had a lot of work to do. "Of course you mean, we allowed them to send us a transmission of some paltry Earther attempt at entertainment."

Kryx didn't look annoyed, not exactly, but he indicated his irritation with a twitch of his left index finger. "The point is, we saw the concert with no light speed delays. It was live."

"And I should care about this because . . . ?"

"Prince Del-Kurj was the headliner." Kryx swung his legs down from the table and leaned forward, a glint in his eyes. "Except he was just Del Arden back then. No one knew he was a Ruby prince." Satisfaction leaked into his voice. "Lord Tarex, the CEO of Tarex Entertainment, was visiting Earth, looking for exotic music acts. Prince Del-Kurj visited Tarex's yacht, and Tarex took off with the prince on board. Tarex had Del for several days, but Allied Space Command wouldn't let the yacht leave orbit."

The incident was coming back to Barthol. "Yes, I remember. Arden went willingly when Tarex offered him a lucrative music contract."

"Willingly?" Kryx didn't hide his incredulity. "Right, a Ruby prince willingly gave himself into slavery and torture, compromising the safety of his family and his empire."

"One should take care how they speak," Barthol told him coldly. "Lest people think a person supports the Skolians."

"Barthol, look at the context." Kryx's enthusiasm was overriding his usual respect. "Lord Tarex forced Prince Del-Kurj to be his provider. The prince was in pretty bad shape by the time the Allied authorities rescued him."

Barthol gritted his teeth. Technically Kryx hadn't violated any protocols by speaking in such a direct manner. He and Barthol were related, so in private, they could dispense with the circuitously exalted speech of an Aristo. But he didn't appreciate Kryx's brash attitude. His nephew seemed to think he had found something useful. Maybe he had. Even so, Barthol needed to punish him. It would be easy; he would cut Kryx out of the loop and take credit for whatever his nephew had discovered.

"The Allieds didn't 'rescue' anyone," Barthol said. "They arrested Arden for harassing Tarex."

"It was probably a cover," Kryx said. "Do you recall the concert Arden gave afterward?"

"Vaguely," Barthol said. "He shouted some insulting song. Only lasted a few minutes."

"Oh yes," Kryx murmured. "That was all he managed before they shut him down. Those are the most furious three minutes I've ever heard. It seems Ruby princes don't like being tortured."

"Enough of this torture business," Barthol said. "He and Tarex had a business arrangement."

"Look at this." Kryx touched a panel in the table, bringing up a menu of holicons. Of course it was illegal for Barthol's civilian nephew to have access to a secured ESComm node, but Barthol didn't care. The laws didn't apply to him.

"After his bodyguards got him out of jail," Kryx continued, "they were supposed to take him to a military base called Annapolis. Instead, for some reason, they allowed him to show up for his concert. Our singing prince literally ran from his flyer to the stage as his band started playing." Glancing at Barthol, he added, "He was still bleeding from the whip lashes of his 'business arrangement' with Tarex."

"So," Barthol said. Good for Tarex. Too bad he had botched the rest of the incident. "The fact that Lord Tarex let a Ruby prince slip through his fingers is stupid at best and possibly treason." Of course no one had arrested Tarex. It wasn't a crime, after all, to lose a prince, and more to the point, he was a powerful man even by Aristo standards.

"Just listen," Kryx urged. "This is a recording of Prince Del's concert."

"Fine," Barthol said. "Play the damn thing." He could be as insultingly direct as his nephew.

Kryx flicked another holicon and the room went dark.

When it lightened, they were standing under a richly starred sky, in a plaza with thousands of people and a white domed building in the distance. An unlit stage dominated the scene. The viewpoint for the recording put Barthol about fifteen meters from the stage, close enough that he could make out a shadowed tower at the back. A lift was rising up in it. The silhouette of a man was just barely discernible on the lift, almost hidden in the darkness.

The lift reached the flat top of the tower, high in the wind. Music swelled, a relentless chord progression, and the audience applauded in the plaza and in the streets beyond, where people were watching the concert on giant screens in the sides of buildings. Red smoke billowed around the tower and lights flared, outlining the man standing at the top. Huge holos of him flared around the stage. He wore leather pants and an open vest that showed his leanly muscled chest.

And his injuries.

Wherever skin was visible, except on his face, the man was bruised or bleeding. The audience obviously assumed it was an effect for the concert, but Barthol had no doubt those injuries were real. As they should be. The man standing there, his arm raised in defiance, was Prince Del-Kurj, the scowling rock scion of the Ruby Dynasty. According to the news broadcasts that followed the concert, Del had been too furious even to let the doctors finish treating him before he went on stage.

Holo-cams swung around the tower and aural-orbs spun in the air, broadcasting the show across the planet and into space. As the music crescendoed, a ramp carried Del down to the main stage. When he reached the main stage, the music hit its highest point. He strode forward like a man possessed, his face set in resolute lines, his gaze blazing. Just when he reached the front edge, the music crashed to a huge finish that provoked the screaming crowd to an even higher pitch.

The music began again. In the relative quiet of the opening, Del called out to the audience in a language that Barthol's desk comm translated. "Are you ready? *Ready to hear some music?*"

The crowd roared their approval. "I've got something new," Del told them. "Something you've never heard. A song for those who share the stars with us." He lifted his chin and shouted into the night. "*This is for you, Tarex.*"

Barthol gritted his teeth. This business was as offensive now as the first time he had heard it, nine years ago. Del sang hard and fast, his rage as intense as the lights flaring around him:

> You dehumanized us; your critics, they all died.
> You answered defiance with massive genocide.
> You hunt us as your prey; you assault and enslave.
> You force us bound to stay for pleasures that
>   you crave.

He was singing to the Aristos, the gods of Eube, the sons of the Carnelian throne, who presided over the greatest empire in human history.

> You broke my brother, you Carnelian Sons.
> You tortured my mother in your war of suns
> You shattered my father; you killed my brothers.
> You murdered my sister, expecting no others.

Well, I'm no golden hero in the blazing skies.
I'm no fair-haired genius hiding in disguise.
I'm only a singer; it's all I can do.
But I'm still alive, and I'm coming after you.

The music thundered, filling the night, and Del's voice rose with what even Barthol had to admit was spectacular power:

I'll never kneel beneath your Highton stare.
I'm here and I'm real; I'll lay your guilt bare.

As the song reached its climax, he threw back his head and screamed:

I'll never kneel beneath your Highton stare
I'm here and I'm real; your living nightmare!

Barthol felt ill listening to him. Del held the final note as the song finished in a crashing chord. But the odious song wasn't done yet. The music began again, dropping into its quieter opening.

"That was for all of you," Del told the audience. "This next time is for *my* people."

"What the hell?" a tech said in the recording. "My people? Isn't that all of us?"

Del sang again—this time in perfect, unaccented Iotic, a dead language spoken by only the Skolian nobility. As he repeated the song, the audience screamed their approval. But Barthol saw the silences, too, people staring with shock as they realized this wasn't a show. It was real.

A woman was moving around the edge of the stage

toward Del. She wasn't in a uniform, but Barthol knew a military officer when he saw one. The prince's people were probably having heart-failure as he sang in a language that blasted his identity to an interstellar audience. A man was coming from the other side of the stage, a giant in military fatigues. Arden kept singing, soaring to a pitch well above a man's normal vocal range. He held the last note even longer this time, with an incredible control of breath.

When Del released the note, the music dropped into the ominous chords of its opening. Del glanced right and left at the military officers, then stalked to the edge of the stage above the shouting, clapping, dancing crowd. One more step and he would fall into them. Barthol thought it was probably why no one had stopped him yet; the crowd might have rioted, and if he fell off the stage, the devil only knew what would happen to him in that seething mass.

Del raised his head and shouted, *"This is for you, Jaibriol Qox."* As if he hadn't yet inflicted enough on the universe, he went through the entire song again, this time bellowing his repugnant lyrics in Highton. Gods, no wonder Tarex had whipped the youth.

Barthol smiled. Kryx had done well.

He had given Barthol the weapon he needed.

V
Plague

"We need the Skolian and Trader delegates to meet in person," Kelric said.

Dehya stared at him. "You must be joking."

They were in a conference room of chrome and platinum hues, at a table with tech-mech panels disguised as gleaming metal artwork. Kelric sat sprawled in a big chair. "How else will we work out the treaty?" he asked. "Everyone and her sister's uncle is trying to undermine the damn thing."

Dehya traced an arc on the chromed table with her graceful finger. Kelric wasn't fooled. Yes, his aunt looked fragile. But in her mind and character, she was one of the strongest people he knew. Although her face had a childlike quality, she was almost the oldest living human, second only to her ex-husband, a retired admiral on Earth. Her stratospheric intellect coupled with the knowledge she had accumulated throughout her life, all one hundred and seventy years of it, had turned her into a greater force than any of his military commanders or the political strategists in the Assembly. To the rest of humanity outside her family, she was a reclusive legend who never appeared in public, Dyhianna Selei, the enigmatic and powerful Ruby Pharaoh.

Right now, though, she was just being obstinate.

"I need your support to make my idea work," Kelric said.

"It's not an idea," she said. "It's a bout of insanity."

"We can figure out how to make it work." He rubbed his shoulder, trying to ease the stiff muscles. His knee joints hurt, too. Damn war injuries. "If anyone can help me do that, it's you."

She tilted her head, studying him. Her eyes were green, like the foliage deep in a forest, but a translucent film covered them, the vestigial inner eyelid she had inherited from her father. In Dehya, the lid was almost invisible, just a trace of gold and rosy hues. Sunrise eyes, people called them. They were beautiful, large and heavily fringed with black lashes, and right now they were filled with her suspicion that he had gone nuts.

"What makes you think I want to make it work?" she asked.

"You supported the peace treaty," Kelric said. "If we plan to trade with the Eubians instead of trying to annihilate them, we have a million details we need to work out, everything from minor import tariffs to how a civilization like ours that considers human freedom an inalienable right is going to trade with an empire whose economy is based on slavery."

"I agree, we need a summit," she said. "But this idea to have us all meet face to face is crazy. The delegates from both governments would probably rather be dropped on a hill of starving vampire-ants."

Kelric gave a startled snort of laughter. "That's a lovely thought."

"Yes, well, I can't imagine a bigger security nightmare than putting a bunch of Trader sadists with delusions of godhood into the same hall as our vociferously contentious Assembly councilors. They'd all want to strangle each other."

"It would be a security problem," he admitted. To describe it more accurately would involve profanity he didn't use around Dehya.

"We can do the summit in a virtual reality simulation," she said. "We stay here, the Traders stay there, and everyone is safe. The Kyle web will give us almost instantaneous communications."

Kelric scowled at her. "It's too easy to lie in virtual reality. And don't tell me about how we have all these wonderful protocols to prevent it. Everyone cheats."

"That may be," she said. "But a virtual summit is the best we're going to get."

"Nothing is impossible."

A hum interrupted their argument, coming from a gold square in the table. Kelric touched the panel. "Skolia here."

A holo appeared above the table, the head and shoulders of Admiral Chad Barzun, Kelric's top naval commander. Normally the granite-haired officer had a gratifyingly calm and solid demeanor, but today he looked frazzled.

"Sir, we have a situation," Chad told him.

Damn. Anything the even-keeled Barzun described as a "situation" was more likely a disaster of interstellar proportions, like a declaration of war from the Traders. "What is it?" Kelric asked.

"It's your brother," Chad said. "Prince Del-Kurj."

Kelric winced. That could be even more stressful than a new war. "What's he done?"

"One of his songs has been released."

"A lot of his songs have been released," Kelric said. "Granted, they're loud. But the last time I checked, shouting rock music didn't qualify as a star-spanning crisis."

Chad cleared his throat. "Sir, it's 'Carnelians Finale.'"

Hell and damnation. Suppressing the "Finale" had been the only tri-lateral agreement ever made between Skolia, Eube, and Allied Worlds of Earth. It hadn't been easy, but they had managed to erase the song off the interstellar meshes before it exploded relations between Eube and Skolia.

Now here it was again, just as Skolia and Eube were embarking on an already nearly impossible peace process.

Aliana grunted as she strained to throw Tide over her hip. It didn't work; he was as immobile as reinforced zirconablock. Not that she'd ever actually seen zirconablock, which was supposedly the heaviest substance in the universe. Like yeah, heavier than a black hole. Tide was still a chunk, though. She barely managed to twist out from under him. Heaving in breaths, her hair straggling in her eyes, she stood there with her arms hanging at her sides. They were in the basement of one of Harindor's "palaces" where his customers injected, inhaled, or imbibed his wares. She and Tide had been working for an hour, doing every whacked out exercise he could think of, and she'd had her fill.

Tide straightened up, huge and looming, and grinned at her. "Getting worn out, girl?"

"Don't call me a girl, vomit breath," Aliana muttered.

"Why? You a boy?" He was amused rather than tired, which just annoyed her more.

"Where'd you learn to fight so well?" she asked, curious despite herself.

His smile vanished.

"What?" she asked. It seemed a perfectly reasonable question.

It was a moment before he responded. Finally he said, "I used to be a Razer."

Aliana stared at him. "Flaming crap."

He laughed. "That sounds unpleasant."

"You were secret police? For *Aristos?*"

He shrugged. "It's nothing."

Like hell it was nothing. "Why aren't you a Razer anymore? I thought it was for life."

"My line malfunctioned." His face had become neutral, impossible to read. "So they decommissioned all of us."

Malfunctioned? It made him sound like a machine. "You mean there are more like you?"

"I don't know if any of the others are left. But yeah, there used to be more."

"How'd you malfunction?" With a smirk, she added, "You going to go psycho on me?"

He stalked over to her. "Listen, byte-babe, shove a mesh-mole in it."

"A what?"

He touched her nose. "Mesh-mole. It's a noxious

piece of code that crawls around your mesh system puking its innards all over your pristine modules, until your system is so mucked up, it can't remember the last time you went to the crap-shack."

Aliana tried not to laugh, mainly because it would interfere with her attempts to glare at him. "That's disgusting, Tide. You're the one told me you went haywire. So what'd you do?"

"I didn't *do* anything. It was another Razer in my line. I don't know what he did. He's dead. All I know is his name. Hidaka. Sam Hidaka."

"I thought Razers didn't have names. Just serial numbers."

He regarded her sourly. "That's why my line was decommissioned."

"Oh. You were too human." That was nuts. She liked him this way, not that she would ever admit it out loud. He wasn't bad looking, either, especially with that impressive scar that ran down his left cheek. He must have taken the injury after he stopped being a Razer; otherwise the Aristo he guarded would have had the scar fixed. Aristos hated imperfection. They were gods, after all. Though if her stepfather Caul was any example of their progeny, she sure as shingles didn't see anything godlike in what they sired.

"You have a name," she pointed out.

He lifted his chin. "Damn right."

She knew she should be afraid of him, but this had to be one of the most interesting things that had ever happened to her. A Razer! "So how come you call yourself Tidewater?"

Now he seemed self-conscious, quite an accomplishment given that usually he looked either emotionless or ready to kill someone. "I liked the tide outside the mansion of the Highton I served. The oceans on the planet Glory are crazy like you wouldn't believe. It's because the planet has so many moons. I loved it when the tide came in. The waves crashed and tore up the beach."

He *loved* it. Everyone knew Razers had no emotions. No wonder they had decommissioned his line. Not that she would call an ability to act like a human being defective.

"Listen, Tide," she said. "I like you this way. So screw whoever decommissioned you."

"I thought you hated me."

"That too."

He smiled. "You're a piece of work, Zina. But listen, don't ever say 'screw whoever decommissioned you.' The decision was made by an Aristo. You could go to the pits for that."

"Oh." Of course an Aristo was involved. She'd never heard anyone call her Zina before, probably for her third name, Azina. She liked it. "I'll be careful."

"Good." He rubbed the back of his hand across his forehead, smearing his sweat. "Anyway, you're making a little progress with the training."

Aliana grinned at him. "I'll whip your ass next time, mesh-mole man."

She thought he'd laugh. Instead he just looked at her oddly. What had she said? For a machine with no emotions, he was certainly moody.

"You mad at me?" she asked.

"No." He strode across the basement to where he'd dumped his gear. "See you tomorrow."

"Sure." What had she said wrong?

No, it wasn't wrong. Her ability to sense moods told her that she had shaken him up, not angered him. It didn't help much, though. She could tell how he felt but not why. She had walls in her mind. They protected her mentally, but she had no idea what to do about them.

After she and Tide parted, Aliana walked home, alone in the night on a road slick with oil and drizzle. A sputtering light orb floated above her, throwing harsh glints on the ground. It was then that she realized what she had said. Tide was a Razer, a machine without a soul or free will, an enforcer who obeyed every command from his owner.

She had called him a man.

"Expecting Skolians to show respect is a contradiction in terms," Barthol Iquar said. "They insult the universe by their mere existence."

Jaibriol sat watching Barthol and his other advisors argue. He brooded in the sunlight that slanted through tall windows around the room. His great-grandfather, Emperor Eube Qox, had terraformed this world to fit his idea of paradise, named it Eube's Glory, and declared himself its god. Now Jaibriol sat here listening to Eube's megalomaniacal legacy, the Aristos, as they debated in their maddening, never-say-anything-straight style of speech. They were in fine form today, so adept at their circuitous arguments, it made his head ache. He wanted to say, *Just make your flaming point.* Of course he couldn't. They spoke directly only to kin, lovers, or slaves. Here it would be the ultimate insult. Aristos had assassinated each other for less, and he was tired of people trying to kill him.

Anyway, he knew the point. A small holo of the

song that had created this disaster played silently above the oval table where they all sat. Even without the sound, he knew the words. He had heard "Carnelians Finale" plenty of times nine years ago, when Del had shouted it to the stars in his magnificent voice. *You dehumanize us, your critics they all died, you answered defiance with massive genocide.* Del was singing to him, Jaibriol the Third, the Carnelian tyrant of Eube.

The worst of it was, the words were true, not for Jaibriol or his father, but for their predecessors, who had perpetrated so many sins on humanity, Jaibriol wondered that they hadn't incinerated in the hell of their own iniquity. That he himself hadn't committed genocide or tortured anyone meant nothing. He let the Aristos continue because the alternative was even worse. If he overtly sought to stop the oppression in an empire where the economy, politics, and social structure were based on that tyranny, someone would just kill him and the atrocities would continue. He had to use more subtle ways to bring about change.

Del would never know the irony, that the emperor of Eube he sang to with such fury was actually his nephew, a Ruby psion—and a member of the Skolian Triad.

The Triad. It was Jaibriol's nightmare. The Ruby Dynasty used it to create a star-spanning mesh in the Kyle universe, a place where a telepath went in mind only, not body. People with similar thoughts were next to each other in Kyle space no matter what their location in the normal universe. It made possible almost instant communication across interstellar distances. Only Skolians could do it. That was why Eube had never conquered them despite ESComm's greater forces. Skolia sailed, Eube lumbered.

Telepaths capable of using the Kyle web were less than one in a million. Aristos called them "providers" and craved their agony with a sadistic addiction they claimed was godlike exaltation. Even if they were willing to use their providers to create a Kyle web, it wouldn't work. Only Ruby psions had the strength to create, support, and extend that vast mesh; such work would tear apart the mind of anyone else. Eube had no Kyle web because only the Ruby Dynasty were Ruby psions, and so far ESComm had failed to keep any Ruby they captured.

Jaibriol gritted his teeth. Neither brilliance nor political acumen had brought him his secret Triad position. It had been a damned accident. If the Fates existed, they must be laughing at him, for last year he had been in the Lock—a Triad command center that ESComm had stolen—when Kelric unknowingly activated it from light years away. The Lock had blasted Jaibriol into the Triad, locking him into a three-way link with Kelric and the Ruby Pharaoh. So it was that Jaibriol had become the tool his forefathers designed him for when they secretly bred the forbidden genes of a Ruby telepath into the Qox Dynasty. He could create a Kyle web—and no one here had a clue.

Someone kicked his foot under the table. He glanced up to find Tarquine watching him. She looked bored, but he knew what she was about. His empress wanted him to pay attention to his counselors before they got him into trouble.

Parizian Sakaar, his Minister of Trade, was speaking. "How more blatant the puppet," he asked, "than to show it in full view of the gallery?"

Jaibriol had followed enough to the conversation to know the "puppet" was Del. Given the Aristo love of hyperbole, especially when it concerned their own greatness, the "gallery" probably meant the rest of the universe, which was presumably watching the Aristos and the purported sins of their enemies.

Corbal raised his eyebrows at the comment. He was seated across from Jaibriol, his white hair glittering in the light from the orbs hovering near the ceiling. He looked relaxed, but Jaibriol knew better. They all wanted an answer to the same question: was it Del who had released "Carnelians Finale"? If so, it was one hell of a hostile act toward the peace treaty. If Jaibriol had to lay odds, he would have bet the person who had put it out there was at this table. Sakaar maybe, who as Trade Minister had a vested interest in controlling the interstellar markets, in particular the slave trade, which the Skolians would never acknowledge as legal. Or perhaps Barthol Iquar, filling his big chair at the end of the table. If Tarquine hadn't offered to name him as heir to the unconscionably wealthy Iquar Line, the general would probably have preferred being dragged through hot tar to signing the document.

Corbal spoke to Sakaar. "In this day and age, even a puppet can act of its own volition."

"Puppets don't make choices," Calope Muze said. "Someone else pulls the strings." An elegant woman with silvery hair, she served as High Judge, the judiciary among Jaibriol's advisors. As his cousin, she was second in line to the Carnelian Throne after Corbal.

Azile Xir spoke dryly. "Puppets and strings should remain inanimate objects." He was Corbal's son and also the Minister of Intelligence. Jaibriol's top spy man. Although Azile was twenty years older than Jaibriol, he was the youngest person here after the emperor.

Corbal snorted. "In my experience, inanimate objects don't exercise their vocal cords, especially with so much energy."

Azile smiled slightly. "Your use of the word energy is kind."

A low laugh went around the table while the other Ministers looked suitably pained at the thought of Del's "energy." Jaibriol doubted any of them would have been caught dead listening to holo-rock if a Ruby prince hadn't been involved.

"Actually," Jaibriol said, "I like his music."

Silence descended while everyone stared at him. They didn't seem insulted by his direct speech, just confused. Except Tarquine, with her deadpan expression. Only Jaibriol knew her well enough to realize she was struggling not to laugh. Everyone else assumed he was making some abstrusely clever insult about Del combined with a pithy political reference, all done in such a convoluted manner that none of them could figure out what the hell he meant. Jaibriol just sat looking royal and enigmatic.

Calope inclined her head. "An appropriate expression of appreciation, Your Highness."

The others nodded as if Jaibriol had said something brilliant. It would have been funny if the situation hadn't been so serious. He had first heard Del sing ten years ago, when Jaibriol had been a teenager, and he had liked the music right off. He even liked "Carnelians Finale," or he would have if it hadn't been about him.

Glancing down the table, he saw Barthol watching him with a narrowed gaze. Not good. Well, so, time to put Barthol on the spot.

Jaibriol said, "I'm curious how our military offices view this business of Earth and her supposed songbird."

"Birds don't exist on Glory," Barthol said in a bored voice. "So I can't imagine why any office would bother with them."

"Unless the songbird is neither from Earth nor Glory," Calop said. "But instead Skolian. It wouldn't be valid for Earthers to think of him as their own or for Eube to consider him such."

"Who knows if Earthers even think," Barthol said. "Let alone if any of it is valid."

It irritated Jaibriol that his top army commander couldn't give a more useful comment on the situation than his scorn for Earth. "We need more than questions about intelligence," Jaibriol said. He wanted the general's assessment of a situation that he suspected Barthol might have deliberately created in secret.

"Indeed," Barthol said indolently. "Your Highness is most esteemed to remark on its lack."

Enough of this, Jaibriol thought. He needed to find out what Barthol was up to, not listen to insults about someone's supposed lack of intelligence, which could refer to him, to Azile Xir, or to who the hell knew what. He eased down his mental shields. The pressure from the gathered Aristos increased until he wanted to jump up, stride around the room, anything to alleviate the painful sense of falling into blackness. But he caught a sense of Barthol's surface thoughts. So that was the general's game: stir up anger by insinuating the Allied Worlds released the song as a back-handed slap against Eube. Barthol was deflecting attention from himself.

Pain sparked in Jaibriol's temples and he withdrew, raising his mental barriers.

Corbal was speaking. "Perhaps the people of Earth are hiding secrets about their borrowed songbird and his music. They would resist hunts by offworlders to uncover such secrets."

Tarquine waved her hand, dismissing his comment. "The only thing Earthers hide when the glorious lions come out to hunt is their own meek selves. If their history is any indication, they would rather pretend the lions don't exist than risk keeping dangerous secrets from us."

Corbal answered with an edge. "The lion is native to Earth, Your Highness. Not Glory."

She regarded him with her exquisitely aloof Highton gaze. "All beasts come from the same place, Corbal dear, if you go back far enough in our ancestry." With a voice like whiskey, she added, "Some of us are just more deadly than others."

For flaming sake. The last thing Jaibriol needed right now was another fight between Corbal and Tarquine. "General Iquar," he said to Barthol. "Your knowledge pleases us. Continue."

A muscle just barely twitched under Barthol's eye; if Jaibriol hadn't looked for such a sign, he would have missed it. He knew what it meant. The general didn't like being asked to support his implications that the Allieds released the song to insult Eube. Tough. Jaibriol had no intention of sitting back while Barthol started rumors that would damage Eube's already shaky relations with the Allied Worlds of Earth.

His headache was growing worse.

The interstellar mesh wasn't one system. It wasn't a million. Not a trillion.

No one knew how many meshes networked human space; every human being alive operated hundreds, thousands, even millions of them. The webs permeated cultures, they saturated people, cities, atmospheres. When meshes could be as small as atomic particles or as long as light years, when they infiltrated every aspect of life, even becoming part of human evolution, it was impossible to keep any place touched by humanity free of them. Individual nodes linked into community meshes, which linked into planetary meshes, which formed super meshes within a star system. Those systems communicated with the Skolian psiberweb through the Kyle network, linking across interstellar space. To gain access to the Kyle, the Allieds petitioned or paid for it and the Eubians stole it, until all of human space was connected across the star-flung reaches of three empires into an ever-evolving entity simply called The Mesh.

As with any form of life, The Mesh could become infected. It developed codes to protect itself. Antibodies. They worked with varying effectiveness, countering contagions it picked up from human civilization or discovered mutated within itself. Usually, an infestation in one network had little effect on another unless they were closely related. It was almost unheard of for an infection to spread throughout settled space, across three empires. A rare, rare phenomenon.

When it happened, people called it a mind-plague.

In the year 2288, only months after the historic signing of the first peace treaty between the Skolian and Eubian empires, a mind-plague exploded across the interstellar meshes.

It was called "Carnelians Finale."

VI
Red

Aliana didn't know which amazed her more, that the guy attacked her or that he believed he could actually do her damage.

She was walking along the lakefront, taking a break from training with Tide. Pebbles and mech-debris littered the shore, either glinting with metallic components or cloudy from composites. Water lapped sluggishly against the rubble, leaving smears of oil that caught prismatic rainbows from the watery sunlight.

A blow hit her from behind, square in the back. She stumbled a step and spun around. A dark-haired youth in a dingy red jumpsuit was raising a club to hit her again. He was almost her height, with a slender frame. She didn't have time to see details of his weapon, other than that it ended in a metal ball the size of her fist. Her hand shot out, and she caught the club as he tried to bring it down. With an easy twist, she ripped it out of his hand.

"Hey!" he shouted, wincing as he pulled his arm against his body.

"What are you doing?" Aliana asked, more amazed than mad.

"Give me that." He pointed to a metal clasp on the collar of her shirt. "Or I kill you."

"Really?" She regarded him curiously. "I'm terrified."

"Do it!" he said menacingly. Or tried. His voice shook.

"Why?" she inquired. "That clasp is worth zilch."

He clenched his fist, raising it as he stepped toward her.

Aliana caught his fist and pushed him away. "I could do this all day, hon."

He glared at her. "You not Aristo over me."

"Hey, asshole, you're the one that hit me."

He pointed to her clasp. "Need that."

"Whatever for? It's a piece of junk."

"Sell. For food."

Aliana looked him over. He wasn't just "slender," he was skeletal. "You don't have any credits, is that it? No way to eat?"

"I fine." He tensed as if to fight, then squinted at her and apparently changed his mind. "Hungry," he added.

"Well listen, mesh-mole, I'm gonna help you. I don't know why, but what the hell." She jerked her head toward the street beyond the rocky beach, about fifty meters away. "Come on. I know a place near here. With food."

"No go with you." He backed farther away. "You hit."

She stiffened, angry. She wasn't like Caul. "Suit yourself." She dropped the club and strode toward the street. Over her shoulder, she said, "You can come, run away, or grab your little club and try bashing me again."

Footsteps sounded behind her. "Not little," he said.

If he had known how to wield the club, it could have been dangerous. She didn't believe he really wanted to hurt her, though. Why she thought that, she couldn't have said, other than it was easier to pick up his mind than with most people. She had no idea why she was helping him, except that it bothered her to see someone hurting. She knew how that felt.

Aliana kept going, with her would-be attacker following. When they reached the street, he came up beside her, acting as if he didn't notice she was there. He hadn't picked up his club, though. Either he trusted her more than he should have or else he didn't know much about weapons.

They walked along the street while armored bug-vans rumbled past, grey and windowless. When they were deeper into the city, an unexpected growl of voices came from a plaza ahead. Uneasy, Aliana stopped at the edge of the open area. Grey and red buildings surrounded it, most with armored plates instead of windows, one-way screens that served as spy portals looking out onto the plaza. A crowd of taskmaker slaves had gathered across the square, watching a giant holo projected on the side of the only building that sported a working screen. She couldn't hear much from this far away except the driving beat of drums.

"Loud," her new friend in the red jumpsuit said.

She glanced at him. "You got a name?"

He ignored her, watching the crowd.

"I have to call you something," she said. "How about Red?"

He continued to pretend he was interested in the crowd.

She motioned at the people. "You want to go see what's up?"

He flinched. "Aristos come?"

Aliana doubted anyone here had ever even seen an Aristo. "Don't worry. They never come to this sleazo slum."

"No Aristos," he said.

"No Aristos. You got my word on that."

He glanced at her. "I go with you."

"Good." She headed across the plaza with Red at her side.

No one paid them much attention, other than a few disinterested glances. She soon saw why everyone had gathered here. The holo showed a gorgeous man in black leather with red hair. He was singing in some language she'd never heard, his head thrown back, his fists clenched, his powerful voice full of fury.

They stopped at the outskirts of the crowd. "Mad," Red said at her side.

"Yeah, no shit." Something bothered Aliana about the singer. He looked familiar, but she knew she'd never seen him before. She would remember a guy who looked that good.

"Provider," Red said suddenly. "Want to go."

"What?" She glanced at him. "You think that guy is a provider?"

"His arm." He pointed at the holo. "Got e-spring burns." He backed away.

"Hey." Aliana pulled him back. "He's somewhere else, not here." Red had it right, though, the singer did have welts, cuts, and burns on his arms. It was part of the show, right? Why else would he go on stage like that?

"Red, look, he doesn't have wrist guards or a collar," she said. "He's not a slave. And he sure as blazes isn't an Aristo, not with that hair."

"Skolian," he said, pulling his thin arm out of her grip. "Singing in Iotic."

Aliana snorted. "Yeah, right. How would you know the language of Skolian royalty?"

"Iotic," he insisted as the man wailed the climatic line of his song.

"I wonder what he's saying," a man nearby said.

Aliana considered Red. "Can you really understand him?"

He shook his head. "Don't know Iotic. Just recognize it."

"You used to work in an Aristo's mansion or something?" It was the only way she could imagine that he might have heard such a high language.

Red wouldn't look at her. "Or something."

The music calmed as the man let go of his final note. The viewpoint of the holo moved out to show his audience, a crowd in some big plaza that dwarfed this little square. Aliana didn't recognize it, but she'd never been anywhere besides this city, Muzepolis, named for its owner, Orzon Muze, the son of Admiral Erix Muze, one of ESComm's Joint Commanders.

Suddenly the singer shouted in Highton, the language of Aristos. *That* Aliana knew; anyone with any sense learned enough Highton to jump to it if an Aristo ever gave them an order. Besides, languages came easy to Aliana. She could almost *feel* what a speaker was trying to say.

"*This is for you, Jaibriol Qox,*" the man shouted. He sang blasphemous words, soaring on the notes until he reached the end, excoriating the highest of the high, the gods of Eube:

I'll never kneel beneath your Highton stare
I'm here and I'm real, your living nightmare!

Gasps sounded as people backed away. Others stood with their mouths open, staring at the singer as if it his vocal cords had suddenly turned into laser cannons shooting them.

"We go!" Red spun around and sprinted away, his long legs eating up distance.

"Hey." Aliana jogged after him and caught up in a few paces. She grabbed him around the waist and pulled him to a stop, her arms wrapped around his lithely muscled body, holding his back against her front, pinning his arms to his sides.

"Calm down," she said. "You didn't do nothing. It's the singer, not you."

"Let go," he said, straining to throw her off. His mind blasted panic.

"Come on." She kept her hold on him. "You got to calm down. You'll make your heart pop."

After a few moments, his struggle eased. Then, gods blast it, he started *crying*. It was silent, and she could barely tell with his back against her front, but with her head alongside his and her cheek against his hair, she saw the tears slide down his face and his expression contort as if he were struggling to hold them back.

"Ah, shoozers," Aliana muttered. "Come on. Don't cry. Here. I'll get you food, okay?"

"I not cry," he said sharply.

"Yeah, I know. I never cry, either." If he could lie about it, so could she.

"Let go me."

"You gonna run away if I do?"

"Maybe."

"I can't feed you if you run off."

"Let go!"

"All right." Aliana felt the panic running out of his mind like water swirling down a drain. She relaxed her arms and let him go. He stood there, tensed as if he expected a blow. When nothing happened, he brushed his dirty red jumpsuit as if he were trying to neaten it up. He stepped away and regarded her sideways.

"Look at me," she said gently.

He looked at her, then flinched and averted his gaze.

"Huh." Aliana wondered what had happened to him. She used to act that way with Caul, her stepfather, when she thought he would hit her. She realized something else, too. As filthy as he was, covered in dirt, he didn't smell, other than the loamy odor of soil. He didn't have the stink of someone who didn't clean himself. In fact, all that dirt *hid* him. No one looked at him. Maybe he did that on purpose. Of course she couldn't come out and ask what was the deal, not yet. It wasn't done that way. But she'd find out.

"So are you coming?" she asked.

He considered her for a moment. "Yes. I go with you."

So they set off together, headed to her home, the cubicle Harindor had given her to live in.

"The question," Dehya said, "isn't how many people have seen the holo." She paced across the parquetry floor of her living room. "It's whether anyone is left who *hasn't* seen the damn thing."

Kelric watcher her, leaning against the edge of an arched entrance to the room. Eldrin, Dehya's husband and Kelric's older brother, was standing by the holo-stage near the wall, watching the holo of Del silently wail "Carnelians Finale." Their mother Roca stood with him. She shook her head, and her hair rippled around her shoulders like liquid gold.

"We have to talk to Del," Roca said. "Convince him to help us put this under wraps again."

"It's impossible." Kelric said tiredly. Nothing could contain this plague.

Dehya paced past him, a diminutive figure is a soft blue dress that swirled around her knees. "We hid that song with best security we have. What happened?"

"Why is it always this way with Del?" Eldrin said. "We forever end up talking about how we have to fix whatever he did."

"Del didn't do anything." Dehya stopped and regarded her husband. "He cooperated with us nine years ago when we suppressed the song. I doubt he has anything to do with it resurfacing."

"He *sang* it," Kelric said. "He knew how politically inflammatory it would be."

Roca spoke quietly. "It's magnificent."

"What, you're supporting this mess?" Kelric growled.

"Of course not," Roca said. As Foreign Affairs Councilor in the Assembly, she advised the two rulers of the Imperialate—the Ruby Pharaoh and the First Councilor—on how to defuse situations exactly such as this. She had won her Foreign Affairs seat by running for election like any other citizen. Combined with her lesser hereditary seat, it made her one of the most influential Assembly councilors. No matter how much she or any of them might like "Carnelians Finale," they had to do their best to counter its effect.

"It's too late to lock it down." Dehya said. "We need damage control."

"How?" Kelric asked. He hoped she had an idea, because he sure as hell didn't.

"Can you get it off the Kyle network?" Eldrin asked Dehya. "You know the meshes better than anyone."

"I can do some deletions," she said. "Especially if you help me. But it's gone too far to erase it the way we did nine years ago."

"Emperor Jaibriol probably released it," Roca said. "Given what he must be dealing with from the other Hightons, he probably regrets ever seeing that treaty. How he convinced his Joint Commanders to sign it is beyond me."

"He didn't release 'Carnelians Finale,'" Kelric said, keeping his mental barriers strong. He had no mental finesse; he was just blunt force. It was frustrating when he needed to pick up nuances from someone's mind, but no one alive could get past his barriers, not even his family. He hid what he knew about Jaibriol.

Roca was watching him. "What's wrong?"

Damn. Her inability to pick up his thoughts didn't stop her from using her too perceptive mother's intuition. He glared at her, mainly to throw her off track. "What *isn't* wrong?"

"We'll do what we can in the meshes," Dehya said. "Roca, you talk with the Allieds."

"Governments aren't the problem," Eldrin said. "No matter how much any of ours may want the treaty, it will fail if the citizens of three empires turn against it. With Del riling everyone up, that's what we're looking at."

"Then we have to calm them down," Dehya said.

"How?" Roca said.

Dehya exhaled. "I wish I knew."

Jaibriol found the lights dimmed when he walked into his bedroom suite at the palace. It was a relief; after his day, he needed refuge.

Suite was a subdued word. Even in the dim light, the walls gleamed, gold and ivory with platinum moldings, all the materials authentic, none created in labs. Chandeliers glittered, heavy with diamonds. An antique lamp with a ruby shade stood near his bed casting dim red light. Dark red drapes canopied the bed, held back by braided gold ropes, and red and gold pillows of gleaming satin were heaped against the headboard. But all that rich, sultry beauty dimmed compared to the woman who lay atop the covers, asleep in the smoky light, long and sleekly curved, wearing nothing more than a black lace shift that barely covered her torso and hips. Her hair shimmered, falling across her face, and her lashes lay long on her cheeks, black against her alabaster skin. Even with no make-up, her lips were red. Her face was soft in repose, the only time his empress looked vulnerable. He never told her; if she knew, she might never again let him see her asleep.

Jaibriol mounted the dais and sat on the bed. He slid his hand over her hip.

Tarquine rolled onto her back, still asleep, her hair falling back from her face, revealing her classic Highton profile, which not only looked like it belonged on a coin, but did in fact grace one. Jaibriol had commissioned it years ago as a peace offering. That was after he had blocked her subtle and exasperatingly illegal attempts to control the market in exotic imported fabrics using her inside knowledge as Finance Minister. He had never realized how much wealth shiny cloth brought into his empire until his brilliantly amoral wife had turned her attention to the subject.

As if Tarquine needed more money. She was already one of the wealthiest human beings in the history of the human race. In fact, including the finances at her disposal as empress, she might be the richest. So why did she need to commit fraud on an interstellar scale? Keeping watch on her was a major headache, and it didn't help that she was so blithely unrepentant.

Yet for all that, she lacked the cruelty inherent to most Aristos. Several decades ago, she had destroyed her ability to transcend. Despite what Aristos vehemently claimed—that transcendence was their exalted right—she had come to the conclusion it was nothing more than animalistic brutality.

"Are you going to sit there all night?" she asked. She raised her eyes halfway, her eyes glinting like red gems under her black lashes. She languidly traced her finger across his thigh.

Jaibriol slid down next to her. As he pulled her into his arms, she undulated against him with an unconscious sensuality. He knew she didn't realize her effect on him because he could lower his empathic barriers with her. That such a powerful, alluring woman had so little idea of her own eroticism made her even more addicting. Eleven years of marriage had done nothing to dull his desire.

Later they lay together, tangled in the satin sheets.

Tarquine dozed in his arms like a deadly wild animal momentarily subdued, until she awoke and resumed prowling. He knew the truth he wanted to deny: he would always be prey to her. She could no longer transcend, but the drive was buried so deep within her that it survived even if the act no longer brought her the ecstasy that had turned the entire race of Aristos into sadists.

The drive that the child they hoped to make would inherit.

"Well, this is it," Aliana said, ushering Red into her home. "It's not much. But it's mine."

She lived in a hive of hexagonal units stacked up in a hexagonal building. Her home was about halfway up the structure. Its only entrance was a door shaped like an elongated hexagon. Inside, she had a combined living room and kitchen, with food processors along the right wall and a media smart-center on the left. The ceiling and floor were horizontal edges of the hexagon, and the walls on either side sloped into points. A table with a few semi-smart chairs stood by the right wall, and a couple of cheap recliners were arrayed around the media smart-center.

Smart, bah. Calling the center's tangle of filaments a brain was generous. As Aliana entered with Red, the center started some propaganda holo about the greatness of Muze Aristos. Of course she would never say *propaganda* out loud. She wasn't important enough that anyone would bother to bug her home, but you never knew what words might tip off some generic monitor in the tech that Aristos sold low-level taskmaker slaves.

The Muze Line owned her. Not that she ever saw

them. She doubted any of them even lived fulltime on the planet, despite its name, Muze's Helios. The only person who "owned" her was Harindor, even if he wasn't the one who put the collar around her neck and the guards on her wrists. He had far more say in her life than the supposedly godlike Muzes, given that she had never even seen one exalted hair on their exalted butts.

Red looked around at her cubicle. "Small."

"Yeah, well, it's better than what you had," she said, suddenly defensive, knowing how paltry it all looked. "Don't diss my home, drill-boy."

Red swung around to her. "No call me that!"

"Hey, sorry." She flushed.

He hesitated, his glance flicking to the kitchen. "Food?"

"Sure." Aliana went to a wall panel and punched in a meal order. She didn't have much, just the usual, but it was all right.

"You not provider," Red said behind her.

Bemused, she turned around. He was standing in the center of the room. It startled her to realize she had trusted him enough to turn away; on principle, she never showed her back to anyone.

"Of course I'm not a provider," she said. "Most people aren't." Only a few thousand providers existed. Most of Eube's two trillion citizens were taskmakers, all slaves, but with complicated hierarchies. Taskmakers at the top had a great deal of wealth or power; those at the bottom, like her, were nobody. Providers weren't in the hierarchy. Their entire reason for existence was to please their Aristo owners. They lived in incredible luxury, but she doubted it was worth it. Pain for your entire life? No thanks.

Red hesitated. "You provider. Aristos just not know."

She gave a snort. "I'm too ugly to be a provider."

"Beautiful. Pretty gold skin."

Right, sure. The wall beeped at her, and she said, "Time to eat."

"Stay away from Aristos," Red persisted. "They find out."

"Don't worry." She pulled two trays of food out of the delivery module. "I'll avoid that big crowd of Aristos hanging around here." She set the trays on the table. The pseudo-steaks smelled great, and the vegetables lit up the white tray with sprays of green, red, orange, and blue.

Red dropped into a chair, his gaze avid. She laid a knife, scoop, and fork next to his tray, but he just picked up the steak with his hand and tore a huge bite out of the meat, eating so fast he hardly seemed to chew.

"Hey, slow down. You'll make yourself sick." Aliana pushed his hand, making him plunk the steak back into its dish. She stuck the fork into the meat. "You know how to eat civilized, right?" She offered him the knife. "You know, cut up your food, use a fork."

He stared at the knife, then at her, then at the knife. Whatever bothered him must have been big, because he stopped trying to eat.

Aliana spoke awkwardly. "Red, I seem to freak you every other minute, hell if I know why. I mean, is it really that crazy for me to think you can use a fork and stuff?"

"Knife." His face paled. "Me not touch. Get punished."

"Why?"

"Not allowed weapon. Not ever."

A terrible feeling was growing in Aliana. She sat next to him and cut a piece of his steak, then speared it with the fork and offered it to him.

Red took the fork and ate the meat.

"Okay," Aliana said. "We'll do it this way." As she sliced up his food, she said, "You need better clothes than that jumpsuit."

"Clothes fine."

She finished cutting his meat. "There. All done."

With no further hesitation, he dug into his meal. He practically inhaled the food, never even pausing to drink his water.

Aliana ate more slowly. "So. About your jumpsuit."

He finished his last bite. "Not need clothes."

"Yes, you do. Yours are filthy. You can borrow a pair of my trousers and a shirt." She touched his arm. "You might have to roll up the shirt sleeves, though. They're probably too long."

Red yanked away his arm. "Clothes fine!"

Her sinking feeling was growing worse. "You've covered up your wrists and your neck," she said softly. "Your wrist guards and your collar. All the signs of who owns you."

He crossed his arms and hunched his shoulders. "Not have to show."

"I want to see them."

"No!"

"Show me," she said. "Or I'll put you out, and no more food for you."

"No." He met her gaze defiantly. "Not cut off my hands."

Good gods. "I'd never do that! Never." She almost

stuttered. "No matter what you got there on your wrists. Not even if it's worth more than this entire hexagon."

"Even if worth more than city?"

Aliana went cold. "Even that."

At first he just looked at her. Then he pushed back his sleeve, uncovering the grimy skin on the back of his hand. He pushed his sleeve farther, above his wrist—

"Gods," she whispered. Even expecting something unusual, she wasn't prepared. *So brilliant.* A slave guard several centimeters wide circled his wrist, made from what looked like solid diamond.

"Is that *real?*" she asked.

Red jerked down his sleeve, covering the sparkle. "Real diamond."

"You got that around your neck, too?"

"And ankles."

"Do the guards and collar include a mesh system that networks into your body?"

His face paled. "Yes."

"So no one can take them off without killing you."

"Except Admiral Muze."

"You're *Admiral Muze's* provider?" Flaming hell! "You mean the Highton Aristo who heads the Muze Line? The joint commander of Eubian Space Command?"

He watched her with his large eyes. "Yes."

"But *how?*" She motioned at him, taking it all in, his raggedy hair and dirty clothes.

"He throw me away," Red said. "I crawl out of trash processor before it process me."

"He threw you out? Like *garbage?*"

"Yes. I garbage. He tired of me."

"I think I'm going to be sick." Aliana stood up and went to a sink by the wall. As she leaned over it, the sink's excuse for a brain sort of figured out what she wanted and turned on a fountain of water. The liquid hit Aliana smack in the face. It was so ridiculous, she choked on a laugh and forgot to be sick.

"You feel bad?" Red asked.

She turned to him, wiping her face with her sleeve. "I'm okay." Lowering her arm, she said, "Are you all right?"

"No more hungry," he said, as if that were enough.

"Does Admiral Muze know you ran away?"

"Not run away," he said matter-of-factly. "Thrown out. Am trash."

"Aren't we all," Aliana said bitterly. "A bunch of rejects. I'm the bastard no one wants. My fight instructor is a decommissioned Razer. And here you are, a thrown-away provider. Don't we make a great crew."

He regarded her warily. "I not understand."

"Neither do I, not really." She sat at the table. "Listen, Red. You say, 'I don't understand.'"

"I did say."

"You used different grammar."

"You teach me to talk good. Yes?"

"I'll try." She winced. "Not that my speech is all that great. But it'll do."

He looked as if he had his doubts. But he said only, "Bath here?"

Aliana motioned to a hexagon portal across the room. "In there. You go clean up. I'll get you some clothes." Softly she said, "With long sleeves and a high collar."

His stiff posture eased a bit. "I thank."

"Sure." She wondered what the blazes she was going to do with her new provider—and what would happen if Admiral Muze found out she had Red.

VII

Triple Strike

WELCOME

It came to Dehya as a sense of greeting rather than an actual word.

Welcome, she answered.

The Kyle mesh spread out like a silvery web, undulating within a blue universe that enveloped her thoughts. Her mind saturated the mesh.

Had Dehya been one of the 999,999 out of every million people who didn't have enough telepathic ability to access the Kyle, she wouldn't have known how a person could mold the web. Had she been just a telop, or telepathic operator, she still wouldn't have been strong enough to notice the changes as the mesh evolved. Were she that one in a trillion who might be sensitive enough, the changes would still barely register. Even some of her own family, the most powerful psions alive, might not notice the more subtle shifts.

Dehya didn't just detect the changes—she caused them.

The Kyle rumbled through her with a power that would kill almost anyone. Yet it had never bothered her. She loved it here. Sometimes she wished she could stay forever. The web itself greeted her, no interface, no links, no nodes. She spoke directly to it, for she created and evolved that mesh until she became a part that ever-growing entity.

Carnelians Finale, she thought.

The blue around her morphed into a meadow speckled with white flowers. Earth. She stood beneath the yellow sun that had shone on the birth of her race. Her people could no longer call Earth their world; they had lost that birthright thousands of years ago when unknown beings had stolen her ancestors from Earth and left them stranded on another world with barely the ability to survive. It had taken those lost humans five thousand years to find their home again, but when they had finally arrived, the people of this blue world hadn't welcomed them.

She supposed it was no surprise. By that time, her people had fractured into Skolia and Eube, two belligerent empires that dwarfed the Allied Worlds of Earth. The only reason Eube didn't try to conquer Earth was because they couldn't spare the resources from their relentless drive to subjugate the Skolian Imperialate. In her more honest moments, Dehya had to admit that if the Eubians didn't exist, demanding all the resources Skolia commanded, her own people might have arrived on Earth as conquerors rather than lost children seeking their origins.

As Dehya crossed the meadow, grass rippled around her knees, green filaments glistening with picoware. Codes flitted within the translucent blades, flicking into existence, then disappearing to some other state of being. The sunlight had a vivid quality, almost vibrant, and a faint smell of flowers scented the air.

A heartbeat underlay it all.

The pulse was so much a part of the landscape that at first Dehya barely noticed. Gradually it increased in power until it shook through her. Not a heartbeat. Drums. As she walked up a hill under the cloud-flecked sky, musical chords joined the drums. They glistened like waves in the air, pulsing through different colors.

She stopped at the top of the hill. The slope rolled away from her feet in a sweep of rippling filaments glinting with a trillion data pathways through the Kyle. Musical data. A song thundered and Del's voice soared on the notes:

I'll never kneel beneath your Highton stare.
I'm here and I'm real; I'll lay your guilt bare.

"And so you have," Dehya murmured. A deeply intense part of her wanted his song to go on forever, shouting the atrocities of the Hightons. The other part, the sovereign who wanted peace, knew they had to stop its spread.

PROCEDURE? the Kyle asked.

Isolate the pathways that this song is taking through your mesh, Dehya thought.

WORKING. Within barely a moment, it thought, **IT IS IMPOSSIBLE TO ISOLATE ALL THE PATHWAYS WITHOUT DAMAGING MY NETWORKS.**

Dehya walked down the slope and filaments rose around her, flashing with the thoughts of a billion minds listening to "Carnelians Finale." *Damage how?*

OBSERVE.

The lights within a nearby reed faded. As they disappeared, the reed crumpled and turned black. Some person in the mesh had just lost their stream of "Carnelians Finale."

Stop, Dehya thought. *Release the block around that pathway.*

LINK REESTABLISHED. Lights flickered erratically within the reed. It turned green, but with a withered look. Somewhere, someone was probably cursing the vagaries of the mesh.

The wind rustled Dehya's hair and sent the filaments whispering against each other. *Do these pathways originate on Earth?* she asked. *All transmitting the song into space?*

YES.

She thought of all the other "meadows" throughout the Kyle, trillions upon trillions for every planet, star system, and interstellar community. It would be impossible to eradicate this song; it had become too intertwined with human civilization. Even crashing the Kyle mesh wouldn't stop it; the music would continue in smaller communities until the Kyle re-established itself.

THE SONG WILL KILL IF NO ANTIDOTE IS FOUND, the Kyle told her. IT IS A PLAGUE OF ANGER THAT INFECTS AND INFLAMES.

Show me.

The meadow blurred until it all ran together. She stood in a vague universe of green with lights glittering in the distance. The green shaded into red as the scene resolved into a room. Telop chairs with empty virtual reality suits were arrayed in the ruddy shadows, each one set before panels blinking with lights:

red, gold, blue, purple. A solitary man occupied one chair, a telop who received messages and sent them through Kyle space. He was listening to "Carnelians Finale" as he worked. Stirred by the song, his anger blasted into the Kyle along with the messages he was routing, like a dark red wave that struck Dehya with great force. She doubted he even realized he was broadcasting his fury.

Dehya surrounded herself with a bubble that filtered six channels: sight, audio, vocal, tactile, smell, and empathy. The red cast of the scene faded as the filter muted the power of the song.

What would happen if we disrupted his stream of the song? she asked.

THAT WOULD ANGER HIM AS MUCH AS THE SONG INFLAMES THOSE WHO RECEIVE IT FROM HIM.

It might be possible to ameliorate—

Dehya never finished the thought. The bubble around her exploded as pain slammed through her mind. She screamed in the dark—

Command centers honeycombed the hull of the Orbiter space station, functional spaces that contrasted with the beauty of the Ground and Sky interior. The most active center was the War Room. Consoles filled its amphitheatre, staffed with telops in VR chairs, their bodies encased in black suits with opalescent sheens, their heads covered by visored helmets. No space was left unused; robot arms with console cups carried other telops through the air as they worked.

Kelric entered high above the amphitheatre, several stories up, on a walkway that circled just below the holodome ceiling. Four catwalks stretched from the walkway to the center of the domed area like giant spokes on a wheel. They terminated at the "hub," a gigantic Command Chair. The dome arched above it, glowing with holos of the nebulae visible in space outside of the Orbiter. If anyone in the amphitheatre looked up, they would see the massive chair silhouetted against that starscape like a technological throne suspended among glittering star fields.

Kelric limped along a catwalk, and it swung slightly with his weight. His leg felt worse than usual today, stiff and unresponsive. When he reached the chair, he lowered himself into it and laid his large arms on the blocky armrests. Lights glinted inside the chair's translucent black surfaces. A hum came from above him as a hood lowered, forming a cavern for his head. A web of conduits settled into his hair, extending threads into his scalp. The chair's exoskeleton closed around him and inserted prongs into sockets in his wrists, lower spine, and neck. A visor clicked into place over his eyes, submerging him in darkness.

Activating simulation modulator transfer in v-space. That thought came from Bolt, the node implanted in his spine.

What the blazes does that mean? Kelric asked.

I'm turning on your helmet. Bolt wasn't supposed to have emotions, but his response felt far too amused to Kelric. His node was having fun with him.

The darkness lightened and left Kelric floating in interstellar space, surrounded by nebulae like cosmic gem dust. **Pretty simulation,** Kelric thought.

It does have aesthetic qualities that humans associate with beauty.

But of course you don't.

Of course not.

He laughed softly. **Bolt, you know that's bull-bollocks.**

You don't have to cuss at me. Then Bolt added, You're right, though, it is pretty.

That it is. So let's go to the planet.

Continuing simulation. The view changed as if Kelric was arrowing through space. Then Bolt added, You know, cussing with alliteration doesn't make it any classier.

Since when did cussing bother you? Kelric asked, curious. **You've heard me do it for decades.** An orange star was swelling in view in front of him. He wondered why Bolt didn't just switch the simulation so they were at the planet.

The profanity bothers your wife, Bolt said.

No, it doesn't. I'm an empath. I'd know if it bothered her.

Bolt transmitted a sense of rebuke.

You're inside me, Kelric thought. **If I don't see it, why would you?**

I'm paying attention.

She swears all the time.

She doesn't mind it from women.

For flaming sake. **Yes, I know, my wife is a barbaric sexist matriarch. Given the opportunity, she'd lock all men up in seclusion.**

I never said that. She's a modern, enlightened woman.

And you're a military mesh node. Not a marital advisor.

Bolt sent him the glyph of a grinning cat.

You enjoy giving me a hard time, Kelric thought.

I would never do such a thing, Bolt assured him. It would have been more convincing if the node hadn't sounded so amused.

The orange star continued to grow larger in front of Kelric as he hurtled through its system. Asteroids flashed by, huge chunks of rock rolling ponderously close.

When will we reach the base mesh? Kelric asked. **My schedule is tight. If I can't check all seven ISC bases in this region before I finish my shift, I'll fall too far behind on my rounds.**

A pause. Then Bolt thought, **Actually, we should already be there.**

Why aren't we? You have control of this—

With no warning, the galaxy burst open, splitting like a rotten fruit. Light drove daggers deep into Kelric's brain and pain roared through him.

And he died.

The dice lay scattered in a rainbow of shapes before Jaibriol. He rested his elbows on the tall table and his chin on his knuckles as he gazed at the playing pieces. Kelric had taught him Quis when they were on Earth negotiating the treaty. Jaibriol would never forget that moment—or hours, maybe—when they had linked minds, and Kelric had flooded him with the rules of the game. Somehow Kelric had known it would help calm the immense energy that had coursed through Jaibriol's mind since he joined the Triad. The patterns, algorithms, strategies, the infinite ways to play Quis: it fascinated Jaibriol. He wished he had someone to challenge. Unfortunately the only person he knew who played it was Kelric. He could just imagine the headlines: *Emperor of Eube challenges Imperator of Skolia to dice game. What does it mean? Is life as we know it ending?!*

"It means I can't figure out the blasted moves," Jaibriol muttered.

"What moves?" a woman said in a dusky voice.

He had enough control not to jerk, but she had caught him off guard, which rarely happened. Then again, she was the only person who could approach him without being blocked by a phalanx of security people and procedures.

He glanced up. "My greetings, wife."

The empress slid her long, sensual body into a wing chair across the table and glanced over his array of dice. "Why do you play with these?"

He wondered how she managed to look erotic and deadly at the same time. "It relaxes me."

Tarquine idly picked up a sapphire octahedron. "Is this an important piece?"

"It could be. Three-dimensional dice are higher in rank than flat ones. So are pieces with more sides." He tapped a garnet square. "Very low rank."

"It's red." Her lashes lowered slightly, veiling her carnelian eyes. "Any Aristo optician can tell you the stratospheric worth of that color."

Calm down, Jaibriol told his pulse, which was having an all too male response. "In Quis, it's just physics. The status of a piece goes by color. The longer the wavelength, the lower the rank. So red is low, purple is high."

"Status. How appropriate." She stretched her arms like a sleek cat, for all appearances relaxed. Since she never relaxed, he wondered how much trouble he was in this time.

"You're in a good mood," he said. "What did you do, cheat some rivals out of their legacy?"

"I never cheat anyone," she purred. "I simply exploit flaws in their finances."

Flaws, indeed. She needed somewhere to turn that prodigious mind of hers before she took over the economy of his entire empire and tangled it into knots just to keep herself entertained. "You should learn to play Quis. We could challenge each other."

"We challenge each other all the time." Her perfect smile curved. "I always win."

He didn't want to debate who won the most arguments, because he would lose. So instead he pushed a handful of dice toward her. The gems sparkled. "The purpose is to build structures. The higher the rank of the structure, of the dice within it, and of the way the structure fits into the story of the game, the more points you get."

She set down the sapphire and nudged a diamond sphere with her index finger. "What story?"

Good question. "I'm not sure, actually." He thought of his solitaire games. "Taken altogether, the structures tell a story. Or predict one. You mold them using various strategies and see what results you get." He gave her a wicked grin. "We'll play a game about you and me playing games. See which of us the Quis predicts will win."

"I don't need dice to tell me that." She leaned back languidly. "Though I must say, that logic was deliciously circular."

Jaibriol thought if she kept looking at him that way,

they would end up working on his need for an heir rather than playing dice. How bizarre, that circular arguments aroused his wife.

"Here." He set an emerald bar in the center of the table. "Your move."

"Is it now." She flicked the diamond ball and it rolled until it hit the bar, then rebounded a bit and stopped.

He set down a topaz rod, bridging his emerald bar and her sphere. "There."

"'There'?" she said. "Does that have a translation?"

"The structure I made using those three dice is called a lamp post. Or something like that. I made it, so I win." He smirked at her. "And I captured your diamond sphere. Which is the highest ranked piece."

"A sphere?" Her elegant eyebrow arched. "It has only one measly little surface."

Jaibriol grinned. "It has an infinite number of faces, wife."

She gave him her iciest Aristo stare. "It most certainly does not."

"Ah, but look." He tapped a line of dice. "Tetrahedron, pentahedron, cube, heptahedron, octahedron. They go from four to eight faces. The more faces, the rounder they get. Let the number of faces go to infinity, and you get a sphere."

"Is that so?"

"It most certainly is."

"Of course I would play the highest ranked piece," she murmured. She slid a ruby pyramid into the center of the table. "And what, your Delectable Highness, can you do with that?"

"You know, Tarquine, I'm an emperor, not a dessert."

"Is there a difference?" she murmured.

Jaibriol decided he was safer treating that as a rhetorical question. Besides, he liked her titles for him better than the overblown honorifics that Aristo custom demanded people use for him, Your Glorious, Exalted Whatever. He wondered if his ancestors had ever exploded from being so full of themselves that their skin couldn't contain their egos.

He set a carnelian pyramid next to her ruby. "Your move."

"Eube and Skolia," she said. "How appropriate."

"It could be," he said. She intuitively seemed to understand how the Quis worked.

They continued playing, their session evolving as he taught her what little he knew of the rules. She caught on extraordinarily fast, and he thought he should be terrified by that fact, but he was enjoying himself too much to care. Quis patterns spread across the table. A story evolved.

It started out as a nebulous idea, but it soon clarified, growing out of whatever subconscious motives they brought to their moves. Tarquine started many new structures, fresh and full of promise, always stressing red and purple, the colors of his throne and office.

And finally he understood.

Jaibriol raised his gaze to look at Tarquine. He felt suddenly wound tight, as if he were about to open a door to an unknown place that he both feared and longed to find.

Her lips curved as she met his gaze. "Am I really that fascinating?"

His pulse was hammering. Music should swell or criers should call out. But they would do none of that here. "When did you find out?" he asked. His voice was surreally calm.

She said, simply, "An hour ago."

"An hour." Jaibriol took a deep breath. "Do you know . . . ?" He couldn't go on.

Her words fell into the silence. "It's a boy."

He stared at her. "You're sure?"

"I'm sure." Her voice was velvet. "Your empire will welcome news of the Highton Heir."

The Highton Heir. *His* heir. The heir to the Carnelian Throne. Gods almighty, she was carrying his son. He felt as if he was struggling to breathe. "Tarquine—"

She did something incredibly rare then. She reached out and took his hand. "He will look like you. Beautiful."

He didn't know how to answer. If his son truly looked like him, as Jaibriol had appeared before he had genetically modified himself, they would have to alter the child's appearance. Jaibriol had been born with multicolored hair, black streaked by gold, with none of the telltale Highton glitter.

The chair heaved under Jaibriol. What the blazes? Meshes networked the furniture, and the table could morph, even act with rudimentary intelligence, but no reason existed for it to react to Tarquine's announcement—

The ceiling suddenly snapped with a great booming crack and collapsed downward, showering them with breaking plasticrete. A growl rumbled through the room. Tapestries swayed and fell while the walls where they hung bowed inward and split open.

Tarquine jumped to her feet as Jaibriol shoved the

table out of the way. A column toppled against a wall, smashing into pieces, and the growl became a roar. Dust billowed in the air while chunks of composite, gems, and stone smashed down around them. As Jaibriol grabbed Tarquine, a jagged weight hit the back of his head. They fell under the rain of debris and he curled his body around her, protecting his empress and their unborn child.

Blackness closed around him.

VIII

Three Paths to Death

The black hover car whizzed above the street like a bullet, whirred around, and came back toward Aliana and Red. It settled on the road, blocking their way. A portal in its side irised open and a woman leaned out, her rusty-red eyes hard in the drizzling morning. A man sat farther back in the car, barely visible.

"Well, aren't you a pretty pair," the woman said. "Get in. We'll give you a ride."

The hair on the back of Aliana's neck rose. That woman had eyes the same color as her stepfather. He used to talk that way when he was drunk, as if he were an Aristo and Aliana was his slave. That was usually before he started hitting.

"No thanks." Aliana grabbed Red's arm, spun around, and strode the other way, tugging him with her.

"Careful," Red said as he strode at her side. "They rich. Important. Not make mad."

"I don't give a drill how rich they are," Aliana said. "They're still slaves." With those eyes, the woman had to be part Aristo, the illegitimate daughter of someone powerful. Just seeing her made Aliana feel as if bugs were crawling on her skin.

The car hummed behind them, its turbines growling. Aliana sped up, pulling Red, and he stumbled as his shoes scraped the pavement. She suddenly knew he had never before worn shoes. His mind blazed with it. She often picked up moods from people, but never with this clarity. She kept her grip on his arm, afraid someone would try to tear him away. He had only been with her a couple of days, but he already felt like a part of her life.

The car came around and settled down in front of them. Aliana skidded to a stop and Red stayed with her, staring at the car.

The woman stepped out and stalked over to them. "Come along," she said. "Both of you."

Aliana tensed. Although the woman wasn't wearing a uniform, she moved like a military tech-type. Even so. Aliana could lose this prowler babe if she sprinted for the labyrinth of alleys that networked the old city. She knew this town better than any half-Aristo spawn. But she doubted Red could keep up, given his problems with the shoes. So she stayed put, tensing for a fight. Good thing she'd been working with Tide.

"Come on," the woman said. "Into the hover with you both."

"Why the hell would we go anywhere with you?" Aliana said.

The man stepped out and lounged against the car, his arms crossed, watching them with an amused look, as if they were his entertainment. Although red streaked his hair, the rest shimmered black like Aristo hair. His eyes were red. He wore a collar like everyone else, but he was obviously in the stratosphere of taskmaker slaves, maybe even more than half Aristo.

The woman's expression hardened. "Someone should teach you respect, girl."

"For what?" Aliana asked. "Why should I respect some random stranger who stops us on the street and tries to haul us off some place where you and that asshole"—she waved her hand at the guy—"can get your kicks making us scream."

The woman studied her as if she were a bug. "You've never been a provider."

"Yeah, well, neither have you," Aliana said. "So what?"

The man wasn't smiling anymore. He came over to the woman and spoke in a low voice. They probably didn't think Aliana could hear. She often picked up conversations that people believed were private. It had to do with feeling their minds and extrapolating their mood to their words. Or something. She didn't know why it worked, but it was useful.

"She isn't wearing provider restraints," the man said. "But gods, her mind is a furnace. The boy, too. Find out who they are."

The woman spoke louder, to Aliana. "Who do you belong to?"

"Same as you," Aliana said. "Garret Muze." Lord Garret was related to Orzon Muze, a cousin of a sister of a brother of who the hell knew what. A minor Aristo, but still an Aristo, so he owned things, like this slum, which more important Aristos didn't even want. Aliana didn't know what the guy meant by "furnace," but she doubted she would like it.

The woman came forward, her laserlike focus boring

into them, and stopped in front of Aliana. "We're part of Lord Orzon's household."

Aliana stood her ground, glad she was taller than this fake Aristo. "Good for you."

The woman's mouth tightened. With no warning, she moved—like a blur.

Shit. Aliana responded by instinct, ducking the blow and kicking out her foot. The woman countered with surreal speed, fast and brutal, as if she had augmentation to her body.

Their fight went *fast.* With her mind so pumped up, Aliana couldn't separate details. She combined the street brawling she already knew with the training Tide had pounded into her every day these past three months. The fight took all her strength, tricks and cheats, and even with that, she felt as if she were struggling with two people. She barely held her own.

Finally Aliana got a choke hold on the woman's neck. She wanted to snap it in two, hear the bones *crack . . .*

"STOP!" Red's shout registered on Aliana. He was yanking on her arm.

Disoriented, Aliana released the woman, who crumpled to the ground. As Aliana's head cleared, she realized she *had* been fighting two people. The man lay nearby, one of his arms bent at an odd angle. Alarms were blaring and people had gathered around, watching avidly.

"Gods," Aliana rasped. What had she done? The man and woman were breathing; in her heightened state, she felt their minds like a blast of heat. They were unconscious but alive.

"We dead," Red told her.

"Like hell!" She grabbed his arm and took off. Red grunted, running clumsily, but he kept up. They had to hide! If Admiral Muze's people caught them, that would be it. They'd kill Red, probably painfully, for having the audacity to want to live, and gods only knew what they'd do to her.

People backed away as she and Red ran, watching with the ugly fascination of a crowd that thinks it's about to witness an execution. No one chased her. Why would they? They had no stake in this and they knew the rules. Mind your business. Keep your head down. She would have done the same.

Aliana ducked into an alley that was so narrow, she and Red had to go single file, their shoulders scraping against the ragged plasti-bricks on either side. At least the wall did nothing to hinder them. The cheap bricks just stayed in place like inanimate objects. Well, yeah, they *were* inanimate objects. She couldn't imagine living in a place where all objects were this dumb, but right now it suited her just fine.

She and Red squeezed through a maze of passages. She had already explored the old city, obsessively mapping its hidden routes in case her stepfather Caul came after her and she needed to lose herself. She could leave home, learn to fight, learn to survive, but she could never get Caul out of her mind, the specter of his fists hitting, hitting, *hitting*. He lurked there like a trap waiting to spring every time she started to think that maybe, just maybe, she would be okay.

Eventually, when her thundering pulse calmed, Aliana slowed to a stop. Red collapsed against the wall. He was breathing so hard, guilt stabbed through Aliana. She was an asshole. To stop Admiral Muze's people from grabbing him, she nearly killed him herself. Real swift.

"I fine," Red said between breaths. "Not even close to dead."

Aliana slumped against the wall, facing the bricks, her palms against their rough surface. "How can you tell what I think so easily?"

"You same as me. More than me."

"More *what?*"

"Don't know," he muttered. "My chest hurts."

"You ever run before?" she asked. That freaking admiral hadn't let him do anything.

He shook his head. "Never."

"Give it a moment. You'll feel better."

They rested there, listening to the slums. People were arguing somewhere, their voices faint and quarrelsome. The air smelled like brine and wet trash.

"We're near the waterfront," Aliana said.

"Lake?"

"No, the ocean docks." She turned and leaned her back against the wall, staring at the opposite wall. "This city is a port for sea ships. You know what those are?"

"They fly above the water?"

"Not above. In it."

"In? Why?"

"Hell if I know." She pushed away from the wall. "You doing better?"

Red stood up straighter. "Better. Yes." Then he smiled.

Aliana froze. It was as if a light had gone on. Even dressed in her worn out shirt and trousers, he was beautiful. Those blue eyes, that mop of brown hair, the perfect features. When he smiled, he was radiant.

Yeah, he was a provider all right, designed, bred, and trained to please, to give you whatever you desired, however you wanted it, without resisting, rebelling, or even thinking. Except wonder of all wonders, he had broken his conditioning and run away. Amazing, how the instinct for self-preservation could defy centuries of breeding for subservient, helpless slavery.

"Why you stare at me?" he asked.

She grinned. "Cause you're just so ugly I can't get over it."

He winced as if she had struck him. "My sorry."

"Red, I was joking! You're gorgeous."

"Not. Admiral threw me away. Am hideous."

"He's an idiot." Gods, she was going to get herself killed if she kept this up, insulting Aristos and pounding powerful people. "Did he, um, I mean, did he make you..." She was too embarrassed to go any further.

"He not want me for sex," Red said. "Only to provide. Has pretty girl providers for sex."

"Maybe that's why he threw you away," Aliana said. "Because you aren't a girl." She drew him away from the wall. "We have to get out of the city. I think we should hide on a boat."

"Not go back to your hexagon?"

"Not a chance," she said. "I don't know if any holocams caught that fight. Most are broken in this part of town. But Red, I beat the cold crap out of those two. And they know what I look like." She shook her head. "We got to run, sweet stuff, far and fast, before they find us."

He didn't look convinced. "How?"

Aliana grimaced. "I wish I knew."

✧ ✧ ✧

"We're losing her pulse," Doctor Sashia shouted. She ran with med techs and Jagernauts down a metal corridor toward an air-speed tube, deep within the Orbiter's hull. The air stretcher floated next to her, protecting its priceless cargo in a cocoon that blocked out physical, audio, visual, tactile, and neurological stresses. The nodes in Sashia's spine linked to the stretcher's EI brain, letting her analyze her patient even as they ran.

The door of the air tube snapped open as they arrived. It took only seconds for Sashia, the techs, and the guards to cram into the car there. As it shot off toward the hospital, Sashia bent over the stretcher and administered a dose of psi-active drugs to her patient. Her hands were clammy.

Her patient—the Ruby Pharaoh—was dying.

"Emperor Qox has lost too much blood!" Doctor Blueson called to his medical team. "Bring me more plasma, nanomed serum five-oh-nine."

Monitors blazed while slave-bots and Razers loomed around Blueson. The emperor lay collapsed on his back, the gaping wounds in his torso pumping blood as the medics desperately worked. Blood soaked Blueson's hands, Jaibriol's shredded clothes, the debris-strewn floor, everything in the ruins of the hall. The empress was in no better condition, and another team was working just as urgently to save her life.

"Gods almighty," a medic in the other group choked. "She's *pregnant!*"

"Stabilize her!" Blueson shouted. He felt as if he were on an out of control racer rocketing off a cliff. He was only a lieutenant, but he had been the closest doctor after the explosion shook the palace. Now he was responsible for the lives of the emperor and empress, and gods help him, apparently for the long-awaited heir to the Carnelian Throne as well.

A woman in the uniform of an ESComm colonel strode into the chaos. The badge on her uniform said *Lyra Qoxdaughter.* Everyone but the medics jumped to attention. Blueson shot her a harried glance but otherwise kept working on the emperor. So much *blood* and he couldn't stop it, not even with adherents and injected meds.

Qoxdaughter knelt next to him. Short yellow hair dusted with grey fell around her face as she helped Blueson close one of the wounds in Jaibriol's torso. She spoke crisply. "Download."

The node in Blueson's spine hurtled data at Qoxdaughter's spinal node. As the emperor's personal physician, she had a far greater rank than Blueson even beyond her military status. She could slave his node to hers and take what she needed. Of course she was privileged. She was the half-Aristo daughter of the emperor's grandfather.

"Your choice of nanomed series is odd," she told Blueson. "I've never seen that combination before."

Blueson froze, holding an air syringe he had been about to use on Jaibriol. If he had harmed the emperor with his inexperience, he would face imprisonment, maybe execution. He kept his voice calm. "I thought that working together, that combination would rebuild his tissues faster."

Qoxdaughter nodded as she tended a gash in Jaibriol's side. "It's working. You may have saved his life."

Blueson exhaled and continued with his injection.

"Thank the gods," he said in a low voice, as much for his own life as for Emperor Qox.

"I doubt the gods had much to do with this," Qoxdaughter muttered.

Blueson didn't think so, either, unless they had decided to destroy Eube by killing the entire royal family in one blow.

"We have to reach him!" Admiral Chad Barzun spoke urgently into the comm on his mech-tech gauntlet. He was standing on the walkway that circled the War Room high above the amphitheatre. The Command Chair hung in the center of the circle, accessible by four catwalks that led to it like spokes. Accessible, that was, until moments ago. In an unprecedented and supposedly impossible event, the independent systems for all four catwalks had simultaneously failed, the locks holding them in place had released, and they had plummeted into the amphitheatre. It had happened in the same instant that a mental earthquake jolted every telop in the amphitheatre and ripped their commander, the Imperator, out of the War Room mesh.

"We can't release the entry hatches," a woman said on his comm. That was Major Qahot, chief of security on the Orbiter. "The War Room is locked tight. I've never seen it like this when we weren't under attack."

"Whatever happened affected Imperator Skolia," Chad said. Kelric was slumped in the Command Chair, unresponsive, his eyes closed. Chad couldn't see him breathing. Was he alive? Dead? No monitors here were working. The consoles were off-mesh, the robot arms were frozen, and the telops were out of their VR suits, all staring up at the holodome. The only light came from the nebulae holos glowing beneath the dome, which were on the emergency generator that kept up life support in the War Room in case of a lockdown during war time.

Two Jagernauts were climbing a metal ladder embedded in the opposite wall, a woman and a man, their black uniforms stark against the silver-white surface. Chad had just finished that same climb on this side of the holodome. He had been lucky; if he hadn't come to the amphitheatre to check the new mesh nodes, he would be locked out of the War Room along with everyone else on his staff. The ladders were a last resort, and right now their safety meshes were as nonfunctional as everything else here, which meant if the Jagernauts lost their grip, nothing would stop their fall.

Chad switched channels on his comm and spoke to the Jagernauts. "Secondary Panquai, how are the rungs?"

The woman on the ladder spoke into the comm on her gauntlet. "Holding fine, Admiral." She had a cable gun in one hand, and it clanged against the rungs as she climbed.

The man coming up after her was Sterven Lamong, a Jagernaut with three armbands around each of his biceps, the sign of a Tertiary, the rank below Secondary. Dark and leanly muscled, he was a male version of Panquai. He had ripped a sheet of mesh composite off a console below and now carried it strapped to his back. It was their best try at a stretcher, given that the mobile units were either inaccessible in their inactive storage bins or outside the War Room.

"Admiral Barzun!" Major Qahot's voice snapped out of his comm. "We've isolated the cause of the lockdown. Sir, it was Imperator Skolia! He did this with his own mind."

Chad swore under his breath. It made a bizarre sort of sense: the *Imperator* was the only "system" with unlimited access to every node in the War Room. Chad's gauntlet comm still worked because it was one of the few nodes off the grid. Kelric had set it up that way deliberately, so that his top commanders would have autonomous systems in case of an emergency.

"Any headway in breaking the lockdown?" Chad asked Qahot.

"We're cutting the walls," she said. "It's slow going. They're damn near impenetrable."

"Do what you can." He watched as Panquai clambered onto the walkway across from him. Lamong swung up next to her and they stood there, two towering mech-warriors in black leathers with silver mesh studs that glinted in the holographic starlight.

Panquai raised her gun. A cable rifle was an independent system, but Chad still tensed as she fired, afraid it would fail. He exhaled with relief as a thick cable shot past the Command Chair and clanged into the walkway only steps from him. As he grabbed it and secured the end around the rail, the smart cable stiffened, creating a bar across the dome.

Panquai and Lamong studied the cable and Kelric. Panquai grabbed the cable and lowered herself until she was hanging from it over the chasm of air, with the amphitheatre far below her. Using her biomech-reinforced strength, she swung hand-over-hand toward the Chair. Lamong followed, carrying their makeshift stretcher.

Kelric hadn't moved. He looked like a part of his cyber-throne that had malfunctioned.

He looked dead.

IX
Awakening

"Bored," Red said, his arms around Aliana's waist, his shoulder wedged against hers.

"No kidding." Aliana pushed farther back in the cargo hold, between the gnarled grey crates. She liked the dark down here and the rolling motion of the ship soothed her, but they had been hiding for hours.

She imagined a healing blanket spread over Red. She didn't expect it to help, but his mood improved. She tilted her head against his, her forehead leaning on his temple and he shifted in her arms, his breath warm on her cheek.

"Aliana pretty," he said.

"I'm big and ugly."

"Pretty." He rubbed his cheek against her hair.

Feeling shy, she shifted in his arms. He put his fingers against her chin and turned her face to him. His lips brushed hers. He paused, waiting, and she held her breath. He kissed her then, holding her face, stroking her cheek with his thumb. Blood rushed through Aliana and she kissed him back, her first time.

"I like." Red murmured.

"Me too."

His hand slid under her sweater. She tensed when she felt his palm on her stomach.

Red stilled his hand. "Not like?"

"If any Aristo found out I kissed you, they would put me in prison or something." She was talking too fast. "I could never afford a provider."

His voice tightened. "Not have to buy me."

She spoke unevenly. "I need time, okay?"

Red kissed her ear. "Okay." He pulled his hand out from under her sweater and just held her.

An engine rumbled above them. It sounded like the hatch in the ceiling opening.

"Damn," Aliana whispered. She dug her heels onto the corrugated floor and wedged them even farther back between two big crates, behind the bulge in one. Red tightened his grip around her waist and they hunkered in the dark, scrunched together.

"Damn stupid bouncer," an irritated man said from somewhere above them.

Huh? That *couldn't* be who it sounded like.

"Did you two have to hide in the least accessible place on the entire ship?" the man asked. Metal clanked, the sound of boots on a ladder.

Light trickled into Aliana and Red's hiding place. She breathed shallowly, silently. But she was getting mad. How the blazes could he be here?

"Aliana, I know you're between the crates," the man said.

Red drew in a sharp breath.

"Go drill yourself," she said loudly.

"I don't think that's anatomically possible." The man sounded amused.

Red's fist clenched against her side.

A lamp shone into their hiding place, lighting their feet. The man crouched down and peered at them under the bulge.

"Tide, go away," Aliana growled.

"Who is that with you?" Tide asked, peering at Red.

Red was so tense, he seemed ready to snap. He kept his arms around Aliana.

"He's my friend," she said.

"Aliana, babe," Tide said. "Did you really think you could stow away and no one would see, in a dockside slum where people spend their entire lives figuring out how to screw the system?" He paused. "Though I must admit, you did a good job. Only one guy noticed. You're lucky he knew me, because he could have called in the head-killers instead of me and claimed a reward for you."

Red peered into the glare from Tide's lamp. "Who?"

"His name is Tidewater," Aliana said sourly. "He used to be a Razer."

"No!" Red pushed back, trying to squeeze into the non-existent space behind them.

"You got a problem with Razers?" Tide asked.

Red didn't answer.

"Right." Tide sat on the rough floor and set down his light. Half of him was visible to one side of the bulge, a dark figure with the light giving him an aura, like the corona on an eclipsed sun. "So Aliana, sweetheart, how come your friend talks fractured Eubian in a Highton accent? Let me see, who would have such bad grammar and yet speak with the accent of the nobility? And be afraid of Razers? Gosh, I wonder."

"Tide, stop it," Aliana said. "Leave him alone."

"You're going to die, stupid girl," he said angrily. "Are you insane? Stealing providers, beating up powerful people, stowing away illegally?"

"What, there's a legal way to stow away?" she asked. "Are you going to rat us out?" She felt tight, ready to explode.

"I'm not telling anyone."

Aliana exhaled. "What did you tell the crew? Hell, Tide, how did you get *on* this boat?"

"It's a ship, not a boat. I'm running deliveries in the flyer Harindor issued me. I told the captain of this rig I needed fuel. It's true."

"How come it needed fuel? You never go anywhere without checking that."

He shrugged. "Seems I forgot this time. Can't imagine why. They're filling it up on the deck."

"And when they're done?" she asked, afraid to breathe, as if that would change his answer.

"Captain invited me to stay for dinner. I'm leaving after that, probably late." Tide paused. "I'm going back up deck. Get a tour, have dinner, take off. If my flyer is carrying more weight than when I landed, well, it's because of the added fuel, right? Couldn't be any other reason."

Aliana closed her eyes. It wouldn't take much for her and Red to sneak onto his flyer while he was having dinner. "Thanks, Tide."

"Yeah well, it's costing me a lot of credit. And if I get killed for transporting you two, you'll need something better than 'thank you' to make up for it."

She gave a shaky laugh and opened her eyes. "Sure. If we all die, I'll make it up to you."

"Deal." He stood up, and shadows encroached on their hiding place. His footsteps receded across the hold. The light switched off as he climbed the ladder. The hatch powered open, then slammed shut, leaving Aliana and Red alone in the dark.

A whirring tugged at Dehya. She floated in a sea of pain.

". . . show any sign," a voice said. "Move a toe. Twitch an eyelid. Lift a finger. *Anything.*"

Go away, she thought.

"Hey!" a man said. "Did you get that from her?"

"Get what?" a woman asked. "She's in a coma."

"Her thought," the man said.

A third voice was fading in and out. ". . . he's a telepath as well as a medic. Sometimes he picks up things from patients."

An authoritative voice said, "Get her husband back here. He's a Ruby telepath."

"The doctors told him to go sleep," someone said. "He'd been here for two days straight."

"Get him," the authoritative voice repeated.

Dryni? Dehya thought. Her husband didn't answer.

She drifted, hurting. Every now and then a clank or hiss penetrated the fog.

Dehya? The thought soaked into her mind.

Dryni? Is that you?

His thought brought hues of a deep blue sky and the sunset. ***Yes, love. It's me.***

Can't stay . . . She drifted into the blur of nonexistence.

✧ ✧ ✧

"I don't need to stay in bed." Jaibriol glared at Doctor Qoxdaughter. He tried to throw off the blankets, but the smart-cloth resisted his efforts, slipping out of his hands and settling around his body again. What fiendish person had come up with intelligent bedding? Jaibriol had grown up in exile, hidden with his family on a world where they had nothing but what they made with their hands. He would never get used to clever furniture, blankets that analyzed his moves, or food that sent him mesh-mail if he forgot to eat. It drove him nuts.

"Your Highness." Qoxdaughter spoke carefully. "If you get up, your wounds might reopen."

"I'm fine." Jaibriol wasn't fine and he knew it; just sitting up made him dizzy. But he couldn't stay here. He jerked away the covers and slid free of the bed before it could resist his efforts. He was still wearing his silk sleep trousers and shirt, but the socks he had pulled on earlier were gone, leaving his feet bare. For saints' sake. He was arguably the most powerful man in the universe, and he couldn't stop the bedding from pulling off his socks. Moving slowly, his head reeling, he fished under the blankets until he found them. Then he leaned against the hospital bed while he put them back on his feet. Qoxdaughter watched him, tensed to respond, though whether to help or hinder him, he didn't know. No, that wasn't true. He knew. She would never dare hinder the emperor.

"Go ahead," he told the doctor as he tugged his socks into place. "Say what you have to say."

She motioned at his bed. "Do you see all these monitors?"

He glanced at the machines arrayed around him. They showed holographic views of his body, as well as graphs and charts and other multi-colored displays floating in the air, gleaming on screens, or glowing on curved surfaces. "Impressive," he said.

"They all tell me the same thing. What you're doing is endangering your health."

"I'm going to see my wife." He stood up straight and gritted his teeth against the pain in his torso. He found it hard to believe that only yesterday an explosion had nearly torn him apart. His body was well on the way to healing, but nothing could fix his fear. He couldn't lose Tarquine.

Qoxdaughter took a breath. "Sire, please—"

"Stop." He lifted his hand. "I'm going, Colonel."

She started to answer, stopped, then said, "Of course, Your Highness."

Even with treatments to dull his pain, Jaibriol hurt everywhere. He knew he should listen to her and lie down. He *wanted* to lie down. But he couldn't rest until he saw Tarquine, not in a holo, but where he could feel her breath against his hand. If someone had come so close to killing them in his own palace, they might try here in the hospital. He knew, logically, his presence would make no difference to the protections around the empress or the child she carried. Even so. He had to visit his wife. He needed to see his family.

Of course Qoxdaughter was family, too, his grandfather's child. She was supposedly half Aristo. If she truly had been, he would have felt the pressure of her mind. He didn't because his grandfather, Ur Qox, had been only half Aristo. His great-grandfather set it up that way so Ur could sire a Ruby heir. And Ur had done exactly that; Jaibriol's father had been a Ruby psion. Two generations of emperors had broken the most entrenched taboo in Eube, claiming a provider's child as their heir, so they could put a Ruby psion on the throne and counter the Skolians. But joke of all bitter jokes, the psion they had created had loathed his throne. Jaibriol's father had gone into hiding to escape a legacy as hateful to him as it was to his Skolian enemies.

Jaibriol knew people believed he had appointed Qoxdaughter as his personal physician because of nepotism. In truth, he chose her because not only was she a damn fine doctor, but also because her presence wasn't an assault on his oversaturated brain. Her medical records had been doctored to say she was half Aristo, but she was only one-quarter, so the Aristo traits didn't manifest in her. Her mind didn't suffocate his.

"Sire?" Qoxdaughter asked.

"Just thinking." Jaibriol looked around. His velvet robe lay on a nearby chair, shimmering blue, its hems embroidered in gold and silver. He walked over and tried to pick up the robe. The chair snapped fasteners onto it, holding the garment, and he had to tug it away.

He glared at Qoxdaughter. "Who programmed this furniture?"

"The tech staff, Your Highness." She kept her disapproval of his behavior out of her voice, but he felt her mood. Her concern for his health battled her fear of displeasing him.

"Have them reprogram this room," he said. "I don't want the furniture, walls, or anything trying to control my actions."

"Yes, Sire."

He pulled on his robe. "How is my wife?"

She spoke smoothly, with the panic hidden in her mind. "We're doing everything possible, everything, using the best—"

"Colonel." Jaibriol put up his hand. "I'm not going to do anything to you if the news isn't good. Tell me the truth."

She let out a breath. "I'm sorry, Sire. She hasn't recovered consciousness."

He felt a constriction in his chest. "And the baby?"

Qoxdaughter spoke quietly. "We don't know yet."

Jaibriol clenched the cuff of his robe, crumpling it in his fist. If Tarquine miscarried, it would be the second time in only months. He wanted to hurt whoever had attacked them, long and horribly, and right now he couldn't care less what that said about him. He went to the door, an elongated hexagon, and it irised open. His four bodyguards were in the foyer outside, their midnight uniforms like shadows against the white Luminex walls. As he walked forward, they fell into formation around him, towering, though he was tall even by Aristo standards.

They headed into the halls of the exclusive medical center, Qoxdaughter walking at his side. Jaibriol glanced at his guards. Like all Razers, they had serial numbers instead of names. ESComm considered them machines rather than human. With his last four guards, he had done the unheard of, encouraging them to pick names for themselves. Those names had died with them on Earth, when they had given their lives to save his during an assassination attempt. Jaibriol had mourned long and hard for their deaths. He had hand-selected those Razers, especially Hidaka, the captain of the unit.

Hidaka, who had known the truth.

Hidaka had witnessed Jaibriol become a member of the Skolian Triad—and murdered an Aristo colonel, the only other witness, to protect Jaibriol's secret. The Razer should never have been able to defy his programming. The moment he had realized Jaibriol was a psion—that the man who sat on the Carnelian Throne was a provider—he should have reported it. Hidaka had been designed, conditioned, and brainwashed to adhere to that principle. Instead he had taken Jaibriol's secret to his grave. Why Hidaka gave him that incredible loyalty, Jaibriol would never know, but he would mourn the captain for the rest of his life.

ESComm Security claimed Hidaka failed to stop the assassination attempt because he was defective. So the idiots decommissioned the entire line. Never mind that Hidaka had acted with great heroism. Never mind that Jaibriol *survived* because of that heroism. Hidaka's "failure" was in what Security discovered in the investigation. He acted too human. So they ordered the destruction of *every* Razer clone in his line. Every goddamned one.

It had been almost too late when Jaibriol discovered what his ESComm "protectors" were up to. He had ordered them to stop destroying valuable Razers, but he couldn't go further without inciting suspicion. His sovereignty was a balance between his authority and his ability to convince the Aristos and ESComm he should hold that authority. So he had never asked his new Razers if they wanted names. Better they remain serial numbers than he draw lethal attention to them.

"This way." Qoxdaughter indicated a hall slanting off from their corridor. Most of the time, the lack of right angles in Aristo architecture no longer disoriented Jaibriol; he was accustomed to the geometry. Even the walls curved into the floor. It was always oblique, indirect, like Aristo speech. He only noticed at times like now, when he already felt disoriented.

They arrived at another hexagon. As it irised open, Jaibriol tensed. He hadn't seen Tarquine since yesterday, when the explosion had ripped through the palace. His doctors said he had bled all over the debris, almost died, that he was alive because he was such an exalted being, etcetera, etcetera. He didn't want to hear it. If he had bled everywhere, that meant so had Tarquine, and no matter how much protocol required everyone to tell the emperor and empress that they were more than human, it wouldn't save her very human life if her injuries were too severe.

Her bodyguards were inside her room, one by the wall, the other near the door. They knelt as he entered.

"Rise," Jaibriol said. He wanted them paying attention to Tarquine's safety, not looking at the floor. Right now nothing mattered but the woman lying on her back on the bed under luminous white smart-sheets, her eyes closed, her breathing slow.

Jaibriol went to the bed and stood gazing at his wife with Doctor Qoxdaughter at his side. He touched Tarquine's cool cheek. Her face look too perfect in repose, like a marble statue.

"Has she shown any sign of change?" he asked.

"Not yet," Qoxdaughter said. "Her coma remains the same." She spoke carefully. "It is inspiring that she was able to get pregnant."

"If that's your way of saying she shouldn't be doing this to her body at her age," Jaibriol answered dryly, "then yes. But she's the empress." He didn't need to tell Qoxdaughter what that meant. The doctor knew he needed an heir. So he said only, "Physically my wife is in her thirties. Essentially."

Qoxdaughter kept looking at Tarquine. "Essentially."

"She will live." He didn't know who he was trying to convince, himself or the colonel.

"Of course." Qoxdaughter continued to watch Tarquine. "She is beyond any normal human."

"Doctor, look at me," he said.

She raised her gaze. "Sire?"

"You say that because you think you have to."

Qoxdaughter spoke quietly. "She is a strong woman, your Highness, and I would say that no matter what."

Jaibriol nodded, though inside he was breaking apart. He had never expected to love an Highton woman, but it had somehow happened, and if Tarquine died, part of him would die as well.

Begin.
Failure.
Retry.
Failure.
Retry.
Failure.
Reinitialize backup of mental files.
Reinitialized.
Begin.
Code begun.

Kelric opened his eyes. He was lying on his back, staring at a silver-white ceiling. Conduits criss-crossed it, glowing white in star designs. Turning his head, he saw his two doctors, Sashia and Drayson, across the room, conferring in low voices. Various monitors around his bed glowed with holos of his brain.

Why am I here? he thought.

Bolt, the node in his spine, answered. **You died.**

What the hell?

If this is hell, it doesn't fit the claims of various literatures. Though some might consider confinement to a hospital as such.

Not funny, Bolt.

I can't be humorous. I am a mesh node. Then it added, **Someone tried to assassinate you, so you were brain dead.**

You mean I really did die?

Yes. I'm sorry.

I seem to be quite alive.

Your most recent neural backup was only minutes old. They restarted your brain with it. You're missing only the last minutes before you died.

Although he knew in theory it was possible to restart the brain from a saved version if they loaded the memory into a living human being, he had never expected to test the theory. **How did I die?**

Someone cracked the War Room mesh and hacked you in Kyle Space.

That's impossible. Only I have that kind of access to the War Room mesh.

Apparently someone else does, too. Either that, or you assassinated yourself.

What a bizarre thought. **How about you?**

I didn't try to kill you, if that is what you mean.

I mean, are you all right?

I'm running diagnostics. I can't find anything unusual.

You wouldn't tell me if you were compromised. Kelric couldn't imagine that Bolt, who had been part of his brain for over half a century, would attack him. He didn't know what he would do if the node was corrupted. Shutting it down would be like cutting out a part of himself.

Have an outside agency run diagnostics on me, Bolt told him.

They probably already are. Kelric tried to remember what had happened just before the attack, but nothing came. **Do you have any records of those moments I've lost?**

I'm missing the time from your last neural backup until they restarted your mind. About two minutes' worth.

Maybe Dehya can help. She has more monitors in the Kyle than ISC. Hell, she's part of the Kyle.

Silence.

Bolt?

I don't think Pharaoh Dyhianna can help.

Why not?

The assassins got to her, too.

"Hell and damnation!" Kelric sat up in bed, knocking the silver sheet away from his body.

Both Sashia and Drayson spun around, as did every medic and tech in the room, all staring at him, their mouths open.

"Pharaoh Dyhianna," he barked at them. "Is she alive?"

Sashia blinked. "Yes." She came over to the bed with Colonel Drayson. "Until about two seconds ago, though, we didn't know you were."

He didn't have time for that. "Where is Dehya?" Kelric swung his legs out from under the sheet. He was wearing a sleep shirt and trousers made from a silvery tech-mesh. His clothes were probably monitoring his vital signs and talking to his doctors.

Sashia made an exasperated noise. "Commander Skolia, stay put! You were just *dead.*"

"I'm fine."

"How did you know about the pharaoh?" Sashia asked.

"Bolt told me."

"Bolt?" Drayson asked crisply. "That refers to one of your spinal nodes, doesn't it?"

I'm not "one," Bolt objected. **I'm the PRIMARY node.**

Kelric held back his smile. "That's right," he told Drayson.

Tell him I need a check, Bolt reminded him.

Kelric spoke to Drayson and Sashia. "Have you run diagnostics on my internal nodes?"

"We've tried," Drayson said. "We can't gain access."

Bolt? Kelric thought. **Let them in.**

Sorry, yes, I'm fixing it. The failsafe security protections kicked in when you died. They shouldn't have any problem now.

"Try again," Kelric told Drayson.

"Good." The doctor went to work, tapping panels on his wrist comm.

"How much did Bolt tell you about what happened?" Sashia asked Kelric.

"Nothing. It doesn't remember." Kelric frowned at them. "What happened to Dehya?"

Drayson glanced up. "We aren't sure. An attack in psiberspace, same as with you. But you had only been in a few minutes. She'd been working for hours, in a lot deeper."

Kelric felt as if he were filling with pressure. "Meaning what? Will she live?"

"We think so," Sashia said.

"You *think*." Kelric clenched the edge of the bed. "Why don't you know?"

"The question isn't her life," Sashia said. "We can keep her breathing." She hesitated. "We can't get her out of Kyle space."

"Why not?" he asked. "Just turn off the machines. It's her thoughts that are there, not her body."

"If we aren't careful, it could cause her brain damage."

"She can't stay there." Kelric knew Dehya sometimes longed to lose herself in the Kyle, to seek its refuge against a universe where she was so sensitive an empath, she had to isolate herself to survive. "She can't," he repeated. "Skolia needs her." *He* needed her.

"We have a team of Rajindias working on her case," Sashia said.

He nodded, trying to relax his shoulders. The House of Rajindia, an ancient noble line, had a talent that all their inbreeding had strengthened. They trained biomech adepts, the neurological specialists who treated psions. If anyone could help Dehya, they were the ones.

Kelric slid off the bed. Considering his recent condition, he felt remarkably healthy. He must not have been for long. "I need some real clothes."

Drayson cleared his throat. "Sir, I don't think it's wise for you to be up so soon."

"I'm pretty sure I'm no longer dead," Kelric deadpanned.

Sashia scowled at him. "Very funny."

He couldn't help but laugh. "Sorry." So much for his sparkling wit.

Drayson looked from Sashia to Kelric. From the colonel's mind, Kelric gathered he didn't know which was more startling, that Kelric had made a joke or that Sashia was so relaxed in her response. Kelric thought perhaps he needed to work on his demeanor around people. True, he couldn't have his officers treating him with Sashia's casual attitude, but neither did he want people to think he was more machine than human. His emotions ran deep and strong; he just didn't know how to express them.

He said only, "What do you know about whoever tried to kill us? How did they reach both Dyhianna and myself?" It was a security nightmare.

Colonel Drayson raked his hand through his bristly grey hair. "We think the Traders are using providers to crack our security."

It was a very real threat, but Kelric doubted it accounted for this situation. "Their providers are psions, it's true. But they aren't strong enough to access our military web at that level." As far as he knew, the Traders had only one such psion, Jaibriol Qox. Kelric felt him as a distant presence in the Triad. If Jaibriol had tried to affect the Triad this way, Kelric and Dehya would know. They would feel it, and he sensed nothing of the kind. The three of them were distantly connected, but even if Jaibriol had died, it wouldn't cause what had happened to Kelric and Dehya.

Colonel Drayson spoke uneasily. "Almost no one has the necessary access to compromise our security the way it happened."

Kelric understood what he left unspoken. Almost no one—except the Joint Commanders of ISC. He had a truly unpleasant array of options for the assassin: Bolt had tried to kill him, ESComm had an unusually high-level provider, or one of Kelric's top commanders had betrayed him.

Sashia spoke carefully. "Admiral Barzun was in the War Room when it happened."

Kelric shook his head. "Chad doesn't have a high enough Kyle rating." However, two of ISC's Joint Commanders could operate on that level: Brant Tapperhaven and Naaj Majda.

Brant commanded the Jagernaut Force, or J-Force, the wild card of ISC: fighter pilots, spies, commandos. Kelric related well to him; they were both Jagernauts, they both had a taciturn nature, and they shared a similar outlook on life.

Naaj Majda was on the other end of the spectrum; she commanded the Pharaoh's Army, the oldest and most conservative branch of ISC. The iron-grey matriarch came down on a hard line against the Traders and despised the peace treaty. Naaj also held a civilian title as queen of the most powerful noble House. With a history stretching back to the Ruby Empire, the House of Majda was an orthodox matriarchy where women owned their men and kept them in seclusion. To further complicate matters, Kelric had married Naaj's older sister Corey decades ago, a union arranged for political reasons. Given that he was a fighter pilot, Corey had hardly expected him to follow the sexist roles of an ancient empire. But she had died only a few years after they married, assassinated by the Traders, leaving a substantial portion of the Majda assets to Kelric.

In the chaos after the last war, Naaj had become acting Imperator. She hadn't liked it when Kelric returned to claim his title after being gone and presumed dead for eighteen years. She had lost a great deal of power and also the Majda assets he owned but hadn't properly dispensed of before his disappearance, on top of which he was a male warlord, which drastically violated her antediluvian view of men. She had plenty of reason to want him gone.

And yet...

Whoever had tried to assassinate Kelric had also acted against Dehya. Whatever problems Naaj had with him, she would never attack the Ruby Pharaoh. The loyalty of the army to the woman who sat on the Ruby Throne was legendary. It went back five thousand years, and Naaj was no exception. She would die rather than see Dehya harmed.

Who else? Admiral Ragnar Bloodmark certainly had reason to resent Kelric. Ragnar was better qualified than Chad Barzun to command the Imperial Fleet. Kelric had chosen Chad because he trusted him more. Kelric also remembered Ragnar's reaction to the Assembly vote on the peace treaty. When the vote had finished, with 78 percent in favor of the treaty, Ragnar's face had contorted into a snarl. It lasted only the briefest instant, but Kelric had seen. Nor had he forgotten the attack that had nearly killed him and Jaibriol Qox during their treaty negotiations. Someone had discovered their hidden meeting on Earth, and Ragnar was one of the few people with the intelligence, the savvy, and the security clearance needed to find that secret.

However, Kelric didn't believe Ragnar would harm

X

Fires of Vengeance

"I've never been in the sky." Aliana was sitting in the co-pilot's seat, gazing out the flyer's windshield. Her shoulder brushed Red's elbow. He was sitting between her chair and Tide's pilot's seat, straddling a control panel. Tide hadn't asked him to move, which surprised Aliana; even she could see it would make Tide's piloting easier if he had access to the panel Red had commandeered instead of Tide having to use the auxiliary panel in the pilot's chair. Red was so enraptured with the view, though, she couldn't have asked him to move, either.

The ocean flashed beneath them, sparkling in the pristine morning light. The sun rested huge and molten on the horizon where the sea met the fiery dawn. Above them, the sky was lightening from the deep purple of night into the pale stone-blue of day.

"It's so pretty," Aliana said.

"You've never flown before?" Tide asked.

"Not once." She felt provincial. "Before Red and I

stowed away, I'd never been more than a few blocks from that cesspool where my stepfather lives." Aliana shuddered. "I swear, sometimes I thought he hated me more than anything else alive. Am I really such drek?"

"No, damn it!" Tide said. "Don't ever believe that."

"Stepman have rusty eyes?" Red asked.

"If you mean, was he part Aristo, then yeah," Aliana said.

"You provider," Red told her. "That why he hit you."

"I am not!" Aliana scowled at him. "Don't make things up."

"Not make up." He touched her cheek, his finger lingering. "Gold skin. Like provider." He lowered his arm. "Pretty, like provider. And your brain hears thoughts. Like provider."

"What the *hell?*" Tide jerked so hard, the flyer swerved. "Are you saying she's an *empath?*"

"Empath. Telepath," Red said.

Aliana's gaze flicked between the two of them. "What are you talking about?"

"He claims you feel people's emotions," Tide said. "Maybe their thoughts."

"Oh, that." Aliana shrugged. "It's no big deal."

Tide made a strangled sound. "I'm going to die."

"Whatever for?" Aliana had never seen him like this. He was usually the man of cool.

Tide tapped a panel that said *autopilot*. Then he turned to give Aliana his full attention. "It's true what Red says, that a lot of providers have been genetically altered to resemble precious metals or gems. Like blue eyes that look like sapphires. Or gold skin. Metallic gold. Like yours."

"Yeah, well, I've never been a provider," Aliana said.

"Did your mother have gold skin?" Tide asked.

"Of course not." Although she didn't like to talk about her mother, it didn't hurt as much now as it had eleven years ago. "She was beautiful. And sweet. But not gold."

"What about your biological father?"

"I have no fucking idea." Aliana crossed her arms and stared out at the sky.

"I'm not trying to hurt you," Tide said. "But you got that gold skin from somewhere." After a moment, he added, "Did your mother work in an Aristo's household? If she was a psion, I could see an Aristo wanting to breed her to another strong psion."

"No, my mother never served an Aristo," Aliana said coldly, watching the horizon. "Never saw an Aristo. Never spoke the freaking *name* of an Aristo." Thawing a bit, she added, "She hardly even lived in Eubian space. She grew up in the hinterlands, on a world even worse than this one. My stepfather brought her here."

A sense of stillness came from Tide. Uncrossing her arms, Aliana glanced over to find him staring at her hard. "What?" she asked.

"What do you mean by hinterlands? A border region with Skolian space?"

"Well, yeah. So it was a crummy place, okay. I can't help that."

"Aliana, could your father be a Skolian?"

"Oh, go drill yourself." What was *with* him, making all these rude cracks? It wasn't like him.

"This can't be," Tide said.

"You bet it can't," Aliana said.

"Skolians have providers?" Red asked.

"If Aliana's father was a provider," Tide said, "She wouldn't be so big."

"Are you done insulting me yet?" she asked.

"I'm not insulting you." Tide took a breath. "You aren't ugly, Aliana. Your stepfather told you that to hurt you. You're beautiful, but not like a provider. They're bred to be soft, pretty, sweet. Docile." Wryly he added, "You're about as docile as a Balzarian she-devil."

Her anger eased. "You got that right."

"Do you know how rare telepaths are?" Tide asked. "At best, one in a million. Maybe one in a billion. Pretty much the only Eubian ones that exist are those bred by Aristos to be providers. So how did someone like you end up in the slums of some unknown planet? It's like finding a billion credit gem in the trash."

Red pushed up his sleeve, and his wrist cuff glittered in the dawn's sunlight. "Can happen."

"Gods almighty." Tide gaped at Red. "Who the hell did you belong to?"

"Admiral Muze."

Tide's face turned ashen. "The Joint Commander of the Eubian Fleet?"

"Yes," Red said. "That right."

"Gods," Tide muttered. "Maybe I should just commit suicide right now."

"Tide, stop it," Aliana said. "You're scaring me. Why would you be in trouble?"

"Oh, nothing much," he growled. "Just for having two of the most valuable pieces of property on the planet and not turning either of you in to the authorities."

Aliana gave an uneasy laugh. "That's not funny."

"No." He turned back to his controls. "Believe me, it's not funny at all."

Aliana didn't understand him; he came from a life she knew nothing about, where people like him guarded the princes of an empire. She spoke slowly, as if the words themselves could end what little joy she had eked out of her life. "Are you're going to turn us into Admiral Muze?"

"Hell, no." His hand was clenched so tight on his navigation stick, his knuckles had turned white. "ESComm ordered my execution just because I have the same DNA as a Razer who died saving the life of the Aristo he protected. The executions stopped, I don't know why, but I've no intention of drawing any attention to myself. I might not survive a second time." His voice tightened. "And damned if I would turn you in anyway."

"You know," Aliana said, "you don't sound like a Razer."

"I suppose that's why our line was decommissioned." His tension eased and he smiled, almost. "My programming is for me to guard whoever I'm assigned to protect. So now I'm protecting you two."

"By calling me a Skolian?" she grumbled, mainly to cover her relief.

"Aliana, listen. It makes sense. Maybe your father was a Skolian soldier." He glanced at her. "Some of them are psions. If your mother's world was in a border region, it's possible a Skolian soldier went there as a spy or on reconnaissance."

Bile rose in her throat. "You mean some Skolian scum raped my mother?"

Tide spoke quietly. "She was forced?"

"Well, actually, that wasn't what she said." Aliana felt as if she were lost at sea instead of above it. She had been so young when her mother told her about her father, not even five yet, but she treasured the memory. "She said she loved him, that he was kind to her, but that he had to go away. Neither of them knew she was pregnant when he left."

"If he were a spy, he would have had to leave eventually," Tide said.

"Good way to learn about your enemies," Aliana said bitterly. "Pretend you're in love with one, get all her pillow talk, and then dump her when you're finished."

"Why pretend?" Tide said. "She wouldn't have anything to tell him if she was a low ranked taskmaker on a slum world. Maybe he really loved her."

"Then why didn't he take her with him?"

"He probably couldn't get her out, especially if he had to leave unexpectedly."

"Yeah, right." His logic made her feel better, though.

"So we go to Skolian embassy?" Red asked.

"Oh, honestly, Red," Aliana said.

"Good gods," Tide said. "That's the answer!"

The answer? It sounded nuts to Aliana. But then, she understood zilch about Skolians, except that she didn't want to meet any. "How do you know about Skolian embassies?" she asked Red.

"Admiral Muze not like them," Red said. "He want them burned. Emperor say no."

Her mouth fell open. "You've met the *emperor?*"

"Seen him. Not come close. He not like me."

"How do you know he didn't like you?" Aliana asked.

"He say Admiral Muze must send me away."

"Oh." She squinted at him. "Then you don't have any good gossip about Emperor Jaibriol?"

Red frowned at her. "Is wrong to gossip about gods."

"Oh, sure," Aliana said. "Like they're really gods."

Tide made an incredulous sound. "Aliana, stop that!"

"Stop what?"

"He's the *emperor.* You're going to get yourself killed if you aren't careful."

She shifted in her seat. "I meant no disrespect." She had, actually, but she saw Tide's point. "Will you really make me go to a Skolian embassy?"

"It may be your only way out of this." Tide glanced at Red. "Both of you."

"Me not Skolian," Red said. "Can't go to embassy."

Aliana sat up straighter. "I'm not leaving Red behind."

Tide exhaled. "All right, listen. I never told you what I'm about to say. If you claim I did, I'll deny it."

"Told us what?" she asked.

"Providers who ask the Skolians for asylum are always granted it," Tide said. "By Skolian law, providers are considered prisoners who have been tortured in violation of interstellar law. A Skolian embassy is Skolian territory. So if they give you asylum, you're free."

"Why would anyone want Skolian asylum?" Aliana said. "It sounds like putting you in a house for the insane." Which was where they'd belong if they wanted to live with Skolians.

"You have a better idea?" Tide asked. "Aliana, sweetheart, you beat up one of Orzon Muze's bastards and his bodyguard and you stole one of Admiral Muze's providers. And if you really are a psion, any Aristo who comes near you will sense it. You're in trouble, babe. You want to be tortured for the rest of your life? A lot of Aristos would enjoy breaking that eff-you spirit of yours."

She stared at him. "Shit."

"Yeah," Tide said. "That sums it up."

"So we three go to embassy?" Red asked.

Tide turned back to his piloting, his gaze shuttered. "Not me."

"Why not?" Aliana asked. "You said yourself, you're in a mess."

"I can't go to the Skolians."

"You'll make us go, but you won't?" She wanted to shake him.

He spoke quietly. "I was a bodyguard for a highly ranked military officer on Glory."

"So?" She clenched her fist. "I'm training to be a bodyguard."

"It's not the same thing."

"Why not?"

He met her angry gaze. "If I defected to the Skolians, I would be committing treason. Their military would take me apart."

"Oh." She felt as if she had rammed into a wall. Of course it was different. Her paltry attempts at training couldn't compare with what he had done in his life. Nor did she want him risking execution for treason. "But what will you do? You said you're in trouble, too."

"I'll manage. As long as no one knows I took you two to the embassy."

"How you hide?" Red asked. "Aristos know everything."

He shrugged. "I was around them for decades, learning their security. Hell, I was *part* of that security. I know a few things myself."

Aliana spoke softly. "I'm sorry, Tide. I never meant for you to be involved."

His expression gentled. "I chose to come after you, babe. That was my decision."

"Why would you make a crazy decision like that?"

He started to answer, but then he glanced at Red and stopped. Turning back to his piloting, he just said, "I have no idea."

"Oh." She didn't know what to make of that.

"You are so damn young," Tide muttered.

"That's curable, you know," she said. When he laughed, she asked, "So where is this embassy?"

He brought the flyer around in a shallow arc, changing their heading from south to east. "This way. Muzeopolis is on a large island to the south, and the embassy is on the mainland."

Aliana could see only water in every direction. But sooner or later, the land would come and the life she had known would change forever.

Burning red mist surrounded Dehya. She couldn't remember why or how she had come here. Music pounded:

I'm no golden hero in the blazing skies.
I'm no fair-haired genius, hiding in disguise.

A man's thought came to her, curling out of the mist. ***When he sings fair-haired genius, he means you.***

Dehya's focus sharpened. **Taquinil? Is that you?**

The red faded into a gentler color, soft and golden. As the universe cooled, the man's thought came again. ***My greetings, Mother.***

The landscape swelled into a shape that resembled the diffraction pattern from a circular aperture, like the wavelets in a pond after she dropped a rock into the smooth water. It grew into a symmetrical peak in the center with smaller ripples circling it. Taquinil. Her son. He existed only in the Kyle, his mind centered in the peak, his thoughts spreading in every direction. The waveform glowed gold, like his eyes in the real universe, against a background as black as his midnight hair. Sparks of light flashed along the ripples.

Taquinil, her firstborn. In the last war, the Traders had reached the Orbiter, attacking that stronghold, seeking the Ruby Dynasty. To escape, she and Taquinil had thrown themselves into the spacetime singularity that defined a Lock, and it had transformed their actual bodies into the Kyle, a universe of thought. The immense energy required for that change had nearly destroyed them. She had eventually returned to normal space, coming out in partial waves, but Taquinil had stayed in the Kyle. He existed now only as a quantum wave function of thought.

Dehya had never quite figured out how to greet a son who had turned himself into a wave. **You look good. For a, uh, waveform.**

A sense of amusement came from him. ***Thank you.***

Taquinil, we miss you.

And I you.

Come home. Meet your brother. He's almost ten. She and Eldrin had named their second son in honor of Eldrin's brother Althor, a Jagernaut who had died in the War. **Come home, sweetheart.**

Maybe someday.

Dehya knew if she pushed, he would disappear. So she just said, **I'm glad to see you.**

I had to come. Someone tried to kill you.

Don't be silly. I'm fine.

No you aren't.

She focused and the scene changed, becoming the green of a sun-drenched forest. Her mind formed an emerald waveform next to Taquinil's gold. All the while, "Carnelians Finale" played in the background: *I'm only a singer; it's all that I can do. But I'm still alive, and I'm coming after you.*

Your uncle Del wrote that, Dehya thought.

Taquinil's wave flashed with red sparks. ***Did he try to hurt you?***

Del? Good gods, no. Why would you ask such a thing?

He resents the Ruby Dynasty.

Sometimes. But he loves us. Dehya had never doubted it. ***He would never deliberately hurt his family.***

Someone attacked you in the Kyle.

Taquinil, stop. Dehya didn't know why he kept insisting on that. Her memory felt oddly hazy, but she didn't want to waste these rare moments with him. ***That song is his rage over the way the Traders have hurt us, the people he loves.***

He released the song onto the meshes. Or it appears that way.

Appears. Interesting choice of words. ***Show me,*** she thought.

They descended through Kyle space. It streamed past them, murmuring with the thoughts of millions, whispering at the edges of her mind or flaring with light. People transmitted data, argued, chatted, conducted research, ran military ops, did uncounted other jobs. The deeper they went, the darker it became, until it was lit only by their gold and emerald waves.

They stopped in a pocket of shadows. Dehya absorbed their surroundings. *We're under a military security mesh. An old one.*

It's no longer used, Taquinil thought. ***A good place to hide.***

Access Kelric Skolia's "module Quis," she thought to the Kyle. It didn't answer.

What is that? Taquinil asked. ***Quis?***

Kelric's top security protocol. He calls it Quis.

His thought turned wry. ***I won't ask how you know his secured protocols.***

Ah, well . . . Dehya had never found a system she couldn't crack. Today she was having trouble, though. Something was wrong. She couldn't reach the ISC programs . . .

Everything suddenly snapped into place. A machine-like thought responded. **COMTRACE ATTENDING.**

She recognized the name; it was a highly secured military node. *Comtrace, access my security analyses codes.*

ACCESSED.

Implement code nineteen. Analyze the web for security breaches.

CODE IMPLEMENTED. Then Comtrace added: **NO BREACHES DETECTED.**

Try code fourteen.

CODE IMPLEMENTED.

Dehya waited.

BREACH DETECTED, Comtrace thought. **PART OF A SECURITY SYSTEM IS GONE. MISSING MOD: FOUR-THREE-B, LATTICE SITE FOUR-TRILLION-SEVEN.**

Only that one mod is missing? she asked.

YES.

That sounds like what I found, Taquinil said. ***For me it manifested as a rip in the mesh.*** A ragged hole appeared in front of them, like a tear in the fabric of the universe.

Someone could pull data through that rip, Dehya thought.

Or send it in, Taquinil said.

Music curled out of the rip and swirled around her in glowing red glyphs:

I'll never kneel beneath your Highton stare.
I'm here and I'm real; I'll lay your guilt bare.

Dehya followed the music through the rip, deeper into the Kyle mesh. Eventually the path turned upward. She followed the song through more layers, each lighter than the last, always upward, until she was no longer in a secured space. The path merged with civilian routes, becoming a road. Eventually it reached systems for the Allied Worlds of Earth. Although she kept following the trail, she knew where it would lead. To Earth. To Del. Supposedly.

You don't believe it, either? Taquinil asked.

Actually, I do.

Why?

Someone accessed Del's mind. She submerged tendrils from her mind into the trail. When the threads had soaked up as much as they could absorb, she integrated them with her thoughts. ***They inserted a virus into his brain that affected the firing of his neurotransmitters, creating fake thoughts as if they were his own. So it appears he used his mind to dump "Carnelians Finale" into Kyle space. He had no idea it happened.***

Are you guessing? Taquinil asked. ***Or are you sure?***

Almost certain.

If someone can affect our minds that way—that's terrifying.

Yes. Dehya didn't want to imagine a universe where terrorists could hijack their telepathic ability. If someone figured out how to control the mind of a Ruby psion, it would give them immense power over the Ruby Dynasty, and by extension, over the Imperialate.

We don't have anything resembling the technology to do it, she thought. *If Ruby psions can't, how could anyone else?*

It should be impossible, Taquinil thought.

She probed more deeply into the trail of Del's operations on the net. *That's odd. Del released the song twice. The first time was a while ago, when it first hit the mesh and turned into a cyber-plague. Then he released it again, a second time. That's why we're picking it up.* She let her thoughts swirl around Taquinil, showing him what she had found.

I see, he thought. ***The second release happened at the same time you were attacked.***

Attack. He kept saying that. A strange sensation rippled through Dehya, as if someone were trying to pull her out of this place.

No, she thought. *Stop.*

Mother? What's wrong?

I have to go! With a gasp, she *whisked* away from Taquinil. A tether was dragging her through the mesh so fast, its layers blurred.

Far away, so very far, someone else was calling her. ***Come back. Come home . . .***

✧ ✧ ✧

Dehya opened her eyes. She was curled in a fetal position under the covers of a bed. Someone was sitting on the edge of the mattress, holding her hand, his head bent, his eyes closed. His dark red hair had fallen around his handsome face, and a hint of freckles were scattered across his nose. Tears wet his cheeks.

"Dryni?" Her voice had an eerie quality, as if she were far away.

Her husband's eyes snapped opened. "Dehya?" His hand tightened around hers.

"Why are you crying?" Her voice was almost inaudible. "Are you here?"

"I always was." Only her mind had gone into the Kyle. "What happened . . . ?"

"You've been buried so deep, no one could reach you. The techs took you out of the chair, but you still didn't come out."

"Not possible . . ."

"No, it's not." He managed a shaky smile. "But you were doing it anyway."

"I'm always there . . . partly." Nothing seemed real anymore . . .

"Dehya, stay with me."

She breathed deeply and slowly uncurled her body. It hurt. Groaning, she stretched out under the silvery-blue sheet. Softly she said, "Our son was there."

Eldrin stroked the hair off her forehead. "Is he all right?"

"Fine. Well, if you call existing as a waveform 'fine.'"

Eldrin gave a wry laugh. "He always was different." His smile faded. "Dehya, don't go back. I can't lose you both. And Althor needs you."

She squeezed his hand, wishing she could live like

everyone else, that her mind wasn't so painfully sensitive. Only her family kept her anchored here. Eldrin and Althor were more than her husband and son, they were a part of her mind. Every time she saw Althor, she felt an immense gratitude that he lived. She and Eldrin would never have more children. The danger was too great, given their close relation. It was a wonder either of their sons had survived. Taquinil had such an extreme telepathic sensitivity, he couldn't endure the normal universe. Althor had been born with so many physical defects, it had taken years to make him whole, and then only with large parts of his body designed from biomech. The Assembly had forced her to marry Eldrin because they wanted more Ruby heirs, but the price it exacted from their children was too high . . . too high . . .

"Dehya, don't let go," Eldrin said. "Don't fall back into wherever you were."

She struggled to focus. She had found something odd, something about Comtrace, the military node most linked to the Imperator.

"Where is Kelric?" she asked.

Eldrin stiffened. "Why do you ask that?"

"Something is wrong." She reached out to his mind, but he had his shields in place, which he never did with her. "Dryni, tell me. What happened?"

After a moment, he said, "He's here, too, in a neural unit of the hospital."

"It got *him*, too?"

"What got him?"

"Something used our minds against us." She rolled onto her back, stiff and sore. "I hardly know how to explain. Like someone hijacked our neural processes and used them to hurt us in ways only *we* could do to ourselves."

"That doesn't sound possible."

"I wouldn't have thought so."

He spoke uneasily. "You need to talk to ISC."

"Is Kelric all right?"

"He's fine, oddly enough."

"Why oddly?"

"Before he was fine, he was dead."

"*What?*" She sat up, then winced as pain shot thought her muscles.

"Dehya, stop." Eldrin tried to nudge her back down. When she scowled at him, he smiled, the color coming back into his face. "Now you look like my stubborn wife."

"Ah, well." He had a point. "What do you mean, Kelric was dead?"

"Well, if you're right, that something caused you and him to do these things with your own minds, then technically, he killed himself."

She pulled off the sheet. "I have to talk to him."

He tugged the sheet back over her. "You have to lie down."

"I'm fine."

"Of course you're fine," he said with exasperation. "You sound just like Kelric. You two are always fine, even when you're killing yourselves to prove it."

"He and I need to talk."

Eldrin met her gaze. "I'll set it up if you both promise to stay in your chairs and not jump up to go work, telling me how fine you are."

She smiled. "All right. Deal." In truth, she was already tiring. But she and Kelric had to figure out what had happened before anyone else was hurt.

✧ ✧ ✧

Tarquine's hospital bed was empty.

Jaibriol stood in her hospital room like a shadow, dressed in black, staring at the bed with its pristine, perfectly arranged smart-sheets. "Where is my wife?"

Doctor Qoxdaughter's face turned ashen. "She was here just minutes ago!"

"Her body couldn't just disappear. Where the blazes are her guards?"

"Your Highness." That came from one of Jaibriol's usually silent Razers, a black-haired man with brown eyes, pure brown, no trace of red. No Aristo blood.

"You've found her?" Jaibriol asked.

The Razer lifted his gauntleted wrist, showing him its comm screen. "She's in the palace library with her guards."

Air seemed to flood back into the room. She wasn't dead. She hadn't passed away while he was in his office, toiling to catch up with the endless work that had piled up. He had resumed his duties today, two days after the attack, over Qoxdaughter's protests, but he hadn't expected Tarquine even to be awake, let alone up and gone.

"Take me to her," Jaibriol said.

The contents of a library even as large as the one in the emperor's palace could fit onto one mesh chip. However, this repository had what few others could claim: real books. Bound in leather, with parchment pages, some were so old that only restoration treatments kept them from falling apart. As much a museum as a library, it housed thousands of the treasures. Jaibriol particularly liked it because the carved archways, ornate moldings, and vaulted ceilings created a serenity that usually calmed him.

Today he wasn't calm. He strode with Qoxdaughter and his Razers into a room where lamps in wall scones shed antiqued light. Four wingchairs upholstered in dark gold were set around a table carved with vines. A woman sat in one chair, her eyes closed, her head leaning against its high back, her dark clothes part of the shadows.

Tarquine.

Jaibriol stopped at the table, filled with an immense gratitude at seeing her that Highton custom forbid him to show. She was breathing regularly and her eyes moved under her lids, whether from a dream or waking thoughts, he couldn't tell. Quis dice lay scattered on the table in front of her. He had left her a new set in her hospital room, hoping the dice would amuse her enough when she awoke that she would stay put, but apparently nothing could keep his restless empress confined to a hospital.

The captain of Tarquine's Razers came over to him and bowed deeply, as Jaibriol had told him to do instead of kneeling. Jaibriol spoke in a low voice. "No one must see her like this." They had kept the assassination attempt a secret, and he intended for it to stay that way.

"We'll make sure of it, Your Highness," the Razer told him.

Jaibriol nodded and went to sit by Tarquine while Qoxdaughter and the Razers moved back, giving them privacy.

Tarquine opened her eyes. "My greetings, husband." Her voice was low. Throaty.

"Why are you here?" he asked. "You should be in the hospital."

"I shall die from boredom in that place."

Jaibriol didn't doubt it. He wanted to ask her how she felt, *talk* to her, give and take comfort, anything to fill the holes in their marriage. But he knew her too well to offer any hint of affection when other people were present.

"I've read the security report on the assassination attempt," he said.

She spoke wryly, "And who almost won the lottery of killing our beloved personages?"

Lottery indeed. If an assassin ever succeeded against them, more than a few Aristos would rejoice. And why? Because of all the evil Jaibriol *hadn't* perpetrated on the human race.

"They traced it to a leak in the palace Security division," he said. "Or what looked like a leak. Further investigation shows the attempt probably came from the Red Point Diamond Aristo Line."

"A Diamond Aristo?" She raised an eyebrow. "How insulting. I would have thought it would take a Highton Aristo to kill us."

He smiled slightly. "Perhaps it does. We are still alive."

She considered him, seemingly relaxed, or more accurately, worn out. But her gaze burned. "And yet supposedly a Red Point Diamond nearly succeeded where everyone else has failed."

"Security found a back doorway that someone snuck into our intelligence networks."

"How clever of Azile Xir."

Jaibriol couldn't tell whether she truly believed that

Azile, the Minister of Intelligence, had anything to do with this, or if she brought him up only because she so disliked Azile's father, Corbal Xir. Given that the elderly Corbal was Jaibriol's kin, his advisor, and the closest Jaibriol had to a friend, he wished Tarquine would try to get along with him better.

"Azile is under investigation," Jaibriol said. Tarquine wasn't the only one who suspected the Intelligence Minister had framed both the Red Point Diamonds and the Security officers. Azile had means and motive. As Intelligence Minister, was he well placed to create the necessary breach in security, and if Jaibriol died without an heir, Azile's father became emperor and Azile was first in line to the throne.

Except Jaibriol didn't believe it. Although he could never be sure of anything he gleaned mentally from an Aristo, given all the protections and mental scar tissue in his own mind, he didn't feel hostility from the Intelligence Minister. If anything, Azile had always shown him a grudging respect, and it had deepened over the years. He just didn't see Azile plotting an assassination.

Jaibriol had spent the last eleven years doing his own intelligence work. He knew secrets about all of his advisors. Azile was illegitimate. Corbal claimed Azile was the son of his late Highton wife, who had passed away years ago, but Azile's mother was actually Sunrise, one of Corbal's pleasure girls, the only one he ever spent time with. Of course Corbal would never admit he was in love with a slave. It didn't matter. He couldn't hide the truth from Jaibriol's Ruby mind. Corbal had committed a crime almost as great as Jaibriol, passing off his half-Aristo son as a Highton. For all that it violated every definition of Highton "decency," it was, Jaibriol suspected, one reason Azile seemed more human to him than most Aristos. He was only half Highton.

Corbal was a more likely suspect than Azile. Jaibriol had used Corbal's secret to blackmail him into signing the peace treaty. That one act had nearly destroyed the precarious bond they had built up over the past decade. And yet . . . Corbal couldn't hide the truth from Jaibriol. He didn't want to be emperor. And as much as he hated what Jaibriol had done with the treaty, he didn't hate Jaibriol. Incredible as it seemed, Corbal cared about him.

Tarquine was studying his face. "So much goes on behind that enigmatic mask of yours."

He allowed himself the hint of a smile. "I suppose that makes me Highton."

"So it does." She paused. "On the outside, you have changed much since I met you."

That was a minefield he didn't want to walk through, that he had learned how to act Highton, even to think like one. So instead, he indicated the dice on the table. "Are you playing Quis?"

"A bit." Although she sounded tired, her gaze was intent. "An interesting game."

"I find it so." He had played solitaire for hours last night. It did more than calm the Triad power coursing through his mind. The more he explored Quis, the more it seemed to build stories. Last night, it had been a dark tale, one of emptiness, of new hopes turned to ashes.

"Join me for a session," Tarquine said.

"Very well." If they couldn't share their grief with words, perhaps this game could offer them a way to find solace together.

He studied the structures she had built. Dark pieces dominated: an ebony ball sat within an onyx ring, a sapphire cube balanced on a jet cylinder. Other patterns bent across the table, fractured and painful. She was solving a puzzle, though he couldn't yet see what riddle she had posed herself.

He picked up a small opal sphere that she had surrounded with dark pieces and set it by a large carnelian sphere. He moved a second carnelian sphere to its other side. That was actually two moves, which was undoubtedly illegal. No matter. Neither of them knew most of the rules anyway.

Tarquine stared with a hollowed look at the small sphere and the two large ones. She moved the smaller sphere away, setting it among dark cubes, surrounding it in a shroud of burial. The room blurred as Jaibriol looked up, his eyes sheened with moisture. He saw the unshed tears in her eyes, in her fierce refusal to cry. Her gaze also blazed with another emotion—hatred for whoever had attacked their lives.

"It's your move," she said, her voice low and deep.

Jaibriol placed a dark octahedron into the midst of dice she was using to symbolize their enemies. Tarquine countered with the onyx ring, setting it within an s-curve of carnelian and gold gems. He recognized her intent; she was describing the Iquar Line, her own dynasty. The onyx ring was her nephew, General Barthol Iquar. It was strangling the Iquar Line.

Jaibriol set a diamond pyramid he used for Corbal into her structure. He wasn't sure why he made the move, since it interfered with her completion of the Iquar story.

"So." Tarquine picked up an obsidian block she

used for her bodyguards and set it between his Corbal pyramid and her Iquar structure.

As they played, a story emerged. At first it told him nothing new, just that Barthol was now the Iquar heir. Gradually another pattern emerged: if Tarquine bore Jaibriol a son and then she and Jaibriol both died, the title of regent for the child-emperor would go to the child's closest relative. Barthol. It would consolidate the two most powerful Aristo Lines, Qox and Iquar, under the general. Barthol would effectively rule Eube. But that could only happen if Jaibriol had an heir; if he died childless, his title would revert to Corbal. It would make no sense for Barthol to seek Tarquine's death if she were pregnant.

Assuming he knew.

Tarquine was watching him with her face half in shadow, her cheekbones gaunt. "I learned I was to bear a child only moments before I told you. I hadn't seen a doctor. No one knew but us."

A deep rage simmered within Jaibriol. "Not Barthol?"

"He had no idea." In a voice edged like a knife, she added, "Patience has never been one of my nephew's virtues."

Jaibriol looked at the dice on the table. The Quis didn't point to Azile as the traitor; they suggested Barthol had framed Azile in a brilliantly convoluted plot that made it look as if Azile had set up the Red Point Diamonds so they appeared to set up the Security officers. Even with the endless Aristo capacity to double-cross, Jaibriol wouldn't have believed Barthol would seek Tarquine's death. He doubted the general was capable of truly loving anyone but himself, but whatever skewed ability he had to feel affection, he had that for Tarquine.

Maybe Barthol had discovered Jaibriol's secret lineage. Yet if Barthol had proof, all he had to do was denounce the emperor. It would destroy both Jaibriol and the treaty. Attempting the much more difficult assassination would be foolish, and for all that Barthol was one of the more vicious people Jaibriol knew, the general was also one of the most intelligent.

Jaibriol met his wife's red gaze. "The Highton loyalty to kin is legendary. I've never known an Aristo Line that didn't value it."

Her voice was ice. "Such loyalty is the bedrock of our lives."

"Even bedrock can crack." If Barthol had tried to kill her, he had stepped over an invisible line even Tarquine would never cross.

Unless she was provoked.

"So." Tarquine settled back into her chair. "The doctors believe it is in my best interest to recuperate in a place of retreat."

Although Jaibriol had no doubt they had told her exactly that, he didn't believe for an instant she would listen. Tarquine would never "retreat" after something like this. "I can't imagine any retreat being sufficient for the Empress of Eube."

"I should go home." She flexed her hand, the long fingers curling in the air as if she were testing their strength. "Back to the estate of my birth, my Line, the family that nurtured my life."

Nurtured, hell. "Your nephew Barthol is running your family estate." Jaibriol didn't want Tarquine anywhere near him.

"Is he?" she said idly. "I had forgotten."

A chill went up Jaibriol's back. "Tarquine."

She glanced at him. "Yes, I do believe I shall go home to recuperate."

"You cannot. It isn't well enough secured."

She waved her hand. "I'm sure you can arrange the necessary protections."

He wanted her here. *Safe.* But nothing would ever be safe, not for Tarquine, not for him, and not for any child they brought into this godforsaken universe.

Darkness moved within Jaibriol. He knew exactly what drove Tarquine, for it burned within him as well—the need to avenge their child. For their son had died within his mother's womb, the only casualty of the attempt against their lives.

He spoke in a shadowed voice. "Give my greetings to Barthol."

XI

A Search for Sanctuary

Tide didn't land at the embassy; he set his flyer down on a public hover-pad in a secluded area of a park where grass rippled and velvet-trees shaded the ground. He claimed he had no permit to park in the city, but Aliana suspected he didn't want to be seen anywhere near the Skolians.

"Nice," Red said, looking around at the sheltered glade as they disembarked.

"The embassy is about half a kilometer from here." Tide motioned toward the north. "Walk that way. Go east at the edge of the park. The embassy is up the boulevard, on a plaza."

"You not come?" Red asked.

Tide shifted his weight. "I can't."

"We'll be fine," Aliana said, even though she was terrified. "We'll just—" They'd what? "Uh—do we walk in the front door?"

"You have to go through their security," Tide said.

"They let provider through?" Red pulled at the

frayed cuffs on his sleeves, which covered his diamond wrist guards.

"They'll let you through," Tide said. "Tell them you're seeking asylum."

"Yeah, that'll make them like us," Aliana drawled. "Greetings, can we go insane with you?"

"Aliana, listen," Tide said. "You have to be careful with what you say. You can't just throw around words."

She squinted at him. "What does that mean, throw around words?"

"I say I am property of Admiral Muze?" Red asked.

"No! Don't say that!" Tide pushed his hand through his hair. "You need to be more subtle."

"How are we supposed to do that?" Aliana asked.

"What subtle mean?" Red asked.

"Gods," Tide muttered.

Aliana scowled at Tide. "You said we could do this!"

"You can." He lifted his hands, then dropped them. "You have to deal with the situation."

She pulled herself up to her full height. "I've been on my own for a long time. *Months.* I can figure this out."

"Legally you're still a child," Tide said. "They'll want the name of your guardian and your owner. If you aren't careful how you answer, they might contact your stepfather."

Well, that was lovely. "I'll kill him if he tries to bring me back to his fucking shit-shack."

"Aliana, watch your language!" Tide said. "You want to convince these people to protect you, not alienate them." He turned to Red. "How old are you? Eighteen? Nineteen?"

"Don't know," Red said.

Tide swore under his breath. "Fine. Great. Let's go."

Relief flooded Aliana. "You'll come with us?"

He looked like he wanted to blow holes in the sky. But he said, "Yeah, I'll come with you."

The crowd almost ruined everything.

Aliana's walk with Tide and Red to the Skolian embassy started out fine. The plaza was beautiful, paved in pale blue and white stones, all interlocking octagons, stars, and pentagons. Stone columns bordered the area and flowering vines wound around them. A crowd had gathered at a holo-kiosk by one column to watch a news broadcast. They were listening to that song by the furious man with red hair. It wouldn't normally have been a problem; anyone could walk around the crowd. But Tide didn't want to be seen.

The embassy stood on the far side of the plaza, beyond the crowd. Its white stone glowed in the sunlight, and wide stairs led up to the entrance through marble columns. Velvet-trees grew around the building and arched over its roof, their long fronds rustling. It was utterly lovely, which was utterly bizarre. The building should have been ugly because it was, well, *Skolian.*

Aliana hoped Tide was wrong about her being half Skolian. How noxious. That could explain why she was so ugly, though. Of course Red said she was beautiful; he was bred to say that. He'd tell her she was beautiful if she had two heads. It didn't make her like him any less, but she didn't feel good about herself. It mattered to her whether or not he truly liked how she looked, and feeling that way scared her.

Tide stood at the edge of the plaza and scowled at the crowd. They seemed fascinated by the singer. Many were angry, though Aliana couldn't tell if they were mad *at* the singer or *with* him. Maybe some of both.

"Listen to that garbage," Tide said. "That's what 'peace' means to the Skolians. It's not enough that one of their princes has to denigrate our emperor. He also has to tell every flaming person in the universe."

"Maybe he not put song out there," Red said.

"He did it," Tide said. "It's been proved. Came straight from him."

"So is the treaty off?" Aliana wasn't sure how that worked. Could you just say, *Never mind, we made a mistake, go away, we'll blow you up another day?*

"Probably," Tide said. "It never had much hope. You can't trust Skolians to follow through with something like that."

Aliana glowered at him. "So these are the people you want me to live with, these Skolians who on purpose screw up a peace treaty. Great, Tide. Just great. Hey, if we go back to war with them, maybe I'll get conscripted into their army and they'll make me come here to shoot Eubians."

"Aliana, no!" Red said.

"It was a joke," Tide told him. He glared at Aliana. "A bad one."

"Yeah, right." It hadn't been a joke. She crossed her arms and fought back the tears burning in her eyes. Damned if she'd cry.

Tide put his hand on her shoulder. "I'm sorry, babe. I just don't see any other options, at least not that I can help you with. I don't have many resources."

"That embassy isn't what I expected," Aliana said.

"Big," Red said.

Tide looked around, studying the area. "You know,

maybe this crowd could work in our favor. With all these people, we might be less conspicuous. Blend in."

"I hope so," Aliana said.

"All right." He took a breath. "Let's do it."

The three of them set off together across the plaza, acting as if they were coming to hear the music. The man was singing in Highton:

You dehumanize us; your critics, they all died.
You answer defiance with massive genocide.

"Bad song," Red said.

Tide had a strange look, and Aliana felt his discomfort. It wasn't anger, exactly—

"Gods almighty," she said. "Is it true? The Aristos committed genocide?"

Tide lowered his voice. "Aliana, *shut up*. Don't ever ask that again."

"Why not?" She knew he was right, but she was tired of people telling her not to think.

"Aristos kill you," Red said.

She frowned at them both, but she said nothing more.

At the embassy, Tide headed for a smaller door to the left of the huge main entrance. They climbed the stairs while breezes pulled their clothes and blew their hair around their faces. Aliana's pulse jumped. This was it. Almost there. She tried to neaten her wrinkled shirt, which wasn't smart enough to smooth out its own cloth.

They came around a marble column and into view of a guard at the smaller door. Red froze, hanging back by the column. Aliana understood. She had seen officers in the police force of Muzeopolis, hard-edged men and women in blue uniforms with scuffed sidearms. They were nothing compared to this man. He was bigger, both in height and muscles, and he wore a black uniform with silver studs. A massive black gun rested in a holster on his hip, glittering like an Aristo's hair.

"Bad," Red said in a low voice.

Tide had kept going, but now he paused, looking around, and came back to them. "He's just the honor guard. A Jagernaut Quaternary."

"Jager-what?" Aliana asked.

"No!" Red backed away. "Not go!"

Tide caught his arm. "He won't hurt you."

"Jagernauts devil," Red said.

"If Tide says he won't hurt us, he won't." Aliana felt ready to burst. "And it's 'Jagernauts *are* devils.'" She had promised to help him with his speech, but she didn't feel any more qualified to do that than to deal with this embassy.

"Can't talk," he said. "Too dumb."

"You aren't dumb. Quit saying that. You're smart."

Red glared at her. "Fine. Jagernauts *are* devils. I not go in there."

"If you don't go in there," Tide told him, "I can't help you."

"Listen, Red," Aliana said. "That guy can't do anything to you." She sincerely hoped that was true. "We can breeze right past him and he has to stay put. Wouldn't you like that?"

He regarded her uncertainly. "I not go."

"Well, suit yourself. You can stay here while we go inside." She hoped the prospect of being left behind would change his mind, because the last thing she wanted to do was to go without him.

"Not leave me here," Red told her.

"I don't know what else to do if you won't come with us," she said.

"Not come." After a moment, he added, "I won't come."

"If you're here when Tide comes out, he can take you back to Muzeopolis." She touched his cheek. "Take care of yourself, Red. I'll miss you."

"Aliana." He took her hand. "Stay."

"You'll be all right." As much a she wanted to keep holding him, she forced herself to let go of his hand. With a deep breath, she turned and set off for the archway. Footsteps came from behind her, and for one excellent moment she thought Red had changed his mind. But it was Tide who caught up with her.

The Jagernaut at the entrance was watching their entire exchange. Aliana tried not to notice his huge gun. She felt Red's fear, both for himself and for her. It was tearing her apart. She couldn't leave him defenseless; gods only knew what would happen.

"Wait!" Hurried footsteps sounded behind them.

Relief poured over Aliana as she turned around.

Red joined them, his glare all for her. "Not leave me." He made it an accusation.

She took his hand and twined her fingers with his. "We'll go together."

Tide was watching them with a strange expression. It felt like . . . what? Loss? Jealousy? She couldn't figure him out, and he was harder to read than most people. His thoughts felt oddly metallic.

Together, they went to the Jagernaut, who was watching them with what seemed more like curiosity than hostility. When they reached him, he spoke in accented Eubic. "Do you want to go inside?"

"They've come to see the Foreign Affairs officer for cross-cultural exceptions," Tide said.

Aliana blinked. That certainly sounded odd. Foreign Affairs for what? Cross-dressers? Probably not, but she had no idea what it meant. The guard seemed to know. Although he had no outward reaction, surprise leaked out of his mind. She expected him to turn them away or at least ask for documents, but instead he simply ushered them inside. A quiet alarm beeped when they walked under the entrance arch, but the Jagernaut flicked several panels on the gauntlet he wore and the alarm stopped. They entered a wide hall with holo-pictures on the walls showing pastoral scenes far nicer than anything in Muzeopolis.

Red's grip tightened on her hand. When Aliana glanced at him, he stared at her with fury.

"What?" she asked in a low voice.

You say he stay outside!

The words burst into Aliana's *mind.* With a gasp, she froze. In the same instant, their guard stopped and swung around to them.

Tide continued for another step, then paused and turned back, his puzzled gaze going from Red to Aliana to the guard. "What's wrong?" he asked.

Sorry, Red thought in Aliana's mind. *Too loud. I go away.* His mind receded from hers.

The Jagernaut spoke quietly to Red. "You're strong. Maybe a seven on the Kyle scale."

Tide's gaze turned hard as he scowled at the Skolian. "You're a psion?"

"All Jagernauts are," the man said. He lifted his hand toward the corridor they had been following. "This way."

Aliana didn't know what to make of this, either Red yelling in her mind or the Jagernaut's reaction. What scale? Whatever it meant, it seemed to work in their favor. She felt the change in the Jagernaut's attitude as if a switch had toggled in his mind. He was no longer wary of Red. He wasn't sure about her yet and Tide he definitely didn't like.

Aliana caught something else, too, something unexpected. The Jagernaut was *nervous*. He had never dealt with a situation like this before. She picked up his mind more easily than she did with most people, except Red. The man knew he had to be careful, that the embassy was isolated in the midst of a hostile empire, and one very valuable member of that empire wanted help. Red was valuable to them! He would help Red. He didn't know if they would help Aliana, though. But *she* knew. She was like Red. She needed to let this Jagernaut know. But how? Well, Red had yelled with his mind, and that seemed to work.

Aliana mustered all the mental force she could imagine and thought, ***Help me, too!***

"*Ah!*" Red pressed the heels of his hands to his temples.

The Jagernaut spun around, his mouth open. "Gods almighty!"

"What?" Tide again looked from Aliana to the Jagernaut to Red. "What's going on?"

No one answered. Red was scowling at Aliana as if she had rudely screamed in his ear. The Jagernaut stared as if she had grown a second head.

Then, very clearly, the Jagernaut's words came into her mind. *Can you hear me?*

Aliana's pulse jumped. "Yes," she whispered.

"Yes?" Tide asked. "Yes what?"

Answer in your mind, the Jagernaut thought to Aliana.

She tried to think more forcefully. ***I don't know how.***

"Ach!" The Jagernaut winced. "Can you moderate that?"

"I don't understand," Aliana said.

"Neither do I," Tide muttered.

"You too loud," Red said, glaring at Aliana.

"Are you a provider?" the Skolian asked Aliana.

"No!" She crossed her arms and met his gaze defiantly.

"Were your parents?" the Jagernaut asked. "Is that why you have gold coloring?"

She wanted to sock him. Yet one more person going on about her skin. *Sex slave baby.* "The hell with you."

"I don't mean to offend you," he said. "Can you tell me where your parents are?"

"My mother is dead," she said shortly. "I never met my father. My stepfather is an asshole."

The Jagernaut exhaled, then flicked more panels on his gauntlet and spoke its comm. "Quaternary Gainor here."

A woman's voice came out of the comm. "This is Lensmark. What's up, Gainor?"

"I have three people asking for cross-cultural," Gainor said.

"Two," Tide said. "I'm not staying. I was never here."

The Jagernaut didn't look surprised. "Make that two, commander. One is about seven on the scale. I don't know about the other. Maybe even more than a nine."

The woman's voice cracked with tension. "Bring them to my office immediately."

"Copy that, ma'am."

"What's going on?" Tide asked when Gainor lowered his arm.

"Secondary Lensmark is the ranking ISC officer at the embassy," Gainor said. "She can expedite your visit."

"I not provider," Red said. Then he added, "I am not provider. Not anymore."

"Not in here, you aren't." Gainor regarded him steadily. "The moment you went through that doorway, you were in Skolian territory. No one can own you here, young man."

Aliana didn't believe it, but at least this Jagernaut hadn't threatened them. She caught an odd reaction from him, as if he thought, *There but for the grace of the gods go I.* She imagined a shroud over her mind, wishing she knew a more reliable way to cut out the moods and thoughts of other people. She picked up random bits and pieces, as if her mind were a ragged, leaky mesh.

They continued down graceful hallways, walking past polished stone sculptures, all of it oddly beautiful, as if the Skolians weren't monsters. Nothing seemed horrific about this Jagernaut, either. Of course, she knew nothing about Jagernauts. Maybe he turned into a monster when the moon came out. Or something.

A realization came to Aliana. Red had denied being a provider. She hadn't thought he could do that. Then again, he'd run away, which he supposedly couldn't do, either. To her, a provider had always seemed like an incredibly expensive jewel owned by an Aristo, nothing you were allowed even to see, let alone touch. Red was turning her assumptions upside down.

They stopped at an archway, this one inlaid with

blue and green mosaics designed to look like triangles around exploding gold suns.

"Nice," Red said.

Gainor smiled, but Aliana felt his tension. It was so strange: she and Red scared this intimidating man. He didn't consider them dangerous; if anything, he felt protective toward them. He feared what would happen to the embassy because they were here, but he never once thought of turning them away. She wished she understood better. Everything was off balance.

When Gainor turned to Tide, his demeanor changed. It was subtle, but she recognized the difference. Gainor distrusted Tide.

"If I take you in there with us," Gainor told him, "Lensmark will want to question you."

"I've nothing to tell her," Tide said.

Gainor nodded, some understanding he and Tide seemed to share. Odd, because Gainor was Skolian and Tide was a Razer, so neither was human according to the Aristos. Yet they were alike somehow and both seemed more human to Aliana than the partial Aristos she'd met.

"Do you guys know each other?" she asked them.

Gainor shot her a baffled look. "Of course not."

"Why do you ask?" Tide asked.

"I don't know. You just seem to understand each other."

Tide's posture altered subtly, as if he were tensed to defend himself. "I have no idea what you're talking about."

"Uh—okay." Why was he mad? Maybe he and Gainor understood each other because they were both military.

Oh. Of course. Tide didn't want them to know he

was a Razer. Well, he should trust her. She wouldn't tell anyone.

"We've never met," Gainor said.

Aliana felt the truth in his words. He was having the same effect on her as often happened with Red, heightening her erratic perception of moods. Apparently she could pick up thoughts on the surface of some people's minds. It was distracting and confusing.

"You can learn to control it," Gainor said.

"Control what?" Aliana felt as if she had wandered into the middle of a play where she didn't know the plot or any of her lines.

"Your mind," Gainor said. "Your Kyle abilities."

"I don't know what Kyle means." She wished they would all stop looking at her.

"You will," Gainor said.

Tide shifted his weight back and forth. "I should go."

The Jagernaut nodded to him. "We'll look after them."

"Do you have to go, Tide?" Aliana asked. "Can't you come with us?"

His voice softened. "I wish I could, babe. But I can't." He gave her a crooked smile. "You remember everything I taught you. You're one hell of a fighter."

"You bet." She wanted to sound cocky, but it came out sad instead. She also wanted to hug him, but of course they never did that. They were too tough. That blurring of her sight, that was because the air in this bizarre place was bothering her eyes.

Tide started to raise his hand as if he would touch her. Then he let out a breath and turned to Red. "Good luck."

"You too," Red said.

When Tide glanced back at Aliana, she again had the sense he wanted to touch her. She was on the verge of throwing her arms around him, entreating him to come with them. But neither of them did anything. He just nodded to her and took off down the hall. At the oddly square corner where his hall intersected another, he paused and looked back.

Aliana raised her hand. "Be well," she whispered.

Tide lifted his hand. Then he turned the corner.

Gainor spoke gently. "What are your names?"

"Aliana call me Red," Red said.

"Do you have any other names?" Gainor asked.

He shook his head. "Just that."

Aliana turned back to them, despondent. "I'm Aliana Miller Azina. I was named for a chemical or something."

"A chemical?" Gainor smiled. "Aliana is a shortened version of Aliana-Lia. It's a popular Skolian name."

"I'm not Skolian!"

Red frowned at her. "But Tide say—"

"Stop it!" Aliana told him. "I don't care what Tide says."

Gainor spoke carefully. "What branch of the military did Tide serve in? The navy?"

"He wasn't military." Aliana didn't actually know if Razers were part of ESComm, but she wouldn't tell this Gainor regardless. He was trying to trick her.

The Jagernaut glanced at Red. "Did he work for the Aristo who owned you?"

"I not know," Red said.

Aliana could tell Gainor wasn't convinced. An alarming thought hit her: if she could pick up his emotions, he might be picking hers up as well.

Gainor spoke, again using that unexpected kindness so incongruous with his formidable presence. "With you, I get some moods, but only a rare thought, and only if it's unusually strong and on the surface of your mind. Like that last one. If you want to protect your mind, imagine a shield around it."

Heat flushed in Aliana's cheeks. This was mortifying. She imagined a fortress surrounding her mind with locks designed to keep Gainor out, out, *OUT.*

He inhaled sharply. "Careful! Don't use it as a weapon."

"Weapon?" She hesitated, uncertain what he meant. She covered her fortress with mist.

Gainor's shoulders relaxed. "Yes. Better."

Another strange thought came to Aliana. It wasn't to his advantage to reveal that he could hear some of her thoughts. He even told her how to protect herself. If he had wanted to trick her, he would never help her that way.

Gainor motioned to the archway. "My commanding officer is in the room beyond this door. She will ask you both about why you came to us. Answer the best you can and you'll be fine."

"All right." Aliana wished this was over. Red stood at her side, steady and silent.

Gainor tapped a code into a tiled panel, and the archway shimmered and faded away. As he ushered them forward, Aliana had an odd sensation, as if an invisible membrane slid over her skin. Maybe the "door" was still there, just changed so they could walk through it.

The room beyond was big. A woman sat at a desk, her dark hair pulled back, her face like an austere statue. She wore a uniform similar to Gainor's, black and sleek, but like Gainor, she had no slave collar or wrist cuffs. So strange. She stood as they came in, her gaze intent on Aliana.

Why look so hard at me? Aliana wondered, but she hid the thought within her mental fortress.

"Welcome," the woman said. "I'm Lyra Lensmark." She motioned to several chairs set about her desk. It disoriented Aliana; she was used to cushions on the floor, scattered around low tables. But she and Red sat down, and Gainor did, too, while Lensmark settled behind her desk. Aliana perched on the edge of her seat, ready to bolt.

"This is Aliana and Red," Gainor said. "They've come to ask for asylum."

"Not political asylum, I take it." Lensmark considered them. "You're both psions?"

"Yes," Red said.

Aliana felt painfully vulnerable, unprotected, ready to burst. "I don't understand this psion thing. Everyone keeps saying it like I should know what it means."

"Provider," Red said.

Not again! Aliana jumped to her feet. "Damn it all, quit calling me that fucking name!"

Lensmark's voice snapped out. "Sit down, young lady."

Startled, Aliana dropped into her seat.

"When you are in my office," Lensmark told her, "you will use courteous language, not cuss like you came out of a sewer hole. Understood?"

"Yes, ma'am." Aliana's cheeks were burning. "I'm sorry."

"All right, let's start over." Lensmark spoke to Red. "You know you're a psion?"

"Yes. I provide—" He looked at Aliana and stopped.

"A provider for who?" Lensmark asked.

"Nobody now. He throw me away."

"Who threw you away?"

"Admiral Muze."

Lensmark's face paled. "Which Admiral Muze?"

"I only know one," Red said. "Joint Commander."

"Gods above," Gainor muttered.

Lensmark let out a long breath. Then she spoke to Aliana. "You have a Skolian name."

No, no, no, no. Aliana wanted to groan. Really, she wanted to cry, but she couldn't do that, not here, not in front of Skolians, not in front of anyone. "It's a chemical. My father worked in an azine factory. My mother worked for a miller. That's why I'm Aliana Miller Azina."

Red shot her an apologetic look, then spoke to Lensmark. "Tide say Aliana is Skolian."

"Who is Tide?" Lensmark asked.

"He's just a friend," Aliana said quickly. "He brought us here."

"Your boyfriend?" Lensmark asked.

Aliana's cheeks heated. "No!"

"He's a lot older than they are," Gainor said. "Military, I'm almost certain."

"Not military," Red said.

They all looked at him.

"He not," Red said.

"How long have you known him?" Lensmark asked.

"I meet yesterday," Red explained.

She raised an eyebrow. "And in your lengthy acquaintance with this man, you can say for certain he isn't a military officer?"

"Yes."

Lensmark considered him. Then she turned to Aliana. "How long have you known Tide?"

Aliana shifted in her chair. "About three months."

"How did you get involved with him?"

"I'm a bouncer at a holo-club. He was teaching me how to fight."

"A girl your age was a bouncer?" Lensmark stared at her. "Where are your parents?"

"My mother is dead." Aliana gritted her teeth, then made herself relax so she could talk. "My father left her before she knew she was pregnant. It was on a hinterland world. Tide says my father might have been a Skolian soldier working as a spy. My stepfather is a half-Aristo asshole."

"What you just told me," Lensmark said, "is astounding in so many ways, I hardly know where to start."

Aliana just wanted to leave. It was all she could do to stay put. And damn it, she'd cussed in front of Lensmark again. She hadn't meant to. The Skolian woman hardly seemed to have noticed, though, she was so distracted by whatever Aliana had said that was so astounding.

"I'm nothing special," Aliana said.

"Did your mother have gold skin?" Lensmark asked.

"Not even close. I don't know about my father."

"A lot of providers have metallic skin," Gainor said.

"My father worked in a *factory*."

Lensmark rubbed her chin. "How tall are you?"

"I don't know." Aliana squinted at her. "You got height restrictions in Skolia?"

Lensmark smiled. "No restrictions. But you're unusually tall and muscular, and I'd wager you aren't done growing yet."

"Does that matter?"

"Your size is related to your parents." Lensmark was being careful again. "It might help us find your father, if he is Skolian. Or was."

Or was. *Was.* Until that moment, Aliana hadn't realized she'd always assumed her father was out there somewhere. On the heels of that unwanted self-knowledge came another: she'd always hoped to find him. Now she didn't know what to do. Did she need to know if her father was a dead Skolian? Hell, she would be Skolian soon, if these people let her. She didn't want this, didn't want to leave everything she'd always known, but she couldn't go back. They would find her, the women and men who served the Muze Line, and she would even rather be a Skolian than become their prisoner.

"I would never do that." The man standing on the holostage in Kelric's living room looked as if he were here in the room instead of many light-years away on Earth. Only the slight wavering of his body every now and then revealed he was a projection. Red hair tousled over his collar, and he looked like a kid, hardly more than twenty. Kelric knew better; physically, his brother Del was in his late thirties.

"Dehya checked it herself," Kelric told him. "The leak on that song came from you."

Del crossed his arms and regarded Kelric coldly. "If you believe I would release 'Carnelians Finale' to destroy the peace process, the hell with you."

A woman's voice came from behind Kelric. "Del, calm down. That's not what he means."

Startled, Kelric looked around. Dehya had entered

the room, a delicate woman in a blue jumpsuit. She seemed too ethereal for the huge, spare living room, which was all smooth stone walls except for the gold silhouette of desert horizon that glowed at waist level.

"Aunt Dehya." Del lowered his arms and his voice warmed. "My greetings."

She smiled as she came up next to Kelric. "It's good to see you, Del. And we know you didn't deliberately release the song. It appeared to come from you, but it was done without your knowledge." Then she added, "Just like Kelric killed himself in the Kyle without realizing it."

Well, damn, Kelric thought. She would have to mention that.

Del stared at them. "Kelric *what?*"

"Something affected our neural processes," Kelric said. He wanted to make this right, so his brother didn't think they doubted him, but he never knew how to talk to Del, how to deal with his brother's emotional intensity and mercurial moods. That was part of what made Del such a gifted artist, but it was so unlike the way Kelric saw the world, it left him at a loss. "We don't know yet how it happened. Essentially, I overloaded my brain until it shut down. Doctor Sashia restarted it from one of my neural backups."

"You're saying someone controlled your thoughts and made you kill yourself?" Del's face paled. "If that's really possible, *nothing* can protect us. Why aren't you terrified?"

He scowled at Del. "Getting emotional won't solve anything." Of course he was afraid. But the last thing Imperial Space Command needed was for its commander to panic.

Kelric, don't, Dehya thought. *To Del, you probably sound like you're discussing the weather.*

This is the way I am. I'm not going to jump up and down screaming.

I know. And I understand. But he doesn't.

Kelric knew what she wanted. Doing his best to put reassurance into his voice, he said, "Del, listen. We don't think this was easily done. It may not even be possible to replicate it."

Del's shoulders had tensed, but as Kelric spoke, his stiffness eased. "Are you all right?"

"I'm fine," Kelric said. He tried to let down his emotional barriers. "It's frustrating. I don't even know what happened in those few moments between my last backup and when I died."

"You backed yourself up and restarted your brain?" Del asked. "I mean, I know it's possible, if you have enough neural augmentation. But it's like—like you're—" He stumbled to a stop.

Kelric had to make a conscious effort not to grit his teeth. "Like I'm a machine?" Del wouldn't be the first person who had described him that way.

"Kelric, no, I didn't mean that. I just don't understand how all this could have happened without any of us knowing." Del reached out to the side, out of the range of the holo-cam, and his arm vanished up to his elbow. It reappeared as he pulled a desk into view. He leaned against it, sitting on the edge. "What about mother and everyone else? Aunt Dehya, are you all right?"

Careful what you tell him, Kelric warned.

He's not a child, Dehya thought. Aloud, she said, "We're not sure what happened to me. Everyone else is fine."

Del braced his palms on the edge of the desk. "What do you mean, what happened to you?"

Don't, Kelric told her. **We don't know if he can handle it.**

He deserves to know, Dehya thought. *He was attacked, too. Trust him.*

Trust. With Del, it was hard for Kelric. In his youth, Del had made some terrible choices, and he had suffered for them. After he had overdosed on drugs, with a violent allergenic reaction, the health nanomeds in his body had gone awry and amplified the damage instead of helping. Del had spent nearly fifty years in cryogenic suspension, until medical science had advanced to the point where they could heal his body and keep him alive. But that was in the past. Kelric would never agree with many of Del's decisions, like staying on Earth to be a "holo-rock" star, but Del had matured these past years and he seemed happier than Kelric had ever seen him before.

Dehya was watching Kelric. She didn't need his agreement to tell Del confidential information; as Ruby Pharaoh, she outranked the Imperator. But she and Kelric had always worked as a team and he respected her judgment.

Tell him what you think he needs to know, he thought. **I won't object.**

Del was waiting, his posture tensed. He had to know they were communicating about him.

"Del, what I tell you isn't for anyone else to know," Dehya said. "Not even Ricki, your wife."

"You have my word," Del said.

"Whoever struck you and Kelric also got to me," Dehya said. "My links to the Kyle web exploded. I was cut off." She spread her hands out from her body. "I couldn't get out of the Kyle."

"Why not?" Del asked. "Couldn't the techs just unplug you from the mesh?"

"They did."

"And you were *still* in the Kyle?"

"That's right."

"I thought that was impossible."

"It is. Mostly."

His smile flashed. "That 'mostly' meaning impossible for anyone except you, I'd wager."

Dehya actually blushed at his smile. "Pretty much."

Kelric almost groaned. How did Del have this effect on women, even Dehya? She claimed his smile was all it took to make all those billions of girls fall in love with him. Kelric didn't understand it, but then, he was no expert on male media idols.

"Aunt Dehya, are you okay now?" Del asked. "You look tired. You should rest."

"I'll be all right," she told him.

He's right, Kelric thought at her. **You should be sleeping. Not cavorting around here.**

Cavorting? Her smile curved as she sent him a image of herself twirling around Kelric while he turned clumsily, too big and too slow to follow her.

Ha, ha, very funny, he grumbled.

Del's gaze was flicking between the two of them. "You have some idea how this happened, yes?" he asked. "So we can stop it from happening again."

"We're working on it," Kelric said. "Something altered the way the neurons fire in our brains. It happened about the same time for both Dehya and me, and we think for you, too. According to the traces of your activity in the Kyle, you actually released 'Carnelians Finale' twice, the second time at exactly the same moment Dehya and I were attacked. We've sent a team to Earth to check you out, make sure you're all right. Based on what Dehya and your cousin Taquinil found, you programmed the release beforehand. You were asleep when 'Carnelians Finale' actually hit the meshes."

"So it wasn't me!"

"It's your neural patterns in the Kyle," Dehya said. "We've verified them."

"I'm sorry," Del said quietly. "I swear, I never wanted to hurt either of you."

"We know," Kelric said. What he really wanted was to bring Del home to the Orbiter, where they could better protect him. He always felt that way about his brother, that he should be a bulwark between Del and the universe, as if he could shield the extreme sensitivity of his brother's mind. Del *felt* things so deeply, he hurt so easily, and he sought solace in the worst places, like the drugs that had nearly killed him so long ago. Of course, Del didn't want Kelric protecting him against anything. He chafed at the authority. Although Kelric could order his people to bring Del home, he didn't want to interfere in his brother's life unless it was necessary. Instead, he found ways to protect Del on Earth, working with their military.

All he said was, "You'd be safer here."

"Maybe I should come to the Orbiter," Del said.

Gods almighty, Dehya thought. **Did he actually say that?**

"You would do that?" Kelric asked, stunned.

"You two are scaring the hell out of me," Del said.

"What if it happens again? What if I lose control or hurt someone?" He raked his hand through his unruly curls. "My song, it's *everywhere,* getting people upset. Either they act like I'm a prophet or else they hate me. I don't feel safe here. And I worry about Ricki."

"Your wife is welcome, too," Kelric said. Although he had never felt comfortable with Ricki, a cutthroat producer in the music business, he had to admit that since Del had married her, he seemed to do all his misbehaving in private rather than in view of the insatiable scandal-mongering reporters for the interstellar media. "I've sent a military escort with the Kyle doctors coming to examine you. You can return with them."

Del nodded with undisguised relief. "Okay. Good. That's what we'll do."

This ought to go down in the history books, Dehya thought. *Del not only agreeing to what you want, but being the one who suggested it.*

I'm just glad he's coming back, Kelric thought. He wouldn't relax, though, until Del was home.

XII

Betrayals

Robert Muzeson had served Jaibriol for eleven years, since the day Jaibriol had assumed his throne. A man of medium height with brown hair and eyes, Robert acted as a personal assistant, staff director, and whatever else Jaibriol needed. Decades ago, during a pirate raid, slave merchants had captured Robert's father, an artist from Earth, and sold him to Robert's mother, a Muze Highton. When Jaibriol discovered Robert was rarely allowed to see his father, he had brought the artist to the palace and became his patron. The father had since developed into one of Eube's premier artists. Even more important, he and Robert became close. Robert looked more like his father every day, from the grey at his temples to the distinguished cast of his face.

He was the only person Jaibriol came close to trusting.

"The report just came in!" Robert strode with him down a columned hall, his usually neat hair disarrayed.

He had paged Jaibriol moments ago, well before dawn. Jaibriol had already been awake; he had little time to rest lately and without Tarquine here, he was too agitated to sleep.

His Razers came with them, stark in their midnight uniforms. Gunmetal collars glinted around their necks, more severe than the dark gold collar Robert wore. Jaibriol hated the slave restraints. He owned billions of people and every one had to wear collars and cuffs with his insignia. He could no more tell them to take those off than he could cut off his own arm. If he tried, the other Aristos would see it as an attack on their dominance. Hell, it *was* an attack. It would destroy his reign, erasing any chance he had to make a difference. But every year, it grated more. He had to find a way to end the oppression that would work instead of just leaving him dead.

Jaibriol lengthened his stride until they were jogging down the marble-columned hall. He was tempted to summon a hall-car, but he could run just as fast. "What I fail to understand," he told Robert, "is why ESComm mobilized without my knowledge."

"General Barthol Iquar ordered it." Robert easily kept up with him. "He made an emergency decision when they couldn't reach you. It is of course contingent on your approval."

Like hell. It made no difference that he approved of Barthol's decision; the general had no business acting first and seeking approval later. Barthol could easily have reached him; this "no time" business served only to undermine Jaibriol's authority.

They ran into the Circle Foyer, a hall tiled in diamonds and snow-marble. Mosaics gleamed on the columned arcade that bordered the room. Jaibriol slowed to a walk. "I'll read from the holofile slate," he told Robert. He normally preferred to speak from memory; it looked better. But he couldn't risk any mistakes in this quickly prepared statement.

As Robert handed him the slate, they paused before a set of double doors that rose as high as the ceiling two stories above. Mosaics in gold, diamond, and carnelian bordered the portals. The Razer captain tapped a code into his wrist gauntlet and the doors swung open.

The Aristos of Eube waited beyond.

High-backed benches ringed the circular hall inside, sparkling like diamond, their backs intricately carved, their seats set with blood red cushions. Aristos in glistening black clothes filled every bench, nobles from all three castes: the Hightons who controlled the government and military; the Diamonds who saw to commerce, production, and banks; and the Silicates who catered to the pleasure of Aristos, including their most important product, the providers. Every person in the room had red eyes, glittering black hair, and perfect faces, as if they had been carved from alabaster.

They looked the same.

They moved the same.

They spoke the same.

They thought the same.

Jaibriol strode down an aisle that radiated like a spoke from a dais in the center of the hall. Surrounded by his bodyguards, with Robert at his side, he reached the dais and mounted its steps. A huge chair sat there, carved from snow marble and inlaid with carnelians and onyx. The Carnelian Throne.

Jaibriol stood by the throne that he never actually sat in and looked over the assembly. In unison, every Aristo present raised his or her arm and clicked their black-diamond finger cymbals. A blended crystalline note rang through the Hall, a rare acknowledgement. Jaibriol might be the most controversial emperor ever to sit on the throne, but he had retained his title despite all the challenges, and as long as he ruled, the Aristos gave him that sign of their reverence.

He waited until the chime vibrated into silence. Then he said, "I come before you to reveal an abomination from those who presume to share the stars with us." It was a typically overblown opening, but expected. Let them hate him for forcing peace down their throats, not for breaking minor Aristo customs. "At three this morning, while the good citizens of this fine city slept, the Imperialate launched a vicious attack." He wanted to shout his anger. "Skolian military vessels entered our space and attacked a Eubian merchant convoy. A *civilian* convoy. They obliterated nine vessels, including several crewed ships." His voice hardened. "Every person on those ships died."

Harsh notes echoed in the hall as Aristos hit their cymbals together, not chimes of honor this time, but the discord of anger. Jaibriol had to believe that whoever had ordered the attack had no ISC backing, because otherwise everything he had thought about Kelric's intent in this peace process was a lie. Not only could this tear apart the treaty, but if Kelric didn't condemn the attack, it would be the equivalent of his declaring war against Eube. That godforsaken song, "Carnelians Finale," was sweeping through settled space, enraging people, inciting Skolians against Eube,

Eubians against Skolia, and also Eubians against the Allied Worlds of Earth, for giving a Ruby prince the forum to shout his inflammatory song and the fame to make it inescapable.

"We will tolerate no such outrage!" Jaibriol's voice resonated. He could show no other reaction, nothing anyone could use to accuse him of valuing the peace treaty above Eube. "The order has been given. ESComm is mobilized to move against Skolia." He prayed Kelric decried the attack in time, because if he didn't, Jaibriol would have to go through with the retaliation. He would deal with Barthol Iquar for giving the order without proper authorization, but he would have had to do it himself if Barthol hadn't acted first.

A flash came from the holofile in his hand. Glancing down, he saw red glyphs scrolling across its surface, the alert for incoming news. As he read the message, a chill raced along his spine. He raised his head to see the Aristos watching him like a huge machine. Except not all were looking at him. Some were staring at their wrist gauntlets, tapping their ear comms, or taking the glazed look of a person communicating with a spinal node, each of them accessing the pervasive mesh that was so much a part of their lives, it was more integral to human beings than their own blood.

Instead of giving the statement he had prepared, Jaibriol read the message appearing on his file. "Even as we speak here, Imperator Skolia is giving the following statement." He let his words ring in the orator's voice he had inherited from his grandfather: "I, Kelric Valdoria Skolia, Imperator of the Skolian Imperialate, denounce the attack on the innocent civilians of the Eubian Concord. Nothing—I repeat *nothing*—in their actions was in any way ordered, encouraged, or authorized by Imperial Space Command. This act of terrorism was designed for one purpose only, to destroy the peace accord between Eube and Skolia. Our government will offer restitution to the families of those people lost in this act of brutal violence, and we will see to it that the perpetrators of this crime pay for their violence. They are under sentence of execution for their treason."

Relief swept over Jaibriol, so intense it felt visceral, followed by shock. He had hoped Kelric would condemn the attack, but he hadn't expected such vehemence. The execution sentence would surely weaken Kelric's support within his own government, bringing him under renewed fire from those who wanted Eube to pay for every sin that Prince Del shouted in his soaring, spectacular "Carnelians Finale."

Emotions from the Aristos flooded Jaibriol, too strong to block even with the mental fortress he had built around his mind. Their fury and frustrated outrage swept over him, for Kelric had just stolen their justification for throwing away the treaty. They didn't want reparations, they didn't want peace, and they sure as hell didn't want to know that ISC hadn't ordered the attack. They wanted war and had ever since that defiant song had smashed through their lives.

Jaibriol didn't know who had ordered the attack and he didn't believe it would be the last assault. He had known the road to peace would be difficult, but he was beginning to wonder if their attempts to follow it would end up bringing on a more violent war than if they had never tried.

✧ ✧ ✧

"Execution!" Roca threw the word at Kelric as they strode along the corridor to the War Room. "Are you out of your flaming mind?"

"This is the *first* chance we've had for peace," he shot back. "They may have destroyed it."

"You don't have to execute them! Arrest is enough. Kill them and our own people will call you a murderer."

"It's not enough to say I'll arrest them," Kelric told her. "You think the Aristos will negotiate a treaty while our military slaughters their civilians in an unprovoked attack and my own brother is screaming to all high hell about their towering evil? I needed a stronger statement."

With no warning, Roca lowered her mental barriers, and her thoughts hit him like a blow. He saw the same image they had all witnessed a thousand times since it had turned into a mesh plague—Del with his head raised in defiance as his voice rang out: *You broke my brother, you Carnelian sons, you tortured my mother in your war of suns.*

Kelric drew her to a stop. "*Nothing* will ever forgive what they did to you. If I could subject every one of those involved to excruciating pain, I would do it." He took a breath, struggling for calm. "But somewhere, sometime, someone *must* say, 'Today I will not seek revenge.' Someone has to say, 'We will stop' and *mean* it, or the bloodshed will go on and on, endless, until we destroy the entire human race."

Her answer came to him low and coiled. "What did Jaibriol Qox offer when the two of you were on Earth? What did you two say to each other, there in secret?" Her controlled façade cracked. "What was so important, Kelric, that you had to commit *treason* to meet him face to face?"

Kelric felt as if he were breaking. In Jaibriol, she had a grandson she would never know. He kept his barriers up, for even she couldn't find what he hid. He couldn't go back on his oath to protect the emperor's secret, not even for the mother he loved.

"The Assembly cleared me of treason," he said quietly. "I would never betray the Imperialate. I'm asking you to trust me."

Roca closed her eyes, then opened them again. "You were my shining, golden child, the miracle who came when I thought I would have no more children." She drew in an uneven breath. "But I don't know you anymore. The military dictator is a stranger to me."

"I'm not a dictator." Did she know she was tearing him apart?

Moisture showed in her eyes. "I don't know what you are."

Of all people, he would never have believed she would doubt him. He had known the price of this peace would be high, but he had never believed it could tear at his family more painfully than the Traders had ever managed.

"No! That can't be true." Panic threatened Aliana as she stood facing Secondary Lensmark, the Jagernaut commander at the Skolian embassy. "You promised! You said you gave asylum to psions. If we leave now, we'll be killed or made into providers."

"We not go back," Red said, his gaze never wavering as he stood at Aliana's side.

"This commando attack on the Eubian merchant ships has changed everything." Lensmark was pacing the room, her leather-clad figure dark against the softly abstract art on the walls. "We've told no one you're here, but the planetary government has clamped down on all Skolians. If we do anything that raises suspicion, gods only know how they might react, and diplomatic immunity be damned."

"Can't we just hide here until it's all over?" Aliana asked.

"Over how?" Lensmark stopped in front of her. "People are ready to explode."

Gainor, the Jagernaut who had escorted Aliana and Red into the embassy, was standing by the wall. He said, "Secondary Lensmark, may I offer a suggestion?"

Aliana wondered why one slave had to ask another for permission to speak. Then again, Skolians didn't consider themselves slaves.

"Go ahead," Lensmark told him.

"We send medical tests to the Imperialate for analysis whenever a Skolian needs specialized work," Gainor said. "Even during this clampdown, I doubt ESComm will halt those. They don't have the facilities to diagnose every Skolian ailment, and they don't want to be bothered with us."

"What do you propose?" Lensmark asked.

He nodded toward Aliana and Red. "We say they're Skolian med techs. Send them with the next off-planet shipment."

Aliana looked from him to Lensmark, on the verge of saying she could do it, mainly because she would do anything to escape. Except she had no clue how to act like a med tech.

"It's risky," Lensmark said. "Sending test results offworld is a lot simpler than sending people. The port authority is doing more security checks than usual, and even in normal times their checks are intensive." She glanced at Aliana and Red. "Do either of you speak Flag or any other Skolian language?"

"What flag?" Red asked.

"I wouldn't know a Skolian language if it jumped up and bit me," Aliana said. An idea came to her. "You could say we were sick. Really sick. No one can treat us here, and people die when they catch what we have. So you want us to leave. Really fast."

"They'd never let you near the starport," Lensmark said. "ESComm would just quarantine the embassy."

"Oh." Aliana was running out of ideas.

"I don't understand what flag," Red repeated.

Lensmark spoke to him in another language, what sounded like gibberish.

And Red answered.

Lensmark blinked. "Not bad. You have an accent, but it's not obviously Eubian. With your broken grammar, it's hard to tell anyway."

"Me not broken," Red objected.

Aliana gaped at him. "Where did you learn Skolian stuff?"

"Languages easy." Red shrugged. "Admiral Muze talk to people in lots of languages. I hear." He touched his temple. "Up here."

Lensmark didn't seem surprised. "Most telepaths learn languages fast." She resumed pacing. "Even if he knows some Flag, I don't see how you two could convince anyone you're Skolian."

"We can act dumb," Aliana said. "We're the, I don't know, the rejected offspring of some Skolian diplomat. She doesn't want us around because we embarrass her." She gave a snort. "It wouldn't be hard for me to act that way. Comes natural."

Lensmark stopped in front of her. "You may be uneducated, but you are *not* dumb."

Aliana hadn't expected that, especially from a hightype like Lensmark. She spoke awkwardly. "Well, you know, I can act dumb. It's what people expect."

"I not need to act," Red said.

Lensmark turned to him. "Don't underestimate yourself, young man. You've a good mind." She smiled at him. "If a lack of verbal ability translated into a lack of intelligence, some of our greatest minds wouldn't exist."

Red's skepticism leaked to Aliana. So she spoke firmly to him. "It's true. You're smart."

His cheeks reddened and he smiled, accenting his high cheekbones in that way she liked so much. She wished they could go somewhere and curl up together. Holding him felt safe. Good. She was always thinking about him.

Lensmark rubbed her chin. "You're both wearing slave restraints." Glancing at Aliana, she said, "Yours aren't wired much into your body, just some minor bio-threads that should be easy to remove." Her gaze shifted to Red. "But the threads from yours are all tangled up with your neural system. An expert will have to map the system before we can remove them."

Aliana blinked. Remove her restraints? She couldn't imagine it. She had worn them in some form or another all her life. She would feel . . . strange without them.

"Mine have traps," Red said. "Risky to take off."

"Don't worry, we won't do anything that hurts either of you," Lensmark said.

"Surely some Skolians have restraints," Aliana said. "Couldn't we say we were like them?"

Lensmark spoke firmly, her gaze intense. "No Skolian wears slave restraints. We are all free."

The Secondary's gauntlet buzzed. She tapped a panel and spoke. "Lensmark here."

"Commander, this is Ensign Idar. We have another petitioner."

"Another?" Lensmark's forehead furrowed. "Is she with you?"

"He, ma'am. And yes, he's here."

"Well, bring him in." Lensmark glanced at Aliana. "Are you expecting anyone else?"

Puzzled, Aliana said, "No one."

The room's door shimmered and vanished. Three people waited outside; two Jagernauts and—

"Tidewater!" Aliana sped across the room, squeezed past a Jagernaut, and grabbed Tide's hands. Happiness washed over her. "You came back!"

Tide flushed as he disentangled his hands from hers. He entered the room with his escort, two uniformed military men, stern and armed.

Lensmark scrutinized Tide as if he were a prisoner. "You're requesting asylum?"

Tide spoke quietly. "I'm asking to defect."

The sudden silence in the room felt like a band pulled taut. Lensmark was so intent on Tide, Aliana wondered that she didn't snap.

"Tide not defective," Red said.

Although Lensmark answered Red, she never took her gaze off Tide. "Those who need our protection ask for asylum. They're the vulnerable ones, people who would die or be terribly harmed if they stayed here." Still watching Tide, she added, "Those who defect are in a position of power, authority, or intelligence that gives them a vested interest in infiltrating our networks. When they ask to defect, they're saying that if we grant them asylum, in return they will give us information about Eube to prove their intent to become Skolian, and that they will accept whatever safeguards we deem necessary to ensure they can't betray us to their superiors."

Well, hell. That was a mouthful of words. "Tide is one of the good people," Aliana said. "He wouldn't betray you."

Lensmark glanced at her and her voice gentled. "I'm sure it seems that way to you."

"I know him really well," Aliana said.

Lensmark considered her. "Then you can tell me what branch of the military he's in."

Aliana stiffened. "I don't know if he's military. That's for him to tell or not." She waited for Lensmark's anger, instinctively tensing to protect herself from a blow.

The Secondary didn't get angry, though. Instead, she nodded as if she respected Aliana's answer. The longer Aliana knew these Skolians, the more they baffled her. An Aristo would have punished her for refusing to answer.

"I used to be a Razer," Tide said.

Lensmark swung back to him. "You're secret police?"

"My line was decommissioned." Dryly he added, "We *are* considered defective."

"Why?" Lensmark asked.

"We want names."

Lensmark waited. When the silence grew long, she said, "So?"

"Machines aren't supposed to want names," Tide said bitterly.

"Gods almighty," the Secondary said under her

breath. "It's a crime, what they do to you all." She spoke in a normal voice. "Were you a bodyguard?"

He nodded, standing between the Jagernauts, his posture wary, his arms by his sides. "For Admiral Muze's younger brother, Lord Orzon."

Red drew in a sharp breath. "You not tell me that!"

"Good Lord," Lensmark said. "This just gets deeper and deeper."

Aliana felt dizzy. Tide had guarded the younger brother to an ESComm Joint Commander, a position high even among the high. And look how Tide had fallen. Except how was it falling when it meant he could be human? At least they hadn't executed him. She had no doubt they would call it something else, like salvaging a broken machine for parts. Bastards.

Lensmark spoke carefully to Tide. "Why do you want to defect?"

"Admiral Muze's men are looking for me." Dark circles showed under Tide's eyes. "After the attack on the merchants, he gave the order to destroy any surviving Razers in my line."

"Why?" Aliana asked. "You had nothing to do with it!" Aristos would never, in a million years, make sense to her.

"ESComm is cracking down on everyone." Tide grimaced. "And that Carnelians song is everywhere. We can't escape the goddamned thing. It's oil on a fire."

"That prince who sings it is a terrible person," Aliana said. "How could he do that to his own brother?"

Lensmark spoke tiredly. "I know you won't believe this, but Prince Del-Kurj didn't release that song. It was done by someone who wanted to stop the peace process. We don't know who."

Aliana just looked at her. Of course Skolians would say that.

Lensmark considered Tide. "If ESComm found out you're here, they would probably drag you out of the embassy regardless of any agreements between our governments. Given the current tensions, they would retaliate against us as well, maybe imprison or execute people from this embassy. Why should we take that chance?"

"I know a great deal." Tide sounded like a coil wound too tight. "From the highest levels of the Highton government. I can tell your military."

Aliana mentally reeled, barely able to absorb the impossible event she was witnessing, a Razer—bred, designed and programmed for loyalty to his Aristo masters above all else—offering to betray the highest of the high.

"I see why ESComm wants your line destroyed," Lensmark said dryly. "If you actually intend to do what you claim."

"Yes, I'll do it."

"You'll have to submit to extensive tests."

"I understand." Tide's voice grated. "Yes, I'll betray them. And yes, that makes me scum."

"I'd say it makes you human," Lensmark said. "To us, freedom is a right belonging to all humans, and the drive to seek freedom from slavery is a powerful, priceless right—a *human* right."

"Then you will give me asylum?" he asked.

"Oh yes," she said, a dangerous glint in her eyes. "Count on it."

XIII
The Hymn of Carelli

Barthol stood alone on a pier far above the surging waves of the ocean. Driven by fourteen moons, the tides of Glory were a glorious testament to the beautiful ferocity of the planet. They thundered below on the private shoreline where the Iquar lands bordered the sea. Giant swells crashed into the columns that supported the tall pier, water jumping high into the air, big round drops glittering beneath the night sky.

The moons made a dramatic presence tonight. The two that orbited closest to Glory were visible, one near the horizon and the other more overhead, but neither was large in the sky; the tiny satellites looked more like big stars. In contrast, Mirella was a great disk overhead. Named for the first empress of Eube, the wife of Eube Qox, it was the largest of any moon as seen from the planet. In honor of his empress, Eube had resurfaced it in carnelian, so it glittered like a huge red jewel.

Viquara, the third largest moon as seen from Glory, was nearly full and almost overhead. Named by the third emperor for his wife, it sparkled white, for he had resurfaced it with diamond in her honor. The second largest moon was a crescent above the horizon. The second emperor, Jaibriol the First, had surfaced it in gold and named it Zara for his wife, who had also been his sister, the only woman he considered worthy of his name. Barthol could relate. Who else was good enough for him, Barthol Iquar, but a woman with Iquar genes? He gritted his teeth. The only candidate worth considering was Tarquine, one of the few people he could neither control nor command.

The current Jaibriol, the fifth emperor of Eube, had of course named the fifth largest moon Tarquine. His alterations to the satellite struck many people as bizarre, but it all made perfect sense to Barthol. Jaibriol treated the moon like a geode, resurfacing it in a steel-diamond composite that shone silver in the sky. Unlike his predeccesors, he had altered the interior as well, turning it into crystalline structures in violet, emerald, and rose, a geode of celestial dimensions. Yes, it fit Tarquine perfectly, may the gods curse her vile ascendance to power.

Barthol considered it too simple to say he hated Tarquine. Her certainty that she dealt with matters of empire better than him grated, yes, but what he hated far more was that she might be right. *No.* He refused to accept that possibility. He was better suited to rule Eube than either she or Jaibriol. The empire would have been far better served had his plans against them succeeded, but Tarquine had outwitted him by surviving when she should have died, she and that wretched husband of hers. Nothing would ease his fisted anger, no matter how many providers he whipped or how many of them he buried his cock inside of, not even when their screams sent him into the highest transcendence. Nothing took away his rage. The universe was wrong. It needed to be righted. He had grown tired of waiting for Jaibriol to sire an heir; he needed to act again, soon, before Corbal Xir inherited the damn Carnelian throne.

Barthol knew he would never sit on the throne, and that was the greatest crime. But he could come as close as Corbal stood now. First rid the universe of Jaibriol and Tarquine. Then produce a "Highton Heir," a baby supposedly hidden to protect him against assassination just as Jaibriol's father had hidden Jaibriol in his youth. Then Barthol would become his regent, and, unlike Corbal Xir, he would know what to do with that shadow power.

The crashing waves jumped higher into the air above him, flaring with phosphorescence. The pier was several stories tall, with columns supporting it like gigantic stilts, but the waves dwarfed it. Barthol loved the wildness of the night, the ferocity of this ocean, the sky strewn with jeweled moons and a wealth of stars. It spoke to a wildness within him that was never sated.

A huge wave smashed the pier and leapt even higher than the platform where Barthol stood. Its droplets glistened against the night sky. He lifted his chin, glorying in that power. To say the chaotic tide was "coming in" simplified a process as complex as his relationship with Tarquine, but the power of the ocean was surging toward a peak. Water misted across him, soaking his hair and clothes. Another wave hit the pier—

And Barthol stumbled.

It wasn't unusual for the force of the waves to affect his balance. One reason he savored coming here was the hint of danger. But the biomech web within his body included hydraulics and joints that not only gave him enhanced speed, reflexes, and strength, they also incorporated libraries that could help him regain his balance, pick himself up, even keep him moving if he was knocked out. Armies of nanomeds patrolled his body. If he was hurt, they would heal him. He couldn't even bruise a knee, let alone fall off a pier.

Today, his biomech faltered at a crucial moment.

Barthol fell to one knee. His body lurched to the side, knocking him to the edge of the pier. He kept toppling, unbalanced, and his skull cracked against a metal ring used to tie ropes. Pain shot through his head as the sound of breaking bone split the night. Barthol gasped, trying to regain control, but he kept rolling. Someone was shouting, his guards probably, but it was happening too fast. He rolled off the pier and plummeted through the air toward the enraged sea.

Node, respond! he thought. *Initiate survival routines. Keep me alive.*

He wasn't sure when he hit the water. The waves were so tumultuous, crashing on the shore, pier, and rocks, that the interface between water and air wasn't definite. He became wetter and wetter until he was submerged, unable to breathe.

Node respond, he thought as his consciousness faltered.

Blackness closed around him.

Jaibriol settled into the violet cushions, running his fingers over their pile, enjoying the rich texture. The black lacquered table before him stood low to the ground. Azile Xir sat across from him, reclining in more of the oversized pillows, and his wife Zylena was to Jaibriol's right, curvaceous in a deep violet dress, as if she were a classic Highton sculpture. Lamps shaded with purple and blue glass cast diffuse light over the dinner party, nothing too bright. A faint perfume of Sharminia incense scented the air. The glimmering embroidery on the pillows disguised a mech-tech network that responded to Jaibriol's every movement, seeking to relax his muscles, but no cushions could mute the pressure of Azile and Zylena's Aristo minds. Jaibriol stayed tense, his head aching, and the cushions kept working, ever so subtly, throughout the evening.

Even so, he appreciated the efforts Azile and Zylena had taken with this dinner. They spared no honor. It felt strange without Tarquine, but as dinners with Aristos went, it was better than most.

Zylena swirled the red wine in her crystal goblet and lifted it to Jaibriol. "Your esteemed health is a joy to the empire, Your Highness."

He wanted to say, *To me, too.* Of course he could never be so direct. He did nothing more than nod, but he added an extra depth to the motion, indicating his appreciation of her words.

The *Hymn of Carelli* was playing in the background, a haunting composition by a slave who had been a favorite of Jaibriol's grandfather. Carelli had created some of the most exquisitely heartbreaking music Jaibriol had ever heard, sublime works of art created by a genius who lived in the gilded hell of an emperor's provider.

"It is auspicious that Empress Tarquine has graced her home with her presence," Azile said. He speared a red spice-olive with a small gold fork and ate with the reserve of someone who could take or leave such an expensive delicacy.

"Indeed," Jaibriol said. Azile was fishing, trying to discover why Tarquine had gone home, other than the official story, that she was doing an annual visit of her family estates. Jaibriol had no intention of elaborating.

As Jaibriol sipped his wine, he stretched out his legs next to the table, across the deep-piled rug of violet and gold. Real gold, for people to step on. He doubted he would ever adapt to the exorbitant wealth Aristos took for granted. Inside, he would always be the boy who grew up in the wilderness with no amenities, no civilization, no *people* even, other than his family.

A thought came from the node in his spine: **Do you wish me to neutralize the alcohol content from the wine you're drinking so it has no effect on your body?**

Yes, good idea, Jaibriol answered. As much as he wanted to be mind-numbingly drunk, he couldn't risk it. He couldn't do much of anything he wanted; it would either put him in danger or weaken his standing among the Hightons. He wondered what was the use of being supposedly the most powerful human being alive when you were trapped by your own power.

What he really wanted to do was return with his family to Prism, the planet where he had grown up. But his parents were dead, and even if he had known what happened to his two brothers and his sister, he doubted they would want to live in that primitive isolation again. They were free somewhere, unfettered by titles. He had tried to find them, with no luck, and he feared to deepen his efforts, lest he draw attention to them. As long as they were hidden and unknown, they were safe.

A girl padded into the room in bare feet, and Jaibriol felt as if the temperature suddenly rose. She was lushly curved, with black hair falling down her back. The blue halter she wore glimmered like sapphire and barely covered her enlarged nipples, with gold chains going around her neck and back to hold it in place. The skirt hung low around her hips, held up by a jeweled belt of sapphires and diamonds, its gauzy blue cloth barely reaching her upper thighs. The sweet curve of her legs showed through the translucent material, as did a g-string held in place by slender gold chains. Her skin sparkled with gold overtones, as did the gold and sapphire collar around her neck and the guards around her wrists and ankles. She was so unbearably beautiful, Jaibriol felt as if he couldn't breathe.

She carried a gold tray with three platters, each covered by a curved dome of platinum. Kneeling gracefully at the table, she bowed her head to Jaibriol.

"You may continue," he said, amazed at how aloof he sounded. The aroma from the platter was making his mouth water. Or maybe it wasn't the food.

"Her name is Sheen," Azile said. "If she pleases, Your Glorious Highness."

Jaibriol wanted to groan. Azile was offering him the pleasure girl for whatever he wished to do with her. And he could think of plenty. Except he couldn't touch her. Among Hightons, where heredity was everything, adultery was punishable by execution. Of course that was all a sham. It only counted as adultery when it happened with another Aristo. It didn't make one whit of difference what they did with pleasure slaves. Providers weren't human, after all, so enjoying their charms wasn't adultery. Jaibriol wondered if the Hightons ever considered the full implications of that. If their slaves weren't human, then they were having sex with animals. How exalted. Anyway, it didn't matter. Tarquine would pulverize him.

That wasn't his only reason, though. He stayed true to his wife because he loved her, God help him. More startling was Tarquine's fidelity. Over the years, he had woven his security network wider and deeper, until he knew everything that went on in his personal realm. He would know if she cheated on him with her slaves. It never happened. True, she was one of the few people alive who could outwit even his security. Hell, she had developed a lot of it. But he also knew from her mind. His formidable empress, incredible as it seemed, remained true to him.

"Your generosity is unparalleled," Jaibriol said. Azile knew him well enough to understand it was "no," phrased to acknowledge the honor the Intelligence Minister intended him.

A man in a tunic and trousers of black velvet stepped forward and knelt next to the woman. Carnelians glittered on his shirt cuffs and the edges of his boots. As the girl lifted the cover off the platter, the tantalizing aroma of steak drifted into the air. The man was holding a gold tine he never let out of his sight. He removed a gold steak knife from the sheath on his belt and cut a piece of the meat, then stabbed it with his tine, swirled it in the sauce on the platter, and ate the food. He similarly took a bite of each delicacy on the plate, including the buttered aparini spears, roe pâté, and a medley of sea sweets.

Jaibriol bit back the urge to dispense with all this

business so they could eat. He had, after all, brought the fellow with him, which is why the man wore carnelians, the royal gem. As much as Jaibriol wanted to eat, he wanted even more to stay alive. He seriously doubted Azile would try to poison him, but he could never be sure of anything.

I'm receiving the data from your tester's biomech web, his spinal node thought. **The food is safe for you to consume.**

Thanks. Relieved, Jaibriol nodded to his taster. The man rose and stepped back, blending into the room's décor. Jaibriol always made sure his taster had the chance to eat his own meals first, of a quality similar to what he was going to taste; otherwise, he would have a few bites of a feast and then have to watch while others dined, which seemed excruciating to Jaibriol.

He nodded to the beautiful girl. "Please proceed."

As she served dinner, Jaibriol eased his mental barriers. The warmth of her empath's mind poured over him. He had to protect himself as much from her as from Azile and Zylena, in her case so she wouldn't realize he was a psion. He also felt Azile's tension. The Intelligence Minister knew he was a suspect in the assassination attempt and hoped this dinner would help allay suspicions. Such an irony, Jaibriol thought, that his empathic abilities—his greatest vulnerability among the Aristos—were also his greatest advantage. In this culture of hidden meaning and tangled intrigues, he sensed people's intentions in ways they would never dream possible for their emperor.

The food was incredible; it was all Jaibriol could do to keep from wolfing it down like a half-grown youth. To slow himself, he spoke with aloof approval to Azile and Zylena. "The Line of Xir defines the word gourmet tonight."

Azile inclined his head. "We find satisfaction in the fields of Tapinazi."

Tapinazi. So that was where this food came from. Jaibriol didn't know much about the region, which was on another continent, but if everything they produced tasted this good, he ought to bring one of their cooks to be his personal chef. He couldn't help but smile. "We haven't yet had time during this dinner to think about Tapinazi."

Azile chuckled and Zylena's lips curved upward, which from Hightons indicated a great appreciation for his joke that he enjoyed the food so much, he hadn't had time to consider where it came from. Jaibriol didn't think he wanted to know what it said about him, that Aristo humor made sense to him now. It had been completely opaque when he had come to Eube eleven years ago.

The provider continued to kneel by the table, her head bowed, her eyes downcast. Jaibriol could tell she was starving. Azile did it deliberately, making her suffer because it caused him and Zylena to transcend. Jaibriol wasn't even sure they knew; it had become so much a part of their lives, they took for granted the pleasant feelings they enjoyed when their providers were uncomfortable. Jaibriol gritted his teeth. He so much wanted it to stop, it was all he could do to keep from offering the girl a place at the table to dine with them.

Azile glanced from the provider to Jaibriol and smiled, apparently assuming the emperor's interest in the girl came from a different type of hunger. It did, actually, but Jaibriol was doing his best to convince himself otherwise.

"She's from a fine line," Azile said. "The Shaltania Diamond Pavilion."

"A many-faceted gem," Jaibriol said.

"It seems the military agrees," Zylena said. "At least, the army."

So that was the latest gossip, that the General of the Army, Barthol Iquar, was buying providers from Shaltania. They had Jaibriol's deepest sympathy.

"One hears many rumors, of course," Azile said.

"Indeed," Jaibriol said, wondering what Azile had to tell him.

"Rumors of military provisions," Azile added, his gaze intent.

Military provisions. Interesting. Jaibriol concentrated on Azile, and through the haze of his discomfort, he caught the Intelligence Minister's meaning. Azile had discovered that Barthol was using psions in an attempt to steal access to the Kyle mesh created by the Skolians. The general had neglected to include that "minor" fact in any of his ESComm reports or updates.

Jaibriol inclined his head to Azile. "A man's title can say much with only one word." Which was his way of saying, *You're clever, Intelligence Minister, to figure that out and even smarter to let me know.* If Azile was seeking to regain favor, he had just taken a big step in that direction.

A hum came from the wrist comm Jaibriol wore as part of his shirt cuff. He glanced at its screen as silver glyphs scrolled over the mesh. In the same instant, a buzz came from across the table. Looking up, he saw Azile frowning at his own wrist comm. The Intelligence Minister glanced at him, started to speak, then waited. The haunting melody of the Carelli hymn played softly in the background.

From the glyphs in his screen, Jaibriol knew Azile was receiving the same message. He brushed the *open* toggle on his cuff, then raised his wrist and spoke into his comm. "Go ahead."

The voice of Robert Muzeson came into the room. "Your Highness, we're receiving a priority message from the Iquar Estate."

Jaibriol's pulse jumped. He met Azile's gaze the table and saw the same look of alarm.

"What is the message?" Jaibriol asked.

"There has been an accident, Sire," Robert said.

One thought burst into Jaibriol's mind: *Tarquine.*

Even as Jaibriol drew in a breath to ask, Robert added, "The Empress is fine."

Jaibriol exhaled. "Good." As his pulse settled, he asked, "What kind of accident?"

"Barthol Iquar was knocked off one of the ocean piers," Robert said. "I'm sorry to bring you such news. He's in a coma."

A chill walked up Jaibriol's spine. "What happened?"

"He hit his head against the pier and fell into the water. It isn't clear which put him in the coma, the head injury or drowning."

"Why the hell didn't his guards pull him out?"

"They did, Sire. They immediately gave aid, and within moments the estate staff had General Iquar in the infirmary at the main house. But his doctors can't revive him."

"I've seen that infirmary," Jaibriol said. "It has better facilities than the hospital here."

"They've spared no effort for him," Robert said. "When the Empress learned what happened, she came down herself to oversee his treatment."

Damn. Tarquine shouldn't be "overseeing" anything. He didn't want anyone to believe she had any connection to the accident. "Where was the Empress before that?"

"At the main estate," Robert said. "She was relaxing with some friends by the sea pools. She is quite improved, Sire." He sounded relieved to give Jaibriol better news. "The trip has been quite beneficial for her health."

The idea of his driven wife "improving" by doing nothing but lounging beside exotic pools would have been funny if it hadn't implied such deadly consequences. *Tarquine, be wise,* Jaibriol thought. If she had caused the accident or if she took advantage of Barthol's condition to exact revenge, she could implicate herself in his death. It was more important to Jaibriol that his wife be well and safe than to make Barthol pay, especially given that their only evidence against the general was the obscure predictions of a dice game neither of them understood that well.

"Thank you for notifying me so promptly," Jaibriol told Robert. "You have done well." He regarded Azile across the table as he spoke, and the Intelligence Minister nodded lightly, accepting Jaibriol's unspoken command that Azile look into the matter.

"I am honored by your words," Robert said. "I wish my news had been better."

The Carelli hymn continued in the background,

its key minor, as if it were mourning the ethereal beauty of its own melody. The singer was a classically trained soprano, her voice so pure she sounded like an angel, especially when she hit the highest notes with an exquisite vibrato.

Jaibriol knew he should be dismayed by Barthol's accident. To lose his Joint Commander in such a difficult time could turn into a disaster. He tried to remember the principles of honor he held so dear, ideas of conscience and judgment that he had respected his entire life, a moral code that would never allow him to sanction the murder of another human being. Instead, he could think only of his heir, the son he would never know, the child who had died in Tarquine's womb.

XIV
Mesh Dreams

"It will never work!" Admiral Chad Barzun stood his ground, his square-jawed face set in firm lines as he challenged Kelric.

All of Kelric's advisors were standing. Given the tension, he doubted anyone would sit any time soon. They had gathered around the oval table in one of the Orbiter conference rooms, their imposing figures reflected in its gold surface. His four Joint Commanders were present, either in person or as holographic simulations. Also present was Barcala Tikal, First Councilor of the Assembly, the civilian leader of the Imperialate, a gangly man with dark hair greying at the temples. Kelric had summoned the Inner Assembly councilors as well: Stars, Nature, Industry, Judiciary, Life, Planetary Development, Finance, Domestic Affairs, Protocol, and Foreign Affairs. Protocol stood next to him, working at a table console, monitoring input from those advisors who were attending as holos, flicking menus above her screen like a maestro conducting an orchestra. Her hair was a new color today, red this time, sparkling like rubies, with mesh studs dusted over it like black glitter.

The Councilor for Foreign Affairs—also known as Roca Skolia—was on Protocol's other side, watching Kelric with a wariness that deeply troubled him from his mother. He hid his response; he couldn't let them see how weary he felt, how isolated.

A solitary woman stood in the head of the table, her delicate frame a dramatic contrast to the others in the room, most of whom towered over her. She was Dehya, the Ruby Pharaoh. Her melodic voice filled the gold-walled chamber. "When Imperator Skolia came to me with this idea of a face-to-face meeting at the peace summit, I reacted similarly to all of you." She looked them over. "I have since changed my mind. I support the Imperator's proposal."

Good gods. Kelric hadn't expected that. This meeting had suddenly become less hopeless.

Naaj Majda, General of the Pharaoh's Army, stood across from Kelric. At six-foot-five, in her dark green uniform with a general's braid on the shoulders, she was a formidable presence. Dark hair streaked with iron-grey framed her ascetically elegant face. "Your Highness," she said to Dehya. "It would be difficult for security to ensure your safety or that of your family in such a meeting."

"We would have to coordinate security with ESComm," Dehya acknowledged.

Naaj gave her a sour look. "ESComm will never coordinate anything with us."

"Ah but, General," Dehya said. "You would have

the chance to meet face to face with your ESComm counterpart. Surely he would value his own safety enough to coordinate."

Naaj snorted. "What safety? My supposedly esteemed counterpart, Barthol Iquar, is brain dead."

The Councilor for Life, a vibrant fellow who oversaw health, human services, and education, made a choked sound, as if he didn't know whether to laugh or be shocked by her statement. Roca gave Naaj an exasperated look. The Councilor for Finance started to smile, then stopped himself.

Barcala Tikal scowled at Naaj. "General Iquar is in a coma. Not dead."

Naaj waved her hand in dismissal. "Regardless of which ESComm commanders come to the summit, they will still deceive, plot against, and betray everyone and her sister's uncle's brother."

Kelric stood listening. Hearing his advisors argue told him a great deal more than they realized. Although they never forgot his presence, they spoke to one another more freely than to him. Naaj, however, was always guarded. Since his decision to execute the commandos who had attacked the Trader merchants, as soon as he discovered their identities, she had barely been civil. She treated him with the respect due one's commanding officer, but that was it. He wanted to believe ESComm had masterminded the attack in an effort to stall the peace process, but he couldn't be sure. He hated suspecting Naaj, because if she had any role in it she had committed treason. But he couldn't deny the possibility.

General Dayamar Stone stood across the table. As Commandant of the Advance Services Corps, the scouts for planetary expeditions, he served as another of Kelric's Joint Commanders. His dark red uniform and knee boots accented his thin frame, but his greying hair was full and unusually thick for a man nearly a century old. Neither her nor Naaj were actually in the room; both were projecting as holos, Dayamar from HQ City on the planet Diesha, and Naaj from the world Raylicon, home to the Majda dynasty.

The only commander who hadn't weighed in on Kelric's suggestion was Brant Tapperhaven, head of the Jagernaut Forces. He was here in person, lounging against a wall across the room like a shadow in the radiant chamber. With his black leather jacket, black knee boots and black pullover, he looked more like a thug than a Joint Commander. He listened intently, his dark eyes traveling from person to person, his telepath's mind shielded. Kelric understood Brant; they had a lot in common, both of them Jagernauts, both taciturn, both empaths who had endured the crucible of warfare and the toll it exacted on soldiers who could feel the deaths of their foes in their own minds.

Today Kelric had to speak, however. "Conducting the treaty negotiations in the usual manner won't work. It leaves too many possibilities for dishonesty. For treachery." He didn't look at Naaj, but if that last word applied to her, she would take his meaning.

General Stone spoke in his gravelly voice. "Putting so many valuable leaders in one place is too dangerous." He motioned around the room, his gesture including everyone. "As you well know."

Kelric took his point; one reason so many of his advisors were here as holos was because Kelric wouldn't risk putting all of his top people together in one room.

"Any more assassination attempts," Chad Barzun said, "and the treaty is dead. Our success in keeping the attempts against you and Pharaoh Dyhianna out of the news is the only reason this treaty has any support."

"What are you talking about?" Tikal demanded. "It has immense support. No one wants more war."

"And no one believes the Traders want peace," Naaj said. "This treaty is a trick. We still don't know how they managed the attack on either Pharaoh Dyhianna or Imperator Skolia, but they almost succeeded. We *cannot* risk putting our leaders and theirs in the same place."

"We don't know that the attack came from the Traders," Dehya said.

"Of course it was the Traders," Naaj said.

"Where the blazes else would it come from?" asked Finance, the councilor who monitored the economic health of the empire. He was all sharp angles, from his gaunt frame to his intellect to his mechanical left arm, which was packed with implants.

Tikal considered Dehya. "It's a good question."

Dehya met his gaze. "It would have to be someone with a high enough authorization to access our most protected mesh nodes."

Silence settled as everyone absorbed her implication. Kelric didn't need to absorb squat. He already knew. The assassin could be one of their own. But who?

He would never forget that flash of hatred from Admiral Ragnar Bloodmark when the Assembly ratified the treaty. Kelric had given them the only justification they would accept to clear him of treason for meeting in secret with the Trader emperor. Peace. Because of the treaty, he had gone free rather than face execution.

In that instant, Ragnar's mask of neutrality had slipped and the admiral's fury had blazed. Why? Ragnar held the second highest position in the Fleet, after Chad Barzun; he might be able to compromise security at a high enough level to reach Kelric and Dehya.

And Naaj. Her attention appeared to be on Tikal right now, but she was present only as a simulation. In reality, she was undoubtedly watching them all. She could project whatever she wanted, even have her systems analyze their behavior and respond to her benefit. Kelric couldn't probe her mind when she was on another planet. Even if she had been here, she knew how to guard against telepaths. To break her mental shields, he would have to attack her with the full force of his mind, which would be tantamount to shooting a gun at his Joint Commander.

Kelric broke the uncomfortable silence. "Having us meet face-to-face has its dangers, I agree. We'll have to work a lot harder on security. I'm willing to accept that challenge."

"As am I," Dehya said.

"Yes, well, you may both be willing," Tikal said. "But the rest of us aren't, not for you two. If either of you dies, it cripples the Imperialate."

"I could die on a routine space flight," Kelric said.

"Which brings up another problem," Stars said in her melodious voice. A slender woman with silver hair and luminous eyes, she was the councilor concerned with transportation throughout the Imperialate. "Everyone must travel to wherever we put this summit. Space flight is yet another danger. If we instead meet by holographic simulation, we diminish those risks."

"We can't hide in a cocoon," Dehya said.

Judiciary considered them. She was tall woman with greying hair swept back from her high forehead, the senior member of the Inner Assembly. "I don't believe Imperial law allows the only surviving members of the Triad to be in the same physical space as the Qox Dynasty."

Kelric regarded her with exasperation. "What, we have a law that says, 'opposing royals may not occupy the same physical space'?"

"It's a matter of interpretation," Judiciary told him.

"We also must consider the economic effect," Finance said in his sharp, quick voice. "As much as we may resist admitting it, our economic health is intricately tied up with the economies of Eube and the Allied Worlds of Earth. You can't untangle them."

Life crossed his brawny arms and glared at Finance. "I fail to see how an in-person summit could risk the economies of three empires."

Finance arched an eyebrow. "Then yes, young man, you do fail."

"As hard as you may all find it to believe," Life said, "human leaders have met in person for ninety-nine point nine nine percent of human history. And somehow their economies survived."

"Life has a point," Nature said, adjusting his spectacles. Formerly a physics professor at Parthonia University, he now served as the Councilor of science and technology.

Finance scowled at him. "And economics is your expertise?"

"It isn't mine, either," Domestic Affairs said, her rich voice a soothing contrast to the others, a trait that served her well as the councilor who oversaw relations among the peoples of the Imperialate. "But I agree with you. This is an emotional issue, and ultimately it is people and their emotions that determine what happens in the interstellar markets. If the summit turns into a disaster, it could spiral into economic crisis."

"You can model the situation to some extent," Industry said. A leanly muscled man of great energy, he oversaw industrial development. At the moment, he was reading something on his gauntlet. Looking up at them, he added, "Even the most sophisticated codes can't precisely predict human behavior, but my analyses suggest that a failure of these talks could result in an economic crisis."

"The talks could fail regardless of how we meet," Dehya said. "Both Imperator Skolia and I believe they have a better chance of success if we meet in person." She turned to the Councilor for Planetary Development, a woman with luxuriant dark hair falling over her shoulders. "Marta, what world are you on right now?"

"Parthonia," Planetary answered. "Why do you ask?"

"When I saw you last month, at the Assembly," Dehya said. "Your hair was short."

If Planetary was startled by the comment, no hint of it showed in her holographic simulation. She said only, "I preferred this length today."

Barcala Tikal spoke to Dehya. "Yes, we see your point. People can change how they look in sims. So what?" He waved his hand at Protocol. "They do it in person, too. Physical presence is no guarantee that the physicality of the people present is genuine."

Protocol raised her eyebrows at him, their red glitter accenting her sparkling red hair. Then she went back to monitoring the holo simulations.

"Barcala, you know it's not that simple," Dehya said. "Look at Nature. Tell me, what is he doing with those spectacles?"

"My glasses?" Nature asked. "Your Highness, I—" When Dehya glared at him, he blinked and fell silent.

"What he's doing," Tikal said dryly, "is staring at you with quite understandable confusion."

"Is he?" Dehya studied Nature, who met her gaze, looking rather self-conscious. "Does he seem innocuous because he really is? Or is he hiding some ability behind those quaint spectacles? Maybe an AI is controlling his image to give him whatever appearance either he or the AI believes will make him most effective at this meeting."

"Uh, actually, this is what I look like," Nature said.

Industry scowled at him. "So why wear those antediluvian contraptions on your eyes?"

"He just likes the way they look," Life said. "That's not the point. It's easy to trick people when you can use your virtual reality arsenal to enhance, augment, misrepresent, and otherwise alter the effectiveness and veracity of what you project to others."

Kelric had no doubt that Nature wore glasses because he liked them. He knew because he had broken an unwritten law of telepaths and probed Nature's mind beyond what he could catch on the surface. Although Nature hadn't known, the probe had left the councilor with a headache. Kelric hadn't liked what he had done; his emotions had overrun his judgment. But those glasses struck him deeply. Decades ago, the Traders had captured and tortured Kelric's father, leaving him blind and unable to walk. After his rescue, the doctors had done their best to repair his injuries. When he could see again, albeit blurrily, he opted for glasses rather than having further operations. Even before his time as a Trader prisoner, he had distrusted the technology of his wife's civilization; afterward, he felt even more vulnerable. Wearing glasses was his way of fighting back. He had eventually died from the injuries that weakened his body, and when Kelric had seen Nature with his spectacles, he'd had the irrational fear that the Assembly councilor would die, too. So he had looked into his mind.

Kelric glanced at his mother. Roca was staring at the table, her face composed but her posture unnaturally still.

Are you all right? he asked her.

She glanced at him. ***I'm all right. It's just hard sometimes, when I remember what happened to your father.***

Yes. Nature reminds me of him, too.

"I don't have to wear them," Nature was saying. "My system here can adjust the focus for this room. I'm just used to having them on. I forget about them."

"I know," Dehya said. "They're fine, Jason." That she used his personal name was a sign that she didn't distrust his motives.

"You're all avoiding her point," Life told them. "People can set VR systems to project whatever they want." He shrugged. "Sure, none of us suspects Nature. He's a harmless preoccupied professor. That's a lot different than what we'll encounter with the Traders."

Nature scowled at him. "Gosh, thank you for the compliment."

"The flip side of that is also important," Domestic Affairs said. "Pharaoh Dyhianna's attitude is mild compared to the suspicion we'll encounter with the Hightons."

"And you don't think people will be dishonest in person?" Finance demanded. He lifted his cybernetic arm. "We're all walking mesh nodes. It's in our hair, skin, clothes, bodies. Nature could incorporate all sorts of sly technologies into his glasses: specialized filters, sensors, high-powered lenses, mesh nodes with AI analysis code, you name it, not to mention they also hide facial expressions. Hell, he could put biomech in his own eyes to achieve a lot of that."

"For flaming sake," Nature said. "I'm not achieving anything but seeing all your faces more clearly. Assuming I'd want to."

"With Hightons," Planetary Affairs said, "we also have more to worry about than what people do for themselves, to themselves, or with themselves in virtual reality."

Domestic Affairs chuckled. "That sounds like it ought to be rated for erotic content if you go further."

Planetary frowned at her. "What I'm saying is that anyone can bring an arsenal of hidden tech to the table. Suppose Nature used that great intellect of his to alter the simulation we send to the Traders of our virtual conference room, giving us an advantage? People react to their surroundings. The Hightons could similarly alter what they send us. We would undoubtedly fool with it, altering it for our gain, and they would alter it again to compensate for whatever they thought we might have done. Carry that to its convoluted extreme and you get one holy mess."

"Amazing I'm so talented at subterfuge," Nature said. "All with my glasses, no less."

"You have the knowledge," General Stone said. "Also access to the necessary experts and systems. You consult with ISC all the time. If we wanted to do what Planetary describes, you would be one of the first people we contacted."

"And we've barely touched on what we can do with virtual sims," Dehya said. "It's possible to do some of these subterfuges in person, yes, but we have significantly more control in face-to-face meetings."

"Fine." Brant Tapperhaven's deep voice broke into the debate. "A face-to-face summit can solve problems. So far I've heard no hint of how we would convince the Hightons to agree."

A startled silence fell, people stunned as much from hearing the taciturn Jagernaut speak as from the impossibility of what he suggested. Kelric knew Jaibriol Qox would be more sympathetic to the idea than the others believed, except Dehya, but he couldn't say that, not here and not to the Traders.

"You have a suggestion?" Kelric asked Brant.

"Nothing that wouldn't sound crazy," Brant said.

"The entire proposal is crazy," Tikal said. "As First Councilor, I protest the whole idea."

That provoked another silence. Barcala and Dehya shared the rule of the Imperialate, Barcala as the elected First Councilor and Dehya as the hereditary Ruby Pharaoh. The uneasy mix of democracy and imperial governance had been Dehya's idea, after she overthrew the Assembly and resumed her throne. Kelric even agreed with her that the blended government would probably be more stable for a modern interstellar civilization. Unfortunately, it also led to situations like this, where the two leaders were opposed. Dehya had ceded only forty-nine percent of her rule to Barcala, which meant she could force her wishes, but doing so could also destabilize their government.

Kelric spoke to Tikal. "You're giving up before we've tried to find solutions."

An image jumped into Tikal's mind, his view of Kelric, an impression so vivid that Kelric picked it up without even trying. To Barcala, he looked like an indomitable warlord from a barbaric time, his face impassive, his muscled arms crossed, his huge biceps bulging. It was a startling contrast to how Kelric saw himself, as a weathered and aging man. He hadn't even realized he had crossed his arms. That highlighted another reason he wanted to meet the Aristos face-to-face. He, Dehya, Roca, Naaj Majda, and Brant Tapperhaven all had an advantage their Highton counterparts lacked: they were psions. As difficult as it was to lower their barriers with Aristos, it was worth the discomfort. But they had to be within a few meters of the Traders for it to work.

Tikal spoke curtly. "If we waste our energies on this, it affects our preparations for the summit. We need to use our time wisely, not chase the mist."

"And if I told you I knew how you just saw me?" Kelric asked. "As a conquering warlord from a bygone era? I mean really, Barcala. Not even on my best days, I'm afraid."

Tikal scowled at him. "Keep out of my brain."

Kelric uncrossed his arms. "I wasn't spying. Your image was so vivid, it came into my mind. Think on this; you've worked with psions for decades and you know better than most how to barrier your mind, yet I caught that image without even trying. The Hightons have none of your experience. They won't even openly admit that psions have any capacity for sophisticated thought, let alone that we can spy on their minds. They don't know how to block us."

Barcala took a breath and slowly let it out. His mental barriers were at full strength now, with nothing leaking past, but Kelric knew he was angry. Kelric didn't blame him; he wouldn't like someone catching his thoughts and then revealing them, either.

After a moment, Barcala said, "I see your point."

Roca spoke. "I agree, the proposal has merits worth considering. But we'll never convince the Traders."

Kelric met Dehya's gaze. Neither of them could reveal why they believed the emperor would agree. But Jaibriol would also have to convince his advisors.

"If we think about it long enough," Life said, "we might figure out a solution."

Kelric nodded to him. This meeting had gone better than he expected, in that at least they agreed to think about it. But how they would convince the Hightons, he had no idea.

Aliana had never seen a med-lab before. It was so bright. The walls, ceiling, consoles, and counters were white Luminex, which glowed with a pleasant, diffuse light. An astringent smell tickled her nose, the scent of a place scrubbed clean. And the room hummed. Every now and then an indistinct voice spoke, not a person, but a machine. Lights glowed on consoles and on the equipment arrayed around the bed where she was sitting. Bed indeed. It looked more the way she imagined a starship, with panels all around and holos rotating above them. Light cables glowed along its edges. And it kept *moving*. It was subtle, but if she shifted her weight, the bed shifted with her. If her muscles stiffened, the bed moved as if it were trying to massage them, which made her tense more, which made the bed move more. She sincerely wished it would stop.

The Skolian doctor had red hair pulled back from her face and caught at the nape of her neck. She was slender, skinny in fact, all bony angles under her white jumpsuit. Even her name sounded bony: Doctor Skellor.

"You'll feel nothing more than a tickle of air," Skellor assured her as she set the muzzle of a syringe-gun against Aliana's neck.

Aliana grimaced when the syringe hissed, not because it hurt, but because she didn't trust whatever Skellor had just injected into her. Nanomeds? Apparently people who didn't grow up in slums took health-meds for granted, but she had never heard of them.

"These med things," Aliana said. "Will they stay inside me? Have baby meds and set up housekeeping?"

Skellor smiled, the lines around her eyes crinkling, which made her look kind despite her being Skolian. "If you mean are they self-replicating, the answer is no. They'll fall apart in a few hours and your body will eliminate them."

"You mean I'll crap 'em out?"

The doctor gave a dry laugh. "Yes."

Aliana supposed she could live with that. "What will they tell you?"

Skellor indicated the machines around the bed. "The meds transmit data about your health to my monitors. Anything from the condition of your liver to the psiamine in your brain."

"Sigh-a-what?"

"Psiamine."

Aliana squinted at her. "Never heard of it."

"It's a neurotransmitter."

"Never heard of that, either."

"It's a chemical," Skellor explained. "Everyone has neurotransmitters, but only psions have psiamine. It's what allows your brain to interpret brain waves from other people."

"Oh. Well, good." Aliana wished she didn't feel so stupid. They weren't treating her as if she were slow, though. They wouldn't tell her these things unless they believed she could understand.

Skellor peered at a holo above a flat screen near the bed. "Secondary Lensmark wants us to send a full workup of your blood into the Skolian medical system. If your father was Skolian, maybe we'll get a hit."

"Ah." Aliana didn't know what else to say. Although she still didn't want to be Skolian, she had to admit, the people here had treated her a lot better than Harindor or her stepfather.

The door across the room irised open into a tall, hexagonal entrance. It relieved Aliana, because many Skolian doorways were bizarre, shaped like rectangles. Skolians used right angles everywhere. It was so strange. Alien.

Secondary Lensmark walked into the room. Aliana hadn't seen her these past two days since Tide defected. Lensmark had been busy with whatever military people at embassies did, like "debriefing" Tide, which sounded to Aliana like Aristo-speak for interrogation. Except these people weren't Aristos. That should mean they were slaves, but they didn't believe that applied to them.

Doctor Skellor straightened up. "My greetings, Lyra."

Aliana blinked. Lyra? Why wasn't Skellor saluting and all? She peered at Skellor's uniform. The embassy insignia glowed on her sleeve, a gold triangle inside an exploding sun, but nothing looked military. Huh. Maybe civilians didn't have to jump and salute.

Lensmark smiled at Aliana. "My greetings."

"Mine, too." Aliana hesitated, uncertain how to address her. "Ma'am," she added.

Lensmark glanced at Skellor. "I'd like to talk to Aliana alone."

The doctor nodded, though she looked worried. "I'll be right outside."

After Skellor left, Lensmark turned her full attention on Aliana. "We have a problem."

Aliana stiffened. So it had come. She had been waiting for someone to say, *It's all a mistake, we can't help you, go on home.* "What happened?"

"Do you know the name Barthol Iquar?" Lensmark asked.

"An Aristo," Aliana said. With a name like that, he had to be Highton. She vaguely recalled hearing it before. "Military, maybe?"

Lensmark pushed her hand through her bristly hair. "He's military, all right. He's the other Joint Commander of ESComm, along with Admiral Muze."

A terrible thought occurred to her. "Tide! They found out he's here."

"No. Aliana, no." Lensmark eased the gruffness of her voice. "It's nothing to do with that. General Iquar has had an accident. He's in a coma."

"Oh." Aliana crossed her arms. "I didn't do it."

Lensmark smiled. "I know." Then she said, "Skolian and Eube relations were already more strained than usual because of the attack on the merchants. Even with Imperator Skolia disavowing knowledge of the incident, it's touchy. Most Eubians don't believe him, in part because of that song his brother sings." She let out a tired breath. "In the midst of all that, ESComm has lost one of its top commanders. It's a mess."

"I'm sorry he's sick," Aliana said. "But why would that matter for me?"

"The problem is, ESComm won't let Skolian ships leave Eubian space. For now, we can't get any of you out. If they knew the three of you were here, they would demand we turn you over to them."

"But why?" Aliana's heartbeat ratcheted up. "Because Tide was a Razer?"

"In part," Lensmark said. "And they'd call you a provider."

"I'm not!"

"I understand. But Aliana, you're an extraordinarily strong psion. To an Aristo, you're like an uncut diamond, unfinished but of immense value." Anger edged Lensmark's voice. "And Red. How that idiot admiral could condemn him to die—" She stopped and waited a moment, then spoke more calmly. "Most Aristos would consider Red a find of great worth. If anyone finds out we have the two of you *and* a Razer who wants to defect, we'll be in deep trouble."

"So you can't take risks? Like trying to get us out of Eube."

"Not yet," the Secondary said. "But we aren't giving up. We just need to wait."

"Why are you hiding us?" Aliana asked, suddenly angry, not at Lensmark, but at the world, the universe, the Hightons, who kept life so ugly. "If you turned us over to ESComm, they'd give you a reward or something."

Lensmark spoke firmly. "I will never turn you over to them, not as long as I have any say in the matter. You have my word."

Aliana flushed. "Thank you, ma'am."

Neither of them said what they both knew, that if ESComm found them here, it wouldn't matter what the Skolians promised.

It had been a long day.

"I want to go home," Larse muttered as he put his virtual reality suit back on. He had just taken it off when his console informed him that it was receiving a message via the Kyle web. He was the only telepathic operator at this middle-of-nowhere outpost, indeed the only one within a many light-year radius. If anyone was going to receive the transmission, it had to be him.

At least this helped justify his job. No one here considered his work necessary. If the Skolian military hadn't been paying for this telop station, his boss would have closed it long ago. They were on the edge of Imperialate space, a nether region where Skolian territory abutted Trader territory. Nothing was out here but their tiny outpost on a ragged asteroid. It frustrated Larse no end that everyone assumed that meant he had nothing to do as a telop. His location made no difference to his work! His position in Kyle space was determined by thought, not spacetime coordinates. Although most messages in the Kyle went through the more densely used pathways, one might come here if its subject was closely related to whatever he was thinking about. He didn't deal with anywhere near as much traffic as the bigger centers, but he still had work to do.

So despite having just finished a twelve hour shift, he dropped back into his telop chair. The helmet lowered over his head and blackness surrounded him. The chair's exoskeleton folded around his body, cool and firm, its motors whirring.

"Access my Kyle account," Larse said.

"Setting up link." That came from Jitters, the AI that ran the outpost. "Psiphons activated."

Clicks sounded as psiphon prongs snicked into sockets in Larse's neck, waist, and wrists. The prongs linked to his biomech web, which had four parts: the sockets, fiberoptic threads that networked his body, a node in his spine, and bio-electrodes in his neurons. Neurotrophic chemicals and bio-shells protected his brain from the implants. Jitter sent signals to the psiphon prongs, which passed them to the threads, which sent them to his spinal node. The node prompted bio-electrodes to fire his neurons, translating the input into thought. Similarly, the system translated his directed thoughts into signals and sent them back to Jitter.

Verify your link to my spinal node, Larse thought.

Verified, Jitter thought. **I'm opening the gate in psiberspace.**

A new thought came into his mind, cool and inhuman: **PROVIDE SECURITY CODES.**

Whoa! That was a node he'd never interacted with before. Powerful. *Access mod 2, path 016 in my biomech,* Larse thought.

ACCESSED. CLEARANCE VERIFIED.

The blackness lightened into a glimmering web that extended in all directions. Larse was a wavepacket, a round hill surrounded by circular ripples that extended into the infinite "lake" of Kyle space. Another packet glowed nearby, carnelian red. Huh. That color was reserved for the Traders.

Identify yourself, Larse thought.

I am an automated transferal protocol, the packet answered. **Source: Skolian Embassy on the planet Muze's Helios. Hosting government: Eubian Concord.**

Interesting. He had never received a message from Trader space. *What are you transmitting?*

Blood test results from embassy personnel.

Couldn't they analyze them at the embassy?

Apparently not, it answered. **Can you route me to a Skolian medical facility?**

Sure, Larse said, disappointed that it was such a mundane request. He scanned various connections until he found a free medical node. *All right, I've got you a good home. I'm transferring you to Steward Medical Center on the planet Sandstorm. They can analyze the tests.*

That will be acceptable.

The transfer only took a few seconds. After Larse finished, he exited the Kyle web, shed his telop gear, and headed home.

Perhaps someday, something interesting would come into his station.

XV

Capture

The doors to the Amphitheatre of Providence rose as tall as ten men, framed by two fluted columns that curved into the floor at the bottom and into a rounded archway at their tops. Mosaics in gold and silver bordered the doors, abstractly beautiful, like stylized flowers.

As Jaibriol and Tarquine approached, the doors swung open. They entered the amphitheatre with four bodyguards and came out on a high balcony. The hall below rumbled with the discussions of the assembled Aristos, over two thousand of them: Hightons, Diamonds, Silicates. Jaibriol reeled under the onslaught of their minds, which had grown worse since his entry into the Skolian Triad. He filled his mind with Quis patterns, letting them evolve, and their geometric beauty shaped his thoughts, shunting the Aristos off like water running over a dry sponge.

He walked to the balcony rail with Tarquine at his side. With his mind calmed by Quis patterns, he sensed her mood beneath her icy Highton veneer. She was a geode, her exterior impossible to read, but her mind like multi-hued crystals, structures of intrigue, ambition, love, and pain from the loss of their child. She was tired, not fully recovered from the assassination attempt even now, several weeks after it had happened. Jaibriol wanted to reach out to her, even just touch her hand, but he could show no such emotion in public.

A robot arm swung through the amphitheatre, its end shaped into a gigantic human hand and burnished like old bronze. Huge gears and cranks operated the hand as if it came from an antique era, but that was for show; it was designed with state-of-the-art technology. Its fingers curled into an open fist, forming a human-sized cup. The hand slowed to a stop at the balcony and docked in front of Jaibriol. Straightening two of its fingers, it created a path from its palm to the balcony.

Jaibriol turned to Tarquine. "I will see you after the session."

She nodded, her alabaster face composed. Screens suspended above the amphitheatre showed them standing here in larger than life holos, visible to everyone below.

As Tarquine withdrew with their guards to sit in the upper levels, Jaibriol walked along the fingers and stepped onto the robot's palm. Its two fingers curled back up, leaving him in a giant cupped hand. A light flashed, indicating the safety protocols were active, preventing the hand from closing into a fist while he was within its grasp.

"Dais," Jaibriol said.

The hand carried him past tiers filled with ornate benches where Aristos and their staff reclined on gilded cushions. A circular dais was rising in the center of the amphitheatre. Four Razers stood on it, awaiting his arrival, and the Minister of Protocol sat at a console there.

When the robot fist docked at the edge of the dais, Protocol rose to her feet. The fist relaxed, its fingers uncurling until Jaibriol stood on its flat palm. He walked across its fingers and stepped onto the dais. He knew force nets surrounded the great disk and would catch anyone who fell, but it still felt strange to stand on a platform without even a rail separating him from the chasm of air below. The robot hand curled into a fist and whirred away, descending into the lower levels of the amphitheatre.

Protocol bowed to Jaibriol. Aristos never knelt. Jaibriol had even found a law from the earliest days of the empire that made it illegal for an Aristo to kneel to anyone. Silicate Aristos bowed to Diamond and Highton Aristos, Diamonds bowed to Hightons, and Hightons bowed to the emperor. When he had first assumed his throne, Jaibriol had kept all the arcane codes of Aristo behavior straight by using his empathic ability to sense from the people around him what needed to be done. It was unsettling to realize how much of it had now become second nature.

He nodded to Protocol, indicating she should resume her seat. With her so close, the pressure of her mind weighed on him more than with anyone else here. One of the Razers on the dais exerted a similar pressure, which meant he was probably more than half Aristo. Jaibriol would have to reassign him to someone else's guard and find a way to do it so the fellow didn't think it was a punishment.

Jaibriol looked out at the tiers of Aristos ringing the amphitheatre. The media orbs spinning in the air would carry his image and words throughout the hall. He spoke and his voice resonated. "We are now convened at this, the two-hundred and twenty-third Summit of Glory."

A chime rang out as the Aristos tapped their finger cymbals, all doing it in the same instant, creating one single note that vibrated in the air. They were like a great machine, one entity composed of two thousand glittering pieces. Some even cloned themselves rather than having children, the ultimate narcissists, unable to envision any greater progeny than themselves.

"We are gratified," Jaibriol said, "by the support offered from this circle of nobility for the challenges faced by ESComm during these difficult days. It pleases us to acknowledge the rising of the sun over Glory." Which was a bald lie. He had just said, *Thank you all for your concern over General Barthol and aren't we all glad the bastard will live after all.* He should be relieved Barthol was going to recover; Eube hadn't lost a Joint Commander and the empress hadn't assassinated her own nephew. But he could never celebrate the survival of his son's murderer.

Another chime sounded from the assembly, followed by silence as they waited for him to continue. Jaibriol said, "We are met this day to consider a petition from those lesser beings who presume to share the stars with our esteemed populations." Which was an absurdly insulting way to present the Skolian proposal, but given its outrageous nature, the more he played to the Aristo sense of superiority, the more likely they were to listen. They were still going to pulverize the idea, but what the hell. He had to try. At least the assembly was listening, all of them sitting there in silence, the forever unrepentant subjects of Prince Del-Kurj's furious "Carnelians Finale," waiting to see why the odiously pitiful Skolians dared petition them.

"It would seem," Jaibriol continued, "that a desire for neighborly relations motivates our petitioners."

A trickle of chimes rolled through the hall like water burbling over stones, the melody of laughter. They felt about as neighborly with the Skolians as a battalion of waroids.

"In matters of trade and treaty," Jaibriol said, "our optimistic neighbors find propitious the concept of an exalted assemblage such as that which graces the Hall of Providence today, but in a setting offered by their Allied neighbors." In other words, the Skolians wanted to meet face-to-face on Earth for the summit. He had no doubt the Aristos understood his implication with the phrase "*their* Allied neighbors." The "Carnelians Finale" song had spurred the Allied Worlds of Earth to change their declared neutrality on Eubian-Skolian conflicts to a wary alliance with Skolia.

Cymbals chimed in an erratic rhythm and voices rose. No one bothered to page Protocol's console with a request to speak, however. The petition was too absurd. Too ridiculously Skolian. It would have been insulting if their emperor hadn't presented it with amusement.

Jaibriol suspected the impulse for the proposal came from Kelric. He understood why. He agreed. He wanted it as well. But the Skolians hadn't offered a way to make this work. They probably didn't have one. If he ordered his people to Earth for an in-person summit because the Skolians requested it, the Aristos would find it unforgivably offensive, dooming the negotiations to failure.

Well, fine. The Skolian Assembly had given him the impossible, so he would give them the impossible back. He let his voice ring in the amphitheatre. "If our audacious neighbors find pleasure in the concept of such a gathering, let us offer them one of the greatest providence." In other words, they could meet right here, on Glory, in the Amphitheatre of Providence.

Cymbals chimed in approving rhythms, and amusement washed over Jaibriol in a great wave. They found his idea a fitting response to the Skolian insolence. *Sure, we'll meet you. Come on over to our house. We slave lords will never let you out again, but that isn't our problem, is it?*

Here is my response, Jaibriol thought to Kelric across the light years, though his uncle could never pick it up over such a great distance. **I haven't said no; I've given it back to you. Find a way to make it work and I'll do it.**

Ragman Mardock had to leave his post in the Steward Medical center. A sandstorm was coming. He needed to move his family into the safe-rooms deep under their house, where they could ride out the fury of the wind-whipped desert. His shift as the operator for offworld communications had four hours to go, but everyone was leaving, hurrying home before the sand blizzard hit.

As Mardock reached to switch off his console, a holicon appeared above one screen, the image of a hemoglobin molecule.

"Damn," Mardock muttered. He flicked the holo and it expanded into a message from some outpost. For flaming sake. It was a request for the analysis of a blood test. Such a trivial message could wait. He started to stand, then hesitated. If they had forwarded the results here instead of doing the analysis themselves, it might be important. He peered at the message—

It blinked out of existence.

"What the—?" Mardock banged the screen, a technique that sometimes fixed malfunctions. It didn't work this time; the message didn't reappear.

"You better not break again," he growled at his console. "I don't have the time to fix—oh." A line of glyphs had appeared on the bottom of the screen: *Incoming message forwarded to Urbanech Medical Complex on Metropoli.*

"Huh." He rubbed his chin. His system had no reason to send the request on to another medical facility. The medtechs here could easily analyze those test results.

Well, no matter. Metropoli was a major center. They could dash this off in no time. It was their problem now, not his. He closed up his station and strode out of his office, relieved nothing important had arrived that could keep him away from home.

Kelric frowned at the Quis dice strewn across the polished table. Playing solitaire was no good. He kept repeating the same themes. He needed someone else's input to help him develop strategies. He wished his wife Ixpar was here. Gods, he missed her. Or his son, a truly luminous Quis player. He needed someone of similar brilliance.

Well, he did have a potential partner who would someday be able to outplay most anyone alive, when she finished learning the game. He touched a tile in the mosaic that bordered the table.

A woman's melodious voice rose into the air. "Kelric, is that you?"

"My greetings, Dehya." He was glad she was answering her comm. Sometimes she became so immersed in work, she forgot to activate it. "Would you like to play Quis?"

"You're working on the summit, yes? The response from the Traders."

"That's right."

"All right. I'll be up in a few minutes."

Kelric grinned. He hadn't actually expected her to drop everything and come. "Good."

Dehya sat back in her chair, her elbows resting on its luster-wood arms. Genuine wood. Kelric liked it because he had grown up on a world without such trees. The space habitat had a few forests, but wood was still a relatively rare commodity.

"You're pondering foliage instead of Quis?" Dehya asked.

"Sorry." Kelric motioned at the Quis dice from their game all over the table. "This is getting us nowhere."

She touched a structure shaped like an open claw of carnelian dice. A ruby sphere and a gold sphere sat inside the claw. "What is this called?"

"Hawk's talon," Kelric said. "If we were playing for money, then whoever closes the claw wins that structure plus whatever is inside of it."

"A ruby and a gold sphere? That's you and me,

surrounded by carnelian dice." She frowned at him. "You can't be thinking of accepting Jaibriol's offer to do the summit on Glory."

Kelric glared at her. "Of course I am. And if you believe that, I have a resort on a swamp planet I'm trying to sell. Like to buy it?"

She laughed, a musical sound. "No thanks."

"I shouldn't be annoyed at him. We gave him nothing he could use to convince his people."

"He could have turned us down. He didn't." Dehya looked over the dice. "Which is pretty much all that this game is telling us."

Kelric tapped another structure, a tower of ruby, gold, and topaz dice. It also contained a sphere, this one designed from both ruby and carnelian. "This is called a desert tower."

"Is it a high rank?"

"Medium," Kelric said. "Except when it's used in conjunction with other desert structures."

"Like a ruby and carnelian sphere."

"It could be." He sat thinking. "That's the problem, you see. That sphere in that tower could be anything. A desert. A ruby. A carnelian. Which is it?"

"It's our game," Dehya said. "We can make it whatever we want." After a pause, she added, "Which is why this isn't working."

Kelric glanced up at her. "What do you mean?"

She waved her hand at the pieces. "We can play this all day long, modeling the summit, but without input from the Traders, we're going in circles. We need to sit at Quis with Jaibriol Qox."

"Sure," Kelric said wryly. "I'll page his comm and ask if he'll drop by for a game."

"He wants a solution," Dehya said. "Without interacting with him, I don't see how we can find one he thinks his people might accept. But we can't interact until we solve this problem." She let out a frustrated exhale. "Which puts us back where we started."

Kelric considered the dice. He spoke slowly, as his idea formed. "When you send a response to Emperor Qox's last message, you should speak from this room. This chair, by this table." He knew the Hightons. They would see the jeweled dice as a deliberate display of wealth. Given how they were always one-upping one another with such displays, it would make sense to them for Dehya to send such a message.

Jaibriol would see the Quis patterns.

Dehya smiled. "Ah, yes. An excellent idea."

Lensmark strode into Aliana's room. "Both of you!" she barked. "Come now! Fast!"

Aliana jumped up from the chair where she had been reading a holobook, and Red scrambled off the couch where he had been dozing.

"What's wrong?" Aliana asked.

"We're going under the embassy," Lensmark said. "We have safe-rooms down there." With no more ado, she turned and left the room as fast as she had entered.

Aliana and Red hurried after her. "Why?" Red asked in the same instant that Aliana said, "What happened?" Somewhere off in the embassy, the pound of booted feet echoed.

"ESComm," Lensmark said as they strode down the hall.

"Ah, hell," Aliana muttered.

"They're searching the embassy," Lensmark said. "We had no warning."

"Do they know we're here?" Aliana asked.

"I don't think so," she said. "They're searching all Skolian facilities." Her gauntlet hummed. As she raised it to speak, she motioned Aliana and Red into a side corridor.

"Lensmark here," she said into her comm.

"It's Quaternary Gaïnor. Ma'am, they're headed your way."

"We're almost there," Lensmark said. "What about Tide?"

"Already down in safe-room two."

"Roger that." Lensmark pushed Aliana into an alcove and stood aside while Red strode into the small area. She followed them across the room and tapped in a code on the wall tiles, her fingers moving so fast, they blurred. With a whir, part of the wall faded into a shimmer.

"Go!" Lensmark pushed Red through the shimmer.

Aliana lunged after him, and the shimmer slid on her skin like a film. She entered a circular room with a hatch on the floor that took up most of the cramped space. Lensmark followed, and when she tapped a panel on this side, the wall solidified, leaving no trace of the entrance.

"Smart," Red said.

"I hope so." Lensmark knelt by the hatch and entered more rapid-fire codes on a panel there. As the hatch hummed and lights blinked around its edges, she grabbed the balled handle and twisted hard. With a hum of well-oiled parts, the hatch spun down into a hole as if it were drilling an entrance. At the bottom, it slid aside, fitting itself into some slot in the wall.

Lensmark indicated a ladder embedded in the wall of the shaft. "Climb."

Aliana nudged Red, and he agilely lowered himself into the hole, gripping the ladder. As he climbed down, Aliana followed and Lensmark came after them. Tubes of cool blue light glowed dimly on the walls. After they were down far enough, the Secondary tapped another panel and the hatch swung back out above their heads. Aliana bit her lip as it rose into place, sealing them into the dim blue darkness. She didn't feel trapped, confined, *buried alive*—

"It's all right," Lensmark murmured, though no one had spoken. "You'll be all right."

Aliana wondered if it was always this way around psions, that they knew her moods so well. Not enough privacy. She needed to learn how to guard her mind.

I swear I'll learn, she vowed. *I'll do whatever I have to, even be Skolian, if I get to live.* She didn't know who she was swearing to; she'd never thought much about the gods and goddesses of Eube, but if some deity existed, she was making a pact. Get her out of this alive and free, and she'd learn whatever the vile Skolians wanted her to learn. Except maybe they weren't vile, because she would far rather be with them than the ESComm soldiers tramping through the building above them.

"Down," Red said below her.

She craned her neck to look and saw Red standing below her. Now that her eyes had adjusted, she could see reasonably well in the eerie blue light. When she reached the bottom of the ladder and stood next to him, he laid his hand on her arm. She swallowed and touched his cheek.

Red looked around. "Looks like warehouse."

Aliana saw what he meant. They were in a large open area, like a metallic cavern lit only by the cool blue lights. "I'd never have guessed this was under the embassy."

Lensmark stepped down next to them. "These are secured areas." She worked on her gauntlet, reading its glowing studs and panels.

"We safe?" Red asked.

"You should be." Lensmark looked up at them. "I have to return to the embassy."

Aliana's shoulders hunched. "You're going to leave us alone?"

"You'll be safer here than up there," Lensmark said.

Red regarded the Secondary uneasily. "Not go."

"I have to," Lensmark said. "The ESComm officers know who I am. If I'm nowhere to be found, they'll be suspicious."

It was all happening too fast for Aliana. "What about Tide? Is he down here, too?"

Lensmark shook her head, her eyes like shadowed pools in the blue light. "He's in another safe-room. We split you up to decrease their chances of them finding all three of you."

A scrape came from across the huge room.

Lensmark spun around so fast, she blurred. She took off running. She was halfway across the cavern! Aliana had never seen anyone move so quickly, not even Harindor's best fighters.

The other side of the cavern was too far away to see clearly, but it looked like its wall had opened into a doorway. Three people stood there, soldiers in dark uniforms with bulky guns, including a big carbine weapon. Aliana had seen Harindor's men with similar, but these guns were even bigger.

"Damn," Aliana said.

"ESComm," Red said.

The blur that was Lensmark suddenly solidified into the Secondary just paces away from the intruders. A man spoke in a deep voice, and in the echoing space of the cavernous room, Aliana heard him even though he was so far away.

"Secondary Lensmark?" he asked.

"That's right." She walked toward the soldiers, her hands out from her sides. "What can I do for you?" The courteous words were undercut by her curt tone.

The soldier said, "Have those two come over here."

Turning, Lensmark motioned to Red and Aliana. Aliana couldn't see Lensmark clearly, but she felt the Secondary's unease as if it were a tangible presence.

Suddenly Lensmark's thought burst in Aliana's mind. *Protect yourself! Shield your mind. And Red's, too, if you can.*

Aliana had no idea how to protect herself or Red, so she just thought, ***Protect*** with as much emphasis as she could. She imagined her mental fortress stronger even than before, guarded, fortified, impossible to breach, surrounding both their minds. Then she hid it with a grey mist until it became invisible. No one could see. No one could know.

Red took her hand. "We stay together." His eyes looked huge and dark.

She nodded, squeezing his fingers. "Always."

They crossed the cavern and their footsteps rang hollowly on the floor. The air was cool on her face and smelled of metal and old stone. Stale.

It was a long walk, but finally they came up next to Lensmark. Up close, the soldiers were even more intimidating, two men and one woman with cold faces.

Aliana wasn't sure how to read the insignia on their stark uniforms, but she thought that the man who had spoken to Lensmark was an officer.

"Who are you?" he asked Aliana.

"W-ward," she answered, deliberately struggling over the word.

He frowned at her. "Ward? Is that your name?"

"Ward of—of state." It wasn't hard to stutter; she was scared enough to make it real. "I fix—things. Carry things. Work with labor-bots. Move, carry, dig."

The female soldier looked Red over. "You don't look strong enough for a labor detail, pretty boy."

"I her brother," Red said.

"They sound like idiots," the other soldier muttered.

"Neither of you has a Skolian accent," the officer said. "You're Eubian."

Red regarded him with his large eyes. "Me Muze property."

Damn! He had just given them away. Almost immediately, though, Aliana realized why. If these soldiers thought they were lying, they would be suspicious, and obviously neither she nor Red could convince anyone they were Skolian.

"Everyone on this planet is Muze property," the officer said. He frowned at Lensmark. "Why are you hiding them down here? Did they come with the Razer you're holding?"

No. Aliana felt ill. They must have found Tide. Had they killed him?

"I have no idea what you're talking about," Lensmark told the officer.

"Don't play games," he said. "We have the Razer upstairs."

"This embassy is Skolian territory," Lensmark said. "Your actions are in violation of the Paris Accord between Eube and Skolia."

"Tell it to Admiral Muze," the officer said curtly. "During your trial for sheltering a traitor."

"I have diplomatic immunity," Lensmark told him. "That protection extends to any refugees who seek shelter within the walls of this mission."

The officer snorted. "You have no immunity. You're military, not a diplomat."

She regarded him steadily. "The Paris Accord extends immunity to military personnel attached to an embassy. That includes me, Major. You're the only one breaking the law."

To Aliana's unmitigated surprise, the officer looked uneasy. The few ESComm soldiers she had seen in the city had always been striding with authority, always unassailable. These seemed markedly uncomfortable, as if they weren't sure they could get away with this. This business of embassies was more complicated than she had realized.

"You'll have to come with us," the officer told Lensmark.

"Where is Ambassador Shazarinda?" Lensmark asked.

"You can direct whatever questions you wish to our legal authorities." He spoke to Aliana and Red, slowing down his words. "You will come now. Come. With us."

"None of us are leaving this embassy," Lensmark said sharply. "Good gods, man, do you want to be responsible for such a serious diplomatic incident?"

The officer flushed, his ruddy face turning even redder. "You should have thought of that before you sheltered a traitor."

"If you wish to extradite someone within this chancery," Lensmark said, "channels exist for negotiating with the diplomatic mission embodied by this embassy."

Aliana blinked. She wasn't even sure what the Secondary had just said.

The officer scowled at Lensmark. "This embassy may enjoy privileges of extraterritoriality, but you are in the jurisdiction of Lord Orzon Muze and his family, who own *everything* on this planet, including the embassy. That's Eubian law, Secondary, and you're in Eubian territory."

"We won't agree to leave," Lensmark said. "Do you plan on dragging us out? Shooting us?"

The officer pushed his hand through his hair, his face strained. "We'll contact Lord Orzon. And you *will* come with us, or we'll drag all three of you."

It was all Aliana could do to keep from clenching her fists. At least no one was paying much attention to her or Red. That was fortunate, because if Red came to the notice of Lord Orzon's father, Admiral Muze, who still owned Red, they would be in even deeper trouble.

The soldiers took them up to the embassy through a chute similar to the one they had come down. As they walked through the wide halls above, Aliana snuck a closer look at their captors. All three had reddish eyes, like Caul, her stepfather. They made her queasy, as if they were a void that could have suffocated her if she hadn't protected herself. Their intense focus on Lensmark made her suspect they knew the Secondary was a psion. Aliana wanted to expand her mental fortress to include Lensmark, but that would mean dropping her defenses, revealing that she and

Red were psions. Lensmark had told her to protect them both. And Red was so vulnerable. He had no idea how to shield his mind. Maybe it was true, what she had heard, that Aristo bred providers that way, so the Aristo could feel their pain more easily. And these were the "exalted beings" she was supposed to worship? What garbage.

They soon entered an unfamiliar room, a place nicer than Harindor's best pleasure palace. His fanciest rooms were rife with big red pillows, purple curtains, and scrolled decorations on the walls, arches, ceilings, and anywhere else he could put the overdone artwork. In contrast, this room was elegant. Paintings decorated its ivory walls in pastoral scenes of deep green velvet trees draped with rosy streamers, all nestled in lush hills dotted with blue-stone outcroppings.

Ambassador Shazarinda was already here. Aliana recognized him from her visit to his office two days ago, when she and Red had officially requested asylum. Tall and slender, with black eyes and a hooked nose, he had impressed her from the moment she met him. She wasn't sure of the right word to describe him. "Gracious," maybe. She had never known anyone with that personality trait before, so she wasn't sure she had it right. Now however, with two ESComm soldiers flanking him, he mostly looked stiff. He nodded to Lensmark, a brief motion, strained and controlled.

Then Aliana saw Tide.

He was standing in the corner, his face so deliberately neutral, she knew he was scared. Two soldiers stood with him and it felt like a punch in the gut to see him trapped that way. Aliana wanted to tell them to leave him alone, but she saw the warning in his eyes, that look he had so often given her when he was training her to control her impulsive anger, the one that meant, *Stay back, stay quiet, stay cool.*

The ESComm officer with Lensmark said, "Ambassador Shazarinda."

"I want it on record," Shazarinda said. "You entered the grounds of this diplomatic mission without permission, and no one here has waived immunity."

"Tell it to Lord Orzon." The officer indicated a console by one wall. "We can contact his offices from here."

Aliana looked at Red and he stared back at her, his gaze stark. As of yet, no one had bothered with the two rough and supposedly slow-witted children, but if they contacted the Muzes, someone would soon ask questions. She was scared for herself, desperately afraid they would learn the truth about Red, and terrified for Tide.

XVI
Simple Messages

Millions of transmissions every hour came into the communications hub of the Urbanech Medical Complex on the planet Metropoli. The message from the Steward Medical Center was buried in the deluge. It landed during a shift directed by Calli Bascel, the only human component in the hub. She was scanning the flow of three-dimensional data with her enhanced vision and optical nerves, which processed the input at mesh speeds and picked out messages that might need human attention. She wouldn't have even noticed the Steward message, except it set off an alarm.

"How bizarre," she said. It was a simple request for analysis of the data from a blood test. Any med-tech could do it. Then she saw the holo-stamp of origin. Ah. A Skolian embassy in Trader space. That was what had activated the alarm. It wasn't unusual for embassy personnel to request a Skolian analysis rather than using a local center run by the Traders. One never knew what Traders might do. Sometimes they blocked Skolian petitions to use their facilities. Even if they honored the request, they didn't always have the proper facilities to analyze Skolian tests. Rumor had it that they sometimes faked Skolian results, which led to health problems, even deaths.

Calli was about to send the message to an appropriate med-tech when it vanished. A line of words glowed on her screen: *Test results forwarded.* She spent several seconds trying to discover where the results had gone. In the meantime, thousands of messages piled up. She finally gave up and turned her attention from the minor request. Wherever it had gone, they could worry about it there.

General Barthol Iquar hated hospitals. He narrowed his gaze at the med-tech examining him.

"Please focus on my index finger," the tech said, holding it near Barthol's nose.

"I see your finger fine," Barthol snapped. "Finish the test."

The med-tech lowered his hand. "My apologies, General. I didn't mean to offend." With deference, he added, "Because of your great value to the empire, sir, we want to do everything possible to ensure your health and well being."

"My health and well being would be a lot better out of this hospital," Barthol said irritably. This idiot was just a tech, not even an important taskmaker. "Get my clothes."

The man flushed, his face turning red. "Sir, please, I'm terribly sorry, but you can't leave."

Barthol's voice turned to ice. "What did you say?"

"The empress t-told us." He stumbled over his words. "She said to give y-you the best treatment. Absolute best. That if any less was provided, we would suffer. She s-said you would want to leave before you should, and we weren't to—to let that happen."

Tarquine ordered him confined? Barthol realized he was clenching the smart-sheet that covered his lower body. He uncurled his fingers and spoke in a slow, deliberate voice. "I told you to get my clothes."

Panic showed on the man's face. He knew the choice Barthol offered him; defy the General of the Eubian Army or defy the Empress. "Sir, please—" His voice cracked.

Barthol didn't believe for one instant that Tarquine was concerned about his welfare. She was trying to assert dominance over him. Bitch. He touched the comm panel on the rail of his bed.

"My greetings, General Iquar," a woman said over the comm. "What may I do for you?"

"One moment," Barthol said. He spoke to the med-tech. "What is your name?"

The man swallowed. "Ren Haquailson."

"Do you have any children?" Barthol said softly.

The blood drained from Ren's face. "Sire! I'll get your clothes." He spun around.

"Get back here!" Barthol's voice cracked in the air.

Ren whirled back faster than he had turned away. "I'm sorry. Your Lordship, Your Glory, great esteemed General, I'm sorry, I'm truly sorry. Whatever you want, I'll do. I swear."

Keeping his gaze fixed on the tech, Barthol spoke into the comm, his voice clipped. "Send the following message to my head of security. The children of Ren Haquailson, a med-tech on the hospital staff, are to be auctioned to a buyer on another planet."

"Please," Ren begged. "I'll do anything you want. Don't take them. They are my life."

Barthol met his gaze with firm knowledge of his righteousness. "They are no longer anything to you. They will belong to whoever buys them." His voice hardened. "Remember that the next time you think to defy your masters. Now get out of my sight. Now!"

After the ashen tech left, Barthol swore. Damn Tarquine! She was the bane of his life. He could take her Iquar title, but he could never own either her power or her sleek, sensual body. If he had to obliterate the entire Qox Dynasty to right that unforgivable wrong, he would rip it apart with his own hands.

The Minister of Protocol, a willowy Highton with short hair, spoke to Jaibriol. "The message came in this morning, Your Highness. We cleared it as fast as possible." She was standing in his office.

Jaibriol was also standing up, leaning against his black desk, which reflected the colors he had chosen today for his office. The walls glowed with the sunset over the Kayzar Sea, a line of red, rose, and gold in a dark blue sky with several moons, including carnelian Mirella, gold Zara, and of course silver Tarquine. He had decided to have an octagonal room today, with rounded corners between the walls, floor, and ceiling. The domed ceiling was the deep blue of twilight, lightened by the orb lamp that hung from its center. Nanobots laced the gems that dripped from the lamp, allowing him to tune the crystals to a vibrant blue that shaded into rose and then gold at their tips. People assumed he chose those hues for the sunset theme, but it was actually a tribute to his mother,

Soz Valdoria, the former Skolian Imperator, whose dark hair had turned rose and then gold at the tips.

One of the wall panels, however, showed a far less aesthetic display than Glory's haunting sunset. Protocol had used it to play a message from the Skolians, their response to Jaibriol about the summit. The playback had finished with an image of the Ruby Pharaoh seated in an elegant wooden chair next to a table. Kelric stood behind her chair, the Fist of Skolia, a massive war god with a square chin and powerfully handsome face. Seeing his uncle always left Jaibriol feeling inadequate. He was acutely aware that Tarquine was in the room, standing several paces away, watching. He could never forget she had owned Kelric for a short time before Jaibriol had met her. The warlord of his enemies had been his wife's lover.

Deal with it, he told himself. *She is your wife. Not his.*

Jaibriol spoke to Protocol. "I find myself pleased by Ministry diligence."

She inclined her head, acknowledging his approval of her work.

"An intriguing display." He motioned at the image. "It invites the commentary of an expert on alien codes of behavior."

Protocol, the only acknowledged expert on alien codes of behavior in the room, went to the panel. As she walked by him, he felt as if he were losing his balance under the force of her Highton mind.

You're gritting your teeth, his node thought. **Should I relax your jaw?**

Yes, Jaibriol answered. **Thank you.**

Protocol tapped several panels disguised as arabesque

designs on the wall. The display showing the Ruby Pharaoh shifted to earlier in the message and began a replay. The pharaoh was saying, "We agree that we must select a neutral place of meeting, regardless of how we are met."

Protocol spoke dryly. "It is amazing how many ways one can find to illustrate one point."

Jaibriol smiled slightly. "So it is." The pharaoh just kept saying the same thing over and over, in different ways. "It is also remarkable how a thousand illustrations may offer nothing new."

"Unless the artist wishes the repetition and lack of depth to be the point," Protocol said.

"How very Highton," Tarquine murmured.

Jaibriol wished she weren't there, watching Kelric. But she was right; the pharaoh did sound like a Highton. Dyhianna Selei was also saying far more than anyone else—except Tarquine—knew.

Jaibriol turned to Protocol. "As always, the insights of protocol add light to the sunset." She had "verified" that Dehya had said essentially nothing.

She bowed. "It is my honor to serve, Your Glorious Highness."

Jaibriol tilted his head, indicating they were done.

Tarquine waited until Protocol left. Then she strolled over to Jaibriol and waved her hand at the panel. "Would you care to explain that?"

He shrugged. "It's Pharaoh Dyhianna saying absolutely nothing at great length."

"I wasn't referring to her words."

Jaibriol knew exactly what she meant. Hidden within that holo, the Ruby Pharaoh and Skolian Imperator had sent a very different message than the spoken words.

Quis dice.

"It's nothing," Jaibriol said.

"Nothing? An interesting game."

"I don't recall discussing a game."

Tarquine came closer, intruding on his personal space. Her voice flowed like dark molasses. "I've heard it said that when the prey plays games with the hunter, such prey is brave indeed."

Jaibriol resisted the urge to yank her close and forget about Kelric. She was trying to unbalance him, prod him into saying more than he intended. She was too damn good at it, but he wouldn't give in, not this time.

"Fortunately," he said, "we have no prey here to play with."

Her smile curved. "Perhaps. Or maybe my toys are here. Singular, that is."

"I would have thought you'd outgrown toys."

The empress touched his nose with the tip of her long finger. "When did you learn to pretend so well, hmmm?" She trailed her finger down to his lips. "Quis dice," she purred. "All over that table. And here I thought you invented the game."

He moved her finger away, his hand curling around hers. "You know I didn't."

She regarded him curiously. "Did Kelric?"

"No." He realized he was still holding her hand. He let it go and stepped back, putting distance between his hormone-addled body and his dangerous wife. It was either that or throw her across his big black desk.

Tarquine watched him with her eyelashes half lowered over her sultry eyes.

"Gods," Jaibriol muttered. She ought to be registered as a deadly weapon.

"Hmmmm?" she asked.

Oh, what the hell. If he didn't tell her what she wanted to know, she'd twist his libido into knots and then go off, stranding him alone in his big office. "Kelric didn't invent it. I'm not sure where it came from. His wife, I think. He and the pharaoh are sending us a message with it."

"He wants you to play Quis." She switched gears smoothly, from seductive to political, with an ease that never stopped astounding him. He didn't think she even consciously realized what she was doing. "But you can't send Quis moves as if you were playing chess by long distance. One message, they can get away with. The gems all over that table look like a deliberate display of wealth. It fits that empty speech of theirs, the way it sounds so Highton. One such display will make no one suspicious. But you won't get away with more than that."

He exhaled. "I know."

A hum came from Jaibriol's wrist comm. Frowning, he glanced down. It was a page from Robert. He touched the receive panel. "Qox here. What is it?"

"Sire, I received a message from the Iquar Estate," Robert said. "General Iquar checked himself out of the hospital and returned home."

"Robert, hold for a moment." Jaibriol toggled off the comm and glanced at Tarquine. "Is Barthol recovered enough to do that?"

Her face and mind both became shuttered. "He hates hospitals. It's an Iquar trait."

Jaibriol tried to fathom her reaction. This happened every time he tried to talk to her about Barthol's accident. Had her nephew outwitted her? Maybe she had nothing to do with his accident? But he didn't see why else she would go home to "recuperate." He eased down his shields and tried to read her mood, but he caught no more than her curiosity about Quis.

"You seem more relaxed in your relationships lately," Jaibriol said, probing.

She regarded him blandly. "I'm always relaxed."

"Right," Jaibriol said. "And I'm always Highton."

"You are the ultimate Highton," she said, as if it were the ultimate compliment.

He tried a different tack. "So is Barthol."

Tarquine made an unimpressed sound, like a brief gust of breath. "Barthol is the ultimate Barthol." She turned back to the holo of the pharaoh and Kelric. "You should replicate that Quis game on the table."

It was exactly what Jaibriol intended to do. He also didn't intend to let her change the subject. "You don't think Barthol is the ultimate Highton?"

Tarquine slanted him a glance. "If you are the ultimate, husband, there can be no others."

Sparring with her was getting him nowhere. It rarely did. This much he knew: if she had wanted her nephew dead, Barthol would be in his grave.

And yet . . . Barthol was an Iquar, thoroughly and without remorse, as brilliant and as hard as diamond. Had he outwitted Tarquine? It would be the first time Jaibriol had seen anyone manage that feat. Or the Quis could be wrong. Maybe Tarquine had discovered it wasn't Barthol who had tried to kill them. If the dice could be that convincing and be wrong, he didn't dare use Quis to help him with Kelric. Too much was at stake.

Jaibriol touched the receive toggle on his wrist comm. "Robert?"

"Here, Sire," his aide said.

"Keep me posted on General Iquar's condition."

"I will." After a pause, Robert added, "We do have a complication."

Jaibriol wanted to groan. Was there ever *not* a complication. "What happened?"

"One of the med-techs tried to discourage the general from leaving the hospital." Robert cleared his throat with the self-conscious scrape Jaibriol recognized. He wasn't going to like whatever came next.

"I take it the general didn't approve," Jaibriol said.

"No, sir. He confiscated the tech's three children and put them up for auction."

"What the *hell?*" Jaibriol stared at his wrist comm as if it had sprouted two heads.

Robert plunged on. "Sire, I fear the father may do something drastic."

"Like what?"

"Suicide."

"For flaming sake." Jaibriol wanted to strangle Barthol. "Send the children back to their father, and transfer him and his entire family to my staff at the palace." Barthol would be furious at the interference, but damned if Jaibriol was going to let him destroy the man's life over nothing.

"Right away, Your Highness." Robert sounded relieved.

"Let me know when it's done," Jaibriol said. "I'll talk to you later."

"Yes, Sire."

Jaibriol toggled off the comm and scowled at Tarquine. "Your nephew ought to be thrashed."

Her face was completely neutral. "He's an excellent commander."

Jaibriol's patience was evaporating. "Yes, well, our

excellent commander will be furious when he finds out I stopped his petty retaliation against the med-tech for having the audacity to, oh-my-God, show concern for your dear nephew's unexalted health."

Tarquine smiled slightly. "I suspect Barthol considers even his illnesses exalted."

"He's not ill," Jaibriol said. "He was hurt. In an *accident*."

"So he was. Fortunate that he recovered."

Blast it, he couldn't read her at all. She had become too damn proficient at shielding her mind. Most Aristos never learned. The only psions the typical Aristo knew were providers, who had no idea how to use their abilities. However, after eleven years of marriage to a Ruby psion who knew all too well how to spy on her mind, Tarquine had become remarkably adept at hiding.

Jaibriol lowered his shields further, enough that he picked up impressions of distant Aristos like painful mental jabs. He reached for Tarquine . . . probing . . . something about Barthol . . . a cold anger . . .

The jabs grew worse until he inhaled sharply and raised his barriers.

Tarquine was watching him with her smooth forehead just slightly furrowed, which from her was a look of blatant puzzlement. "You shouldn't let Barthol upset you. He's not worth it."

"It's not that," Jaibriol said. "My head just hurts."

"Your nanomeds should be fixing it."

"They can't fix my being emperor." He turned back to the holo of the pharaoh and the Quis dice. "It's true, I could play that game using their patterns. But should I rely on what it tells me? If the dice are wrong, I would be a fool to depend on them for strategy."

Her voice took on a shadowed quality. "Depend on them, Jaibriol."

A chill went up his spine as he turned to her. "And if they mislead?"

Her gaze never wavered. "They do not."

Since Tarquine's miscarriage, a deep anger had pulsed within him. It surged now, pushing at the cage of his self-control. She still believed Barthol had killed their son.

"Come," Tarquine said. "Let us play this game the Skolians offer us."

"Very well." Perhaps with Quis she could say what she wouldn't tell him aloud about Barthol. "Let us sit at the dice."

Headquarters City on the planet Diesha served the Skolian military. The command centers for ISC were spread throughout the Imperialate, so that even if many were destroyed, it wouldn't cripple the military. But HQ City hummed with the heartbeat of ISC, its largest and most active center. In psiberspace, it manifested as a huge network in the Kyle mesh.

A medical transmission flashed into the HQ mesh, whisking along like a spark of light. It stopped at no console. No human operator saw it. Only automated AI sentries registered its presence. They read the layers of security code the message had accumulated, processed the data those codes provided, and added their own layers. After the transmission accreted more security codes, the ISC system calculated a new destination for the message and hurtled it back into the web.

So a simple request for an analysis of a blood test continued on its way.

believed Del's talent was genuine. It was only when his producers at Prime Nova brought them in and had Del perform for them live, up close and personal, that they acknowledged his astonishing virtuosity was genuine. His dazzling quality, depth, and six-octave range were real.

Those closest to Del knew he had grown up on a rural world that eschewed technology. Although he'd had access to such advantages if he wanted them, it had never occurred to him to enhance his voice. He simply trained, almost from birth, though he hadn't realized he was doing it. He just sang all the time, doing exercises he made up. No one on his home world liked holo-rock, including his family, the Ruby Dynasty. It wasn't until he sang on Earth, in their lucrative and cutthroat world of entertainment, that he discovered people actually wanted to hear him. His ancestors had been genetically engineered to develop their voices as instruments, but it was the years of never-ending training that gave him what critics called "the voice of an unparalleled rock angel."

The biographer seemed more interested in Del's charisma, however, than his talent. Like many youths on his home world, Del had learned a form of martial arts called *mai-quinjo.* It left him with a dancer's lithe grace and musculature, which for him translated into an erotic grace, not only when he moved, but even in his still postures, his hips tilted, his body relaxed and lean, as if he were about to melt into a sensual dance. It mortified Del; he never wanted anyone to see him dance. But after Prime Nova had coaxed him into working with a choreographer, his sales had soared.

It was no wonder people fell in love with Del. He

looked like a misbehaved angel, with large eyes fringed by ridiculously long eyelashes. When he sang, his face could go in a heartbeat from unbearably beautiful to the snarl of passion. In his black leather, he was the ultimate pretty bad-boy, the rock god everyone wanted in their bed.

"What are you reading?" a man asked behind him.

Mac turned with a start. Del was standing there, watching him curiously. Mac held up the holofile. "The latest version of your biography."

Del winced. "I hope it isn't as embarrassing as the last one."

"He's toned it down." Mac set the file on a table by the chair and stood up. "Ready for your speech?"

"I'm trying." Del paled, which accented the freckles across his nose. "How many people do you think are out there?"

Mac had wondered himself. He flicked through a menu on his wrist comm. "According to the latest figures, twelve thousand are gathered in the plaza and surrounding streets. Broadcasters are estimating the interstellar audience in the tens of billions."

"Gods," Del muttered. "Just to hear me stumble through a few words?"

Mac wished he could ease Del's stage fright. The prince had long ago overcome his fear of singing in public; indeed, he thrived now on performing. But giving speeches still petrified him.

"You'll do fine," Mac said. "Just think of it as a song without a melody."

"Just another live song," Del said, with a self-deprecatory laugh. "That's what got me into this mess, when I sang 'Carnelians Finale' live."

"It's one hell of a song," Mac said. And apt. God only knew if the Hightons would ever stop in their single-minded urge to subjugate the sum total of all humanity. But they and the Skolians were finally trying to make peace and Del wanted it to succeed as much as anyone else.

Mac's comm hummed. Glancing at its small screen, he said, "Security has finished their checks. We can go on in, if you're ready."

Del straightened his shoulders. "Yeah, let's get it over with."

The safe-room exited into a studio full of talk and commotion. Mesh consoles crammed with equipment lined the walls, all occupied by media techs or security people monitoring the room, building, city, planet, and offworld links. Del's three bodyguards were standing around the water dispenser across the room, talking, ready to ensure that no one tried to attack, assault, assassinate, or climb up on the balcony and kiss Del while he was giving his speech.

Gerard, the senior mesh-tech, came over to them. His blue VR suit glinted with threads that carried more information in their hair-thin conduits than the combined memory of some entire towns. "We're all set," he said.

"Thanks." Del fidgeted with the end of his belt, then realized what he was doing and stopped.

Gerard indicated a doorway across into the room. "That's your entrance."

"Yeah. Okay. Good. Thanks." Del was talking too fast. He went where Gerard pointed them, flexing his fingers, curling them into a fist, relaxing them, flexing again.

Mac walked at his side. "You'll be fine."

"If I don't screw this up," Del said.

"You can't screw it up. You have a recording of the speech in your wrist comm, right?"

Del glanced at his wrist, where the silver comm glinted. "Yeah, it's there."

"So no worries." Mac filled his voice with reassurance. It continually amazed him that a man as successful as Del could have so many self-doubts. "If you forget, the comm can give you verbal cues over the audio-plug in your ear."

The captain of Del's bodyguards joined them at the balcony doors. A lanky woman sporting dark spiked hair, she was every inch the no-nonsense type with her standard-issue shirt, slacks, and blazer, all severely cut. She looked as if she could take on a pack of wildcats without a flinch. Her badge read *Jett Masters* and a pulse revolver rested in a holster on her hip.

Jett nodded to Del. "We're ready to activate the security field, Your Highness."

"Thanks." Then he added, "You can just call me Del."

"Okay, Del." She attached a silver clip to his vest, the device indistinguishable from the studs on the leather. "This controls the field. You'll be surrounded with energy deflectors just like when you perform live."

Del gave her one of his blazing smiles, that celebrated flash of brilliant white teeth. "I've never figured out what that means, 'energy deflector.' "

Incredibly, the tough-as-nails Jett blushed at Del's smile. Mac inwardly groaned. It surely violated some conservation law of the cosmos that so many women reacted that way, even this hardened security officer.

At least Jett recovered faster than most. "The field

doesn't literally deflect energy," she said. "It affects electronics, optics, superconductors, even solid objects. It helps deflect threats by interfering with what drives them. We also have laser carbines mounted in hidden locations, EM pulse generators, sound blasters, optical blinders, and an armed human contingent."

"This is just a speech," Del said with a laugh. "Not a military engagement."

"I know. But better to have too much than too little."

"You know, my brother Kelric would really like you."

Jett blinked. "You mean Imperator Skolia?"

"Yeah, him. He loves this tech stuff."

She inclined her head to him. "Thank you."

Del looked confused. "Uh, yeah. Sure."

Mac held back his laugh. Given the strained relationship between Del and his brother, it probably hadn't occurred to Del that a military officer would take his comment as a compliment. Something about her response did strike Mac as odd, though he wasn't sure what.

"Okay," Del said, more to himself than anyone else. "Let's do it."

Jett touched a panel on her gauntlet and the door whisked open, revealing a balcony with potted plants around its edges. Breezes tousled Del's hair as he walked forward with Jett and Mac. He went to the edge of the balcony and rested his hands on its rail, staring at the plaza below. Gusts of air blew his curls back from his face. People filled the wind-swept area. As soon as they saw him, applause broke out and voices surged with appreciative calls. Giant holos of Del appeared on buildings, projecting his image to the streets beyond, where more people had gathered to hear Skolia's expatriate rock god have his say. Del waved at the crowd and flashed his grin, and the applause swelled. Only Mac could see what didn't show in the holos, the whitening of Del's knuckles as he gripped the railing with his other hand.

Aural-orbs spun in the air, swirling with colors that indicated their broadcast frequencies and the media outlets that owned them. A blimp floated above the city, its surface projecting the image of a sea ship, as if an ancient frigate was sailing the sky above Washington D.C. Smart-cranes with media stations at their ends were poised above the buildings bordering the plaza; big enough for two people, maybe three, the stations were also packed with tech, including EI-controlled cams and media consoles. Not all of them carried crews from the conglomerates, however. One had two Marines standing at attention, both armed with EM pulse rifles.

Del spoke in a low voice. "Gods."

"You'll do fine," Mac said. Times like this made him wonder if Del would ever decide his career wasn't worth the toll it exacted. The moment "Carnelians Finale" had revealed his identity to three empires, he had lost what few freedoms remained in his life. He had already been living the constrained lifestyle of a celebrity, but that had been nothing to the limitations imposed when it became known he was a Ruby prince. He could never appear in public without these precautions.

A tech's voice came over their earplugs. "Del, you're good to go. This channel is private. If you toggle the red button on your wrist comm, it will put you into the public address system."

"Thanks." Speaking to himself, he added, "Okay, here goes." He touched the red panel on his comm and it turned green.

"Hey," Del said. "Hello."

His voice resonated from every orb and speaker in the plaza. The techs weren't enhancing it; the same genetics that had gifted Del with his spectacular ability to sing also gave him that glorious orator's voice. Ironically, it reminded Mac of the Trader emperor, Jaibriol Qox, whose voice had a similar quality.

People called out greetings, kids were jumping up and down, and the general clamor swelled. Del held up his hand for quiet and laughed when half the crowd waved back to him. He waited until the commotion died down and then said, "Thank you all for coming. For listening. Wherever you are." His opening wasn't as smooth as what he had planned, but he was speaking from memory rather than using the prompt in his audio comm.

"We've heard a lot in recent months about my song, 'Carnelians Finale,'" Del said. "I've come here today to talk to you about that."

The crowd fell completely silent.

"The song is about my family," Del said. "And about the wars my people have had with the Eubians for centuries. The wars and their aftermath." He stopped, and his hand on the rail was shaking. He lifted his chin. "I did not release that song! After all these killing centuries of warfare between my people and the Eubians, we want *peace*." He took an uneven breath. "I would never undermine the efforts of my family and Emperor Jaibriol to negotiate the treaty that Skolia and Eube have signed. Never!"

Murmurs spread through the crowd. A few buildings showed the audience now rather than Del. It was hard to read their mood; their expressions and body language were as varied as the people. Some looked relieved, others disappointed, others uncertain. Their tension was like an elasticized band pulled too tight.

"Nothing will change what my family has suffered," Del said. "But someone has to say '*Today I will not seek vengeance.* Today, I will look beyond the violence and extend the hand of peace.'" His voice rang out as he left behind his careful speech. "Because if we cannot find it within ourselves to extend that hand, our children will pay the price, all of them, as we fight endless wars, grinding each other in the machinery of our hatred until nothing remains of the human race, not Skolian, not Eubian, not Allied. I ask you, entreat you, not to let anger pull apart our efforts to find peace, especially not the anger from my song. Let us begin a new era for humanity, one of a better harmony."

Del stopped and the crowd was silent.

Good Lord. Mac hadn't expected that. The same passion that drove "Carnelians Finale," wrenching out of Del's deepest pain, had infused his words here. The crowd rumbled with the sounds of people stunned and hopeful, angry and puzzled, so many emotions blended together. Del had pulled away their moorings. Skolians hated Traders, Traders hated Skolians. That was all they knew. This was probably the first time a major political figure had made such a statement: *Let us forgive.* Whether it would calm the furor over Del's song, Mac couldn't tell, but if anything could help, it was this.

Del lifted his hand to the crowd and they responded with an upsurge, waving and calling his name. As he stepped back from the rail, the commentators in the media cranes talked full speed into their holocams, already analyzing Del's words for their interstellar audiences.

When Mac joined him at the back of the balcony, Del touched the green panel on his comm and it turned red. He gave a shaky smile. "Well, okay. It's done." With a wince, Del added, "I hope my family doesn't get upset about my changing the script."

Mac spoke quietly. "It was a good speech."

Inside the console room, the techs were spinning down, more relaxed. Many nodded to Del or complimented him on the speech. The tension was easing. It had gone well.

Jett walked at Del's side. "Would you like to return to your flyer?" she asked.

Del smiled at her with relief. "Yeah, that'd be good. Thanks."

"Here, this way." She ushered them toward a side door.

"What made you decide to change the words?" Mac asked as they walked with Jett. Del's other two bodyguards came with them, two bulky Marines assigned to him by Allied Space Command for this event.

"Truthfully, I'm not sure. It just came out." Del pushed back his mop of hair. "Kelric would say I'm too emotional, that I should control my feelings more."

Mac smiled. "I'll bet you your next paycheck he likes this."

Del laughed easily now, his voice rich and full. "If you're willing to bet that much, I better not. You're too good at figuring out odds." They went through the doorway, with Jett in front and his other two guards behind. "All that math, it's incomprehensible hieroglyphics to me."

Mac nodded, distracted. Jett had ushered them into an unfamiliar corridor, leading them toward an elevator at its end. "Captain Masters, where are we going?"

"We have a hover car downstairs," she said. "It will leave the building via secured tunnels." She glanced at Del. "So you don't have to go out into that crowd."

"Thanks." Del massaged the muscles in the back of his neck. "When I started performing, before I was well known, it bothered me that people said I shouldn't go in a crowd. I wanted to meet them. I mean, they actually liked my music. But the better known I got, the crazier it went. People would grab my clothes and hair." He reddened. "Women threw lingerie. A few times I was trampled when the crowd knocked me down. It was nuts."

"We'll make sure nothing like that happens," Jett assured him.

The elevator turned out to be a pleasant chamber carpeted in amber, with mahogany walls and a luminous disk on the ceiling, like a pool of radiance shedding light. Yet it felt wrong to Mac. It was like when Jett had thanked Del for comparing her to Kelric. He didn't understand what troubled him; all her responses were normal and expected, and the Marines looked unconcerned as they stepped inside the elevator chamber.

"Captain, where does this elevator go?" Mac asked as the doors closed. "I thought I knew all the exits from this building."

"HQ recently installed it," Jett said. "Special treatment for VIPs."

Again, a perfectly normal answer, but it felt...what?

Fake, Mac thought. *It's fake.* He didn't know why he thought she or the Marines were acting; he had no reason for it other than his gut reaction.

"No, let's go out the way we came in," Mac said. He turned toward the control panel—and found only the smooth wall. "Where are the controls?" He swung around to Jett. "Stop this elevator."

"I'm sorry, Mister Tyler." She looked genuinely apologetic. "This is a secured chamber. It won't stop until we reach the hover lot in the basement."

Del spoke coldly. "I'm not stupid, Masters. If you can start this lift, you have the codes to stop it. Do it now. I'm not going anywhere."

"I believe you *are* going somewhere, Your Highness," she said. "With us. You won't be making any more speeches." The other two guards were watching Del and Mac with impassive gazes, silent bulwarks behind Jett, their hands resting on their holstered guns.

"Are you crazy?" Mac asked. "You can't take him with you."

Jett ignored him as she spoke to Del. "Many people, both Allied and Skolian, believe your song must be heard. This 'peace' treaty is a falsehood propagated by the Traders to weaken us, with the ultimate goal of conquest over all humanity." Her voice hardened. "We're making sure no one else uses you as a propaganda tool, not the Traders, not the Allieds, and not your own family."

Del stared at her. "You're out of your flaming mind."

"You won't even get him out of this building," Mac

said. "Let alone anywhere else." According to the files he had seen, these Marines had been vetted by both the Allieds and Skolians. But if they were taking Del, he didn't believe the military had any hand in it. This came from somewhere else.

"We have private transportation arranged," Jett said.

"Gods, this is rich," Del said with an angry laugh. "I can't even trust the people who are supposed to protect me from the nut cases out there who want to 'keep me from being used' by whoever they don't like this week."

"You're looking at a court-martial," Mac told Jett, his voice as hard as the knot forming in his stomach. This couldn't be happening, not now. Was there *anyone* out there who wasn't trying to destroy the damn peace process?

The sensation of descending stopped and the elevator doors slid open. Outside, a man and a woman in black jumpsuits waited in the hover lot. The woman was holding a laser carbine, but the man had a different type of gun, an air-loaded syringe pistol. A hover-van with tinted windows waited on a pad behind them, dark and sleek.

"No." Del raised his hands, palms outward, as if to push away the commandos. "Damn it, no." He swung around to Jett. "I'm not going with you."

"I'm afraid you have to." Jett glanced at the man in the lot and he raised his syringe pistol.

A familiar stab of fear went through Mac. "You can't shoot him! He's allergic to many drugs. He's not even native to this planet. You could kill him!"

"We're aware of his health," Jett said. "The shot will only knock him out. Unless he comes of his own free will." She raised her hand as if inviting Del to dinner. "After you, Your Highness."

Del, stall, Mac thought, shouting the words in his mind. He wasn't a telepath, but Del was a powerful enough psion that if Mac projected his thought with sufficient strength, Del might pick it up even through the mental shields he used to protect his mind.

Del glanced at Mac, his forehead furrowed as if he were straining to hear a whisper.

Stall them! Mac thought. Allied Space Command monitored Del. Even if Masters and her people had temporarily nullified that security, they couldn't keep this up for long. If he and Del stalled long enough, someone would find them.

Del crossed his arms and regarded Jett implacably. "I'm not going anywhere."

"Suit yourself." She nodded to the man with the syringe gun.

As had often happened during Mac's Air Force days in an engagement, his time sense slowed down. The man with the syringe seemed to move in slow motion, training his weapon on Del. Mac didn't give a rat's ass what Jett Masters claimed about their precautions; he couldn't let whatever was in that gun hit Del. When the man's finger touched the firing stud, Mac threw himself in front of Del. He didn't hear the shot, he felt only a stab of pain in his neck, but that was enough; he recognized the pressure-driven dart of a syringe gun. With a grunt, he lurched past Del and crashed into Jett. He was dimly aware of the Marines converging on them as he and Jett slammed into the wall.

The world went dark.

Aliana had never expected even to leave Muzeopolis, let alone visit a Skolian embassy. The idea that she might leave the *planet* was so far outside her experience, it never entered her mind.

Until it happened.

She had no choice. The soldiers had taken them from the embassy despite outraged protests from the Skolians. Aliana was just grateful ESComm hadn't executed anyone, especially Lensmark, who she particularly liked despite the Secondary being an Imperialate soldier. The Skolians should be grateful they were alive, yet instead they were furious at ESComm. Aliana wished she could be angry, too, but mostly she was terrified.

"Zina?" Red's voice was soft in the darkness.

Aliana lifted her head. She was slouched in a big beanbag, here in the two-room cabin where the soldiers had locked up her and Red. He had been in the other room, asleep in a pressure hammock slung between two bulkheads. She could have closed his door, but she couldn't bear to cut herself off from him, her only friend within light years. She had no idea what the soldiers had done with Tide and it was killing her. This had happened because he helped her and Red. Even knowing ESComm would have looked for him anyway when the order came to kill any survivors of his line, she felt responsible.

"I'm over here," she said, ensconced in the soft beanbag. It shifted around, making her more comfortable.

"I come over?" He sounded closer.

"Yes," she said softly. "Please."

A hand touched her shoulder. The fresh scent of his clothes tickled her nose, and the smooth cloth of his jumpsuit brushed her neck when his arm moved past her. The material crinkled as he settled to her in the big lump of a chair.

Aliana hesitated, feeling shy. But they had so little time left with each other. She didn't want to waste it. She put her arms around him, tentative, afraid he would pull away.

"You smell good," she said.

"You, too." His cheek moved against hers as if he were searching for something. He turned her head, bringing her lips against his. Then he kissed her softly, with such sweetness. It felt good, like warmth against the cold of their fear and isolation.

Fear. Common sense finally kicked in and Aliana pulled back. "Red, no. We can't."

"Yes, can," he murmured, stroking her hair.

"I'm not an Aristo. I can't have you."

"Not want Aristo." His voice caught. "They never love. They hurt and hurt and *hurt.*"

She couldn't imagine what hells he had lived. "I'm so sorry," she whispered.

"Not want to die." His usually rich voice had a hard edge. "Aristos say I never think. No mind. Nothing. Just provide. But I *think.*" His voice rasped with an anger she had never heard him give words to. "I feel. I dream. I laugh and I cry. I want to *live.*"

"Ah, gods." Tears gathered in her eyes. It was all there, in him, the humanity the Aristos had denied, that they had bred him never to show, just like the humanity within Tide. She had no way to save his life, no way to help either of them. ESComm was sending them both to Admiral Muze, who was on the planet Glory. She didn't know why they included her, except that she was a side issue caught up with Red and

Tide. She knew only that Admiral Muze had wanted to kill Red for some cruel and arbitrary reason she would never understand.

She brushed her lips over Red's nose, tickling it with her tongue, and he laughed, his voice catching at the end. He kissed her again as they slid down in the beanbag. It molded around them, cradling their bodies. Red undressed them both with such expertise, she didn't realize what he was doing until his palms slid over her bare skin and she felt his smooth chest against her body. He knew exactly how to touch her, how to make her want him, his touch playful and kind.

Their minds blended until Aliana couldn't tell where his started and hers ended. She knew then what he wanted, what he needed, that he had never been touched in love, never in his life, only hurt until he wept from the pain and his loneliness. When her skin brushed his, he tensed as if for a blow. When she caressed him instead, his startled relief suffused her mind.

He made love to her with kindness and desperation. The damp skin of his face pressed against her cheek, his tears mixing with hers. It was the first time—and probably the last—that either of them would know how it felt to share love.

XVIII

A Simple Test

Jaibriol walked the cliff path with two of his bodyguards in front and two following. They were high above the ragged shoreline where the enraged waves of Glory's ocean battered the black sands. The wild landscape reflected the tumult in his mind as he prepared to face Admiral Erix Muze, his naval Joint Commander.

Although Jaibriol had never felt comfortable with Muze, he preferred him to Barthol. Until this business with the peace treaty, he and Erix had maintained a wary détente. The moment Jaibriol had blackmailed Erix into signing the treaty, threatening to execute him for a crime he hadn't committed, that had changed. The cold, uncompromising nature of Highton law allowed the emperor to put to death *anyone* in the family of a traitor, even though Erix had nothing to do with the sins of his first cousin, Colonel Vatrix Muze, who had tried to assassinate Jaibriol last year.

Supposedly tried to assassinate.

Jaibriol was the only person alive who knew Vatrix

had never tried to kill him. The colonel had caught him crawling out of the Lock after Jaibriol had unwillingly joined the Skolian Triad. Hidaka, the captain of Jaibriol's Razer bodyguards, had also witnessed it—and he had blasted Muze into ashes with a laser carbine so the colonel could never reveal Jaibriol's secret.

Even now, many months later, Jaibriol could barely absorb the immensity of what Hidaka had done. The Razer had known exactly what he witnessed. Hidaka had been built, bred, and programmed for one purpose: to serve Hightons. Jaibriol had valued Hidaka's intelligence and loyalty, but he would have never, in a millennium, have expected Hidaka to murder a Highton colonel to protect so huge and unforgivable a secret, that the emperor was a Ruby psion. Hidaka's loyalty had outweighed a conditioning his creators forced on him even before his cybernetic birth from a mechanical womb. The Razer Hidaka had risen to an ideal, his belief, however naively, that Jaibriol could make the universe a better place for humanity.

And so Hidaka had died. He had given his life to protect Jaibriol when the emperor met with Kelric on Earth. All of their bodyguards had died, Skolian and Eubian alike, sacrificing themselves to protect two sovereigns who were committing treason by meeting in secret. From that sacrifice had come a miracle. Deep in the night, Kelric and Jaibriol had hunkered together, the only survivors, stranded in the wilds of the Appalachian Mountains, and written the peace treaty.

Jaibriol gritted his teeth. How did ESComm respond to this great sacrifice and miracle? By murdering Hidaka's entire line. In the warped universe of Highton logic, they punished the Razer for sacrificing his life. Why? Their investigation had uncovered signs of Hidaka's humanity, hints that he was developing self-determination. It was far too great a threat to the Aristos that the Razers—the most dangerous of all their human creations—could think for themselves. By the time Jaibriol had discovered what was happening, it was too late; none of Hidaka's line had survived.

Or so he had thought before today.

Jaibriol's aide Robert was waiting up ahead. He bowed deeply as Jaibriol joined him. "My honor at your presence, Your Highness."

"My greetings." Jaibriol had long ago told Robert not to kneel, before he realized other Aristos considered it a threat when their emperor did away with the expected deference. They saw each of his changes as a chink that weakened the fundamental structure of Eube; too many chinks, and slaves would think they were human. Which was exactly what Jaibriol intended. But if he pushed too hard, his sway over the Aristos weakened. It was a balancing act, easing constraints bit by bit, humanizing Eube without losing his ability to make changes.

"Has Admiral Muze arrived?" Jaibriol asked.

"Ten minutes ago." Robert indicated a path that sloped away from the cliff, down into the mountains, ending in a clearing circled by black marble pillars and high peaks. A retinue waited there, the admiral's tall form in their midst. Muze's black hair glittered in the pale sunlight that diffused through the misty air, water vapor from the waves below that survived even this high in the mountains. Sunlight sparkled in the veils of mist, softening their view of the clearing so that Muze's retinue looked like spirits in a celestial palace. It never ceased to amaze Jaibriol that a race as unrepentantly brutal as the Hightons produced such ethereal beauty in the worlds they created.

He walked down the path with Robert and his bodyguards. As he came within the circle of the pillars, everyone in Muze's retinue went down on one knee, their heads bent, including the admiral's two Razer bodyguards. Muze bowed to Jaibriol.

Jaibriol lifted his hand, indicating they could rise. People who knelt to him always managed to see that motion even though they were supposed to be staring at the ground. He didn't care where they looked; he would have dispensed with the entire process if it wouldn't have led to so much grief. But it had its uses, such as now, when he wanted to hold the upper hand with Erix.

Jaibriol spoke to the admiral. "It would please us to enjoy the company of ESComm's finest." By disguising his order for Erix to walk with him as a compliment, he offered more honor than a rigorous adherence to Highton custom required.

Erix nodded, the tilt of his head expressing his appreciation of the phrasing. Jaibriol didn't extend his invitation to Erix's retinue, but Robert stayed behind as a courtesy. Jaibriol could have allowed them to come. Although it might have softened Erix up to let him bring his Razers, Jaibriol didn't want the pressure of their partly Aristo minds. It was difficult enough to deal with just the admiral.

He and Erix strolled along the high cliff, accompanied by Jaibriol's Razers. The wind blew through their shimmering hair. A black marble rail ran along a waist-high wall to their left; beyond it, the black cliff face dropped in great sweeps to the beach far below. The black sands sparkled in the sunlight while waves leapt high above the spiked outcroppings of glittering black rock that jutted up in the water along the shoreline.

"A beautiful sight," Erix commented.

"Indeed," Jaibriol said. "A sight fit for our empire's visionaries."

Erix's face remained cold. He knew what Jaibriol meant, that those who supported the treaty were enlightened. He offered no sign of agreement.

Steeling himself, Jaibriol eased down his barriers. The force of Erix's mind increased like the pressure of water against a flexible barrier, ready to burst and flood him with pain.

Security protocols activated, his spinal node thought. It controlled the biomech in his body, which could moderate his responses, even automatic actions like his sweat or heartbeat, and stop him from visibly flinching under the onslaught of Erix's mind.

The admiral had no idea that Jaibriol had extended a mental probe. He took for granted what every Aristo considered an undisputed truth; no other Aristo could know what went on in his mind. The "gods" of Eube had decreed that Kyle abilities made providers weak, less than human, but Jaibriol knew the truth, why Aristos were fanatic that no genes of an empath or telepath "contaminate" their DNA. Psions could spy on their minds, in that one simple act bypassing the convoluted modes of interaction that Hightons used to hide their feelings. Aristos tortured psions into subservience not only for transcendence, but also as punishment for possessing a gift no true Aristo could ever own.

If only you knew, Jaibriol thought. He could only skim the surface of Erix's thoughts, but that was enough. It was no surprise to discover the admiral would never forgive Jaibriol for blackmailing him or that he considered the peace process a mistake. What Jaibriol didn't expect was that he had earned Erix's respect. In the universe of Machiavellian Highton intrigue, Jaibriol had shown himself to be far more inspired than Erix expected. As much as the admiral abhorred the actual treaty, he couldn't help but admire the way Jaibriol had pushed it through. He hadn't thought Eube's young emperor was devious enough to pull off such a coup.

Jaibriol hardly considered it a compliment that Erix considered him good at being Highton, but it gave him a way to deal with the admiral. He could only take Erix's mind in small doses, though. He raised his barriers, muting the painful force. Ironically, his discomfort caused Muze to transcend at a low level, one he wasn't aware of, but that eased his antagonism about this meeting.

Jaibriol indicated a marble bench in an alcove carved into the cliff wall on their right. "It would be good to relax, perhaps view the latest mesh broadcast. Or similar." In other words, *give me your report about the embassy situation on your son's planet, Muze's Helios.*

"It would be my honor, Your Highness," Erix said.

After they sat down, Erix pulled a slender tube off his belt and unrolled it into a gold screen, which he laid on his lap. Holicons appeared around its edges, morphing every time he flicked one, until finally a larger holo formed above the screen. It showed a group of people, both ESComm officers and civilians.

Erix indicated a man with dark hair in the center. "One can find substantial defects in a Skolian embassy." Disgust edged his voice. "Should it please your honored Highness, ESComm is prepared to dismantle and study any defective equipment."

Jaibriol couldn't answer. He felt as if someone had socked him in the stomach. The man in that holo, the traitor who had tried to defect to the Skolians—it was *Hidaka.* Except it wasn't his dead bodyguard, but rather, another clone from the same line, one with the same "flaws" in his constructed personality, the flaws had made Hidaka extraordinary. *Human.*

Somehow Jaibriol spoke in a detached voice. "It might be advantageous to debrief so anomalous a defect." In other words, *Bring him here. I want talk to him.*

Erix didn't look surprised. "Of course, Your Highness."

"I'm intrigued that such anomalies aren't isolated," Jaibriol said. The report on the embassy situation had mentioned two slaves who were with the Razer.

Erix spoke dryly. "Especially when such anomalies involve one's own property." He indicated a boy on the edge of the group.

Jaibriol studied the youth. So that was Erix's escaped provider. The admiral's security people had traced him to the embassy, which was how they had found the Razer. The boy was standing off to one side, almost fading into the background. It wasn't clear why he had been with the Razer.

"Astonishing that the Skolians acquired an item of

such value," Jaibriol said. In other words, *How the hell did your provider end up in a Skolian embassy?*

Muze shrugged, looking at the holo instead of Jaibriol. "One can tire of even a valuable painting or vase, no longer wishing it to clutter their home. In such cases, it is efficient to dispose of the object. After all, one can always replace it."

Dispose? Jaibriol felt ill. Erix would kill a slave just because he was tired of having him around? Gods, were both of his Joint Commanders such monsters?

Except Erix was lying. His face offered no hint that he cared, but Jaibriol felt his remorse. He hadn't wanted to kill the provider. He had reacted in anger when another Aristo implied he was sleeping with the boy. Of course Hightons slept with whatever slaves they wanted, and some didn't care about the sex. Erix did care; he only slept with his pleasure girls, which was why he professed to throw away the male provider. But he knew perfectly well his staff had left the boy a way to escape. If this situation hadn't come up, Erix would have never bothered to reclaim him.

Jaibriol wondered what it said about how he lived, that he found Erix's remorse a good sign. What the admiral did to his providers was unconscionable, and if that boy hadn't broken his conditioning and climbed out of the waste compactor, Muze would have murdered him simply out of irritation with another Highton's verbal jabs. But that insight offered Jaibriol a way to save the provider; he needed to give Erix an alternative to killing the youth that allowed the admiral to save face.

Jaibriol spoke with a nonchalance far different from he felt. "Others may enjoy property that doesn't meet the standards of our exalted kin." He paused as if mulling over a thought. "The daughter of an aide on my staff celebrates her ascendance to adulthood soon. She deserves a gift." In truth, he had little idea when the daughters of the people on his staff had birthdays, but he could undoubtedly find a suitable one and give her the boy.

Erix inclined his head. "You are generous."

Generous? He felt like a monster. How many slaves had died for each he could save? He hadn't even yet accounted for the other slave they had found with the Razer. "Perhaps the young lady celebrating her birth would enjoy a matched pair."

Erix waved his hand in dismissal, then indicated another figure in the holo. "I doubt such large size and unattractive features would produce much of a match."

Jaibriol looked where Erix indicated—and nearly lost his carefully built composure.

It was true the girl was unusually tall, but she wasn't ugly. Hers was a beauty of strength and power, traits no Aristo wanted in a slave, except for the purpose of destroying it. But that wasn't what made him feel as if his stomach dropped through the ground. God above, hadn't anyone *seen* it? Was it so utterly absurd that they all missed it?

The girl was a feminine version of Kelric Valdoria, the Skolian Imperator.

"We don't even know if he's alive!" Roca strode down the hall with Kelric and First Councilor Barcala Tikal.

"The Allieds have a lot to answer for," Kelric said. How could they have *lost* Del?

"His speech could have made a difference," Tikal said. "It was even better than what he showed us beforehand. He entreats people to calm down, let Eube and Skolia heal their rifts—and what happens? Some fanatics grab him from the heart of Allied Space Command. It will inflame everyone all over again." He banged his fist against his thigh in frustration. "This group that claims they took him, The Minutemen of Valor—we've never even heard of them."

"I don't care about the speech." Roca's golden face was flushed, her legendary eyes furious. "I don't care about the damned treaty. I just want my son home." She scowled, first at Kelric, then at Barcala. "What the blazes is a 'Minuteman' anyway? A man who does it all in a minute?"

Kelric choked on his laugh. "Mother, for flaming sakes!"

Tikal glanced at Roca. "I do believe you're embarrassing our mighty warlord, Councilor."

Kelric had heard far worse from his female commanders. But none of them were his mother. He decided to pretend her comment was purely innocent. "Minuteman is a historical term from the United States on Earth. They were rebel soldiers chosen for their ability to take up arms fast."

"Anyone who hurts one of my children," Roca said, "is no hero." She regarded Kelric implacably. "They deserve to die."

"Roca," Tikal warned.

She turned her iciest gaze on him. "What?"

"If you tell the Allieds that, it will only inflame matters."

"What I say to you two and what I say in public

are two different things," Roca answered. "But I mean what I say. If these people hurt Del, they'll pay."

Kelric knew her anger was a shield she used to help her deal with her fear for Del. "We'll get him back," he told her. "I swear."

"Yes, well, the question is how," Barcala said.

They had reached two doors that ended the corridor, portals of glass and chrome. Tikal keyed in a code and the doors swung inward under his push. His spacious office lay beyond, with its glass and chrome tables, modern furniture, and an extensive media center taking up one wall.

Tikal strode to the big mesh table he used as a desk and traced his hand across it, shifting around holicons. "Here's another update," he said, reading the three-dimensional glyphs as they formed over the table. "Nothing new." He looked up at Kelric and Roca across the table. "The kidnappers still haven't told us what they want."

"They have what they want," Kelric said. "They ruined his speech. They want people angry, not appeased."

Roca rubbed her eyes, her anger slipping into exhaustion. Kelric recognized the signs; she needed that anger to keep going. He spoke more gently. "It will work out."

"I just don't see how we can go forward with this treaty business," she said.

"We can't give up," Tikal said. "That's what they want. If we stop, we're letting them win."

"And if they kill Del to make their point?" she asked.

"They won't kill him," Tikal said. "It would achieve nothing except starting a war between us and Earth."

"Killing Del would be stupid," Kelric said. "And

they aren't. Everything they've done so far shows they know exactly what they're doing."

"I hope so." Roca took a deep breath. "At least Mac Tyler is with him. He's not alone."

There was that. Kelric liked Del's manager, a former Air Force officer who had gone into the music business after he retired. "Maybe our people have more news." He checked his gauntlet mesh, paging through messages. "The transport we sent to pick him up is in the Solar System. They'll reach Earth in a few hours."

Tikal continued to move glowing images around on his table. "Nothing else new—" He broke off as a flashing red icon appeared. In the same instant, Kelric's gauntlet buzzed and Roca tapped the audio comm in her ear.

"What the hell is *that*?" Tikal flicked his hand through the holo.

"I'm getting an emergency page," Roca said, her head tilted as she listened.

Kelric touched the *receive* toggle on his comm and a message scrolled across his gauntlet screen in red glyphs: *The Ministry for Foreign Affairs of the Palace Protocol Division in the Qox Palace on Glory has contacted the Protocol Division of the Inner Skolian Assembly.* It was the first step in the lengthy dance needed for the Eubian emperor to send a message the Skolian government.

"Hell's bells," Tikal said. "It's a message from Glory."

"From Emperor Jaibriol's protocol people," Roca said.

"They're routing it to both my staff and Dehya's staff," Tikal grumbled. "It's ridiculous. They should just send us the damn message."

Roca smiled at him. "If we don't let them do their thing, Barcala, they get upset."

Kelric only half listened to them as he studied the images accompanying the announcement from Glory that had arrived as a prelude to the message from the emperor. He didn't even know what he was looking for. The glyphs went on and on . . .

Kelric saw what he sought.

It appeared disguised in a frame of artwork. The Traders always included such a border to open a government communiqué. A distinguishing characteristic of such designs, especially for the emperor, was their artistic originality. They were never the same. The greater the beauty, the more they believed it glorified the sender. Kelric had never seen one like this. The intricate work included a pattern so subtle, it was almost invisible. Quis symbols. Jaibriol had sent an answer to the session Dehya and Kelric had left on the table. The emperor must be learning Quis at an incredible rate, to create such a sophisticated response.

Kelric barely listened as the official message wound its way to Tikal and Dehya. It would no doubt be some standard statement, Jaibriol re-iterating what they already knew.

The real message was in those dice patterns.

Dehya's private office glowed in sunrise colors, the walls rosy near the floor and shading into blue at the ceiling. A starry night glimmered on the ceiling. The screens of her mesh stations glowed, gleamed, and glistened around her, alight with images. It was all beautiful, but what she found most captivating was the brilliance of the EI that ran it all. She had been working on this Evolving Intelligence for decades, until it had become an extension of her own mind.

She called it Laplace, after an Earth mathematician who had created radiant equations.

She shifted her weight in her chair. "My guess is that these Minutemen on Earth who grabbed Del aren't connected to whoever attacked Kelric, Del, and myself in Kyle space."

"Why?" Laplace asked. "The Allieds may claim they don't believe telepathy exists, but what their military says to the public and what they know are different matters. They're well aware of what we do with the Kyle, and they are undoubtedly working to learn it themselves."

"The style of the attacks is too different." Worrying about Del was making it hard for her to concentrate, which sent her in circles; the more trouble she had thinking, the more she worried that she couldn't help him, which made it even harder to think.

"Take a breath," Laplace said. "Relax. Clear your mind."

Dehya smiled slightly. "What, are you reading my mind?"

"Over the years, your thought processes have become more predictable."

"I'm glad someone thinks so. Most people say I'm incomprehensible."

"So talk to me," Laplace said. "We'll figure this out."

"The kidnappers acted directly against Del," Dehya said. "It was overt. Direct. Blunt. The other attacks happened in Kyle space. They were abstruse and convoluted."

"More Highton," Laplace said.

"Maybe. But Hightons are only that way with each other, not with those of us they consider slaves. Given that, Del's kidnapping is more what I'd expect from the Traders than the Allieds. But the Kyle attacks were done by a sophisticated psion with training, which the Traders don't have."

Except, of course, Jaibriol Qox. Kelric didn't think Jaibriol would attack them. Dehya was less certain, but not by much. Jaibriol was in the Triad. Her sense of him was distant and unformed, but she was aware of him at the edges of her mind. She didn't think he had done this. Similarly, if he had died while in the Triad, she would have felt the shock as a distant loss, just as she had sensed it when Roca's husband Eldrinson had died while he was a Triad member eleven years ago. She hadn't experienced that for Jaibriol.

"How do you know the Eubians don't have a provider capable of such attacks?" Laplace asked. "They have a Lock command center, and it contains consoles that a trained telop could use to access Kyle space. With enough work, ESComm could hack our Kyle networks."

Dehya grimaced. "They would need a psion nearly as strong as a Ruby. That's incredibly rare. The only reason more than three or four of us exist is because we've deliberately bred for them. Even with that, it's hard to make more. Cloning doesn't work. A woman who isn't a strong psion can't carry one of us to term. Hell, Laplace, I could barely carry my own children, and I *am* a Ruby. If the Traders have a way to make more of us or were fortunate enough to discover a psion with such power, *and* they've figured out how to use the Kyle at that level of sophistication, *and* they've cracked our highest security—" She just shook her head. She couldn't go on.

"It does seem unlikely," Laplace said. "I calculate the probability as tiny. But not zero."

"What it seems is terrifying," Dehya said. "If they

can achieve all that, the only reason they haven't destroyed us yet is because they don't fully realize what they're doing."

"So far, it seems the most likely possibility," Laplace said. "Unless you have another."

Dehya thought for a moment. "The attack against Kelric and me damaged our neural processes. In Del's case, it didn't cause damage, it spurred him to release 'Carnelians Finale.' It looks like the same person did all three attacks, based on the path of their work that we've so far unraveled in web, but we don't know that for certain." She wanted to believe it was a one-time attack that couldn't be repeated, but whatever had caused Del to release "Carnelians Finale" was different enough to suggest more than one source. "Laplace, bring up my analysis of the attack on Kelric. I want the models where I assumed various plans on the part of the attackers and then evolved those plans to see if they could result in what happened to him."

"Done," the EI said. "Do you want me to run those same models on Prince Del-Kurj?"

"That's right. See if they predict what happened to him as well as they do for Kelric."

A line of red glyphs suddenly flashed on Dehya's main screen.

"Well, that's dramatic," she said.

"It's a message from your protocol office," Laplace told her.

She scanned the glyphs. Wryly she said, "It seems the Traders want to elevate us with their glorious correspondence."

"I'm monitoring its progress through our diplomatic channels."

"See if anything in it resembles Quis patterns."

"Checking." Then Laplace said, "I have the results for the analysis on Prince Del-Kurj."

"It failed, didn't it?"

"Yes, it did. I can't use the same model for him that describes what happened to Imperator Skolia. Such a model fails for every scenario, then goes wonky and spews out a lot of mesh code."

Dehya scowled at her mesh screens. "My code never goes wonky."

"All right," Laplace said. "I'm analyzing the non-wonky code it spewed all over. The situation with Del is too different to predict its outcome with the Kelric model."

"It's odd," Dehya mused. "It's as if whoever attacked us left behind a neural signature. The signature of whoever tampered with Del in the Kyle is different than the one for me and Kelric."

"You think two people are involved?"

"Unfortunately, yes, even if it's supposed to look like one," Dehya said. "According to what we've dug up in Kyle space, all three of us had our brains affected at the same time. I was in a Triad Chair on the Orbiter and Kelric was in the War Room, but Del was asleep."

"Maybe the attacks weren't really at the same time."

"Well, he released the song twice, the first time before we were attacked. The Kyle space paths for the two releases are tangled up together. It's hard to separate them because events in the Kyle are related by similarity, not by time." She thumped a panel her with frustration. "How did they get to him? None of us show any evidence of drugs, physical tampering, or anything else. The only possibility that makes sense is that they affected our neural processes through Kyle space. But he almost never goes into the Kyle."

"A psion's mind is more vulnerable during sleep," Light said. "Maybe a telepath reached him on Earth while he slept, and Del went onto the Kyle web without waking up."

"It's possible, I suppose. But who? It would have to be an immensely powerful psion."

"I'm running your models again," Light said. "If you remove the assumption that the tampering came through the Kyle web, they all spew wonky code."

She decided to let the "wonky" go this time. "So either it didn't happen while Del was asleep or my models are drilled."

"I don't believe it's anatomically possible to 'drill' a mesh code," Laplace said. "According to my files on profanity, 'drill' refers to the act of reproduc—"

"I know what it means!" Dehya said, laughing. "You know, you evolving codes create new parts of yourselves all the time by splicing other parts together. That's like reproduction."

"Yes, well, I don't have sexual relations with other codes. By the way, the message from Emperor Jaibriol has finished clearing through the protocol offices."

"Good. Has Kelric contacted you?"

"Yes, he wishes to meet with you at his house. He says, 'Bring your Quis dice.'"

A thought came to her. "Can you code my models for the Kyle attacks into Quis patterns?"

"I can do that. Do you want me to project the models as a game you can play?"

"Yes. But not now. I need to meet with Kelric."

"He's says he'll be home in ten minutes."

Dehya stood up and stretched her arms. "Upload the message from Emperor Jaibriol to my spinal node." She headed for the archway out of her office. "Did you find Quis patterns in it?"

"In a border." Laplace paused. "Did you know that you have a message waiting in your main queue that is labeled as urgent?"

Dehya stopped at the doorway. "No I didn't. What is it?"

"Well, oddly enough, it appears to be a request for an analysis of blood tests."

"Appears? Can't you tell?"

"It's buried in layers of security code."

Baffled, Dehya returned her station, stepping inside the array of screens. "Why ever would someone want me to analyze blood tests?"

"I've no idea. It originated at a Skolian embassy on the Eubian planet called Muze's Helios."

How strange. "File it under 'incoming, top priority.' I'll look at it after I see Kelric."

"Pharaoh Dyhianna, I can't file it. My security codes aren't high enough."

That stopped her cold. "Your codes are my codes. I can access anything." Technically, she couldn't access Kelric's most secured files or those of the Assembly, but she had long ago circumvented their protections.

"It has to be you," Laplace said. "Physically. It wants DNA, fingerprints, and retinal scans."

"That's truly odd." Dehya slid her finger into a slot below the screen. A light played over her eyes while the console analyzed her fingerprint and scraped a skin sample for the DNA check.

A new voice spoke, cold and impersonal. "Identity verified. Invoking Zeta protocol."

"What for?" Dehya asked. Her Zeta protocol involved such a high level of security, even Kelric couldn't break it.

"I'm downloading the message," Laplace said.

"What does it say?"

"Nothing really. It's exactly what I thought, a request for a blood test analysis."

This became more bizarre by the moment. Dehya brought up the message and scanned the layers of code it had accumulated. Why had they sent these tests out for a Skolian analysis? A procedure this simple could be done within the embassy.

Dehya spoke uneasily. "Laplace, analyze the blood tests."

"I'm not a medical unit."

"The procedure is trivial. Any EI could do it. Hell, an AI could." Dehya slowly sat back down. "Like the AI at the medical center on Sandstorm." Except that AI hadn't returned any results to the embassy, it had instead forwarded this message. From Sandstorm, the message had followed an ever more complex path, ending up deep within the ISC mesh, which had sent it to her.

"Analysis finished," Laplace said.

"Put it on the screen."

"Projecting."

Dehya read the glyphs—and read them again. And again.

"Gods almighty," she whispered.

XIX
Revelations

Ships came into many hubs on the planet Glory. Taken altogether, the ports served billions. Some were military, others civilian, and some served both. Some were only for Aristos; others, larger and less extravagant, were for taskmakers. Commercial hubs catered to corporations, trade ports catered to the slave trade, and the cargo ports were for shipping goods other than people.

One small port was unlisted on any public, private, or commercial system. Hidden high in the Jaizire Mountains, it served only one person. The emperor.

Jaibriol stood on an upper level of the exclusive terminal and watched the ship from Muze's Helios land. It was an ESComm transport, its main purpose to carry three members of Admiral Muze's family, all high-ranking officers in the Eubian Fleet. As an afterthought, or so it appeared, Jaibriol had asked them to send along the three prisoners from the Skolian embassy.

You have no idea, he thought as the ship landed. **You have no idea what you carry.**

Unfortunately, neither did he.

Aliana was suffocating.

It was the Hightons. She felt claustrophobic when they were near, as if she had too little air to breathe. Three of them stood here in the shuttle, ESComm officers, tall and cold-faced, their skin as white as a precious stone. Their black hair glittered, splintering the harsh light in the shuttle. Their red eyes looked like crystals. They were beautiful in a terrible way, like heartless gods who could kill with a mere glance and would neither care nor even realize if that happened.

Now that the shuttle had landed, the Aristos stood by the hatchway and talked among themselves, ignoring everyone else. Aliana had no idea if this was normal, that they could step into this little ship, fly down to the planet from the bigger ship that had taken them here from Muze's Helios, and just walk off the shuttle. She had some hazy idea that landing on a new world involved many procedures and long lines, but nothing like that seemed to be involved here.

Six ESComm soldiers were in the ship, including the pilot and co-pilot, who both had dull black hair and rusty-red eyes, which made them look part Aristo, like her stepfather. They were far more refined than Caul, though. No one spoke to her. They barely seemed to notice her. She stood alone at the back of the shuttle, feeling trivial.

They hadn't let her and Red sit together on the way down. He was standing now on the other side of the craft, flanked by two soldiers. Someone had cut his hair, brushed it until it shone, and put him in clothes cut from a dark blue velvet that shimmered, both the pants and the long-sleeved shirt. His diamond wrist guards sparkled beneath his cuffs, and his shirt was cut to show his jeweled collar. His clothes, slave restraints, demeanor, everything about him was so much more exorbitant than anything Aliana had ever imagined, it was hard to believe he was real. Seeing him this way gave her a tendril of hope, though. Surely they wouldn't go to so much trouble to make him look like a valuable provider if Admiral Muze just intended to kill him.

They had given Aliana a functional blue jumpsuit to wear, nothing at all fancy. No one paid attention to her as long as she obeyed and stayed out of their way. She wanted to spy on them with her mind, but she couldn't risk opening her mental fortress. It was better that way; she feared the mental pressure of the Aristos would crush her and Red if she let her defenses weaken.

She still had no idea what had happened to Tide. She wanted so much to see him, to make sure he was all right. Except he wouldn't be all right. They had probably started interrogating him. She flinched inside, wanting to find him, wanting to help, anything, but she was just a low-level taskmaker with no value, no resources, nothing.

An orb glowed on the pilot's controls, shedding gold light. The pilot leaned over it and spoke in a low voice. Someone answered in Highton, but Aliana couldn't make out the words. She watched Red for clues. He was closer to the front and he knew Highton well. When his face paled, she felt as if the ground had dropped out from under them.

The pilot went to the Hightons and spoke with

respect. They nodded, their icy perfection never thawing. With no other warning, the hull next to them shimmered and opened to the day outside. Radiance poured into the ship, tinged with gold, purer than the sunlight of Muze's Helios. A patch of sky showed beyond the hatchway, its color too blue, without the faded quality of the sky back home. Aliana didn't see any other airlock, not what she expected, the kind with two solid doors. If that shimmer was an airlock, then the embassy used them even on the planet. That they needed airlocks in an embassy was a sobering comment on their lack of safety.

Someone touched her arm. Startled, she turned to see one of the soldiers. "Stay with me when we leave the ship," he told her. "Don't talk. Kneel when it's appropriate."

She wanted to ask how she would know when it was appropriate, but he looked so severe, she just nodded.

Two soldiers left the shuttle. She had little doubt that they went first so if any danger turned up outside, they would be killed instead of the Hightons. Apparently nothing happened, because the three Aristos disembarked, their grey uniforms crackling as they moved. Red's guards escorted him out next, and his clothes glistened in the gold sunlight slanting through the hatchway.

Aliana's guard went forward and she followed him, squinting as they neared the exit, not because the sunlight bothered her, but because . . . well, she didn't know why. She wanted to protect herself, and squinting was pretty much the extent of her ability to do anything. That and maybe her mental fortress, if it was even doing anything.

The landing field was a silvery expanse decorated with blue lines and elegant gold and red symbols where the lines intersected. It was lovely and unexpected. The wind blew through her hair, ruffling the gold curls that fell around her shoulders and down her back. The air smelled impossibly pure and clear, reminding her of sweet water running over rocks. Mountains rose high on all sides, peak after peak carpeted in green forests thicker than any foliage she had ever seen. So much sensation, so much richness. She needed time to absorb it all.

The guard drew her to a halt. She saw why; up ahead, the three Hightons had stopped. A newcomer had joined them on the landing field, a man who looked like them, except his uniform had more gold, especially the bars on his shoulders. The four of them stood talking, looking so much alike, Aliana wondered if they were clones. Probably not; they weren't identical. But she would have bet they were kin.

Red's guards stopped him well back from the Hightons. The moment she saw his face, she knew what Highton had come to meet the shuttle. It wasn't only Red's fear that told her, but also the hatred. He was staring at the man who had tortured him for over a year and then, on a whim, condemned him to die.

Aliana clenched her fists, struggling for control. She wanted to run at Admiral Muze, attack him, do to him what he had done to Red, make him *suffer.* A few months ago she might have tried, even knowing they would shoot her before she went a few steps. But she was learning to control her temper. She didn't know what she could do for Red, but getting herself killed wouldn't help him.

Beyond the Hightons, another shuttle stood on the field gleaming like platinum. It was so sleek, Aliana realized it was artwork rather than a real ship. Or at least she thought so until an oval shimmered open in its hull and a flight of stairs morphed down to the ground. Four men in black uniforms with carnelian red on their cuffs appeared in the hatchway. They descended to the field and stood flanking the stairs, two on each side, giants with emotionless faces and powerful forms. They weren't Aristos; none had any hint of glittering hair or red eyes. They wore large gauntlets packed with tech, and silvery mesh piping threaded their uniforms. It all made them seem inhuman. And yet she recognized something about them, something familiar . . .

It hit her like a cold wind. They were like *Tide*. It wasn't only their builds, but the way they held themselves, as if they were poised to attack or defend. These were Razers, the secret police and bodyguards of the Aristos. So who were they guarding?

When the answer to her question appeared in the hatchway of the platinum flyer, Aliana understood exactly what her guard had meant about kneeling. She gaped for one second at the celebrated face of the man and then dropped to her knees, bowing her head. The emperor had come to meet them.

No sound broke the silence except the keening wind. Aliana couldn't absorb it all, so she decided to pretend it was perfectly normal for the greatest man alive to show up. Once she put that idea into her mind, she could think again. She raised her gaze, keeping her head down so no one would see she wasn't looking at the ground. The emperor was standing with Admiral Muze and the other Hightons, his four bodyguards hulking around him. Everyone else was on their knees, including the bodyguards of the other Hightons. Her own guard was kneeling next to her, reduced to the same slavish show of obligatory worship as everyone else.

Eventually the emperor lifted his fingers slightly and the soldiers all stood up. A low tone hummed on the gauntlet of the guard next to Aliana.

"You may rise," he told her in a low voice.

Aliana stood up. So did everyone else at exactly the same time, as if the emperor's presence had turned them into a machine. Jaibriol Qox the Third. Who would have thought she would come this close to the greatest being alive? He looked younger than she expected. She was glad he was so far away; it meant she didn't have to struggle against the pressure of his mind. She felt Admiral Muze even at this distance, a faint pressure adding to that of the other Hightons. The emperor didn't register, though. Or maybe all their minds blended together to create a single miasma of misery.

Two thoughts came to Aliana. The first was that she had never heard the words "miasma of misery" in her life. Yet not only had she thought them, but she understood them. The other thought was that for one insane instant, she was certain the emperor *knew* she was there.

Kelric sunk onto the sofa in his living room and sat, his booted feet planted wide, his elbows resting on his knees, his forehead on his palms. So tired. He couldn't stop thinking about Del. Surely he would sense it if his brother had died. Del still lived. He had to believe that. But in what condition?

He wanted to go to Earth, throw away caution, forget he was the Imperator, and find his brother. Such a rash act would play into the hands of Del's kidnappers, further disrupting the peace process. Gods, it was one thing after another, like being struck again and again, until he felt so worn down he wondered if the summit would ever happen. No one wanted it: not his people, not the Traders, not the Allieds. What the hell was wrong with them? Did they *want* to keep fighting until they wiped out the human race? If they couldn't even establish the terms of a treaty they had already signed, maybe *homo sapiens* didn't deserve to keep existing. But damned if he would give up. He would find a way to rescue his brother, meet with Jaibriol, and make the treaty work, and he would do it without anyone dying from assassination.

Gods only knew what Jaibriol Qox was dealing with. And Tarquine, his empress. Kelric didn't want to worry about Tarquine. He didn't love her. Sometimes he had hated her. But they had been lovers, no matter how much he wanted to forget. Why she had paid such an exorbitant price to buy an aging man as her provider, he would never understand. He had escaped and come home to claim his title while she went on to marry Jaibriol Qox, the epitome of youth and vitality.

"Kelric?" The soft voice came from across the room.

He looked up with a start. Dehya was standing in the entrance of his living room, a small figure within a huge archway. He didn't need to ask how she entered; he never closed his home to her. She watched him with her sunrise eyes, so large and distant. Her face was paler than usual, her skin almost translucent. He had intended to meet with her hours ago, to go over the message from Jaibriol, but the time had somehow slipped by.

"What's wrong?" He stood up, rubbing the small of his back. "You look as if you've seen the death of the human race." He meant it as a joke, but it didn't sound funny.

"Ah, gods, Kelric," she said.

He went over to her. "Is it Del?"

She shook her head.

Kelric waited. When she said nothing, he thought, **Dehya? What is it?**

"I can't," she said aloud. "I've been in the Kyle web for hours. My mind is worn out."

"Have you been searching for Del?"

"All day." She had that strange distant look, as if she were still partially in the Kyle. "I've also been running models, trying to understand what happened to the three of us."

"Did you find anything?"

"Clues." Her luminous eyes were so wide. "That's not what I need to talk to you about."

A woman's rich voice came from the hall beyond the archway. "Kelric?"

He looked past Dehya. Roca was coming up the wide corridor. As Dehya turned around, Roca squinted at Kelric, then turned to Dehya, her sister. "He looks fine."

"I am fine," Kelric said. "Why wouldn't I be?"

"I sent her a message that she had to come right away." Dehya sounded exhausted. She hadn't even pulled back her hair; it fell in a lustrous but tangled black sweep over her arms and down her back to her waist. "I wanted to talk with you two first before we told anyone else."

Roca joined them. "Is it Del?" Her voice caught. "Please don't tell me it's bad news."

"It's not Del," Kelric said. "I've no idea what this is about."

"I received a coded message from ISC on my personal account," Dehya said. "Highest security level. It came from Trader space."

He stared at her. "Why the *blazes* would ISC send you private messages from the Eubians?"

Dehya paced away from him, into the living room. As he turned to watch her, she stopped and faced them. "It's because of a hidden monitor I set up on the interstellar meshes. It caught a message. A Skolian embassy on the world Muze's Helios sent a blood test offworld, asking to have the results analyzed."

"Why send it offworld?" Roca asked. "Analyzing blood tests is trivial."

"It was for a Eubian taskmaker."

"Why ask us to look at it?" Kelric said. "Who sent it?"

"A Jagernaut Secondary called Lyra Lensmark."

"I know Lensmark," he said. "She's a good officer. Calm, tough, rational." Lyra also had more diplomatic skills than most Jagernauts. That was why he had assigned her to an embassy in such a sensitive location.

"She was being careful," Dehya said. "I think."

"You think?" Roca asked.

"The taskmaker asked for asylum," Dehya said. "She's a psion. But I don't think that's why Lensmark sent the blood tests offworld."

It was starting to make sense to Kelric. "Lensmark was smart to seek a Skolian facility. I wouldn't trust ESComm to respect the Paris Accord if they found out she was harboring a psion."

"I think that's exactly how it was meant to look," Dehya said, her voice strained, like leaves blowing over a distant plain.

"Appears?" Roca said. "Dehya, what are you trying to tell us? Whatever is going on in your mind, either I can't follow it or else you're blocking me."

"I'm sorry." Dehya took a breath. "I've been in the web so deep, I'm having trouble pulling out."

"You're not *connected* to the web," Roca said.

"I know." Dehya's voice sounded distant. "But part of me is there."

Unlike the rest of his family, Kelric had seen Dehya like this before, when she had been working long hours in the mesh and was struggling to come out. He had discovered that direct, literal questions helped her focus.

"What did Lensmark write on the request?" he asked.

"Not much," Dehya said. "The girl isn't a provider, but Lensmark is sure she's a psion."

"So what's the problem?" Roca asked.

Dehya looked from Kelric to Roca, her face as delicate as porcelain. "The girl has gold skin. Gold eyes. Gold hair. She's tall. Very tall. And strong. Much too strong for a provider."

Kelric felt as if she had punched him in the stomach. He didn't want to hear this. It had to be coincidence.

The blood drained from Roca's face. "A lot of providers have gold coloring."

"That isn't what set off my monitors." Dehya's voice drifted eerily. She shook her head as if to reset her mind. "My zeta monitor is hidden throughout the meshes. Its main portion sleeps most of the time. It wakes only if its outermost shell detects certain genetic markers."

Kelric's pulse ratcheted up. "Ruby genes? Is that what you're trying to say?"

"I've analyzed the tests over and over," Dehya said. "They give the same results every time. It's probably why the girl's mother got pregnant; Ruby genetics play havoc with birth control methods." Turning to Roca, she took a deep breath. "Somehow, seventeen years ago, your son Althor fathered a daughter with a Eubian woman."

"No." Roca's voice cracked. "That's impossible."

"The tests give a 99.7% probability that he's her father."

"How could Althor have a Trader family?" Kelric said. "Even if he did somehow manage it, he'd never leave them with the Eubians."

"Unless he didn't know," Dehya said.

"You're saying I have a grandchild who is a *Trader?*" Roca asked.

The pharaoh closed her eyes, and for an instant her body looked translucent.

"Dehya, come back," Kelric said.

She opened her eyes. Her gaze was so distant, he wondered if she would phase out of real space. How long had she been submerged in the Kyle trying to verify the truth of this claim?

"The girl has all the Ruby genes," Dehya said. "All of them. *Every* one." Her eyes were huge, like green pools. "She is a Ruby. An heir in the direct line of succession to the Triad."

"No." Kelric didn't want this to be true. He didn't want to discover that a member of his family, one he had never even met, was trapped with the Traders. If ESComm realized they had a Ruby psion, they wouldn't give a flying drill about peace, not even with Jaibriol at the helm. They could make a Kyle web, break the Skolian monopoly on faster-than-light communications, and conquer the Imperialate.

"It's no mistake," Dehya said. "You can't fake that genetic signature. It's too complex."

Roca crossed her arms and scowled at Dehya. "You're forgetting something, aren't you?"

Dehya tilted her head. "What?"

"Althor didn't like women."

"He liked women fine," Dehya said.

"Oh, you know what I mean," Roca said. "Why do you think he was in a three-way marriage with Vaz and that boy Coop? He only married Vaz because the Assembly wanted him to have a wife. It was Coop he wanted."

"He has another daughter," Dehya pointed out. "Eristia and her mother Syreen lived here for years, and Syreen still does. Althor may not have married Syreen, but he loved them both."

"Yes, well, why do you think he didn't marry Syreen?" Roca demanded.

"He went both ways," Dehya said. "You know that, Roca."

"That's only because the Assembly was always pressuring him to get married, make babies, all that diddlecarp. He was trying to make everyone else happy and making himself miserable." She lowered her arms, suddenly looking very tired. "He just wanted his own life."

Kelric had never understood why the universe had seemed determined to fuss over his brother's sexual preferences. It wasn't anyone's business but Althor's. But the Assembly had been unceasingly annoyed that one of their invaluable Ruby Heirs didn't want to make Ruby babies.

Regardless, though, Althor made up his own mind. "He married Vaz because he liked her," Kelric said. "If he had an affair with this woman before that, then he cared for her, too." He thought of his brother's military records. "He did some covert work among the Eubians fifteen to twenty years ago." Althor had died eleven years ago, in the Radiance War, so what Dehya described wasn't impossible. "ISC regulations wouldn't allow him to bring back a Trader citizen, and if someone had broken his cover, he would have acted to deflect attention from his lover. So yes, he would have had to leave. But if he had known he had a daughter, he would never have left her or the mother behind."

"All right," Roca said. "Let's say, for the sake of argument, that this girl is a genuine Ruby Heir. Then we *must* get her out of Trader space. The mother, too, if we can."

"It won't work," Dehya said miserably.

"Why not?" Kelric asked. "You said the girl was at the embassy."

"I've been investigating," Dehya said. "ESComm broke in and took her, along with a provider who wanted asylum and a Razer who had asked to defect."

"Hell and damnation!" Kelric wanted to punch the wall. "A *Razer* wanted to defect? And we lost him, too?"

"Yes." Dehya lifted her hands, then dropped them. "The provider, a boy, belonged to Admiral Erix Muze."

"If they broke into the embassy," Roca said coldly, "they violated the Paris Accord."

"They pulverized it," Dehya said. "Roca, we could use your expertise as Foreign Affairs Councilor on that, to make sure none of the embassy staff are harmed or taken into custody."

"Count on it," Roca said. "What about the Eubians?"

"The provider, Althor's daughter, and the Razer were all sent to Admiral Muze," Dehya said. "He found out about them because someone recognized his provider from footage of a street brawl between the girl and two of Muze's illegitimate grandchildren. Apparently Althor's daughter was protecting the boy."

"That's impossible," Kelric said. "A low-level slave would never fight high-level taskmakers. They're bred and conditioned from birth to obey."

"If she's Althor's daughter," Roca said, "she's a far different breed than the usual taskmaker."

"I couldn't find much about her," Dehya said. "She's never registered on our spy monitors. If Lensmark hadn't found a way to warn us, we would never have known she existed."

Kelric felt heavy. He walked away from them, deeper into his living room. He didn't know how to add this incredible development to everything else that weighed on him.

"Kelric?" Dehya said.

He turned to face her. "You and I need to play Quis."

"I know," she said.

"For flaming sake." Roca glared at them. "Your answer to this mess is to play *dice*?"

Dehya smiled at her sister. "It helps us plan."

"First you two nearly die. Then Del. Now this." Roca's voice cracked. "It's too much."

Kelric came back over to them. "We'll figure it out."

"You need to give up this idea of meeting Jaibriol Qox face-to-face," Roca told him.

"Why?" Kelric asked. "This has nothing to do with that."

"Well, fine," his mother said. "You can accept his invitation to have the summit on Glory, and while we're there, miraculously avoiding their attempts to make us all prisoners, you can rescue this Ruby Heir we had no idea existed, grabbing her out from under the nose of Erix Muze. Hell, Kelric, while you're at it, you can create a few new galaxies, too."

He laid his hand on her shoulder. "We *will* solve this."

"I hope so," she said softly. "Because I don't know how much more of this we can take."

"We'll manage," Kelric said. "We'll fix it."

He just wished he knew how.

XX
The Next Move

The Mentation Chamber was tucked into the Orbiter's hull, close enough to the poles of the rotating sphere that the gravity was significantly lower than Earth standard and the floor slanted sharply. The outer surface of the chamber was dichromesh glass reinforced to withstand the radiant emptiness of space. It curved outward and offered a glorious view of jeweled nebulae in the deep black of the interstellar void. Dehya stood before the window, remembering the words of an ancient poet. His identity had faded in the blur of history, but one line of his works survived: *Magnificent sea forever bright, forever cold and forever night.*

The click of dice came from behind her, followed by Kelric's musing voice. "The seeds of the game we sent Jaibriol Qox are all here in the patterns he sent us."

Dehya turned around. Kelric was seated at a carved table, which stood on a dais that compensated for the tilt of the floor. Quis structures covered the table, reproducing the session Jaibriol Qox had coded into his last message. Kelric was studying them with that incredible gift of his to understand patterns. Dehya liked watching him. It was hard to understand why he terrified people. Couldn't they see the luminous intellect and affectionate man inside that huge frame? Yes, he was a phenomenal warrior. But she would always remember how she had first known him, as a baby snuggled in a sling on Roca's hip, a golden cherub gurgling and happy. He had grown into an inimitable man, but she understood the gentler side he hid within.

"It's like a frozen frame of the game," he said, intent on the dice, his face bathed in starlight. "We sent him a frame of ours, he played that game, and he sent us this frame."

Dehya came over and sat across from him. "The problem is figuring out how he produced these patterns. I see the seeds, yes, but modeling how he reached this point in the game is difficult."

Kelric looked up. "The closer we get to figuring out his moves, the better we can understand his intent."

She mulled over the patterns evolving in her mind. "You know, we've assumed he played solitaire. But I don't think he did."

Kelric regarded her uneasily. "That would mean he taught someone else." He motioned at the structures. "Someone talented enough to help him come up with this work of art."

"Who do you think?" Dehya asked. "You know the Hightons better than most." She thought of Tarquine Iquar. It didn't surprise her that Jaibriol had married the Finance Minister. True, an emperor was expected to choose a beautiful young Highton for his empress, the flower of supposed maidenhood, after which she dedicated her life to fawning on him. That was the antithesis of Tarquine Iquar. But if Jaibriol truly was the son of Kelric's sister Soz, and he had grown up on a world with no other human beings except his family, then his *only* model of an adult woman during his formative years was a force of nature who had become one of the most formidable warrior queens in the history of the human race. It was no wonder he chose Tarquine as his wife.

"The empress," Dehya said. "Jaibriol taught her Quis."

Kelric scowled darkly. "Then gods help the human race."

Dehya couldn't help but smile. "Don't look so dire."

"Quis was developed by the women who rule the Twelve Estates on Coba." His metallic face showed alarm, which in Kelric's understated universe could mean he was envisioning a disaster of unmitigated proportions. "It's how they establish their authority. And Tarquine Iquar could leave any of them in the dust when it comes to political acumen and intrigues. If she realizes the power of Quis, who knows what she could do."

"You put a lot of trust into Jaibriol Qox when you taught him Quis."

His thought came to her mind like a tap the door. **Dehya?**

She eased down her barriers. *Our Jagernaut body-guards are outside this chamber.*

I turned on a cyberlock tuned to our brains, he answered. **It surrounds this chamber. Even if they were strong enough to catch hints**

of our thoughts from outside, which they probably aren't, the field would block them.

Dehya nodded. It was a good idea. The cyberlock affected the neural processes of anyone who crossed the field from either within or without. On its lowest setting, it caused vertigo. On its highest setting, it fatally disrupted neural structure in the brain. The one Kelric had activated affected neither him nor her because they both had a key for it within their brains. Designed from their own neurons, it knew to protect them. The cyberlock affected neural firings, so it would also veil their thoughts from any telepaths outside its field, providing an extra layer of security.

How many people know you taught Jaibriol Qox this dice game? she asked.

Just you.

No one else?

Tarquine Iquar, apparently. He paused. **I taught him Quis by opening my mind and dumping the rules for the game into his. We shared thoughts during that time. He has great strength of character. I don't believe he would betray us.**

Maybe not deliberately. That doesn't mean he won't. Or that his wife won't.

He could use it to his advantage, that's true. So can we. A dangerous glint came into his eyes. **And no one plays Quis as well as I do.**

Dehya smiled. *You shouldn't be so insecure about your ability.*

Ah well. He didn't look the least bit abashed.

She finally put into words what they both knew but never said. *Jaibriol is part of the Triad.*

Kelric met her gaze. **Yes.**

Yes. One simple word. *Yes, the leader of our greatest enemies is part of our ruling Triad.*

We must meet with him in person, she thought. A face-to-face meeting was the only way they could truly communicate with the third Triad member. By telepathy.

Dehya brushed her fingers along the table. A section slid out to her right, an opalescent screen with colorful holicons floating above it. She flicked her fingers through various menus until she reached her workspace on this Quis session.

"Laplace, attend," she said.

"Attending," her EI answered.

"Access all files on Tarquine Iquar," Dehya said. "Draw from every source you can find, including my accounts, Assembly accounts, anywhere."

"Include all ISC files," Kelric said. "You have full access on my authority."

"Security verified," Laplace said. "What shall I do with the data?"

"Use it to create a profile for a Quis player," Dehya said. "Then re-run all my models for the game on this table with Tarquine Iquar as a second player, starting with the initial Quis session and evolving to this one. Give me the result that best matches the session here."

"Analyzing," Laplace told her.

Within moments, a holographic Quis game appeared on the mesh screen. Laplace said, "I was able to play a game that evolves to match the one on your table exactly."

"Gods help us," Kelric muttered. "He taught her Quis."

Luminous glyphs appeared on the screen, offering data with the words they represented and also in their dimensionality and the way their colors shaded through blue and rose. Studying them, Dehya said, "That's odd."

"What is?" Kelric asked.

"I think the empress left hints about herself in her moves, probably unintentionally."

Kelric tapped the table and a mesh screen slid out to his right, mirroring the one Dehya had summoned. He spoke to the air. "Show me the moves you predict were made by the players Jaibriol and Tarquine, starting from the first Quis session and ending at the one here."

Quis holos appeared and evolved as if players were moving the pieces. Kelric was so intent on the game, he seemed in a trance. But then he said, "You're right. She's here. She's mourning."

"Mourning?" Dehya hadn't caught that. "Who?"

Kelric spoke quietly. "The death of their son."

Good gods. Had Jaibriol finally sired the Highton Heir? "We've nothing on the birth of an heir to the Carnelian Throne. Given the pressure they're under to produce one, you'd think they would announce it to the universe."

"It's all so vague." Kelric continued to study the game. "I doubt they meant to put any of it into the session."

As Dehya watched the moves evolve, a picture formed in her mind, enhanced by Kelric's insights. "The child wasn't born yet. It died very recently. That's why it affected their dice."

"Good gods." Kelric looked up at her. "Are you getting a date for the child's death?"

A chill went up Dehya's back. "The same time you and I were nearly assassinated."

"That's one hell of a coincidence."

"Or not."

"Even if Jaibriol had died, it shouldn't have affected us so dramatically," Kelric said. "We probably would have sensed his passing. But it wouldn't have almost killed us."

Dehya nodded. "It seems more likely someone tried to kill us all at the same time."

"Why time the attempts to coincide? It just looks suspicious."

"Maybe it wasn't the same person. One assassin might have used the work of another."

"Whoever attacked us knew a great deal about ISC security," Kelric said. "Whoever attacked Jaibriol's child had to know similar about ESComm. If they are working together to kill both us and Jaibriol Qox, then we're all in a hell of a lot of trouble."

She regarded him bleakly. "Or it could be a double-agent. But who would want *both* the Highton and Ruby Heirs dead?"

Someone who knows Jaibriol is a member of the Triad, Kelric thought.

Could you tell, when you linked with him on Earth, if anyone else knew?

No one. I think Tarquine realizes he's a Ruby. Probably Corbal Xir also knows that much.

Maybe one of them tried to kill him.

Not Tarquine, I don't think, Kelric thought. **Maybe Xir. If Jaibriol dies without an heir, Corbal becomes emperor.**

He wouldn't have to kill the child, just reveal

that Jaibriol isn't a full Highton. The Aristos would never let his child rule, then.

Before I lived among the Traders, I'd have agreed. Now I'm not sure. To them, bloodline is everything. Kelric touched a ruby sphere in their Quis structures. **They wouldn't let a Ruby psion rule, it's true. But a child who legitimately descends from Eube Qox and is more than half Highton, so he's not a psion? Gods only know. Tarquine would certainly never consent to her child losing the throne.** With a grimace, he added, **One thing is for certain: it would be one unholy mess.**

So killing the child might be the simpler solution.

Possibly.

Wryly she said, *Or we could be completely wrong.*

True.

This much is clear from the dice, Dehya thought. *The loss of their son affected them deeply.*

Family is important to Jaibriol. It's crushing him. Kelric let her see his memory of Jaibriol, the love the emperor had felt for his family and his loneliness at losing them.

No wonder he's mourning, she thought. *It must be killing him, being part of the Triad, surrounded by Aristos, with no respite.*

Ai, Kelric murmured. **It's why I gave him Quis.**

An idea was forming in her mind. *How did Soz meet Jaibriol's father?*

I'm not sure. On the planet Delos, I think.

Kelric, listen. Everything in his Quis suggests that if we can find a way to let him save face with the Aristos, he'll agree to our proposal for the summit. He's given us everything we need to find an answer we can live with, too. She waved her hand over the dice. *It's all here, who he needs to convince among his key people and what objections they will have.*

It's an act of trust that he is telling us so much about his key advisors. He paused. **Are you thinking we should suggest meeting on Delos instead of Earth?**

He should be the one to suggest it. His advisors will never agree if they think it's our idea. And we need to give him ways to counter their arguments. Make them think they're putting one over on us by agreeing to this.

Kelric picked up an opal ring and threaded it into the structure of a tower. **Let's see what we can come up with.**

So they planned their next moves in an interstellar game of Quis.

Del lifted his head into complete blackness. Where . . . ?

"Mac?" he mumbled. "Are you here?"

"Yes." His manager's voice came from nearby in the dark. "How do you feel?"

Del sat up, groggy and disoriented. "Like someone hit me in the head."

"Are you injured?"

"I don't think so. Where is this?"

"I don't know," Mac said. "They knocked us both out. I woke up here."

"*Who* knocked us out?" Del rubbed his neck, sore from sleeping on the corrugated floor.

"Jett Masters and her people. I don't know who

they're working for." A rustle came from nearby, Mac sitting up it sounded like. "Someone opened a panel a while back and left some food and water, if you're hungry. But that's it. No one has come in here or spoken to us."

"I couldn't eat right now," Del said. "At least it smells good." He inhaled. "It's strange. Like someone is baking a cake."

Mac grunted. "I didn't know people still did that."

"It's a big fad in Ricki's crowd. Genuine baking, mostly because no one knows how."

"Ricki must be going nuts, worrying about you."

"I know." Del thought of his wife, her streaming blond hair, giant blue eyes, and voluptuous body. She looked like an angel, became a seductress in his arms, and turned into a devil in the cutthroat universe of high-powered entertainment conglomerates. He could sense her even from far away, like a distant song. Which was supposed to be impossible, but he didn't care, because it was true. "She's upset. Mad and scared, but she won't let anyone see how afraid she is. If I were these people who kidnapped us, I would be more afraid of her than anyone's military."

Mac gave a dry laugh. "Yeah, I know what you mean."

Del felt around in the dark. When his hand hit a wall, he scooted over and sat against it for support. After a few minutes, when his stomach settled, he said, "I don't get it. What do they expect to accomplish by kidnapping us?"

"To undermine your speech about 'Carnelians Finale,' I'd imagine," Mac said.

"Blasted song," Del muttered. "I meant every word of it. Do you have any idea how hard it was for me to make that speech? But damn it, what I was singing about is never going to stop unless we quit trying to kill each other. What do these people want, more war?"

"They don't trust the Traders." Mac sounded tired.

"Neither do I. But grabbing me doesn't do any good." Del hated to imagine what his family was thinking now. He caused them no end of grief, even when he was doing his best to live his life in a way that would honor their principles as well as his own.

"Jett Masters and her people are real Allied officers, not imposters," Mac said. "I've seen their records. But Allied Space Command would never sanction this operation. I'd wager some other group planted Jett and the others in ASC."

"How extensive do you think their organization is?" Del asked. If this group that had taken them had a strong foothold among the Allieds, it didn't bode well for Skolian relations with Earth.

"I've no idea," Mac said.

"I wonder if they had anything to do with releasing 'Carnelians Finale.'" Del still couldn't believe he had done it. He wished he could remember. Dehya believed someone had tricked him. Even that seemed impossible; he didn't have enough knowledge about the networks to put his song out there with such wide coverage.

"Jett Masters certainly seemed affected by your song," Mac said.

"See, that's what I don't get," Del said. "Why would Allied military types react so much to a song about my family? They have no stake in Skolian-Trader affairs, not unless we get dragged into another war and they have to fight. You'd think they'd want peace. It keeps them alive."

"I guess they believe the Traders are duping your people."

"Maybe they aren't from Earth." It never ceased to amaze Del that he sang in the birthplace of the human race. For millennia, Earth had been a myth among his people. Then one day, Earth's children had showed up, their lost siblings. And now he lived here, where the sky seemed the right shade of blue even though he had grown up on a world with a lavender sky. Everything here felt right, the air, the sunrises, the gravity—

Gravity?

"We're not on Earth!" Del said. "The gravity is too light."

"I'll be damned," Mac said. "You're right! That must be why I feel queasy. I get spacesick from Coriolis forces. We're must be on a ship that's rotating to create a sense of gravity."

"Great," Del said, scowling. "Just fantastic. We're in space." He climbed to his feet, leaning on the wall. "You know, this could be the bulkhead of a cargo hold."

"I explored while you were sleeping," Mac said tiredly. "The walls are smooth. I couldn't even find the seams of a doorway or the panel that delivered food."

It worried Del that Mac sounded so drained. Although his manager looked like a robust man in his forties, Mac was seventy and slowing down each year. "Hey, are you all right?"

"Just my stomach," Mac said. "I'll be fine."

Del wasn't sure he believed him. It was another mark against whoever had kidnapped them, that they had dragged Mac into this.

Del checked the hold, but he didn't find anything,

either. It was dark, no hint of light, which was probably deliberate, to keep them off balance and confused.

Off balance . . .

"That's it!" Del said.

"Did you find something?" Mac asked.

"I realized something about 'Carnelians Finale.'" He headed toward Mac, moving his hands in front of him. "Say something, so I don't run into you."

"You sound like you're right in front of me."

No kidding. Del stepped to the side and walked into a slanting bulkhead, thumping his forehead. Wincing, he slid down and sat with his back against the wall. "Whoever put us in here is probably listening to everything we say."

"Probably," Mac said. "Does that mean you aren't going to tell me what you realized?"

"Not now. But I will." Del turned his thoughts over and around. He, Dehya, and Kelric had all been attacked. It had nearly killed them, yet hardly affected him at all. A trail in Kyle space led to him, with a "fingerprint" exactly like a neurological map of his brain, all braided into the paths for Kelric and Dehya. The record of his operations in the Kyle showed him releasing "Carnelians Finale" twice, the first time when the song initially hit the meshes and then again when Dehya and Kelric were attacked. The data about the first release hadn't appeared separately; it was tangled up with the data for the second release. That was how the Kyle worked; subject matter rather than spacetime coordinates determined location, so even though Del had released the song twice, it showed up as one Kyle pathway because both releases involved the same process. Del didn't like it. It seemed an independent verification should exist of the first time he had released the song.

"Unless the first time never happened," Del said.

"Hmmm... what didn't?" Mac sounded half-asleep.

"I'll tell you later." Damn! He needed to talk to Dehya. What if the Kyle path incriminating him was fake? Normally Dehya could tell. But it was tangled up with what happened to her, and she had nearly died. Even so, his idea seemed unlikely. Only someone with a detailed neurological scan of his brain could fake his neural signature, which meant his private doctors or a top ISC officer. He couldn't imagine them committing treason, besides which, they would never have been so clumsy about it. If not for what had happened to Dehya and Kelric, Del would have thought the evidence implicating him was an amateurish subterfuge. But to isolate Dehya in Kyle space and explode Kelric's links using his own brain required an expert with a terrifyingly sophisticated knowledge of the Kyle.

"Grasping at straws," Del muttered.

Mac yawned and shifted in the dark. "Heh?"

"It's an ancient English idiom." Del hesitated. "Mac—"

"Hmmm?"

"I don't want to die out here for someone's fanatical politics."

"I doubt they'll kill us. It won't get them anything."

"Maybe they've demanded a ransom."

"Possibly."

"They might turn us over to the Traders."

"If they like your song, I doubt they're Traders. That song excoriates the Aristos."

"Yeah, but it works to their advantage to make people mad even if they hate the song." Del snorted. "Hell, I wouldn't have been surprised if the Traders had released it."

Then it hit Del. Someone else might have a scan of his brain. Lord Axil Tarex, the Aristo who had captured and tortured him—the Highton who had provoked Del to sing "Carnelians Finale." Tarex could have taken one without Del knowing while Del had been his prisoner.

"Maybe that's it," he said.

"Del, what are you talking about?" Mac asked.

"It's nothing. I just need to rest." He lay down and closed his eyes. What he was about to do almost certainly wouldn't succeed, but he would try anyway, just in case.

Del had never worked as a telop. He rarely used the Kyle web. He knew nothing about the tech. He took after his father, who had never understood the gleaming technology of his wife's people. But like his father, Del was at home in the Kyle itself, as if he were a sea creature who knew nothing of marine science or technology yet could swim with ease.

As Del's thoughts drifted, he relaxed his barriers, the mental walls he created to protect his empath's mind. He was taking a risk, leaving himself unprotected as his awareness spread into space. He couldn't access the Kyle; he had no gateway, no tech, nothing. He was much too far away to contact Dehya by telepathy. But maybe, just maybe, he could send an impression of his ideas.

At least he could try.

Aliana missed Red.

A silver flyer had brought her to the palace without him. Scared and uncertain, she had sat by its window and gazed at the mountains while the sun set in fiery red hues. As night fell, they flew above Qoxire, the capital of Eube. City of legend. It was even more splendid than the tales claimed, with its soaring crystal arches and luminous towers, spire after golden spire reaching into the sky. The city had sparkled in the night like a myth awash in magic.

The "suite" where the palace guards left her was bigger than the entire shack where she had lived with her stepfather. It wasn't one room, but several, all connected by arches bordered with mosaics in rose and emerald tiles. The ceilings curved in high vaults, paneled in ivory, emerald, and blue. An orb lamp hung from the highest point and dripped blue crystals that were too fine to be glass; they had to be real sapphires. Niches in the wall held urns lacquered in gold and blue with delicate birds painted on them. Gold draperies hung on some alcoves, held back by braided ropes, their tasseled ends dusted with carnelians. The gold carpet was so thick, it covered her toes and was sheer pleasure on her bare feet. Incense with a sweet, hypnotic scent burned in a gold pot, a tendril of smoke curling into the air.

Unfortunately, she had only herself to share these miracles. The soldiers had taken Red in a different flyer. She hadn't seen Tide since they left Muze's Helios. Aliana longed to know if they were all right. She didn't know what to do, except keep up her mental defenses as Lensmark had told her to do, for herself and for Red.

A hum came from behind Aliana. As she turned around, a wall across the room shimmered into another horseshoe arch. Two Razers stood framed the entrance, with more people behind them, their black hair glittering—

Ah gods. Aliana dropped to her knees, her head bowed.

Footsteps entered, soft on the carpet. A man spoke in Highton. "You may wait outside."

Was he talking to her? She snuck a look, lifting her gaze a bit but not her head. A man's elegant black shoes gleamed nearby. More muffled footsteps sounded, people leaving, and the man walked out of view. The room became quiet. It wasn't empty, though. She sensed another mind.

The man spoke. "You may stand."

She started to rise, then hesitated. What if he hadn't meant her?

"Aliana," he said softly. "Stop kneeling."

Raising her head, she him a few paces away, the only other person in the room.

Emperor Jaibriol.

He was even more beautiful in person than in the broadcasts. His face was a sculptor's dream, with high cheekbones, a perfect nose, and large eyes. He was the quintessential Highton, from his black diamond hair to his alabaster skin. His black clothes were cut perfectly for his body, accenting his broad shoulders, slim waist and long legs. Carnelians glinted on the cuffs and collar of his shirt. His red eyes were more the color of rubies than carnelians, vivid and pure red. Most of all, though, he somehow looked *human*, not like other Hightons, who were too icy to be mortal.

And just where had she learned the word *quintessential?*

She stood up slowly. Jaibriol just waited. Probably

she'd already insulted him unforgivably. The people who had brought her to Glory had barely talked to her at all, let alone offered any clues about how to behave with an emperor. For lack of a better idea, she used one of the first phrases she had ever learned in Highton. "You honor me with your presence, Your Glorious Highness."

Jaibriol smiled slightly. "Do I?"

That was certainly an odd thing to say. Of course he did.

He indicated something behind her. "Let us sit."

Turning, she saw the brocaded sofa flanked by armchairs, gold and blue, with a polished wooden table in front, all on a blue rug with carnelian tassels. Feeling like a trespasser, she went where he indicated and almost sat down. Mercifully, she caught herself in time. She stood waiting as he came over and settled onto the sofa. When he nodded, she sat in the armchair, on the edge of its seat. She was afraid to breathe too deeply, in case he heard and was offended.

Jaibriol's wrist comm hummed. He touched a panel and a man's voice rose into the air. "He is here, Your Highness."

"Good," Jaibriol said. "Send him in."

Confused, Aliana glanced at the archway. It had become a solid wall again, but as she looked, it shimmered back into an entrance. Four Razers stood there, dark and big, with black guns on their belts, their eyes like windows into the heart of a machine. They came forward—

With Tide!

He walked in their midst, so much like them, they could have all been brothers. Even knowing him as

Harindor's top fighter, far better than all the rest, she had never realized he could look so harsh. He wore no uniform, however, only dark slacks and a blue dress shirt, elegant in its cut. She tried to catch his gaze, but he wouldn't look at her. She couldn't understand what terrible thing that other Tide had done, the one who had caused ESComm to kill all his brothers. Why should acting human deserve execution?

A few paces from the sofa, the Razers stopped and one of them shoved on Tide's shoulder. He went down on one knee, his head bowed.

"You may rise." The emperor sounded bored. Aliana gritted her teeth. Tide deserved better.

Tide rose, his gaze downcast.

"The rest of you may wait outside," Jaibriol said.

The Razers stared at him, their strict faces furrowing. One started to speak. Jaibriol did almost nothing, just barely raised his eyebrows, but it silenced the Razer. All four bowed at exactly the same time, like machine parts working in unison. Then they strode from the room, dark figures casting shadows on the gold carpet.

It wasn't until the archway turned back into a wall that Jaibriol acknowledged Tide. He lifted his hand, motioning toward the other armchair. "You may sit."

Tide went where the emperor indicated and sat, his face composed but his jaw rigid. His posture was more tense than Aliana had ever seen from him before, including even the day he came to the embassy to defect.

The emperor spoke in a low voice. "You look just like him." His voice had none of the curt snap Aliana associated with Hightons. He sounded *shaken.* Something else was strange, too, she wasn't sure what . . .

"You're the last of your line," Jaibriol told him. "All

the rest are dead." With an unexpected bitterness, he added, "All eleven of them."

"I'm sorry, Your Highness," Tide said.

Aliana couldn't believe he was apologizing for being alive. Gods! He seemed hunched up mentally, ready to defend himself—or to hear his sentence of execution. He wasn't a psion, so he wouldn't feel the pressure of the emperor's mind, but—

Wait! *That was it.* That was what felt strange about Jaibriol. No mental pressure. Even with her barriers in place, she sensed other Aristos like a distant force that would consume her mind if she relaxed her defenses. She felt none of that here.

"You have nothing to apologize for," Jaibriol said to Tide. "Hidaka saved my life."

Tide gave a start, a barely discernable jerk of his shoulders, but Aliana understood. *Hidaka saved my life.* The emperor had to mean the Razer whose sin of humanity had resulted in the death of his line. Yet Jaibriol called him Hidaka. *By his name.* He acknowledged the Razer's humanity.

Tide waited, his muscles so rigid that his shirt couldn't smooth out its wrinkles.

"I'm assigning you to my bodyguard," Jaibriol said.

Tide's mouth fell open. "Sire! I—did you—I don't understand."

Aliana's instant of joy turned into dismay. The emperor wouldn't put a defector on his bodyguard. He was toying with Tide. Or so she thought, until Jaibriol said something even stranger.

"I appreciate your undercover work at the embassy," he told Tide. "Your insights on their operations have been of great use."

Aliana's mouth dropped open. Tide was a *spy*? She would have never guessed. In fact, watching Tide, she was certain he would have never guessed, either.

"I, uh—thank you," Tide said.

"Since the ESComm raid disrupted your work at the embassy," Jaibriol continued, "we are pulling you off that assignment. You will join our palace guard, instead, and accompany us to Delos."

Aliana didn't know what she had expected, but this sure as flaming stars wasn't it.

Tide was trying not to look confused. "The Allied planet Delos?"

"That's right," Jaibriol said. "For the summit with the Skolians."

Tide finally recovered enough to form a complete sentence. "You do me an incredible honor, Your Most Esteemed Glory."

For one instant Aliana had the ridiculous sense that the emperor wanted to say *You're the only one in three empires who seems to think so.* Of course he didn't make such a bizarre statement.

Instead, Jaibriol turned to her. "You will also come to Delos with us."

She stared at him blankly. She couldn't imagine any reason why he would want Aliana Miller Azina in even the same galaxy with him.

"One more thing," he told her. "You will *never* leave this suite without my authorization. You keep off the meshes, out of sight, out of mind. *Do you understand?*"

Startled by his vehemence, she blurted, "I promise, I won't, I mean I will, Your Highness, Your Greatness, Your Glory—" She shut her mouth when Tide gave her a *stop babbling* glare.

Jaibriol sat considering her. The silence stretched out. Just when she thought it would become unbearable, he said, "The staff at the Skolian embassy thought you were a psion. However, none of my people detect the slightest Kyle ability from you." He paused. "Oddly enough, they can't verify that boy is a psion, either, even though he was previously registered with a rating above seven."

Aliana didn't know why they didn't find whatever they expected. All she could think was that the emperor must know what had happened to Red. ***Please, please, don't say he died.*** She remembered his touch, strong and gentle at the same time, his soft words, his dimple when he smiled. Desperate to know what had happened to him, she imagined her mental walls thinning, just *here* with the emperor, to find out what he knew—

Warmth! Gods, so much power.

Jaibriol's expression didn't change the slightest bit, yet Aliana had the oddest sense, as if he had gasped inside his mind. Then the warmth was gone. *Completely.* He was a cipher, unreadable, his mind a blank. Confused, she imagined her mental fortress intact again.

"This boy," Jaibriol said to her. "The one you call Red."

Her pulse surged. "Yes, Sire?"

"Did something happen to his brain in Muzeopolis?"

"I don't know," Aliana said. "When I met him, he was starving."

"That shouldn't affect his Kyle ability." Jaibriol's gaze bored into her. "I'm going to leave him with you. I want both of you to stay here, out of the way. Out of sight."

She was going to see Red! "Your Most Glorious Highness, yes, we will, I promise."

Tide was watching her with an odd look. She couldn't read his carefully composed expression, but she sensed...

envy? Of Red? That made no sense. The emperor had just given Tide a far greater honor, more than his life, more even than his previous job. Tide was to be a personal bodyguard of the emperor himself. He had no reason to envy a couple of low-level slaves confined to their rooms.

The emperor turned back to Tide. "Robert Muzeson will process your transfer to the palace guard when we finish here."

"Thank you, Your Highness," Tide said. "I won't disappoint you."

To Aliana's unmitigated surprise, Jaibriol said, "I know," in a far gentler voice than she had heard from any other Aristo. Then he rose to his feet. "That is all."

Aliana and Tide jumped up. She caught a flash of mortified panic from Tide; they weren't supposed to sit if the emperor was standing. Well, if he stood up without telling them, how could they help it? Honestly, Hightons were strange, with their protocols and procedures. But Jaibriol was going to let her be with Red, and he had let her see Tide, and that meant everything.

The emperor summoned his guards back into the room. As the Razers entered, Aliana shuddered. What she felt from their minds was neither the pain of an Aristo nor the warmth of a psion. They were . . . inaccessible. They gave her a darkened sense, more of night than day. Would Tide become like that? She didn't know what it would mean, but it was better than his death.

Jaibriol spoke to Aliana. "Remember what I told you. Stay out of sight."

With that, he left the room, striding out with Tide and his night-souled bodyguards.

. . . not Tarex . . . his ship? . . . Allied . . . Tarex could fake . . . all fake . . .

Fake what? Dehya kept walking, but Del was fading into the fog. **Wait! Come back.**

His thought drifted . . . ***two-thirds Earth gravity . . . air smells like vanilla . . .***

Then he was gone.

Jaibriol stood in his darkened suite, thinking he should tell the lumos to come on. But he was so tired, even that seemed an effort.

Aliana was a psion—and that was an understatement of magnificent proportions. She had been reading him even when they both had mental fortifications so strong, they were blocking every Aristo within kilometers. When she lowered her barriers, clumsily trying to probe his mind, it was like a sun had gone nova. He had felt that kind of power only once in his adult life, when he and Kelric had met on Earth. This girl had that same golden, blazing warmth.

Not only that, but with no training, she was protecting the boy Red so well that no hint of his ability had registered with any Highton here or on the ship that brought them to Glory. According to the reports, Red had picked her at random in a clumsy robbery attempt. Jaibriol didn't believe for one moment that choice was arbitrary. Even if the boy hadn't consciously oriented on Aliana because of her mind, he must have sensed her luminous power.

Incredibly, no one else had a clue. He had checked every record he could find. Aliana had never been tested. She had been hidden in one of the worst slums on Muze's Helios, so thoroughly disguised by her poverty and inconspicuous existence that no one had guessed.

She had to be a Ruby heir. She had their golden metallic beauty. Was she a full Ruby psion? If not, she was damn close. What the blazing hell was he going to do with her? She could be the most valuable human being alive in Eubian space, a Ruby Dynasty hostage worth her weight in fortified platinum. Except it was more like having a vial of nitroglycerine in his pocket. One wrong step and it could blow him up.

A drowsy voice murmured in the darkness. "Are you going to stand there all night?" Dim light appeared, cast through the red and gold shade on an antique lamp across the room. It stood on a black lacquered nightstand next to the canopied bed. Tarquine was sitting up, reclined against the headboard, rubbing her eyes. The bed covers had fallen down to her waist, leaving her shapely torso uncovered, her lithe curves covered by flimsy red lace.

Jaibriol exhaled. After this excruciating day, he knew what he needed. He stalked across the room, undoing the high collar of his shirt. As he climbed the dais where the bed stood, he unfastened the carnelian links that held his shirt cuffs closed. Tarquine watched him, her long lashes half-closed over her eyes.

He sat on the edge of the bed and pulled off his shirt. As he leaned down to kiss her, he grasped her silken lingerie and yanked. It ripped easily, pulling away from her body, a scrap of lace in his fist. Tarquine kissed him with her palm cupped on his cheek, her long fingers curving around his jaw. Pulling her under his body, he let himself submerge into her hypnotic sensuality. She knew exactly how to touch him, yet she no idea what she did; she was simply being Tarquine, a draught of potent whiskey, a drug he would crave for the rest of his fractured life, the deadly creature he loved at his own peril. For some unfathomable reason she wanted him, not only the coldly unassailable emperor of Eube, but also as the passionate, idealistic youth who had grown up with nothing but his family's love in the wilderness of an uncharted world.

He didn't finish undressing; he just pulled open his trousers and drove deep within her. She raised her hips to meet his. He wanted her hard and fast, with a fire no Aristo would ever admit to feeling. Nor could she hide from him; her arousal saturated his mind with the same forbidden intensity. Her fingernails scraped his shoulders, leaving marks the nanomeds in his body would repair. He arched his back and groaned, shoving deep into her, pinning her to the bed.

Jaibriol felt the animalistic craving within her, shadowed and buried—that drive to brutality that Aristos called transcendence. She had exorcised her ability to transcend because she believed it was wrong, but her desire for that sublime ecstasy was still there. Every time they made love, he felt what she wanted to do to him, what she held back. Every time he lay with her, he balanced on that edge of her darkness. He was never safe, but it never stopped him from needing her, even now, when he was as angry as he was aroused, when he took her with an edge of violence himself, using passion to vanquish the Ruby powers that threatened his mind, his ability to rule, even his sanity.

✧ ✧ ✧

Jaibriol lay on his back, one arm thrown over his head on the sable pillow. Tarquine lay next to him, her eyes closed. Her breathing had slowed and her mind drowsed. Sated.

Eventually he said, "I received a response from Pharaoh Dyhianna."

"Hmmm . . . when?"

"A few hours ago." He stared up at the velvet curtains of the bed, which were held back by braided cords. "I'm surprised your security people didn't catch it."

"You distracted me," she said, her voice low.

Jaibriol put his arm around her. As long as she was distracted, she wouldn't ask him about the tall girl with gold skin. He would have to disguise Aliana's coloring.

"What did our Skolian queenling say?" she said. "Or perhaps I should ask about her dice."

Jaibriol rolled onto his side, facing her. "She offered a solution for convening the summit. I think I'm going to accept it."

Her lashes lifted, revealing her red gaze, suddenly awake and intent. "What solution?"

"We meet on the world Delos." Jaibriol propped his head up on his hand, resting his elbow on the bed. "Our people build half of the summit hall and theirs build the other half. We have control of whatever we build and full rights to inspect whatever the other side creates. The Allieds will monitor it all with their security."

"No. It's too dangerous."

"Anything will be dangerous. Hell, Tarquine, we could be killed in our own home."

She studied his face. "Delos is that world the Allieds

call sanctuary, yes? I have heard what they say. A place where 'Eubian and Skolian may walk side by side, in harmony.' It is balderdash."

The room seemed too quiet. He had checked its security, and he knew she had protected their privacy with her own systems, which outdid even ESComm's best. They were truly alone here, no one listening, watching, recording. Still, he feared to speak the answer on his lips.

"What is it?" Tarquine asked.

"My parents met on Delos."

He waited for her to tell him the lie, that his sainted mother, the gods exalt her soul, was the Highton woman all Eube assumed had birthed and raised him, an Aristo of the revered Kaliga Line. She knew the truth, but neither of them ever spoke it aloud.

Instead, tonight she simply said, "How did they meet?"

It was the most dangerous conversation he had ever had. Even here, he couldn't go further than that one sentence, *My parents met on Delos.*

Tarquine waited. When he didn't answer, she murmured, "No sanctuary exists for those flawed gods who rule the stars."

"We aren't gods, no matter what Eube Qox claimed."

"We are what we need to be." She traced her finger across his lips. "Let no blasphemy cross these, husband. This fickle universe worships its deities one day and reviles them the next."

He closed his hand around hers and lowered it to the bed. "We are going to Delos."

"It is astonishing," she said, "how well the nanomeds we carry in our bodies can monitor our health."

"And you bring this up because . . . ?"

"Be certain what you choose for this summit. If you choose wrong, we could all die."

" 'All' suggests many people. Who?"

"Three. You. Me." She placed his palm over her stomach. "The son we created tonight."

He went very still. "You can't know already." Given her age, she required special medical treatment to conceive. Yes, she could prime her body for it. But nothing could be certain within only an hour after they made love.

"The child is conceived," she said softly. "My body is ready. You will have a son." In a parched voice, she added, "I have twice lost our heir. I will not have it happen again."

"Stay here." He touched her cheek. "Don't come to Delos."

Her gaze never wavered. "I will be at the summit."

Jaibriol wanted her there, but he wanted more to protect her and their child. "You cannot."

"I will."

He could forbid her. And then? He would have her enmity. When most husbands and wives argued, it damaged their lives. When he and Tarquine battled, it damaged an empire.

"I will go to Delos," he told her. "If you come, you are choosing to endanger our child, the Highton Heir. It is your responsibility, Tarquine."

Her voice cooled. "I act as I believe right, given the choices others make. If their choices are foolish, they must live with them."

"You may also be choosing for our son."

"If you insist on going to Delos, so are you." She

splayed her hand against his chest. "No sanctuary exists for us, Jaibriol." Softly, she added, "Just as none existed for your parents."

For that, he had no answer. His parents, who had met on the forgiving soil of Delos, had died in the unrelenting hatreds of two empires.

"I was asleep." Dehya paced away from the marble bench. She, Kelric, Roca, and First Councilor Tikal had met here, in a park surrounded by meadows on three sides and ethereal City on the fourth. A breeze ruffled her hair and skitterbugs clicked and hummed in the pure air.

"What you're describing can't happen," Tikal said. "Del couldn't reach you through Kyle space. It had to be a dream."

Dehya turned back to them. Kelric was standing by a white column, leaning against it, his muscled arms folded. Light from the Sun Lamp shone on his gold hair and skin. Roca and Barcala were sitting on a marble bench, Roca in a rose-hued dress, her long, long legs crossed. Barcala had leaned against a column at the other end of the curving seat, one foot up on the bench with his leg bent, his elbow resting on his knee, his other foot on the blue-tiled ground.

"It's true," Dehya admitted. "It should be impossible for Del to reach me."

"But?" Roca said.

Dehya tried to focus. At times like this, when she had been deep in the web, it was hard to talk. She didn't feel fully in this universe. During sleep, that feeling could become even stronger...

"Dehya," Kelric asked. "Are you still here?"

"Yes." *Focus.* She made a sweeping gesture to encompass the Orbiter. "This space station, the Lock here, so much of what we do in the Kyle—it's all based on ancient machines from the Ruby Empire. We've never found good records to describe how they were created or why they work. I've studied the Locks all my life and I'm only beginning to understand them."

"So what are you saying?" Tikal asked. "That Del was working on it, too? No offense, but your rock star nephew is about as likely to do Kyle research as he is to turn into a fish."

She winced, not from his words but for his veiled hostility. After the coup that overthrew the Assembly, ISC had almost executed Tikal. He lived because of her choice to split the government, but he had never again trusted her.

"I meant we don't fully understand the technology," Dehya said. "When I'm sleeping, my mental barriers fade. Could Del reach me? It's unlikely, yes, but maybe not impossible."

"Too many people live on Earth," Roca said. "Billions. Even if he could reach across space to you, all those other minds would be like static blocking what little you might pick up."

"On Earth, yes." What was it Del had told her? ***Two-thirds Earth gravity . . .***

"It's rotating," she said. "That's why the gravity is lower."

They blinked at her. Barcala said, "Are you talking about the Orbiter?"

"No." What else had Del said? Her mind drifted . . . Axil Tarex and neural scans . . .

"Dehya?" Kelric's voice came from far away.

Dehya mentally shook herself. She had asked them to meet here in the hopes that the fresh air and breezes would help her stay focused in real space. "I think Del is being held on a ship. One large enough to rotate so that it provides an apparent gravity about two-thirds that of Earth." It hit her, then, what she had been missing. "A Trader ship."

Kelric stiffened. "He said that?"

"No, I don't think he knew." She thought back to her visits to Earth. "Certain areas on the planet Glory are known for a flower with a distinctive smell. People from Earth associate it with the scent of an Earth plant used to make a food flavoring."

Kelric said, "And this matters because . . . ?"

"Del told me he smelled vanilla," Dehya said. "That's the food flavoring."

Roca squinted at her sister. "He smells vanilla and from that, you infer that the Traders took him?"

"He also mentioned Axil Tarex," Dehya said.

"For flaming sake!" Tikal said. "You only now get to that part?"

She winced. "Sorry."

Kelric gave Tikal a wry glance. "You get used to the way she thinks after a while."

Dehya started to frown at him, then decided he had a point. "I think Del believes Lord Tarex scanned his brain and created a neurological map."

"It's not impossible," Kelric said. "But the equipment Tarex would need is hardly standard issue for a private yacht. Also, according to our intelligence, he has very few direct connections to the planet Glory. He certainly doesn't live there. It's not impossible his ship would smell like a specific region on that planet, but it seems unlikely."

"Not his ship, maybe," Dehya said. "But possibly one that belonged to someone in the emperor's inner circle."

Kelric went very still. "You think Jaibriol Qox ordered Del's abduction?"

On the surface, it was a logical question. Of course, she doubted Jaibriol had anything to do with it. She said only, "It could be any number of people. Someone in ESComm, I would guess."

"It still doesn't explain how whoever took Prince Del-Kurj managed the kidnapping," Tikal said.

"Something to do with the neural scans of his brain," Dehya said. "It could connect to the Kyle space attacks, too."

Roca stiffened, her gaze shifting to Kelric. "The Traders have your neural scans, too."

"And your brother Althor's," Tikal said. "From when he was a prisoner of war."

"*Althor.*" Kelric stared at Tikal. "Hell and damnation."

"Gods," Roca said. "This gets worse and worse."

"Worse than what?" Tikal asked. "Why do you all suddenly look like you're at a funeral?"

Dehya cleared her throat. "It has to do with the other thing we need to talk to you about."

"I'm afraid to ask," Tikal said.

Kelric glanced at Dehya and Roca.

Go ahead, Dehya thought, and Roca nodded.

Kelric spoke to Tikal. "My brother Althor fathered a daughter seventeen years ago with a Trader woman."

"We think the girl may be a Ruby psion," Dehya said.

"And she's on Glory," Roca said. "Where ESComm has Althor's DNA and neural scans."

Tikal stared at them. "Please tell me you're joking."

"I'm afraid not," Dehya said.

"Flaming hell," Tikal said. "How can you all be so *calm?*"

"If you think we're calm," Roca told him dryly, "we're a lot better at hiding our reactions than we thought."

"And you're sure about this?" Tikal asked. "Absolutely sure?"

"Ninety-nine point seven percent sure," Dehya said. "The girl sought asylum at a Skolian embassy on Muze's Helios, and a military attaché there, Lyra Lensmark, sent us her blood tests to analyze."

"How did this Lensmark figure out about the girl?"

"We don't know," Roca said. "We can't reach Lensmark. ESComm is blocking our messages."

Tikal scowled. "They have no right to refuse us communication with the embassy staff."

Roca spoke dryly. "Apparently ESComm has forgotten the Paris Accord we all spent so much time hammering out all those years ago. But we're negotiating with them."

"Do they know the girl is your kin?" Tikal asked.

"We don't think so." Roca pushed her hand through her hair and sent it rippling around her body like a gold waterfall. "I've found no indication they have any clue about the girl's identity. Their main concern has been the man who brought her in and a youth who came with them. The boy is a provider belonging to Admiral Muze and the man is a Razer who claimed he wanted to defect. Apparently the Razer was actually a spy planted by ESComm. No one seems interested in the girl. She's what they call a slum rat, a child who grew up in poverty."

"Hidden in plain sight," Dehya murmured.

"So how did Lensmark know?" Tikal asked.

"We're aren't sure she knew anything for certain," Dehya said. "However, according to the DNA analysis, this girl has gold skin, gold eyes, and gold hair. Lensmark would have seen that."

Tikal glanced at Roca and Kelric, and they looked back at him like the male and female aspects of a golden being, radiant in the Orbiter sunlight.

"So let me see if I have this straight," Tikal said. "Someone in the emperor's circle with a probable link to Lord Axil Tarex may have kidnapped Prince Del-Kurj by infiltrating Allied Space Command and possibly using Del's neural patterns, secretly scanned by Tarex and given to ESComm. The Traders also have Imperator Skolia's neural scans, which implies they could do similar to him. In addition, they have scans and DNA records of the late Prince Althor, and they also have his illegitimate daughter, who just may be a Ruby psion, which they will probably realize if they do any searches on her DNA profile."

"That about sums it up," Dehya said.

"Any other disasters you want to tell me about?" Tikal said dourly. "Maybe the universe is going to blow up?"

Kelric smiled slightly. "It stopped doing that."

Dehya knew Kelric's dry humor helped him deal with crises, but most people didn't even realize when he was joking. Tikal just shot him an exasperated look.

She wished she could talk to them about Jaibriol. But just her and Kelric knowing was too risky. Suppose one of them were captured? They had protections in their minds, traps that activated under the duress of interrogation and erased their knowledge by destroying neural pathways. Better to have amnesia than unwillingly betray their family, people, empire. But no traps protected their knowledge about Jaibriol. To create such traps, they would have to tell the surgeon what to protect, which they could never do. She and Kelric had to find a way to do it themselves, even if it meant doing brain surgery on each other.

Right now, her mech-enhanced brain was shifting into an accelerated mode, pushing her limits. She was tired. She had lived too long, one hundred and seventy years. Her brain had too much in it. She wanted to turn off her mind, like a node put to sleep, but she couldn't rest, not yet.

Tikal was speaking and one channel of her mind registered his words. "Dehya, ESComm doesn't have your neural scans," he said. "I can see how they might have used Del's and Kelric's to attack them in Kyle space, but how did they get to you?"

"I'm not sure," Dehya said. She was missing something Del had tried to tell her. She went to another bench, a curve of white marble on fluted supports, and sat down cross-legged, comfortable in her white jumpsuit. Closing her eyes, she rested her hands in her lap.

Access memory, Dream, Prince Del-Kurj, she thought.

Light, her spinal node, answered. **Accessed.**

Distantly, she heard Tikal talking to Roca and Kelric. "What is she doing? Meditating?"

"Just thinking," Roca said. "She does it that way sometimes."

"I've known her for decades," Tikal said. "Never seen her do that before."

Kelric's voice was a distant rumble. "She does it more and more lately."

Their voices faded as Dehya increased her concentration. Del's words replayed in her mind, misty, vague: . . . ***not Tarex . . . his ship? . . . Allied . . . Tarex could fake . . . all fake . . .***

Dehya sent a thought to Light. *Del thinks he's on an Allied ship.*

Possibly, Light answered. **Or he could mean Tarex wants him to think that.**

If Tarex wanted to mislead him, he wouldn't let his vessel smell like a Trader ship.

Unless Tarex wants Del to think someone from Glory kidnapped him.

Oh, it could be a million things. Tarex this, Glory that. What did Del mean, "All fake"?

I don't know.

Dehya pulled up files in her mind, some stored as biological memories, others stored in her spinal nodes. She labeled each file with a Quis die. Then she manipulated the dice, playing Quis with them, and in doing so, ran multiple analyses in her mind on the dream about Del.

After a moment, Dehya opened her eyes and regarded the others. "It's all fake."

Tikal's face paled. "Dehya, what the hell are you doing?"

"Doing?" She looked around, but she saw nothing unusual, except a mist blurring the park.

"That's been happening lately," Roca said uneasily.

"What happens?" Dehya asked.

"Your voice," Roca said. "You sound ghostly. Otherworldly."

"The plains of blue," she murmured. She had learned

the phrase from Roca's son Shannon, the only other one of them who could access the Kyle without technology. Except maybe Del could do it, too. Of all Roca's sons, he was the most like Shannon.

Kelric spoke gently. "Dehya, you need to tell us what you mean. Focus."

The models running in her mind were distracting. ***Light, move the calculations about Del into the background.***

Done, Light answered.

Her workspace quieted, freeing her to concentrate on the others. She said, "I think we can't figure out how someone tampered with our minds because this so-called tampering was fake."

"Both you and Imperator Skolia nearly died," Tikal said. "I'd hardly call that fake."

"I don't mean in that sense." She switched her thoughts into a linear mode. Presenting them that way to people seemed more successful, especially when she added extra details floating in her mind, those she usually absorbed without directly thinking about them. It made her feel annoyingly verbose, but it seemed to work. Given what was at stake, it seemed better to be just annoying rather than both annoying and confusing.

"I'm still analyzing," she said. "But this is what I think so far. What happened to Del only appears connected to the attacks on Kelric and me. If Tarex has Del's neural scans, ESComm must have them, too. Also, if ESComm has agents in the Allied military, General Barthol Iquar would be the Joint Commander with the most interest in their actions, since the Eubian army is more involved in covert operations than their fleet. And he lives on Glory." She paused. "Then we have these Minutemen. Are they a Trader group in disguise? It's a logical name to use if they're claiming to be Allied citizens. It resonates with the history of the country where Del lives. They say they want people to hear 'Carnelians Finale,' which has been a major impediment to public acceptance of the peace process. Well, Barthol Iquar is almost certainly a staunch foe of the peace process. However, he signed the treaty—gods only know how Jaibriol Qox pulled that one off—and it would be treason for him to undermine it. So he sets up this fake Allied group to do his dirty work. He uses Del's neural scans to create a Kyle pathway that links Del to the release of 'Carnelians Finale,' because not only does that shift blame away from ESComm, but it also appears as if a Skolian prince is the one committing treason. However—"

"Dehya, wait!" Roca held up her hands. "Slow down. We need time."

"Sorry." Dehya waited, feeling foolish. Apparently she still wasn't communicating well. She needed to work on that.

Kelric smiled at her. "We're recording what you're saying on our nodes, then replaying the recording. Just give us a few seconds."

"Ah." She sat with her hands in her lap and ran mental analyses of her Del dream.

After a moment, Kelric gave Roca a questioning look. When she nodded, he glanced at Tikal, who also nodded. So Kelric spoke to Dehya. "All right. Go on."

She put her calculations into the background and returned to linear mode. "Barthol Iquar is a Highton. So a high probability exists that he isn't a psion."

"A 'high probability?'" Roca asked. "I'll say. It's impossible."

"Why would you suggest otherwise?" Tikal asked Dehya.

"Because Aristos are human," Dehya said. "Regardless of their claims about their eternally annoying exaltation. Do you really believe no Aristo has ever passed off an illegitimate child as an Aristo? We may think they're incapable of love, but any human can love, no matter how weak they believe it makes them. Five generations of Aristos exist now, long enough for some Kyle DNA to have worked its way into their gene pool."

"Highton empaths?" Tikal squinted at her. "It's a contradiction of terms."

"I can't see how they would survive," Roca said.

"It would be a nightmare," Dehya said. How Jaibriol managed, she couldn't imagine. It was a testament to his strength of will that he hadn't committed suicide. "I think it's safe to assume General Iquar can't manipulate Kyle space himself. He might use providers, but their work would be clumsy. They don't have training, and Eube has no infrastructure to access Kyle space. But if General Iquar could steal access to ours, it wouldn't be impossible for him to use a provider to manipulate the web."

Roca shook her head. "What happened to you and Kelric would take far more than a few inexperienced providers sneaking into Kyle space. The training and web access it requires are far too sophisticated. How would ESComm do it?"

Dehya spoke grimly. "That's the unpleasant part."

"The rest of this *isn't?*" Tikal asked.

She wished she had a better theory to offer. "ESComm would need an agent in ISC or the Assembly, someone high up. Very few people could manage that access to us." She forced out the names. "Roca, you're one. Tikal, you would be, but you aren't a psion, so you'd need to work with someone who is. The others are General Naaj Majda, Admiral Chad Barzun, Admiral Ragnar Bloodmark, General Dayamar Stone, and Primary Brant Tapperhaven."

They all stared at her. At least, Roca and Tikal stared. Kelric didn't look surprised.

"You know damn well I didn't do this," Tikal said curtly.

"I didn't say anyone had." Dehya hated this. "Just that you're the ones with access. Kelric and I have it, too. I could have acted against him or he could have acted against me."

"That's crazy," Roca said. "Besides, you were both attacked."

"We're in the Triad," Dehya said. "If one of us attacked the other, it would backlash against the attacker. What happens to one of us, happens to both."

Both of them.

Except the Triad had three people.

"This is just great," Tikal said dourly. "We all could have committed treason."

Three people. Jaibriol's son had died in his mother's womb, maybe at the moment Dehya and Kelric experienced the attacks. Was that the connection? It still didn't fit. She and Kelric had been in the Triad with Kelric's father when he had died, and although they both knew he had passed, neither of them had suffered a backlash. True, he died peacefully, surrounded by family. But Dehya had also been in the Triad with Kurj, who had been Imperator before Soz and Kelric. He had died violently in battle. She had felt him go, yes, but it hadn't nearly killed her. The death of an unborn child who was only half Ruby, as heartbreaking as it may have been, wouldn't nearly kill both her and Kelric.

Had Jaibriol attacked them? She didn't believe it. They would have recognized such an attack, especially from another Triad member.

Dehya talked slowly, thinking. "Maybe we *did* experience a backlash, both me and Kelric." She considered them. "From the attack on Del."

"Del?" Kelric asked. "What do you mean?"

"The second time he supposedly released 'Carnelians Finale,' it happened when you and I experienced those Kyle attacks." Dehya concentrated on him, hiding her thoughts but hoping he realized she meant a lot more than Del. "What if we were just collateral damage?"

Tikal gave her an incredulous look. "You're saying ESComm went after Prince Del-Kurj and got you and Kelric *by accident?* That's some collateral damage."

"If it doesn't involve betrayals by our top people," Roca said, "I'll gladly consider it."

Kelric was watching Dehya closely. "Go on."

"What happened to us could have been an unintended side effect of the tampering with Del," Dehya said. "As members of the Ruby Dynasty, we're all connected. If Del could reach me through Kyle space while I was asleep, think how much stronger the link would be if I had been in the web."

Tikal regarded her doubtfully. "It still doesn't seem likely."

"It does have a low probability," Dehya admitted. In fact, it was essentially zero. She and Kelric would sense if Del was attacked, certainly, but it wouldn't nearly kill them, besides which, he hadn't been attacked, only manipulated. But a murder attempt that nearly killed the third Triad member—*that* was a different story. What if the Highton Heir had died in violence aimed not at him, but at his father, the emperor? In the Kyle, events were related by similarity, not location. If the same person who tried to kill Jaibriol had also been the one who implicated Del, using untrained telops, he could have unknowingly linked what Jaibriol experienced to the release of "Carnelians Finale." That release had a huge impact on the summit—which Dehya and Kelric had been working on almost continually for many months. In Kyle space, that would have linked the murder attempt against Jaibriol directly to Kelric and Dehya. It would explain why the attack against Del appeared so clumsy while that against Dehya and Kelric seemed so sophisticated. No one had attacked them; the backlash had nearly killed her and Kelric because they and Jaibriol were in the Triad. The sophistication of the attacks came from their own minds. That they had *both* been in Kyle space when Jaibriol experienced whatever happened had magnified the effect.

Dehya knew she was guessing, playing mental dice games, but it made a hell of a lot more sense than the other possibilities. She watched Kelric, silently urging him to go with her comments about Del. They needed a scenario people would accept, because Dehya couldn't tell them the truth.

Kelric met her gaze. "If what you suggest is true, then whoever implicated Del must have left a trace

XXII
Leto's Children

"Delos," Jaibriol repeated, straining to keep his annoyance in check. "The Allied planet." He was ready to throttle Barthol.

The general walked with him, nearly as tall as Jaibriol, but not quite. Jaibriol felt how much the comparison angered Barthol, that his bulky physique, despite its power, wasn't perfect by Aristo standards, not quite broad enough in the shoulders or narrow enough in the hips. He had genetically sculpted his body to come as close to the Highton ideal as he could manage without compromising his health or longevity. It appalled Jaibriol, the extent to which his advisors were willing to go so they would all be the same, all seeking the same uncompromising standard of Highton perfection.

Regardless of what he thought of Barthol, the general did his job well. Jaibriol had no cause to replace him as a Joint Commander and what looked like every reason to keep him. Politically, removing

Barthol would be dangerous; he was well liked among the army brass, not the least because he walked the edge between expected Highton behavior and breaking the rules in ways that Jaibriol suspected many of his top officers would like to do. Barthol's ouster would set the army at odds with the palace. Jaibriol had worked for years to build his support within ESComm, and the peace treaty had alienated a good portion of his backing. He couldn't risk losing any more.

Admiral Erix Muze, who was walking on Jaibriol's other side, was easier to deal with. He had Barthol's talent for military command, but without the general's inhuman edge. The three of them were strolling through the palace gardens, accompanied by Jaibriol's four bodyguards, dark monoliths with metallic minds. Jaibriol hadn't included Tide; he needed to understand the Razer better before he relied on a man who had tried to defect.

Every time he saw Tide, he felt as if he were turning upside down. Tide was Hidaka, yet he would never be Hidaka. He had the same intense loyalty that in Hidaka had become an unswerving fidelity to the emperor. How it manifested in Tide, he didn't know, for Tide's life had taken a different path. He had never witnessed the emperor join the Triad, never protected Jaibriol by murdering a Highton colonel who witnessed the same, never lied about what he had seen, all to protect the emperor even though he had known—from the instant Jaibriol had dragged himself out of the Lock—that Jaibriol was a Ruby psion.

Tide had never died to save Jaibriol's life and make the peace treaty a reality.

Jaibriol didn't know what to expect from this Razer, a man he knew so well and yet not at all. So he had created a cover: Tide had been on assignment, spying on the Skolians, and ESComm had blown his cover when they raided the embassy. That story had the added benefit of allowing Jaibriol to disapprove of the raid, which had violated the Paris Accord and damaged their relations with the Imperialate, without appearing to side with the Skolians for harboring a defector. ESComm wasn't happy with him for "neglecting" to notify them of the operation, but such covert dealings by the palace were classic Highton intrigue and surprised no one. In fact, Jaibriol had the impression Erix Muze enjoyed thinking the Skolians had been so well taken in by a false claim of defection.

For now, he had to concentrate on convincing his Joint Commanders that Delos was a good place for the summit. If they backed him, it would garner him the support he needed from his other advisors. At the moment, though, Barthol wouldn't even acknowledge he knew Delos existed.

"For a name like Delos, I imagine some sort of germ," Barthol was saying. "It might give one hives."

Erix smiled, far more amused than Jaibriol by Barthol's professed lack of knowledge. The admiral said, "I have heard that in the mythology of Earth's ancient Greeks, the island of Delos is a sanctuary. They have a work called *The Homeric Hymns,* including passages about Apollo, a god in their pantheon. This quote is from his mother Leto:

> "Delos, if you would be willing to be the
> abode of my son Phoebus Apollo and make

> him a rich temple—; for no other will touch you, as you will find: and I think you will never be rich in oxen and sheep, nor bear vintage nor yet produce plants abundantly. But if you have the temple of far-shooting Apollo, all men will bring you hecatombs and gather here, and incessant savour of rich sacrifice will always arise, and you will feed those who dwell in you from the hand of strangers; for truly your own soil is not rich."

If Jaibriol hadn't learned so well to control his expressions, he would have gaped at the admiral. He hadn't expected poetry, of all things, from his literal minded military commander. As a statement supporting the choice of Delos for the summit, not only was Erix's response unexpectedly eloquent, but the admiral had clearly taken some time looking into the world and its background. As much as Jaibriol often chafed at Highton discourse, at its best, it could be a thing of subtle beauty.

"Your knowledge of Earth poets is appreciated," Jaibriol told him.

Barthol snorted. "It sounds to me like this Zeus fellow fucked the girl Leto, and she dropped his provider son on a barren island where nothing grows."

And then, Jaibriol thought, there are other forms of Highton discourse.

Technically, Barthol hadn't violated Highton principles, since he hadn't directly addressed the topic of the summit, but he left no doubts as to his opinion of the Allieds and their worlds. Jaibriol was tired of sparring with him, particularly since Barthol obviously knew far more about Delos than he claimed. He just said, "Where would you have expected her to give birth?" If Barthol had a better idea where to put the summit, he sure as blazes hadn't suggested it yet.

Barthol waved his hand as if to encompass the palace and all of Glory. "Mount Olympus."

"I'm sure Zeus's wife would have appreciated that," Erix said dryly.

Security protocols activated, Jaibriol's spinal node thought. It controlled his response, hiding his reaction, but nothing could stop his burst of fury. Tarquine had lost her child here in the place that Barthol—who might have been the assassin—so blithely titled Mt. Olympus, land of the Highton gods.

Stay calm, Jaibriol told himself. He wouldn't play the twisted game of brutal discourse Barthol invited. If he let the general push him into responding with anger, he risked revealing too much. The moment he found proof that Barthol had murdered his son, the general would pay. All that stayed his hand now was the lack of evidence and Tarquine's puzzling silence on the topic.

Jaibriol's voice came out with a detachment far different from what he felt. "In the Greek tales, it profited Zeus that the woman Leto gave birth on Delos. It exalted that king of the gods to have the humans in his life positioned so he could control them without their knowledge." Let Barthol figure that one out. He might even like what Jaibriol implied.

The idea had come to him after he decoded the last message from the Ruby Pharaoh. Verbally, she had said no more than a bland agreement that they should meet somewhere neutral. She and Kelric had disguised the Quis patterns in a detailed border that framed the Skolian insignia. An unusual touch for ISC, to put artwork in a communiqué, but exactly what Hightons expected.

Beautifully complex patterns saturated the Quis they had sent him. The message was clear: *Pick a neutral place away from Earth and set it up so your people have an apparent advantage in security, maybe utilizing a secret they think we don't know, say perhaps the use of Kyle space by ESComm. Make your advisors think it is a trick to dominate us. But leave a back door in Kyle space that we can use to ensure our safety. You—and only you among the Aristos—can do that. Give us that back door and we will accept your terms.*

It didn't surprise Jaibriol that they had figured out ESComm was using providers in Kyle space. As far as he knew, ESComm had accomplished little with their fledgling telops, but he suspected Barthol had attempted more in secret. Although Jaibriol had no evidence that the general had released "Carnelians Finale," his instincts pointed to Barthol rather than Prince Del-Kurj as the culprit.

"Zeus didn't go to Delos in this little tale of gods," Barthol said.

It startled Jaibriol to realize how much had gone through his mind in the moments between his last comment and Barthol's response. Since he had updated spinal nodes, his thoughts often jumped into an accelerated mode without his realizing it. He wondered who Barthol was comparing to Zeus: Jaibriol or himself?

"True," Jaibriol said. "But then, Zeus didn't have the advantage of Highton intelligence."

Erix smiled slightly. "It's amusing to think what he might have accomplished with the help of ESComm."

Barthol gave a snort of laughter. "Greek God Space Command. How entertaining. Wouldn't have worked, though. Zeus was too busy begetting whelps."

Well, weren't his Joint Commanders in a good mood today. Jaibriol eased his barriers. Through the painful haze of their Highton minds, he felt Barthol's contempt. The Zeus jokes were stabs at Jaibriol for having no heir. The general loathed him even more now, since Jaibriol had interfered in his punishment of the taskmaker whose children Barthol had intended to sell. Jaibriol gritted his teeth and probed further, but if Barthol was responsible for the assassination attempt against him, it wasn't in the general's surface thoughts.

Jaibriol picked up more from Erix, perhaps because the admiral's mind didn't exert as much pressure. Erix was satisfied with the discussion about Delos and considered Jaibriol's idea creative. He found Barthol amusing, edgy for a Highton, with an appreciated wit. It stuck in Jaibriol's craw that people would find someone as morally bankrupt as Barthol entertaining, but at least he had Erix's support on Delos.

He caught another thought from the admiral. Erix was grateful to him for dealing with the provider, saving the boy from execution. Gods. The seeds of a conscience were in there. Perhaps in a few decades, if Erix survived until his eighties, he would develop a moral code that Jaibriol understood, as had Tarquine and Corbal. How many more decades would it take to reach a stage where they might like each other? For that, he wanted to weep, that if he endured long enough, he might someday, in his second century of life, have a few friends. If he was even the same person by then. Surrounded by the Hightons every day of his life for so many years, he sometimes felt as if the universe had turned upside down, that he was the aberrant one and they the norm.

Pain spiked in Jaibriol's temples and his vision blurred. To probe their minds more deeply would send him to the hospital. He pulled back, raising his barriers. He had to hold true to his ideals. He couldn't lose sight of what his parents had taught him in the first fourteen years of his life, in that lost and dreamlike time before he had become Jaibriol the Third, emperor of Eube.

"Greek mythology has its intriguing side," Jaibriol said. "I would like to discuss this more, what the gods might have done to remake Delos according to their wishes."

"Indeed," Erix said.

"Oh well, of course, Your Glorious Highness." Barthol sounded bored.

Jaibriol gritted his teeth. Steeling himself, he lowered his shields and took one last look at Barthol's mind. It was excruciating, made worse by his realization that the general was transcending from his discomfort. He found nothing new; Barthol loathed the entire concept of the summit and didn't give a damn where it took place—

And then Jaibriol hit a secret worth more than a platinum mine.

Prince Del-Kurj.

The Kyle streamed past Dehya, a blue mist with sparks for the thoughts of people using the web. Kelric was working in tandem with her, using the Command Chair in the War Room while she used the one in the Triad Chamber. Eldrin had also joined them in Kyle space, accessing it as a telop rather than a Triad member, helping to serve as an anchor for Dehya. She knew what they feared, that she would otherwise fade away into Kyle space forever.

Now that she knew what to look for, the signs of Del's supposed actions with "Carnelians Finale" were easier to find. She submerged into the deep grotto where Taquinil had discovered the security breach. She showed Kelric and Eldrin the rip in the mesh. *They were able to hide this from our security because it's been so long since ISC used this part of the mesh.*

I didn't even know this sector was still here, Kelric thought. **I thought we had cleaned up all these old files.**

The ISC network has evolved for centuries, Dehya thought. *This section was deactivated a century ago, but it ended up buried under newer systems and was never fully dismantled.*

Frustration tinged his usually stoic thoughts. **It's impossible to track it all, trillions of nodes, always changing. And that's just the active mesh sections.**

We do our best, Dehya thought. *What matters is that we found the breach.*

As did ESComm, Kelric growled.

Eldrin's thought came to them with a sense of distance created by his less powerful telop chair. ***Are you sure it was ESComm that used this breach? As much as I hate to say it, someone in ISC would have better access to this area than ESComm.***

Kelric's mood darkened as if a shutter had closed. **What you're asking me to do is impossible.**

I cannot point to one of my top people as a traitor. Who? Naaj Majda? Ragnar Bloodmark? To accuse either, I would need iron-clad proof.

Why Naaj or Ragnar? Dehya asked, troubled that he picked the two officers she most trusted. *Brant Tapperhaven has always been a maverick. You like him because he was a Jagernaut. You relate to him, that whole taciturn fighter pilot thing. But he's the one most willing to break rules.*

Oh, I don't know, Eldrin said. ***Ragnar is a damn asshole.***

For flaming sake, Dehya thought, irked.

He interferes with our lives, Eldrin told her.

This isn't the time, she thought. *That has nothing to do with Ragnar as a military officer.*

Are you sure? Kelric asked. **You asked if my friendship with Brant affects my judgment. It's a good question. You should ask the same about your friendships with Ragnar and Naaj.**

That gave her pause. He had a point. *Have you noticed,* she thought, *that every time we try to discuss this breach in the web, we end up arguing about something else?*

Both Kelric and Eldrin were silent. Then Kelric thought, **No.**

Actually, she's right, Eldrin said. ***It happens whenever she and I talk about this business with Del and "Carnelians Finale," but only when we're in Kyle space.***

You think ESComm planted some sort of disruptive code that affects us when we broach the subject?

You know what? Dehya said. *I think yes, that's exactly what they did. This business with "Carnelians*

Finale" is subterfuge. Someone released the song twice, and the second time, they linked it to Del. Maybe they tried to link it both times, but they couldn't manage at first because they didn't know what they were doing. Just look at this breach. A rip? They didn't even hide it. She couldn't imagine Naaj, Ragnar, or Brant doing such sloppy work.

If ESComm is using untrained providers, Kelric thought, **they probably knew they'd leave a trail. Maybe they booby-trapped the pathway to distract anyone who investigated.**

It's possible, Dehya thought. Now came the big lie, because they needed to convince Eldrin. *We were caught in it because of our link to Del. When they tampered with him, a backlash hit us.* That was the story they would spread, to draw attention from a more probable scenario, that the backlash came from an attempt against the life of the third Triad member.

It seems unlikely, Eldrin thought. ***If it were possible to affect the Triad through Kyle space that way, nearly killing you and Kelric, they would have tried it before.***

They have Althor's daughter, Kelric answered. **A Ruby psion. She might be able to cause such an effect.**

Dehya's relief vanished. Yes, the Traders had Aliana. ESComm had taken her into custody *after* Dehya and Kelric had nearly died, so she probably had nothing to do with what had happened to them. But the danger remained. Although ESComm couldn't create their own web, they could steal web access and use Alaina's power in Kyle space.

A metallic thought intruded on them: **Communication incoming.**

Identify yourself, Kelric thought.

Node IMIN: Imperial Intelligence A5a.mil.

IMIN, my staff can deal with messages, Kelric told it.

This one is from Comtrace, IMIN answered.

Kelric immediately thought. **Transfer us to Comtrace.**

A new thought formed, powerful and inhuman, coming from Comtrace, one of ISC's most powerful Evolving Intelligences. **TRANSFER COMPLETE.**

What is the message? Kelric asked.

IT COMES FROM THE PALACE ON GLORY, Comtrace said.

Has it cleared the protocols yet?

IT IS IN PROCESS. I CAN SPEED ITS PROGRESS, IF THE PHARAOH WISHES.

Yes, do that, Dehya said.

It was time to find out Jaibriol's next move in their interstellar game of Quis.

Aliana curled closer to Red under the velvety covers. He murmured in his sleep and pulled her into his arms. So strange, to have someone share her bed. Who would have thought it could be so nice.

Red laughed drowsily. "Most of human race likes it."

"I can see why." She had never trusted anyone enough to hold him at night or wake up with him in the morning. Given how fast night came and went on Glory, with its sixteen-hour day, she and Red had done a lot of that recently. They couldn't leave this suite where the emperor's guards had put them, but far worse fates existed than living in this gorgeous place with Red.

"All Aristo live this way," Red said.

"It isn't fair that so few of them get so much while the rest of us have so little."

"They Aristos," he said matter-of-factly. "We nothing."

"I suppose." She tickled him under the arm. "You definitely feel like something."

"Ai! Stop!" Red burst out laughing and grabbed her hands.

"You seem happy," Aliana said. "I never heard you laugh before we came here."

His smile faded. "Never have reason to laugh. Just cry."

"I don't understand how anyone could hurt you that way. They're monsters."

She expected some platitude about Aristos being exalted, but instead he said, "Emperor Jaibriol is different. I not feel his mind."

"Red, he's the *emperor.* I doubt his brain is empty."

"I mean he different from other Hightons."

"I was too busy being intimidated to think about it," she admitted. "But you're right, being around him doesn't hurt. I think he's like us. His mind, I mean."

Red gave a surprisingly harsh laugh. "He Highton. Not like us. Never like us."

"Well, I think he is," she said, feeling stubborn.

"No Highton is ever provider."

"I didn't say that."

"Yes. You did."

"He's left us alone. That's what matters." They had seen no one but the servers who brought them wonderfully sumptuous meals. The closets here were full of clothes and the cupboards full of anything else they could want. It was merciful respite. She didn't know if executioners would come for Red in five minutes, tomorrow, five years, or never. It turned this refuge into a bittersweet dream, a tenuous interlude caught inside a bubble that might disappear any moment.

Red stroked her hair. "Definitely alone."

She smiled and tickled him more, making him laugh, and then they were kissing. They played for a while, rolling in the silken sheets, teasing and caressing. Loving. Eventually, when they had worn each other out, they drifted back to sleep.

A hum came from across the room.

She lifted her head. "What was that?"

"Someone outside," Red mumbled.

Aliana pulled on the soft blue robe she had thrown on top of the covers and slipped out of bed. She padded across the room to the wall with the entrance panel. Hesitating, she peered at its glowing buttons. Finally she said, "Greetings?"

A familiar voice came out of the air. "Zina, let me in."

"Tide? Is that you?"

"Yes." Even with a mechanical cadence, his voice had a distinctive sound.

She grinned. "Come in!"

"You have to open the door."

"Oh!" She paused. "How do I do that?"

"Give it permission."

"Um, sure, I mean, yes, door, you can open."

The wall shimmered, a pearly light in the dark room, then faded, leaving an open archway with Tide in it, a looming man in black trousers and tunic, with heavy boots that came to his knees and a gun holstered on his hip. Aliana had been ready to throw her arms around him, but now she held back, confused. He didn't look like Tide. He was a Razer.

He walked into the room. As the wall solidified, he said, "Can we turn on the lumos?"

"Oh. Sure." She hesitated, uncertain what to do. She tried, "Lumos on. Not bright."

The light came up, diffuse and soft.

"Aliana?" Red was coming across the room, dressed in a dark gold robe.

"For flaming sake," Tide said. "They put the two of you in here together?"

"What's wrong with that?" Aliana asked.

"You're children," he growled.

Aliana glared at him, forgetting she was intimidated. "I am *not* a child."

Red came to stand at her side and smiled disarmingly. "Am glad to see you, Tide."

The Razer exhaled as if his anger were leaking out a hole Red had poked in the balloon of his ire. "Thank you." Then he added, "But you can't call me Tide."

Aliana bit back her rebellious response. Blasting the Aristos for denying Tide his name after the emperor had given him back his life would be stupid. Besides, something else was going on with him, she didn't know what. Something about Red hurt him. Aliana wanted to ask why, but she knew Tide wouldn't tell her, especially not in front of Red.

"You two better be taking precautions," Tide said.

"I won't get pregnant, if that's what you mean," she said. This suite had everything they needed. Feeling clumsy, she said, "We're good together. Really." She took Red's hand. "It's nice."

Tide smiled then, though he seemed sad. "After

everything you two have been through, you deserve happiness. If you can give that to each other, I'm happy for you."

Aliana felt her face heating. This was all too much personal talk. Besides, she was worried about Tide. "Are you supposed to be here? The emperor said we can't see anyone."

"I'm assigned as the escort for both of you," Tide said. "We're leaving the planet at dawn."

"Leaving? For *where?*" she asked.

"What His Highness told you. To Delos."

Her voice trembled. "I can't do that."

Tide's voice gentled in a way she was certain no other Razer would let happen. "I'm sorry. But you have no choice."

"I'm afraid," she said. Red squeezed her hand.

"I'll look out for you both." Tide raked his hand through his newly cropped dark hair. "None of this makes sense. I tried to *defect,* for gods sake. So the emperor tells everyone I was on a spy mission and puts me on his personal bodyguard. Don't get me wrong; I can't begin to say how grateful I am. But it's crazy. I don't understand."

"You look like his other bodyguard," Red said.

Aliana blinked. "What other bodyguard?"

Red glanced at her. "Razer who save emperor's life on Earth."

"How do you know that?" Tide asked.

"Emperor say so." Red answered. "He tell you."

"You weren't there," Tide said. "So how would you know?"

Red hesitated, looking uncertain. "I'm not sure. From his mind, I think."

"I'm picking up his mind, too," Aliana said. "Like words I've never heard before, but suddenly I know what they mean."

"Don't *say* that." Tide lowered his voice. "You can't talk that way, either of you. Stay behind your mental walls or whatever you're doing to hide. You're going to be on a ship packed full of Aristos."

Red's face paled. "I not go."

"You have to go," Tide said.

"No!"

"Red, listen," Aliana said. "They don't know we're psions. They won't make us providers."

He shook his head with a sharp motion. "They know I am provider."

"But you don't work anymore," she said. "So they aren't interested."

"They think neither of you have any Kyle ability," Tide told them. "Eventually they'll test you, but for now you're safe." He considered Aliana. "The problem is, you *look* like a provider, at least your coloring." When she opened her mouth to tell him exactly what she thought of that, he held up his hand. "Don't get mad at me. I can't help the way you look. But listen, don't worry."

"Why not?" she growled.

"They're going to disguise you."

"Why? I don't want a disguise."

Tide lifted his hands. "I don't know why. One never questions Hightons."

"Why not?" Aliana asked crossly.

"Because no one is paying attention to you two right now," Tide said. "Not with everything else that is going on. You want it to stay that way."

"All they think about is Delos summit," Red said.

"That's putting it mildly." Tide grimaced. "It's all going to hell. Everything was already a mess, and now some Allied group has kidnapped that damn Skolian prince and worked everyone up, just when the furor was dying down. I can't believe anyone thinks this summit will achieve anything but disaster."

"What prince?" Aliana asked.

"Angry singer," Red said. "The one with the mad song."

"Oh, him." Aliana wasn't surprised someone had grabbed him. He had certainly caused a lot of trouble.

Red frowned at her. "Zina, how you know he do anything? You think 'He make trouble.' Everyone thinks that. But maybe it's not him."

"Sorry." She didn't really have any ill wishes for the singer.

Tide looked from Aliana to Red. "Was that just a figure of speech?" he asked Red. "Or were you really responding to what she was thinking?"

"Not speech figure," Red said. "It was what she think."

"No!" Aliana said, remembering Lensmark had told her to protect Red. "He says that all the time," she told Tide quickly. "He doesn't *really* mean he knows what I think."

"Yes, I do," Red said.

"No you don't!" She sent him a fierce look.

Tide was watching them as if he were seeing an avalanche crashing down. "Is that the best you two can do to hide that you're still psions?"

Aliana tried to sound nonchalant. "I don't know what you mean."

"Gods," he muttered. "On the trip to Delos, I want you both to stay away from everyone. Stay in your cabin. Don't interact with anyone if you can help it." With difficulty, he added, "Keep each other company, if that's what it takes to hide you."

There it was again, his pain. Aliana wished she understood what hurt him. He had his life back now, even better than before. Why would she and Red matter? They were nobody.

"He already say why," Red told her. "You child. Off-limits. To him."

Tide's forehead creased. "What?"

"It's nothing," Aliana said, flustered. She had no idea what Red meant, either. Too much was happening too fast. "This summit can't be safe."

"It's all confused." Tide paced away like a boxer full of agitated energy. "The Skolians claim Prince Del-Kurj didn't release that song and their military didn't attack our merchants, that these are set-ups by people trying to disrupt the peace process." He turned and came back to them. "The Allied Worlds of Earth claim these Minutemen have nothing to do with them. ESComm says it's all nonsense, that the Allieds and Skolians are in collusion."

Red squinted at them. "Why they bother to have summit?"

"Gods only know," Tide said. "Hell, maybe even they have no idea."

"Why does the emperor want Red and me?" Aliana asked. "We can't help."

Tide spread his arms out from his body. "Truthfully, I've no idea."

Neither did Aliana. But they might soon find out, if they were leaving at dawn.

Their respite here was coming to an end.

XXIII
Rocked Star

"Damn," Dehya said. "We were right about ESComm training telops."

She and Kelric were in the Mentation Room, bathed in starlight, playing the latest Quis session Jaibriol had sent them. Except this time the verbal message hadn't been a bland non-statement. He had sent a detailed proposal: Meet on Delos. Their governments would build the amphitheatre for the summit together, each side monitoring the other, with the Allieds mediating.

The Quis told a different story: ESComm had infiltrated the Delos mesh through Kyle space, using providers who had little idea what they were doing. The fact that ISC didn't know gave ESComm a large advantage, one they intended to exploit.

"So ESComm ripped that hole in our mesh," Kelric said.

"We need to decide whether to sew it up or leave it as a trap," Dehya said absently, intent on the dice. "The intricacy of these patterns, the details—a lot is here, if we can figure it out."

Kelric shifted several dice. "Something is different. I'm not sure what."

Dehya worked with him, manipulating real dice while she ran Quis simulations in her mind. So many possibilities. So many paths.

"Gods all-flaming-mighty," she suddenly said. "This isn't about the summit. It's about Del!"

Kelric looked up with a start. Then he returned to the game and worked his magic. As they deconstructed the patterns, a new story became clear.

Jaibriol knew what had happened to Del.

The siren jarred Del out of sleep. He sat up too fast and nausea surged over him. The hold was as dark as always, but an alarm screamed through the air.

Del scrambled to his feet. "That's an ESComm warning siren for a military attack!"

Mac's voice came from near him in the dark. "ESComm? As in, Eubian?"

"Hell, yeah," Del said. "These people are Traders!" He turned in the darkness, trying to orient himself. "We have to get out of here."

"No kidding." The clang of a fist hitting metal came from the direction of Mac's voice. "Hello!" he shouted. "Is anyone there? Can you hear us?"

Del walked forward, holding his hands in front of him, striving for calm despite his racing pulse. His palms hit a bulkhead and he felt his way along it. When he reached what he thought was the place where their food came, he scraped the surface, dug at it, pounded, but nothing worked.

"Come on," he muttered. The siren kept screaming. Del hit the bulkhead with his fist. "Let us out!"

he yelled. He kept waiting for a new siren to add its voice to the clamor, the warning that the hull had been breached, the whoosh of air rushing out of the cargo bay out into space—along with him and Mac.

"I can't hear a blasted thing over that alarm," Mac said.

For lack of a better idea, Del shouted in Highton. "Ship, answer! What is the emergency?"

A booming metallic voice spoke. "This ship is under attack. Proceed to the lifeboats."

"We can't proceed," Del said, startled that it had actually answered. "We're locked in here."

"You are prisoners."

"Yeah, well, we're going to be dead prisoners pretty soon."

"Entrance opened," the ship said.

The wall glowed as a hatchway appeared nearby. It wasn't rectangular or oval, like on Earth ships, but an elongated octagon. Harsh light slanted into the cargo bay. Squinting, Del held up his hand to protect his dark-adapted eyes.

"Come on." Mac grabbed his arm. "Let's *go.*"

They ran through the hatchway and into an octagonal-shaped corridor with bulkheads like burnished white gold. Glowing blue rails ran along them at waist height. At regular intervals, red tiles flashed in the walls, pulsating with the vibration of the siren.

"Do you recognize any of this?" Mac asked as they ran, shielding their eyes. "Is it like Tarex's yacht?"

"Not at all. It's bigger, a rotation ship maybe." Del pointed ahead, where the deck sloped upward until the disappeared behind the curved ceiling. "I think we're in the wheel."

"It looks military to me," Mac said. "Definitely *not* Allied."

The ship's metallic voice spoke. "You will find shuttles in bay six on this level." The blue rail on the wall turned emerald. "Follow the green pointers."

Del kept running. "I haven't seen a single crew member."

"My guess?" Mac said. "This entire ship is being run by the five people who took us."

"That's nuts. They wouldn't jeopardize the mission with such a small crew."

"It was probably that or nothing." Mac was breathing hard. "If this is ESComm, it must have taken years, decades even, to infiltrate Allied Space Command with agents high enough to position themselves on your guard detail. That could make this a desperation move, the hope that they can succeed in kidnapping you even without a full crew."

Del continued to run, though he held back his full speed so Mac could keep up. "This ship could stop us."

"Right now, I'd bet its priority is getting you out of here alive and still a prisoner."

"And we're helping it," Del muttered. His eyes had recovered enough that he could see the hall without squinting. The ceiling looked exactly like the deck, with gold and silver panels. If the ship stopped rotating, the "gravity" would cease and bottom could just as well be top.

They reached an intersection where corridors branched off right and left, up and down. The green rail curved into a shaft above them like a glowing emerald pathway.

"Ship!" Del said in Highton. "Can you give us a ladder?"

The chute above them whirred, and a ladder slid down from its rim until it clanged the deck at Del's feet. He climbed upward with Mac right behind him. At the top, they clambered out into a docking bay filled with small, gleaming ships, silver and blue, each with a black puma emblazoned on its hull.

"Gorgeous," Del said as they jogged across the bay. He spoke to Mac in English. "You were in the Air Force before you retired, right? Can you fly one of these?"

"I've no idea." Mac slowed down as they ran into the midst of ships. "These aren't lifeboats. Some look like single-pilot reconnaissance craft." He paused by a sleek beauty. "This is a racer. It's meant to go fast." He ran his hand over the hull. "I don't see a way inside, though."

Del spoke in Highton. "Ship! We need to board this craft."

"You may board," the ship said. A molecular airlock shimmered in the racer's hull and vanished, revealing an interior crammed with equipment and seats for a pilot, co-pilot, and two passengers. "I'm coding your travel route into the racer's AI."

Del swore under his breath. Although an AI wasn't as smart as an EI, it could easily take him and Mac to wherever the Traders wanted.

"We can pilot the racer," Del told the mothership.

"That is unacceptable," the ship answered.

Sirens continued to blare, and somewhere a clanging vibrated through the ship. Mac paused in the hatchway. "If a battle is going on out there, we may have a rough ride."

"We won't have any options," Del said. "The mothership is locking us out of the racer's controls."

"If we stay here," Mac said, "we could be killed by whoever is attacking this ship."

"Maybe they've come for us," Del said. If they launched into space, they *might* wrest control away from the racer AI. Then they could go where they wanted, assuming no one shot them down. But if they couldn't control of the racer, it would take them away, either saving their lives or stealing them out from under the noses of their rescuers.

"We don't know who is attacking," Mac said. "Allieds? ESComm? ISC?"

"If someone has come to rescue us," Del said, "we can meet up with them better if we're in the racer than if we're running around this ship."

"Not if the racer won't let us communicate with them. They might blow us up."

"They might blow up this entire mothership!"

Mac clenched the side of the hatchway. "If they came to rescue us, they won't do that."

"Then they wouldn't blow up a racer, either," Del said. "If this really is a Eubian ship, it would rather kill us than let us be rescued. It's that gruesome death-before-capture Trader thing."

Mac smacked his palm against the hull. "I wish that damn alarm would stop screaming! It's impossible to think straight."

"What the hell," Del said. "Let's go! We'll take our chances."

"Deal." Mac strode into the racer and Del jumped up after him. The moment he was onboard, the airlock reformed behind him, solidifying into the double-layered hull.

The racer spoke, sounding less metallic than the

mothership. "Seat yourselves in the pilot and co-pilot's chair. I will activate your exoskeletons."

Del dropped into the co-pilot's seat. He wasn't sure he wanted his "exoskeleton" activated, whatever that meant, but he understood too little about star ships to know whether or not he needed it. His chair whirred and a cage folded around his body, enclosing him in a flexible network of struts, equipment, and virtual reality gear. A heads-up display lowered over his head, flooding him with data. He shoved it back so he could see the cockpit. Three-dimensional glyphs formed in the air, along with star maps and confusing displays of graphs and machine parts. One panel glowed with what looked like a weapons manifest.

"Uh, Mac," he said. "This is military."

Mac was studying the panels around his seat. "It's fast. That's what we need."

"Yeah, fast and *armed.* It's a freaking warship."

"That, too." Mac was toggling panels on the pilot's controls, running through displays. "It's been two decades since I've flown a fighter. Back then, we had even less data about ESComm space craft than we do now, and what little we knew then doesn't match what I'm seeing here."

"Can you fly this thing?"

"I can't even get into the nav system. Look at that!" Mac pointed to a display of stars and numbers evolving in the air. "The AI is plotting our course. I can't make it stop."

The hum of engines rumbled through the craft, while lights pulsed in green, red, gold and blue. Mac swung his seat around to Del, ensconced in his exoskeleton like a fighter pilot. "If that's your people out there, they would have brought Jag fighters, yes?"

"Hell, yeah." Even with as little familiarity as Del had with the military, he knew Jag squads were the most effective units for in-close military operations. He ought to know. Four of his siblings had been fighter pilots: his sister Soz, his brother Kelric, his brother Althor, and his half brother Kurj, his namesake.

"Jagernauts are all telepaths, right?" Mac asked. "With their abilities enhanced by neural implants and links to their ships."

"I'm not supposed to tell you anything about that," Del said.

Clangs came from outside as the racer slid along its launch rail.

"Del, listen," Mac said. "When we're out of the mothership, nothing solid will be blocking your mind except the racer's hull. I want you to drop your mental barriers and blast this area with a message. If any telepaths are out there, you might reach them."

"I might," Del said. "But the chances aren't great. The electromagnetic fields of our brains fall off as the Coulomb force. That means that within a few meters of wherever we are, our reception of other people's minds goes essentially to zero."

"For normal people, yes. But don't other telepaths have a better chance of picking you up? Especially Jagernauts, with all that augmentation you're not supposed to talk about."

Mac had a point. "They might."

"Prepare for launch," the racer said. Its front screens activated, showing the docking bay. The bay doors opened like mammoth jigsaw puzzle pieces pulling apart and a rumble shook through the ship. With a jerk that shoved Del back in his seat, the racer surged forward, hurtling along its rail. As the g-forces increased, the exoskeleton compensated, cushioning Del's body. In a roar of engines, the racer shot past the bay doors and into space.

They hurtled out of a huge ship, a wheel rotating around a hub. Projections covered its hull, weapons ports and other structures Del didn't recognize.

They were in the midst of a battle.

Small ships were firing on the wheel, gold and black vessels that darted around it, making up in speed what they lacked in size. Among them, deadliest of all, were four single-pilot fighters that glowed like alabaster. Jags. Smart missiles raced through space and beams flared. An incandescent explosion silently burst on the wheel and sent debris hurtling out into space.

"Those are Skolian ships attacking the wheel!" Del said.

Mac nodded, intent on his controls. "See if you can reach them."

Del closed his eyes and tried to lower his barriers. He had spent so much of his life making sure his defenses protected him, blocking the onslaught of emotions from other people, that it was difficult to let go. His adrenaline-pushed agitation made it hard to focus.

Calm, he thought. *Stay calm.* His shields began to fade. He felt vulnerable, exposed to attack, but he kept working. When his shields were all the way down, he "shouted," ***This is Prince Del-Kurj! We're in ESComm racer QT8. Don't fire on us! Mac Tyler and I are prisoners in the racer. We have no nav control. Don't shoot!*** He repeated the message over and over again, imagining his thoughts projected in all directions.

After what felt like an eternity, Mac said, "Are you getting anything?"

Del opened his eyes. The forward screens showed them racing away from the battle. According to a display on his armrest, only one minute had passed since he started.

"I sent a message," he said. "I've no idea if anyone caught it."

"Try again," Mac said.

"Okay." Marshalling his strength, he shouted: ***This is Del-Kurj. We're prisoners in racer QT8. If you're out there, if you pick this up, you have to stop the racer.***

A woman's voice burst into the cockpit, speaking Skolian Flag. "Racer QT8, this is Secondary Panquai, captain of ISC Blackhawk Squadron. We are receiving you. Good work! We can pick you up more easily out here. I'll dock with your ship and tow you in."

The racer spoke. "Onboard communication systems breached."

Del grinned. "You bet."

"Do not respond to Blackhawk," the racer told him.

Mac was touching different panels, trying something, Del didn't know what, but he would have bet his next royalty payment it was the ship-to-ship comm. Sure enough, the lights on the comm panel suddenly flared green.

"This is Mac Tyler," he said. "Panquai, can you read me?"

"We're receiving," Panquai answered. "Is Prince Del-Kurj with you?"

"I'm right here," Del said.

"Your racer is preparing to fire on us," she told him. "It's also preparing to invert."

Damn! One racer couldn't outgun a full Jag squad, but if it inverted out of normal space into superluminal space, the Jags would never catch it. The screens showed them arrowing away from the wheel ship accompanied by four Jag starfighters. Two ESComm ships were in pursuit, drones probably if Mac was right that the wheel ship had almost no crew. They couldn't keep up with the racer or the Jags.

"Panquai, what do you want us to do?" Mac asked.

"We're trying to break into the nav-attack system," she said. "It's too damn well protected."

Mac spoke in heavily accented Highton. "Racer, release nav and weapons."

"Negative," the racer responded. "If the Jags try to gain control of me, I will fire on them."

"You don't have chance against a Jag squad," Mac said. "You know this."

"I calculate a two percent probability that I can defeat them," the racer said. "I calculate an eighty-six percent probability that Prince Del-Kurj and yourself would be killed in such an engagement. I have informed Blackhawk Squadron that I am prepared to fight, and that if they damage my systems, I will detonate myself and kill you both."

"For flaming sake!" Del said. "Don't do that."

A woman's thought came into Del's mind. *Prince Del-Kurj, this is Secondary Panquai. Can you receive me?*

Del jerked at the unexpectedly clear message. He had never interacted with a telepath while their abilities were enhanced by the neural technology of a Jag starfighter.

Yes, he thought. ***I'm receiving you.***

We're going to try something, she thought. *I want you to envision, in your mind, the displays all around you. Let me see them.*

Del focused on the panels, creating pictures in his mind. ***Is it coming through?***

It's blurred. Can you project more clearly?

Del added more details to his mental picture. ***How's that?***

Better, she said. *My mind is converting the pictures into data my Jag can download. Anything you see, no matter how small, might help. We don't have much time; your racer will invert within minutes.*

Do you want me to look at the pilot's controls, too?

If you can. But yours should duplicate his.

Del concentrated harder, forming images of the controls in his mind. Mac watched him, staying silent; probably he knew Del was in a link with the Jagernaut.

Good! Panquai suddenly thought. *We have enough. Now open the nav-attack console and do the same for its interior circuitry. The AI will try to stop you, but it's easier to confuse than an EI. Distract it.*

Del glanced at Mac. "Can you open the weapons and navigation panels?"

"Open it, yes. But I can't transfer control from the ship to you. We're locked out."

"That's okay," Del said. "Just bother the AI as much as you can."

As Mac unfastened a panel from his controls, the racer said, "Stop doing that."

"We play hopscotch," Mac answered.

Prince Del-Kurj, get as much as you can as fast as you can, Panquai thought.

"No you aren't playing hopscotch," the racer told Mac. "Replace that panel."

Del focused on the silvery circuits that Mac had uncovered. He knew nothing about the tech, and he wasn't sure his image was accurate, but he supplied as many details as he could.

"You see, this is problem," Mac told the racer in stilted Highton. "This panel, I not wish to replace. Your refusing to give us ship defies the Jabberwocky and Mad Hatter. If you fall down a rabbit hole, you are really in a mole hole, which is maybe a black hole, which means you are trapped forever and elongated infinitely."

"That makes no sense," the racer said. "You're mixing references to children's stories from the culture of Earth with theoretical astrophysics in a clumsy attempt to confuse me."

"Am I?" Mac said. "To me, the military context is obvious."

"The Mad Hatter has a military context?"

"Well, obviously," Mac said. "Why think you he is mad?"

"There is no military context!" the racer said. "Cease your actions or I will flood the cockpit with sleeping gas."

"You won't," Mac said. "You want no harm for either of us, especially not Prince Del-Kurj."

"Gas released," the racer said.

"Shit," Del muttered. ***Panquai, the racer is gassing us. I don't know if I'm allergic.***

We're getting close, she thought. *Hang in there. Send images for as long as you can.*

Del struggled to concentrate. That little white conduit, maybe that was important. The symbols there, he didn't recognize what they meant, but Panquai might. The gas continued to hiss, until he sagged back in his seat, dizzy and nauseous. ***Panquai . . . can't keep my eyes open . . .***

It's all right, Panquai said. *Hang on!*

"Preparing to invert," the racer said.

"*No!*" Mac said. Del managed to open his eyes enough to see Mac struggling to sit forward.

"Mister Tyler, I'm locking your exoskeleton," the racer said.

"No, don't—" Mac groaned as the frame around his body tightened, forcing him to sit back.

A pictorial display above the forward controls indicated the ship was jumping in and out of quasis, or quantum stasis, protecting them from the immense accelerations it needed to reach relativistic speeds so fast. Del couldn't read Highton any better than he could read English, but he recognized the numbers on the display: they were going to invert in only forty-two seconds.

Del just barely remained conscious, though whether it was because of his body's eccentric reaction to medicine or the racer hadn't really intended to knock him out, he didn't know. The AI had achieved what it wanted, incapacitating both him and Mac.

Secondary Panquai, he thought. ***We . . . invert in thirty seconds.***

We'll get you, she thought.

The seconds flashed by. Twenty-five. Twenty. Fifteen.

We're almost in! Panquai thought.

The rumble of the engines surged as the racer activated the inversion engines.

Ten seconds.

Five.

One.

NOW, Panquai shouted.

A giant fist of pressure slammed Del back. He groaned as his vision blurred. One thought jumped out of his fragmented thoughts; the racer's quasis generators had stopped working. He prayed the Jags could extend their fields to this racer, because if they couldn't, these accelerations were going to smear him and Mac all over their seats.

"I can't survive this," the racer said. "Self-destruct initialized."

"No!" Del yelled. ***Panquai!*** he shouted. ***The racer is going to expl—***

The universe went black.

The populace tended to stay inside during the day, which burned with heat in the long hours of sunlight. They came out after the sun was long vanished from the sky. The air was cool now, chilly but bracing, and the city hummed, vibrant with energy, awash in color and music in the deepest hours of night.

Jaibriol had come to Delos once before, when he traded himself for his uncle Eldrin, the Ruby Consort, and assumed his throne as emperor of Eube. Before he had taken that final step, he had wandered around New Athens, savoring his last day of freedom. The city bordered an ocean on one side and rose up into the hills on the other. The houses thinned out at the higher slopes and became mansions separated by parks. He remembered the musical fountains and flowerbeds, including flute-blossoms that chimed in the wind. The homes there were shaped like galleons afloat in foliage sculpted to resemble waves, all in hues of green, white, and ocean-blues. The rare boulevard wound through the parks like a ribbon of silver.

The harbor lay southeast of the city. Breakers rolled in over knife-coral reefs, which jutted out of the water in spires. It had fascinated him to watch sparks flash as iridescent fliers darted in and out of the coral. Gates and channels were cut through the reefs, allowing ships into the harbor. Waves glowed purple and gold from phosphorescence and smashed against the coral, jumping high into the air, bursting in sprays of foam.

Tonight Jaibriol saw the city and ocean through a sheen of light that rippled around his balcony like a faint aurora borealis. It was the only outward sign of a cyberlock, an implant in his brain. When activated, the lock produced a field tuned to its owner's brain waves. If penetrated by anyone whose neural signature wasn't imprinted in the lock, a low-keyed field sounded an alarm and a mid-keyed field knocked out the intruders. For the entire time he was on Delos, Jaibriol's cyberlock would be high-keyed: set to kill.

His wrist comm hummed. With regret, he turned from the view and walked past the open glass doors into his living room. White carpet spread around him, glimmering. The furniture resembled wood, but with a glowing quality, swirled with gold and upholstered in rose-patterned cushions. A media center gleamed to one side, glossy with screens and Luminex consoles. Paintings of Greek landscapes hung on the pale gold walls.

Jaibriol touched a panel on his comm and it turned gold. Suddenly he felt better, no longer disoriented. It was how he knew it was safe for someone to approach him; he had just deactivated his cyberlock.

"Jason?" Jaibriol asked.

The EI that ran the suite answered in a pleasant male voice. "Yes, Your Highness. Would you like me to admit the party that has rung your doorbell?"

He hadn't heard any bell, just the hum on his comm. "Who is it?"

"Your aide, Robert Muzeson."

"Yes, let him in."

A door whisked open somewhere beyond the entrance across the room, where two ivory columns rose up from the floor and curved into a pointed arch at the top.

A moment later, Robert walked through the arch, dressed in elegant black trousers and ivory shirt. He bowed deeply. "I'm honored to see you, Your Highness."

"My greetings." Jaibriol motioned to two wingchairs. "Did you get any sleep?"

"Not yet." He waited while Jaibriol sat, then settled into the other chair. A white orb painted with rose and gold vines hovered in the corner, shedding diffuse light over them.

"The preparations are almost complete for the summit," Robert said. "The Allieds have finished coordinating the construction of the amphitheatre for both us and the Skolians."

"How did it work out?"

Robert's wince said as much as his words. "About as well as you might expect. We don't trust the Skolians and they don't trust us. But it's done."

"Show me."

Robert pulled a gold tube out of a sheath on his belt and tapped it against his knee. As it unrolled into a screen, holicons appeared above it in neat rows. He flicked one of the Allied insignia, a blue wreath, and a much larger image appeared of a building high in the Delos hills, a structure built to resemble a tall ship. As Robert flicked more holicons, the view zoomed in. Then they were inside the building, in a conference room, at a crystal table. Its seats were a cross between the recliners Hightons preferred and the chairs used by Skolians.

"It looks exactly like the models ESComm and ISC came up with," Jaibriol said.

"I should hope so," Robert said dourly. "Given the arguing over *every* excruciating detail."

Jaibriol smiled. "Ah, well, it's to be expect—" He stopped as his comm shrilled. At the same moment, the holicon of a red emergency beacon appeared above Robert's mesh screen, its brightness swamping the other images.

Jaibriol tapped his comm. "Qox here. What is it?"

"Your Highness! This is Major Iquarson. We've intercepted an encrypted ISC message and broken the code. ISC has attacked more of our ships!"

Jaibriol swore under his breath. Had yet another fanatic set up another crisis in the hopes of squelching the summit on the eve of its commencement? Robert was bringing up menus above his screen so fast, the holos blurred in a smear of colors.

"What happened?" Jaibriol asked the major.

"A Skolian military unit attacked a Eubian wheel ship—a *civilian* ship—belonging to Axil Tarex, the CEO of Tarex Entertainment."

Well, bloody hell. Jaibriol didn't know whether to be relieved or even more worried. Kelric and the Ruby Pharaoh must have translated his last Quis message. Lord Axil Tarex, CEO of Tarex Entertainment, may the gods scorch his greedy soul, had been part of Barthol's ill-advised attempt to kidnap Prince Del-Kurj and stir the interstellar pot of outrage over "Carnelians Finale." Barthol had assigned all five of ESComm's spies on Earth to the mission, which meant he had effectively thrown away decades of building their covers, all for an abduction that could start another war.

"What happened to the crew and passengers of the wheel ship?" Jaibriol asked.

Major Iquarson spoke grimly. "The Skolians captured them all."

Jaibriol glanced at Robert's mesh screen. His aide had located a file showing the battle, a surgically precise attack by the Skolians. The so-called "civilian" wheel ship was firing back with what looked like military armaments.

"I see," Jaibriol told Major Iquarson. "And did this ISC message happen to mention *why* the Skolians attacked Lord Tarex's ship?"

A pause came from the major. Jaibriol supposed he should have kept the sarcasm out of his voice. But he was fed up. For Barthol to collaborate with Tarex on the kidnapping had been a bad idea; doing it without telling the emperor had been stupid. If Jaibriol hadn't picked it up out of Barthol's mind, gods only knew what would have happened. Right now one concern wiped out all others: if Del hadn't survived the rescue, this summit was over and done with before it even began.

"The ISC message we intercepted was brief," Iquarson told him. "It just said they had seven people, everyone who had been onboard the wheel."

"Only seven people?" Jaibriol asked. "Including the crew?"

"Yes, Sire."

Although Jaibriol knew a wheel ship with a good EI could, in theory, operate with no crew, he sure as blazes wouldn't want to travel on it. He could see why Barthol didn't want a lot of people involved, though; the fewer who knew about their contraband prince, the less chance someone would compromise the mission. EIs were easier than humans to program, as Barthol was so fond of saying in his constant drive to design an army of cybernetic soldiers.

"Do you know the identities of the crew and passengers?" Jaibriol asked.

"Not for certain," Iquarson said. "Either it carried seven Allied citizens, or else two Allieds and five Eubians."

Jaibriol would have laughed if he hadn't been so angry. "Seven Allied citizens as the only crew on Lord Axil Tarex's wheel ship?"

"It does seem far-fetched," Iquarson admitted.

Jaibriol continued to watch Robert's record of the battle. It showed a racer arrowing away from the battle with four Jag fighters keeping pace and two Eubian fighters chasing them.

"Who was on the racer?" Jaibriol asked.

"We don't know, Sire," Iquarson said. "They appear to be fleeing."

"Did the Jags catch them?"

"Yes, just barely. The passengers in the racer made a valiant effort to destroy themselves, but the Jags dishonored them."

"By rescuing them?" Jaibriol asked dryly.

Iquarson apparently missed the edge in his voice. "Yes, Sire. I'm sorry."

Jaibriol had never understood this suicide-to-retain-honor business. If the people in that racer were who he suspected, he was immensely grateful the ship had failed to kill them. "So ISC has everyone from the mothership?"

"As far as we know," Iquarson said. "We'll keep you apprised as we learn more."

"You do that," Jaibriol said. "And tell General Iquar I want to see him. *Immediately.*"

"Yes, Your Highness. Right away."

"Very well." Jaibriol flicked off his comm.

Robert was watching him. "You don't seem surprised."

"I wish just *once* someone would surprise me with good news." Jaibriol pushed to his feet and paced across the uselessly gorgeous rug, which like so much else in his life achieved nothing except beauty. He needed so much more from the people and environment that surrounded him, like morality and trust. He wanted to excoriate Barthol. He wanted even more, though, for this beleaguered summit to succeed, and that meant reining in his desire to stake the general across hot coals.

"Would you like me to prepare a statement for you on the incident?" Robert asked. "I can also monitor the meshes to see if the Skolians come up with an apology."

"Apology?" Jaibriol swung around to him. "For what? Rescuing Prince Del-Kurj?"

Robert gaped at him. "You think he was on the wheel ship?"

"That's right," Jaibriol said. "If the Skolians know Tarex owned that ship rather than these Minutemen of whatever, they have grounds to pull out of the summit." His best hope was that they had found Del because of Jaibriol's Quis message, and that the Imperator would make allowances because of that.

The military had obviously armed Tarex's ship. Of course, Barthol would claim ESComm had no connection to the operation, just as ISC claimed they had no connection to the attack on the Eubian merchants. And Tarex had never signed any peace treaty, so he couldn't be accused of treason for trying to recover a singer he had considered his possession ever since he held Del prisoner nine years ago under the guise of "signing" him to his music label. The Skolians would consider his actions criminal, but according to the Eubian legal system, Tarex had broken no laws.

The EI that ran the suite spoke. "General Barthol

Iquar and his bodyguards are at the entrance. Shall I grant them entry?"

"Just Iquar," Jaibriol said. "Not his guards." It would anger the general, but tough. "Make sure my Razers stay with him."

Within moments, the thud of boots came from beyond the archway. Jaibriol stood in his living room, watching the entrance. Two of his bodyguards appeared in the arch, giants with gunmetal collars and massive gauntlets that not only included their slave guards, but also miniature weapons platforms. As they stepped aside, Barthol stalked through the archway, his grey uniform like a shadow. Two more of Jaibriol's Razers followed, including Tide. Barthol's face showed only detachment, but hostility blazed from his mind.

The general stopped at exactly the appropriate distance from Jaibriol and bowed from the waist exactly as expected, not one centimeter more. Jaibriol wouldn't have been surprised if Barthol had his biomech web controlling the amount he bent so that he didn't give even a fraction more respect than his life demanded.

"My honor," Barthol said. "At your Glorious presence." His pause before the honorific left the words hanging as if he had almost forgotten them. It balanced on the edge of insult, and he no doubt believed he could get away with it because Jaibriol needed him at the summit.

"So it is," Jaibriol said, knowing Barthol would take it as an affront. He slowly walked around the general, pacing with deliberation, while Barthol looked straight ahead, his posture ramrod straight. His mind was like a grinding machine that relentlessly eroded Jaibriol's barriers.

Steeling himself, Jaibriol probed the general's thoughts. Barthol was furious. He hadn't expected Jaibriol to figure out his role in Del's capture, and he sure as hell hadn't expected the Skolians to rescue the prince. That Barthol already knew about the rescue hit Jaibriol with another unpleasant realization; ESComm had reported to its army commander first, before the emperor.

Damn.

If he lost his already shaky ESComm support, this summit would be in even more trouble. He felt reasonably certain about Erix Muze, at least as confident as one could ever feel about a Highton, but Barthol could cause him no end of problems.

Jaibriol paused behind the general. "Have you ever wondered, Barthol, why the late night hours have such a terrible reputation with poets?"

"No," Barthol said. Then he added, "Your Highness."

"They always write about the despair those hours can inflict on the human soul."

"Do they now?" Barthol said. "I don't read poetry."

"No, I imagine not," Jaibriol said. "A pity, that."

Barthol shrugged. "Poets often prey on the pity of callow youth."

Robert stood up, his mesh screen clutched in one hand, blurring the holicons that floated around it. Jaibriol shook his head slightly and Robert made no further move, though his jaw stiffened.

Jaibriol finished his circuit and came in front of Barthol. He stood regarding the general, looking *down*. A muscle twitched under Barthol's eye.

"Music is a form of poetry, don't you think?" Jaibriol said.

"I imagine those who write music would like to think so," Barthol answered.

"There are those who say it can bring about the rise and fall of empires."

Barthol lifted his shoulders again, a brusque motion. "Such delusions aren't reserved only to those who write little ditties."

"Of course, other composers could care less," Jaibriol continued, as if Barthol had said nothing. "They just want to sing. But what they sing, now that is what causes the furor."

"I wouldn't know," Barthol said. His arms were by his sides, innocuous, except that his middle finger on his left hand rested on top his index finger, which implied he was the one who couldn't care less.

"Some singers inspire any number of dramatic responses," Jaibriol said. "Fans scream, women profess their love, concert halls fill. Conglomerate executives amass prodigious wealth. Perhaps even a war begins. All from one song."

"Slaves waste their time in all manner of silly ways," Barthol said. "That's why they're slaves and not Aristos."

"And yet," Jaibriol said, "music always has its place. Force it to go somewhere against its will, and the resulting discord can destroy those who would attempt to steal it."

Barthol's fist clenched. "Music is a waste of time. Often it deserves to die."

In a deceptively quiet voice, Jaibriol said, "Music never dies, General. It survives wars, famine, plague, and the fall of empires. The same cannot be said even for our most powerful warriors. The songs written about their deeds will live on long after they have died."

"History is written by the victors," Barthol said. "The songs we sing are part of that history, vaunted today." He regarded Jaibriol steadily. "And crushed tomorrow."

Robert's face had gone pale and the Razers were tensed as if ready for combat, their hands resting on their holstered guns.

"Spoken well, with such experience," Jaibriol murmured. "Those who live with their failed deeds today know what it means to pay the price tomorrow."

"Ah, but 'price' implies a trade," Barthol said. "Have you noticed, Most Gloried Highness, that those who demand too high a price find themselves with no trade at all when a new day dawns?"

Jaibriol knew if he pushed Barthol any further, the general would withdraw his support for the summit, which was supposed to be about trade relations. So he just inclined his head. "Trade is always complex. It will be our pleasure to see its success."

Like hell, Barthol thought, with such bitter disgust that it came to Jaibriol's mind even though the general was the antithesis of a psion. **My only pleasure would be freedom from your wretched existence. I failed to kill you once; I won't again.**

Aloud, Barthol said only, "It will be an auspicious day," and in doing so, he backed away from the edge of their verbal battle before they fell so deep into it, one of them unforgivably insulted the other.

Security protocols activated, Jaibriol's spinal node thought, hiding his response to Barthol's thought. *I failed to kill you once; I won't again.* With that thought had come a vivid image in the general's mind of Jaibriol lying in the wreckage of the library where he and Tarquine had nearly died.

Somehow Jaibriol stayed calm as he raised his hand, giving Barthol permission to leave. His Razers escorted the general out, all of them striding through the archway. Inside, rage seared his thoughts.

"Well, wasn't that rousing?" a throaty voice said behind Jaibriol.

He turned with a start. Tarquine was standing in the archway to their bedroom, leaning against one side of it, her arms crossed, her black hair mussed around her shoulders from sleep.

"How long were you listening?" he asked.

"Long enough to wonder if you and my nephew were about to declare war on each other."

Jaibriol couldn't say what he had picked up from Barthol about the attempts on their lives. He glanced at Robert. His aide met his gaze, then unclenched his fist, which had crumpled his mesh screen. He smoothed out the screen, rolled it up and slid it back into its sheath on his belt.

"Your Highness," Robert said, "shall I prepare a statement on the situation with Tarex?"

Jaibriol nodded, wishing *he* could crumple something with his fists, anything to ease his tension. "Get as much background as you can on the situation. Lord Tarex is a Silicate Aristo, the CEO of Tarex Entertainment. It's unlikely the people who kidnapped Prince Del-Kurj were his agents." Given the verbal slugfest Robert had just witnessed between Jaibriol and Eube's General of the Army, it wouldn't be hard for him to figure out where the agents came from.

Robert spoke carefully. "This will make tomorrow's summit interesting."

Jaibriol smiled rather wanly. "You're a master of

understatement." He had a long night ahead of him. "Write a first draft of the statement and mesh it to me so I can work on it."

Robert bowed to him. "Right away, Sire."

After Robert left, Tarquine came over to Jaibriol. "He's a good aide."

"Yes, he is," Jaibriol said. "I thought you were asleep."

"It seems I can't stay that way."

More than anything, he wished she were on Glory. Away from this mess. Tomorrow, Kelric and Tarquine would meet in person for the first time since Kelric had escaped from her eleven years ago, after she had bought him at the highest price ever paid for a slave in the history of Eube. Tarquine kept her thought on that subject buried too deep for him to find without mentally breaking her barriers, which he would no more do than he would physically attack her. He didn't want her to see Kelric, didn't want Kelric to see her, didn't want to live with this constant fear that he would never measure up to that golden warlord.

"Jai?" she asked. "Where are you?"

"Your nephew is in a bad mood tonight," he said.

She spoke dryly. "If the essence of Barthol could be condensed into a mineral, he would be a vein so extensive within the planet, everyone on the surface would be in danger of collapsing into the depths of the crust when he finished mining the ore."

As a description of how deeply Barthol could undermine their lives, that was certainly apt. "After that incident with the fellow whose children Barthol tried to sell," Jaibriol said, "I looked more deeply into your nephew's affairs. It wasn't the first time he did something like that. Not even close."

Her expression became shuttered. "Barthol is a Highton."

"So are you. So am I. So is Corbal. So are a thousand other people. I don't see them tearing apart families and pushing people to suicide for some stupid, trumped-up offense."

The empress shrugged. "We are all different."

"Tarquine, you know this is serious," Jaibriol said. "If all Aristos treated their taskmakers like Barthol, it would weaken the empire. He owns several billion. If he makes their lives so miserable that they feel they have no reason to live, they'll rise up against him." Personally, he would find it sheer pleasure to watch Barthol's slaves revolt. But then what? If the emperor didn't put down such a rebellion, the Aristos would believe he was abetting a revolution, which would destroy him. The genocide Del sang about in "Carnelians Finale" was no euphemism. Jaibriol's predecessors had wiped out entire races, even destroyed planets as punishment for a rebellion. Jaibriol had made inroads in easing the slavery of Eube, including in the provisions of this treaty he and the Skolians were supposed to discuss tomorrow, if it didn't collapse under the weight of its own divisive existence. But he had a long, long way to go.

"Whatever you may think of him," Tarquine said coolly, "Barthol is my nephew."

"Family."

"Yes." She paused, watching him, her gaze unreadable. "But not family like our child, Jai. And that child *will* be a son."

He stared at her, forgetting Barthol. "Then it's true? You're pregnant?"

She said, simply, "Yes. I am."

His first thought was to insist she see a doctor, many doctors, the best in the empire. They couldn't leave the care of their son to their own treatment, especially not after Tarquine had twice miscarried. Except he knew an even harsher truth, one they couldn't risk any doctor discovering: the child she carried was barely more than half Aristo. He would inherit half the Highton genes from his mother, but only one-sixteenth from Jaibriol. The Highton Heir would be one-half Ruby.

Jaibriol dreaded Tarquine coming to the summit. When the Skolian public learned the truth about Prince Del-Kurj, emotions would explode. It would be unforgivable that ESComm kidnapped the prince who sang "Carnelians Finale" just after Del's speech asking people to set aside their anger. The Imperialate would demand justice. The Aristos would inflame the situation with their blatant approval, congratulating Tarex for capturing the provider who had dared shout to the stars that he would never kneel beneath their Highton stares. During all that furor, Jaibriol would have to deal with ESComm attempts to sabotage the summit using the embryonic Kyle technology they had mangled together. And gods only knew what else Barthol had planned.

"Tarquine, go back to Glory," he said. "Take our son home. To safety."

"I can't do that," she said.

"*Why?*"

Her voice quieted. "Jaibriol, trust me."

She was asking for one of the few things he could never give her. Loyal yet amoral, brilliant yet uncompromising, prodigiously wealthy yet never satisfied, the woman who would give life to his son also killed those who stood in her way. How could he ever trust her?

"You endanger our heir," he said. "My heir. Your heir."

Her voice turned flat. "My heir is Barthol."

Barthol. The would-be despot who wanted Tarquine dead so he could inherit her Line, her lands, perhaps even the regency of the Carnelian Throne. She had given him that legacy to make Jaibriol's treaty a reality. He wanted to say *I'm sorry,* but Hightons never spoke those words they considered a weakness.

So instead he said, "You gave me honor."

She looked away from him, out the glass doors of the balcony. "Barthol's son is here, too."

Jaibriol barely knew Hazar, Barthol's eldest child and heir, who had no interest in anything except his own hedonistic pleasure. "I didn't think Hazar cared about politics."

Tarquine turned back to him. "He doesn't. But he will someday rule Iquar." She grimaced as if she had bitten into a sour fruit. "Let us just say it has been suggested that he at least appear to be learning his responsibilities."

Jaibriol had no answer. As much as he disliked Barthol, he knew the general was capable of leading the Iquar Line. It would be a brutal rule, but the Iquars would prosper. Hazar was another story. When Tarquine had named Barthol as her heir, she had ceded power to a branch of her family that might someday irreparably damage her Line.

Jaibriol couldn't fix what his treaty had cost her.

So he gave her the only exchange he had to offer, his acceptance of her refusal to leave. "When you take your place at my side in the summit," he said, "the empire will know the great value I place in your counsel."

She inclined her head, accepting his unspoken apology.

The graceful response now would be to let the matter drop. Yet something kept tugging at him. "Tarquine—have we ever talked about the Skolian Jagernauts?"

"We talk about Skolians far too much," she said. "I am quite thoroughly tired of them."

"I suppose." He felt the same way. But it was odd the way he had so easily picked up Barthol's thought. It made him think of the Skolians. "You know they have mech-enhanced telepathy."

"You believe that little myth of theirs?"

That surprised Jaibriol. She knew it wasn't a myth. She probably had more intelligence on the Jagernauts than ESComm, not only because she kept her own dossiers, but also because she had once owned one of the most important Jagernauts alive. She knew the implants in their brains could boost their neural activity. Something felt wrong here. It wasn't her response, more her *lack* of one.

"Other people besides Jagernauts use the technology," he said.

She raised her sculpted eyebrow. "And I should care because . . . ?"

Why, indeed. He wasn't even sure why he was pushing it on her. "Anyone who can afford the procedure can have a brain implant that enhances neural activity."

Exasperation flashed on her face. "Yes, my most gloriously talkative husband, anyone can. People can put anything they want in their brain, plant flowers, mine for ore, play tiddle-widdle. Why anyone would wish to do so is an entirely different question and one which I have no idea why, at this particular moment, we are discussing."

"It can change how a telepath picks up their thoughts." He thought of his Razers with their metallic minds, hard to read, different than human.

"Maybe it does," she said. "Why do you care?"

Because I picked up your nephew that way, he wanted to answer. But he couldn't speak such words. Instead, he said, "We have no idea what tricks anyone might try tomorrow. They will have Jagernauts there."

"I'm sure ESComm is prepared."

Even though her response seemed genuine, it felt off. She had perfected the art of verbal deflection so well that even he, a psion, had trouble reading what lay beneath her Highton exterior. She was hiding something and had been since Barthol's accident. He wanted to believe the general had recovered because Tarquine had stepped back from murdering her own nephew. Or maybe she had tried and failed, as impossible as it seemed. He didn't believe she had discovered Barthol had no link to the death of their son, not after what he had just picked up from the general.

Then it hit him. He had been refusing to acknowledge another obvious choice, the one that was so very Highton. Tarquine and Barthol could have joined forces.

Jaibriol suddenly felt ill. It couldn't be true, that his empress would enter into a pact with Barthol to reclaim the rule of her Line, perhaps even of all Eube, without having to slaughter her own kin. Tarquine carried the Highton Heir now; she no longer needed Jaibriol to ensure her legacy.

"What is it?" Tarquine asked. "Why do you stand there so silent?"

"It is nothing," Jaibriol said. He could say no more.

If Tarquine had betrayed him, it would destroy a piece of him that could never be repaired.

A piece of what made him human.

XXV
Traders

The Flagstorm battlecruiser known as *Pharaoh's Shield*—the pride of the Skolian Fleet—rotated majestically in space. As the transport carrying Del approached the cruiser, he floated in an observation bay, looking out a wall-sized view screen, awestruck. The cylindrical body of the great ship was twelve kilometers long and one kilometer in diameter. A giant tube extended down its center, circled at intervals by huge rings. Spokes extended from the rings to the cylinder's rim, allowing the ship to turn and so create a sense of gravity for the thousands of people who lived within it. Lights flashed on its outer hull or ran across it like trains of radiance, a testament to the never ending activity within the antennae, pods, cranes, and flanges on its myriad surfaces.

A flotilla of smaller ships accompanied the cruiser: Starslammers and Thunderbolts; razor-edged Scythes; unfolding Jack-knives; bolts, masts, tugs, and booms. Jags shot through the fleet, luminous and brilliant, the flotilla vanguard, all of it set against a dazzling backdrop of nebulae. Del's only experience with star travel had been as a civilian, usually on a commercial star liner or yacht. The Firestorm took away his breath.

A man spoke behind him. "Incredible, isn't it?"

Del maneuvered around to see Mac floating in the open hatch of the bay. His manager looked much better than the last time Del had seen him, twenty hours ago, when they had woken up in the crammed cabin of a Jag starfighter just moments after it had rescued them from the racer determined to blow them up. In a startling act of compassion for an AI, the racer had knocked them both unconscious in preparation for the destruction.

Blackhawk Squad had thrown the racer into quasis in the instant it detonated, freezing the molecular structure of the ship. The racer's molecules didn't stop vibrating or whatever molecules did, but they couldn't change their quantum configuration, which as far as Del understood, meant the ship had been in a sort of suspended animation. Secondary Panquai, the squad leader, had eased off the quasis enough to extract them before the racer blew. Waking up from that drugged sleep to find himself alive had definitely been one of the better moments in Del's life.

He grinned at Mac, holding a grip in the bulkhead, floating in the microgravity. He was glad to see Mac up and around; his manager had been spacesick during most of the past twenty hours, while Blackhawk squad brought them to this transport and the transport brought them here.

"Can you believe my *brother* commands that!" Del gestured at the battlecruiser. "I mean, I knew he was the Imperator and all, but nothing ever brought it home like this."

Mac pushed off from the hatch and drifted toward Del. "It's hard sometimes with family to see their lives away from how we know them." He grabbed a handhold by the screen, and he and Del hung there together, watching as *Pharaoh's Shield* grew larger.

A half-sphere capped the far end of the cylinder, but the end they were approaching was open to space. Gigantic thrusters circled its perimeter, each many times the size of the transport. Their small ship sailed past as a docking tube opened ahead, like a bud unfurling its petals. They flew into the pod and the petals closed behind it, cutting off Del's view of space.

"Kelric and I have argued so much," Del said. "Especially when I was younger."

"You and he are very different," Mac said. "But Del, even a bystander like myself can tell that for all that you two may have diametrically opposed personalities, your brother loves you."

"It's hard sometimes to believe." Wryly he said, "It's ironic, you know. The thing I've done in my life that they most hate, my being a rock singer on Earth, is what gave me enough confidence to believe that I was, if not worthy to be in this family, at least worthy of their love."

"Of course you're worthy!" Mac said. "You don't have to be a war leader or a politician. Be yourself. That's a unique, remarkable feat."

"Well, it's unique, anyway." Del sensed someone behind them, a strong psion. Maneuvering around, he saw Secondary Panquai in the hatchway. The Jagernaut's close-cropped hair reminded him of a bristle-brush, except it looked a lot sexier on the lean, muscular warrior, the perfect complement for her black leather uniform. Del had never been comfortable with military officers, but he'd let Panquai take him anywhere she wanted. Well, not really. His wife Ricki was even more dangerous than this Jagernaut. He missed her. At least ISC had let her know he was all right.

"Hey, Panquai," he said.

She nodded, as calm and stoic as ever. "Ready to board the cruiser, Your Highness?"

"Sure," Del said, though apprehension replaced his good mood. He would have to face Kelric soon. Even when he'd done nothing wrong, he felt intimidated by his brother.

They disembarked from the transport into a spherical decon chamber with the ubiquitous Luminex walls. As they floated there, the chamber checked them for every contaminant known to humanity and probably a few more. Apparently they were clean, because a portal soon opened, allowing them to drift into a tunnel with blue rails along its sides. Del thought they must be in the central tube of the cylinder, the axis it rotated around, because he was still floating. The ships he usually traveled in were designed to minimize any perceived discomfort of their passengers, including microgravity, and he had never realized how much fun it could be to float around like this. Mac looked a little green, though, so Del kept quiet.

A bullet-shaped magcar, black and gold, waited across the tunnel, upside-down relative to them. Grinning, Del flipped upside-down and hauled himself into the car, followed by Panquai and Mac. As the door snicked closed behind them, they strapped into their seats.

"Prepare to launch," a voice said.

Del blinked. Launch?

With a jerk, the car set off like a projectile hurtling in the bore of a gun. The sides of the tunnel were visible on view screens.

"This is amazing," Del said. "Where are we going?"

"Down the length of the ship," Panquai said. "Twelve kilometers."

Mac leaned his head back and closed his eyes. "Tell me when we get there."

"Don't go to sleep!" Del said. "You'll miss the fun."

Mac slitted open his eyes enough to glare at Del, then closed them again.

When the car finally stopped, it let them out into a set of airlocks, not membranes but solid chambers with circular handles they had to crank around. They worked their way through several and floated past the final hatchway—into mech-tech wonderland.

They had reached the bridge of the battlecruiser, the hemisphere that capped one end of the cylinder. The airlock let them out in the center of the hemisphere's flat base, which had to be at least a kilometer wide. Unlike the Orbiter, which was designed for beauty, this habitat was optimized for efficiency. A crane shifted aside as Del, Mac, and Panquai floated through the equipment around the hatch and into the more open area beyond. The bridge was *huge.* Crew members worked everywhere, upside-down far "above" them, sideways to the left and right, or right-side-up "beneath" them. Mini-flyers navigated the open space. A huge robot arm terminated in a command chair in the center of the hemisphere, facing away from them. Lights flashed and glittered as if they were in a fantastical city.

With no warning, the hull screens came on—and the *entire* hemisphere became a view portal, like a giant window. Suddenly Del was floating in the glory of space with nothing more than the cable he was clutching to keep him in place. A world hung before them, blue, green, and violet, all swirling with clouds. The spectacular vista was so vivid, Del gasped for breath as if he were actually in space.

"My God," Mac said next to him.

Secondary Panquai, who was on the other side of Mac, grinned at them. "Impressive, eh?"

"I've never seen anything like this even on an Air Force cruiser," Mac said.

Del could barely absorb it all. He had never thought of ISC as powerful, not compared to ESComm, which had many more ships, bases, and weapons. As a member of the Ruby Dynasty, he lived with the knowledge of that deadly discrepancy every day of his life, knowing his family was responsible for maintaining the Kyle web, the Imperialate's one advantage over the Traders. Mac's comment brought home the scope of ISC in a way Del had never understood before. The feeling it gave him was too big to put in words. Perhaps someday he could write it into music.

"I don't feel any gravity," Del said. "We won't fall, will we?" The curving hull was half a kilometer away.

"You won't," Panquai said. "They aren't rotating the hemisphere. When it turns, you can feel a pull like gravity on the hull, but you wouldn't here." She smiled. "Hang on, though, if you don't want to float away and bump into the crew."

Del had no wish to interfere with anyone. It would make him look like Kelric's scattered-brained rock star brother, a reputation he had spent the last decade trying to dispel.

"So where do we go from here?" Mac asked.

"Follow me," Panquai said. With a shove against a crane, she launched toward a cable that stretched across the hemisphere. Del followed, delighted, flying through the air. He caught the cable behind Panquai, his hair swirling around his head, and Mac came sailing in behind them. They pulled themselves along, skimming through the hemisphere, using whatever was nearby for a handhold, always headed toward the center. The hum of the bridge was a melody of engines, consoles, and boards, vibrating deeply like the beat of a great drum, or higher like chimes or strings, a choral symphony of tech.

Panquai pulled up alongside the command chair and floated around in front of it. With one arm hooked around a cable to hold herself in place, she saluted whoever sat there, clenching her hands into fists and crossing them at the wrists, right over left, as she raised them.

"Secondary Panquai, Captain, Blackhawk Squadron," she said. "Permission to come aboard, sir."

Del wasn't sure why she was asking for permission for what she had already done, but he was so nervous that he barely heard the familiar voice rumble, "Permission granted. Good work, Panquai."

So. This was it. Del floated around in front of the command chair. Kelric sat there, a giant with gold skin, metallic hair streaked by grey, and molten gold eyes. With his square jaw and handsome face, he looked more like some artist's conception of a war god than a real person. Then he grinned at Del and shattered the image, becoming the brother Del had always known.

"My greetings, Del," the Imperator said. "Welcome."

"Hey, Kelric." Del wondered if he should ask for permission to come aboard. At this, their first face-to-face meeting in two years, it seemed they should have more to say, especially after all that had happened. *Welcome* felt anti-climatic.

"Mister Tyler, welcome as well," Kelric said, nodding to Mac.

Mac managed to bow to Kelric even though he was weightless and hanging onto a cable. "I'm honored, Commander." He motioned at the bridge around them. "This is incredible."

"Ah, well." The comment seemed to make Kelric uncomfortable the same way that Del felt when people told him he was an incredible singer. Del never felt he measured up.

"So that's Delos?" Mac said, indicating the view screens behind them. "It's beautiful."

Looking around, Del had to agree with Mac. He would write a song for that jeweled world hanging so bright and promising against the unforgiving depths of black space. Okay, that was a little melodramatic. He'd have to work on the words. Mac was right, though, it was gorgeous.

Del turned back to Kelric. He wanted to hug his brother, say how happy he was to be here, to be alive, all those things that Kelric would feel were embarrassingly emotional. Since they were pretending this was casual instead, Del just said, "Is that where the summit will be?"

"That's it," Kelric said. "In just a few hours."

Del didn't know what else to say. Kelric had never been easy to talk to. But perhaps they didn't need words, because here he could feel Kelric's mental power. Del saw him in person so rarely, he tended to forget that about his brother. Kelric was like a sun, warm and golden in a way that had nothing to do with his metallic coloring. Regardless of how the Imperator looked, that was no machine behind those gold eyes. It was a man, a good man.

Del smiled. "You look great."

Kelric blinked. "Thanks."

"But shouldn't you be on the planet?" Del asked. "I thought the summit was today." His internal clock was thrown all out of whack after living in darkness for days and then traveling on the transport, which had no day or night.

"Most of our party is down there," Kelric said. "Except for Mother, Dehya, and me. We've been waiting for you to get onboard."

"You didn't have to do that." It embarrassed Del to hear that he was the one holding up this historic and monumentally beleaguered summit.

Kelric gave him a wry smile. "You try telling Mother that."

Del couldn't help but laugh. "Point taken."

"Come on." Kelric unfastened his safety webbing. "Let's go see her."

Roca was crying, talking, and hugging Del at the same time. "Ah, gods, honey, we've been so worried." She stepped back, holding his upper arms with her hands, tears on her face. "I'm so very, very glad to see you."

Del was acutely aware of everyone watching them: Kelric, Mac, Panquai, bodyguards. But none of that mattered. They were in the cylindrical shell of the ship, which had full gravity, and he easily pulled his mother into another hug. Then Dehya was there, and he held her, too, amazed at how fragile she felt. It was such a relief to let his tension and fear go. He had been holding it all inside, striving to stay calm for days in the dark. Until this moment, he hadn't really believed it was over.

They finally separated and Del wiped the heel of his hand across his face, smearing away the tears. He glanced at Kelric—and had the shock of his life. A tear showed on his brother's famously stoic face. Kelric was standing back, hiding by being silent, but he wiped his face with the heel of his hand exactly the way Del had done it. That moment meant more to Del than any words.

"Well, so." Roca reddened as if suddenly remembering they were in a room full of people. "Did Kelric talk to you about what he'd like you to do?"

"To monitor Kyle space," Del said.

Kelric came over to them, his usual self again. "You'll be looking for your own neural signature." He nodded toward Panquai, who was by the wall. "The Secondary will work with you."

"Are you sure you want me to do this?" Del said. It meant a great deal to him that Kelric had requested his help, but he wasn't sure he knew how. "I don't have any experience as a telop."

"It's a forgery of your own neural signature," Kelric said. "It's like sensing your own mind. Now that we know what to look for, you can probably find it by matching your thoughts to the forgery."

Dehya spoke. "No one else can do it, Del. It's you that they've forged. The only other signature for a living Ruby psion they can copy is Kelric's, and he'll be at the summit. As his brother, you're far more likely to recognize his mental signature than one of his officers."

As much as it relieved Del that they no longer believed someone had tampered with their minds, but that she and Kelric had been caught in an attempt to forge his neural signature, he still didn't see how it had nearly killed them. They seemed convinced, though. What stunned him more was that they trusted him to play such a crucial role in their security. Suppose he failed?

"I'll do my best," Del said.

Dehya's expression softened. "You will. Believe that."

"You really think they'd attack you during the treaty negotiations?" Del asked.

Roca snorted. "They're ESComm. Of course they would."

"So it was ESComm that took me and Mac," Del said. "Not the Allieds."

"That's right," Kelric said. "We have all five of their agents in custody."

Del thought of how they had shot Mac when his manager tried to protect him. "Serves the drilling bastards right." When Roca frowned at him, he said, "Sorry."

Kelric grinned at Roca. "I've heard you say far worse."

All the military officers gaped at him. Del didn't blame them; he had seen Kelric smile plenty of times when they had been boys, but he doubted most people even realized the Imperator knew how. The grin turned Kelric's face radiant; in that instant, Del could see why the queens on the planet Coba had gone to war over his brother.

"What?" Kelric said, when everyone had stared at him for a few moments.

Roca smiled. "It's nothing."

"We should go down to the planet," Dehya said. "The summit is set to open in a few hours."

"Are you sure you'll be all right there?" Del asked. "New Athens is packed with Hightons, and our battlecruisers aren't the only ones in orbit."

"Don't worry," Roca said. "We'll be fine."

Del hoped so, because part of their safety would depend on his ability to figure out if the Traders were using his or Kelric's forged signature to tamper with their security.

He hoped he was up to the task.

During the trip to Delos, Aliana stayed with Red in the ship's cabin where Tide had left them, a place with a blue rug and chromed furniture. It was much smaller than their palace suite, but still nicer than any place she had known before Glory. She and Red ate meals delivered by machines, wore clothes they found in the cabinets, and held each other for comfort. The only time they saw anyone else was when a woman came and changed Aliana, making her hair blond and her skin normal, with no metallic cast. She had lenses that turned Aliana's eyes blue. By the time the woman finished, Aliana looked like someone else. She didn't like the disguise, but apparently it was reversible if the emperor changed his mind.

At Delos, Tide hurried them through the disembarking process; she saw almost nothing of the ship in space or the shuttle that took them to the planet. She felt too heavy here and the air had a tang. She saw only enclosed places: corridors, tunnels, and this chamber where they were standing as it rose up in some building. Tide stood with them, cold, dark, and silent, wearing bulky gauntlets and a heavy gun on his hip, more like a deadly machine than a man.

The wall in front of them suddenly opened, its gold doors pulling back. Outside, three more Razers waited. As Aliana walked out with Red, she tried not to stare at them. Her heart was beating too fast, and Red's mind was going numb, as if he were retreating within himself.

Tide spoke with the other Razers. Except he didn't *say* anything. Their gauntlets flashed, some code they all seemed to understand without speaking a word. The four of them turned as one, surrounding Aliana and Red, and led them down a gold hallway. She had heard no other sounds, nothing but silence. At the end, they stopped at two tall doors, crystal and gold. Right angles were everywhere, disorienting Aliana, not just the doors, but the corners where walls met each other, the floor, or the ceiling. She felt off balance, as if she were going to fall.

Tide's fingers played across his gauntlet and its lights flashed blue. The doors swung open like portals into some unknown land. Their escort took them into a suite where chandeliers dripped diamond teardrops and floating orbs shed pearly light. Aliana couldn't take it all in; the wonders slid off her mind like rain sluicing off waterproof clothes.

The living room was full of people. Several tech-mech types were gathered around an extravagant media center. The life-sized holo of a man stood on the holo-stage, a Skolian it looked like, judging from his uniform. He was speaking to a Eubian woman in this room while other people at consoles monitored the exchange.

Then it hit Aliana: the *emperor* was in the room, surrounded by men in grey uniforms with red braid on their sleeves. The woman next to him mesmerized Aliana. As tall as the emperor with a leanly beautiful face, she had flawless skin and her black hair glittered in a waterfall to her shoulders. She exuded a sense of power simply by standing there. The Empress Tarquine. Both she and the emperor wore clothes that looked like dark gems spun into fabric. *Black diamond cloth.* Aliana had heard of it, but had never touched the fabric or expected to see it up close. Only Aristos could wear such garments.

The Razers stopped Aliana and Red a distance away from the emperor. Aliana needed no prompting; she went down on one knee with her head bowed, aware of Red doing the same. The other Aristos she had met had blatantly projected their own belief in their importance, their conviction that they deserved reverence. The emperor neither cared about his power nor needed anyone to worship him, yet somehow, that only made him seem more deserving of such respect.

One of the Razers touched her shoulder. Looking up, she saw the emperor and empress watching them. Apparently Jaibriol had given the signal they could rise, because Red was standing up. So she did, too, her head swimming from the astringent atmosphere.

Jaibriol spoke to a man at his side. "Robert, have them wait at the back of the room. When I call for the boy, bring them both to the holo-stage."

The man, "Robert" apparently, nodded. "I'll take care of it, Your Highness."

The people at the holo-stage had finished whatever they were discussing. The Eubian official, a willowy woman with dark brown hair, came over to the emperor and bowed deeply. "We are ready, Your Highness."

As the Razers drew Aliana and Red back in the room, the emperor and his retinue went to the holo-stage. The taskmaker woman continued speaking to Jaibriol. "You and Pharaoh Dyhianna will appear simultaneously. Due to your relative ages and length of rule, you are expected to speak first." She hesitated. "If that is unacceptable, Your Highness, we will demand another arrangement."

Jaibriol spoke in his impeccable Highton. "It will be fine. Skolians need these protocols." With those few words, he granted them a wealth of knowledge; the Skolians were weaker, needing such protocols to bolster their confidence in the presence of a god-emperor. Aliana didn't know if that was really true, but it was impressive how easily he made it sound that way.

She spoke in a low voice to Red. "That's amazing how he talks."

Red jerked at the sound of her voice, then shook his head at her. He mouthed the word *Highton.* He seemed otherwise frozen, barely even able to breathe. That was when she realized another Highton was present.

Admiral Erix Muze.

Aliana felt as if the air left the room. This was the man who had tortured Red. He was standing at the back of the media center, watching the proceedings with an intent gaze that she suspected missed nothing. Red's fear was like an elastic sheet stretched tight, ready to snap into ragged pieces. Aliana imagined her mental fortress growing stronger, protecting him even more.

Jaibriol stepped onto a dais with screens around its back and settled in a chair there, facing the now empty holo-stage. Robert stood next to the dais. The techs were working at consoles arranged in an arc behind the holo-stage so they wouldn't be visible to any Skolian who appeared on it. As they toggled panels, the emperor's chair "changed" into a white throne inlaid with carnelians and diamonds. The holo was so well done, Aliana would have thought it was real if she hadn't just seen them turn on the projection.

"Ten seconds," someone said.

Aliana wondered if the pharaoh would kneel to Emperor Jaibriol. Probably not. Skolians seemed to think they weren't slaves. It had shocked Aliana at first, but after what she had seen of Aristos, she rather liked the way Skolians thumbed their noses at them.

"Five seconds," the tech said. The curving screens that backed both the holo-stage and the emperor's dais rippled with abstract swirls, gold and black.

Someone else said, "We're running—now!"

A woman appeared on the holo-stage, seated in a gold chair inlaid with red gems. The Ruby Throne? It looked as real as the Carnelian Throne where the emperor sat. All these chairs named after jewels. As furniture went, they didn't look particularly comfortable.

The pharaoh was a delicate woman with black hair piled on her head and tendrils curling around her face, as shining as Highton hair but without the distinctive glitter. She had large eyes, green maybe, but with a translucent rosy sheen. Aliana had expected someone hard and stern, not this ethereal beauty. The pharoah had the softness of a provider, but her gaze showed strength rather than vulnerability, contradicting her fragile appearance.

The emperor and the pharaoh regarded each other. The strained emotions in the room built until Aliana felt ready to snap.

Emperor Jaibriol spoke in Highton. "The Line of Qox acknowledges the Ruby Dynasty."

The woman answered in a melodic voice, speaking Highton with a lilting accent. "The House of Skolia acknowledges the Qox Dynasty."

"We are gratified to hear of your nephew's good health," Jaibriol said.

"It is indeed fortunate," the pharaoh said, her voice and expression neutral.

For flaming sake, Aliana thought. They had gone to all this trouble and preparation so the emperor of Eube could tell the pharaoh of Skolia that he was glad her nephew wasn't sick?

"News of his health will gratify my people," the pharaoh said.

Jaibriol studied her. "I imagine they will also have an interest in news of how he recovered."

"Perhaps," she said. "But such a matter is private."

Well, sure, Aliana thought. Despite the odd subject, the pharoah's response seemed reasonable. It wasn't anyone's business how the doctors treated whatever had been wrong with her nephew. Yet for some reason everyone in the room had come to attention, as if the pharaoh had just made a vital offer rather than a bland comment. Then again, Hightons never seemed to say anything like normal people. If Skolians were similar, who knew what this conversation actually meant.

"A worthy sentiment," Jaibriol said. "It could be intrusive on his privacy to make his treatment public." He paused. "Or the condition it treated."

The pharaoh spoke carefully. "Some cultures require confidentiality agreements protecting the privacy of their patients."

Aliana was enjoying the bizarre exchange. Now they had a confidentiality agreement, and why ever would the emperor care about Skolian medical practices? Maybe they were talking about the loud Skolian prince, and he had lost his voice so he couldn't sing about Hightons anymore. She discovered she was disappointed with that thought.

"I imagine the terms of such an agreement would be of interest to all those involved," Jaibriol said.

"A proposal might be considered." Quietly the pharaoh added, "Even welcomed."

Someone in the room exhaled. Aliana looked around, noting the relief among the people here. Knowing the pharaoh might welcome a proposal from her nephew's doctors on how to keep his health a private matter apparently made a lot of Eubian people happy. She tugged on Red's sleeve. When he glanced at her, she gave him a questioning look. He responded with the barest shrug. He didn't understand what was going on, either.

The emperor glanced at Robert, who seemed to know exactly what the look meant. Robert bowed and left the dais, walking toward the back of the room. Aliana watched with mild curiosity—until she realized he was headed straight to her and Red. As she stiffened, Robert stopped in front of them.

The aide spoke to Red in Highton. "You will stand

on the dais by Emperor Jaibriol. Don't speak unless he asks you to." He glanced at Aliana. "You may come, but stay back."

"Why would they want us up there?" Aliana asked.

Red shot her a warning glance. Then he bowed to Robert. "Yes, sir. Is my honor."

Aliana closed her mouth and followed them, wondering what she and Red could possibly have to do with a nephew of the Ruby Pharaoh and his doctor's confidentiality agreement. The pharaoh and Jaibriol continued their exchange as she and Red came up to the dais. Aliana hung back, unsure how to act.

Robert nudged Red forward. As Red stepped onto the dais, he averted his eyes, looking at neither the emperor nor the pharaoh.

The pharaoh spoke gently. "Young man, can you hear me?"

Red looked up. "Yes, Your Glory."

Robert spoke in a low voice to Red. "The pharaoh is always 'Your Highness.'"

Red spoke quickly. "Yes, Your Highness."

Aliana thought the pharaoh had an odd look about her. No one else seemed to notice. They seemed to see her as a beautiful object, like an exotic vase of great value. They appreciated her beauty but didn't much like anything else about her. Their thoughts had a hard edge, their anger that this person sat on a throne. However, they had a grudging respect for her Highton speech, which apparently included her ability to say nothing much at all as if it were a profound statement.

Even so. Aliana still thought the pharaoh had an odd look. Maybe no one else saw it because the much greater oddness of having to treat her as an equal with the emperor swamped out everything else. But something was off about the way she and the emperor interacted. Strange, that. Aliana wished she could figure out what bothered her.

The pharaoh was speaking to Red. "You asked my people for asylum."

"I not mean to offend," Red told her.

"You gave no offense," she said kindly. Turning to the emperor, she said, "I understand he has a high Kyle rating?"

"His tests put it at 7.6." Jaibriol was speaking in Highton, but his style had changed, become more direct, as if they were now discussing business.

Aliana wasn't sure what 7.6 meant, but the emperor had just lied to the pharaoh. As far as he knew, Red had lost whatever made him a psion, his brain burnt out by his trauma on Muze's Helios, which as she understood it, would make him zero on this scale of theirs. Jaibriol was misleading the pharaoh and everyone here approved. Except, no, he wasn't lying. Or she didn't think so; it was hard to read him from within her mental fortress.

Jaibriol glanced at Robert with one of those silent communications they seemed to know so well. Robert nodded—and took Aliana's elbow.

What the blazes? No, she couldn't go up there; that wasn't in the script. But Robert nudged her forward. With her heartbeat ratcheting up, she stepped onto the dais. She felt exposed up there. It gave her a better view of the media center, however, including screens that showed images of the emperor in his chair with Red next to him. She was standing slightly behind Red, a tall girl with yellow hair, blue eyes, a blue jumpsuit, and a narrow collar around her neck. She hardly recognized herself.

"This girl also asked for asylum," Jaibriol told the pharaoh.

"I see." Dyhianna regarded Aliana with luminous eyes. She looked so *real.* Even knowing it was a holo, Aliana felt as if she were in the presence of the actual person, as if she could reach out and touch the pharaoh. She struck a chord in Aliana, though Aliana couldn't have said why she found a sense of familiarity with a Skolian.

"She is also a psion," Jaibriol continued. "A rating of three or four."

Huh. The emperor was being strange again. Tide said no one here knew she was a psion. So why say three or four? To convince the pharaoh to take her, probably. Aliana had thought Skolians didn't buy providers, but that seemed to be exactly what they were doing. They would want more than a zero. Maybe the emperor knew the Skolians at the embassy believed Aliana's rating was nine. If that was true, though, why undervalue it? On the surface, his reason for misleading the Skolians was obvious; they were Skolians, so they deserved to be tricked. Except the summit was about to start, and he would want them amenable to his wishes, not angry because he cheated them.

Of course, if he knew she was a nine and the other Hightons thought she was zero, then he looked good to the Hightons for putting one over on the pharaoh, but he would please the pharaoh by giving her a higher rated provider than he claimed. So he won all around.

Whatever his reasoning, Aliana wished he would finish. Her head *hurt.* Admiral Muze was watching them from behind a console. Just looking at him made her temples ache.

The pharaoh was speaking. "Two psions, five spies. That split would unbalance a scale."

"That depends on what you're weighing on each side," Jaibriol said.

"Perhaps." She contemplated him, her face composed. "Five spies who took a prince."

Jaibriol spoke carefully. "The loss of the Eubian merchants weighs heavily with some, bringing demands of execution. Perhaps it is time to let that weight ease."

The pharaoh inclined her head. "And in doing so, give more balance."

Jaibriol returned her nod, which as far as Aliana could tell, meant they were agreed. But on what? Not to kill someone who had misplaced some Eubian merchants? For that and two psions, the pharaoh would give him five spies, all because her nephew had been sick and was well now. Sure, right, that made sense.

Even so, it amazed Aliana how well the pharaoh dealt with the emperor. They were two of a kind. Yes, she knew it was insulting to compare the emperor to a Skolian. But Aliana actually rather liked the pharaoh, at least more than she liked Hightons.

As Robert maneuvered Aliana and Red away from the dais, the sovereigns continued their convoluted non-conversation. Aides, officers, and techs closed in, cutting off Aliana's view of the proceedings. But the empress, who was standing a bit off from the others, was staring at her, and a chill went up Aliana's back.

Then they were out of the suite. Aliana looked at

Red, and he closed his eyes, then opened them again, watching her. She knew how he felt. It was a relief to be out of there, away from the Aristos, especially Admiral Muze. She had seen it in Red's mind, flashes of the Highton who had brutalized him with the arrogant cruelty of one who believed it was his exalted right. To live with that every day, to know it would never get better; no, it was far better to scrabble in a slum, starving and freezing, than to live in luxury as a provider.

Four Razers accompanied them to the lift, but only Tide went down with them. As soon as they were alone, Aliana spoke to Red. "Are you all right?"

He nodded jerkily. "Was hard. Seeing him."

She made a face. "I didn't like him, either."

"Aliana," Tide warned.

"What happened in there?" she asked him. "Are they selling us to the Skolians?"

"Trading," Tide said. "You two for five agents that the Skolians captured."

"What was that bit about dead merchants?" she asked.

"I'm not sure," Tide admitted. "I think the emperor is saying they won't demand the execution of the Skolian commandos who killed the Eubian merchants."

Interesting. "So the Skolians got back their angry prince," Aliana said.

"Apparently," Tide said.

"I thought people from Earth take prince," Red said.

Tide shrugged. "Everyone claims something different."

Aliana doubted he would tell them any of his theories, but she tried anyway. "Why trade me to the Skolians? And why say I'm 'three or four'? That means they think I'm a psion, right? But not a very strong one."

"Well, yes," Tide said. "That's exactly what it means."

"But the emperor was—" She bit off the word "lying." More carefully, she said, "I thought everyone at the palace believed I wasn't a psion."

"You are probably an empath," Tide said. "They haven't had time to test you formally, so the emperor may be guessing."

She thought back over the meeting. "Why was everyone relieved when the Ruby Pharaoh said that her doctor would welcome a confidentiality agreement saying he couldn't talk about the singing prince being sick or whatever happened before they rescued him from the ESComm soldiers who kidnapped him while they were pretending to be Allied soldiers?"

"Good gods," Tide said. "You picked up all that?"

"Mostly from the emperor and the pharaoh," Aliana said. "A little from you just now."

He stopped looking astounded and went back into Razer mode, which made him a lot harder to read. "The pharaoh didn't mean a doctor. She was telling the emperor that if he traded you and Red to her for the ESComm agents, she wouldn't make public what happened to Prince Del-Kurj."

"Why?" Aliana asked, fascinated. "She's giving back the agents. Why agree to more?"

Tide shrugged. "Maybe she wants this summit to succeed."

"They both do," Aliana said. "Both her and emperor Qox."

"You think so?"

"I'm sure of it."

Tide looked amused. "You know a lot about the motivations of emperors and pharaohs."

Aliana flushed. Of course she didn't know. Actually, she did, but it sounded foolish when she said that, so she kept her mouth shut.

"Why Skolians take us?" Red asked.

"You're psions," Tide said. "That makes you valuable to them."

"You're coming with us, aren't you?" Aliana said. "Like you were going to defect?"

Tide spoke harshly. "I was on a mission. I would rather die than defect to the Skolians."

Aliana suspected he was protecting himself. Maybe he meant it, maybe not. She had thought she knew Tide, but there was far more to him than the enforcer who had worked for Harindor.

"Admiral Muze not want emperor to give us to Skolians," Red said.

Aliana stiffened. "No! He can't stop us."

"Actually," Tide said, "ESComm has to approve the exchange. They haven't yet."

That wasn't what she wanted to hear. "They'll let it happen, won't they?"

"I wouldn't presume to know their thoughts," Tide said, in full Razer mode.

Aliana felt queasy. If the exchange didn't go through, she and Red could both end up as providers. The Skolians would reveal what happened to their prince and the summit would—

Would what?

She didn't want to find out the answer.

XXVI
Island of Sanctuary

The building called the Amphitheatre of Leto resembled a great galleon constructed from crystal. Trees surrounded it, aqua and sea-green, sculpted like waves and tipped by foamy white blossoms, each a spray of petaled tubes that sang when the wind blew across them. The Allieds had raised the amphitheatre within only days, working with both Skolian and Eubian architects. On a clear winter morning in the hills above New Athens, the Trader Emperor and the Ruby Pharaoh came in person to the same planet, the same city, the same building. No such meeting had ever before occured. More protections were in place than had been seen at any other summit for any the three major civilizations that comprised the trillions strong population of humanity.

So began the first day of the Delos Summit.

Birds were flying outside the floor-to-ceiling window of the chamber where Kelric stood. He had never seen such a species, bright red with blue wings. He enjoyed watching them soar in the violet-tinged sky. This chamber was in a "mast" of the building, a tower room with its narrow window-wall offering a panoramic view. In the distance, New Athens sprawled across the land, a city of wide streets and airy markets that were mostly empty now in the burning heat of the day. Beyond the city, the ocean waves crashed against the reefs.

It seemed fitting to Kelric that the summit was here on a world of sanctuary instead of on Earth. This peace they sought would join two bitterly estranged branches of Earth's lost children, who had been sundered long before they rediscovered the legendary home of their species.

A note chimed behind him, high and clear. Turning, he saw Dehya coming through the archway of the chamber, a slender woman in a simple white dress. Her black hair was piled high on her head, caught by slender braids.

"Is it time?" Kelric asked.

"We have a few minutes." She joined him at the window. A cloud floated below the glass, and birds arrowed through it, streaks of red.

"World of sanctuary," she murmured.

"Perhaps," Kelric said. They could hope.

She looked up at him. "That girl on the dais was Aliana."

"So they claim." He shook his head. "She had normal hair and skin. Blue eyes. No gold."

"Kelric, she looks like *you.* But with her coloring disguised, it's hard to make the connection unless you're looking for it."

"I hope that's it." It had shaken him to see a girl

who might be his kin wearing Trader slave restraints. Did Jaibriol suspect the girl's identity? When they had suggested the exchange of the ESComm agents for the two psions who asked for asylum, Kelric had feared ESComm would refuse. The youth was a valuable provider. If Dehya had agreed to take only Aliana, it would have looked like an absurdly unbalanced exchange, drawing exactly the attention to the girl they were trying to avoid. Although he was gratified that their plans for the trade had so far worked, they were nowhere near completion. He wouldn't believe Aliana was safe until they had her away from Delos.

Dehya spoke quietly. "We should join the others."

He let out a breath. "Yes, let's go."

They left the chamber together, Kelric limping. His leg ached more than usual, perhaps because of the heavier gravity here. Compared to the vibrant youth of Jaibriol Qox, he felt aged and slow. Dehya seemed so small. His job was to protect the Ruby Pharaoh, not put her in a building full of Aristos. Still, they had made the best decision they could, given the situation. Besides, Dehya only looked fragile. She had a strength of will like a steel rod.

A cluster of people waited in the conference room: Roca, First Councilor Tikal, General Naaj Majda, Admiral Chad Barzun, and various bodyguards. It was a resplendent group. Naaj wore her green uniform with gold braid on the shoulders and cuffs, and medals on the tunic. Her belt had the Majda hawk tooled into it, the insignia of a queen. Chad stood next to her, smart in his blue Fleet uniform, his grey hair cropped short. Roca was a vision, a statuesque woman in a rose dress that set off her gold skin.

Tikal wore conservative trousers and an elegant white shirt. Grey streaked his brown hair, but his lean face showed only a few lines, making him look younger than his sixty years.

Kelric had chosen a simple uniform, a dark gold tunic with a stripe across his chest and trousers that tucked into boots. Like his predecessors before him, he wore none of the medals, ribbons, and pins he had won during his career. He had only a wide band on each of his biceps to indicate his rank of Imperator.

He looked around at the newly constructed room. A good portion of his participation in the summit would take place here. Its eastern wall was also a window and sunlight poured through the polarized glass. The ceiling slanted upward, its highest point more than four times his height, braced by beams cut from a gold wood. Light orbs spun in the upper reaches of the room like swirling moonstones. The table was round, making every seat equivalent. A twin of this room waited in another "mast" of this building, the tower dedicated to the Eubians. The third mast contained the center where the Allieds had set up the monitoring stations for all three governments.

Tikal was talking on his wrist comm. He looked up as Kelric and Dehya joined him. "Major General Yamada is coming up in the lift. He should be here in a minute or so."

"Good choice," Kelric said. Yamada had been in charge of the military forces on Delos eleven years ago, when Jaibriol had traded himself to the Eubians for Eldrin, Dehya's husband.

As Roca came over to them, Kelric thought, **How are you doing?** This summit would be the first time she came face to face with Hightons since she had been a Eubian prisoner. It had been many years, but she still suffered from nightmares.

I'll be all right, she answered.

General Yamada arrived within moments. A stocky man with a wide face, he had two stars on each shoulder of his blue uniform and a multitude of ribbons and medals on his chest. A striking woman walked at his side. Her dark blond hair was streaked by gold, and she wore a smart blue skirt and jacket. Kelric recognized her as Kate Dolan, the Delos Ambassador to Skolia, one of Earth's top diplomats. The Allieds had given this summit their highest priority.

After all the formalities were observed, Yamada said, "The Eubian delegation is waiting to enter the amphitheatre. Major General Holland is accompanying them. We'll time it so that both of your parties enter at the same moment."

Kelric nodded, accepting the conditions they had all decided on well before this moment.

It was time to begin.

Jaibriol entered the amphitheatre with Tarquine at his left and the Earth general on his right, followed by Corbal Xir, Azile Xir, Barthol Iquar, and Erix Muze. The civilians wore black diamond clothes, and the military officers had on black dress uniforms, a sharp contrast to their alabaster faces. They looked like a starkly beautiful chess set. Except in chess, the queen acted in the defense of the king. Jaibriol no longer knew what was true for Tarquine, and it weighed on him far more even than the minds of the other Hightons with them.

They stood on a high balcony looking out over the tiers of seats, ring upon ring of them, with a circular dais in the center. The domed ceiling curved high above the hall, veined by crystal panels that reflected the light orbs. It was smaller than the Amphitheatre of Providence on Glory; only a few hundred delegates sat in these tiers. But they were a markedly distinguished group, the elite of his empire and the Imperialate. More than half of the Eubian delegates were Aristos, and though they were too far away to impact his mind directly, he felt them like a distant pressure. He stood with Tarquine, his hands resting on the crystal rail, and looked out over that phenomenal assemblage, the first of its kind ever convened.

What riveted Jaibriol, however, wasn't the delegates; it was the group on the balcony directly across the hall from him. The Ruby Pharaoh entered with the Assembly First Councilor and another Allied general. Kelric came in behind them, massive and towering, a dramatic contrast to the delicate pharaoh.

Jaibriol wasn't tempted to underestimate Dyhianna Selei, a mistake so many people had made and regretted. She had survived the Radiance War, assassination attempts, and Eubian infiltrations, then gathered her forces and overthrown her own government. The Skolians claimed they split their government evenly between the Ruby Dynasty and the democratic Assembly, but Jaibriol didn't believe it. If ever it came to a challenge between the two, their military would support the pharaoh.

Dyhianna Selei was also the Assembly Key of the Triad, the liaison between the Assembly and the star-spanning web. The Mind of Skolia. Kelric was the Military Key, the Fist of Skolia. Kelric's late father—Jaibriol's grandfather—had been the Web Key, the Heart of Skolia.

Three keys to the Web: Mind, Fist, and Heart.

What does that make me? Jaibriol thought. The Heart of Skolia? He couldn't have come up with a less apt description if he had tried. He gazed across that amphitheatre at his family, the kin he could never acknowledge, and felt as if he were breaking.

It was excruciating to be this close and yet cut off from them. The same was true for Aliana. He had analyzed her DNA in secret. It matched that of Althor Valdoria, who had been an ESComm prisoner years ago. Aliana was Jaibriol's first cousin. He could never tell her, never breathe a word of it to that gloriously powerful psion. But he could disguise her coloring to hide the resemblance between Kelric and an "inconsequential" taskmaker no one had yet bothered to notice.

The delegates were all watching the royal parties, waiting. They were already organized into task forces, and they would later split into their groups, Skolians and Traders together, to discuss the multitude of details needed to put the treaty into effect, setting up trade relations between their empires. The main conferences, the ones that would determine how Eube and Skolia would attempt to coexist in the same galaxy, would be between Jaibriol's people and the Pharaoh's party in the tower conference rooms.

The dais was rising in the center of the amphitheatre, crewed by Allied personnel. A robot arm had docked at Jaibriol's balcony, waiting for his use. It ended in a gigantic bronzed hand exactly like the one in the Amphitheatre of Providence. A similar arm was docked at the Skolian balcony, except that it ended in a Luminex console cup.

Major General Holland spoke at his side. "Your Highness, they are ready."

Jaibriol took a breath. "Let us begin, then."

The general spoke into his gauntlet comm. "On three." Across the amphitheatre, Major General Yamada was also speaking into his comm.

Holland paused, then said, "Copy that. One, two, three."

Jaibriol raised his hand in the same instant the Ruby Pharaoh raised hers. A single chime rang out in the amphitheatre as the Aristos tapped the diamond cymbals they wore on their thumbs and index fingers. Lights flashed from the Skolian consoles.

On the dais below, an Allied woman stood next to a console. She spoke in a clear voice that carried throughout the amphitheatre:

"The Summit of Delos is begun."

Streaming blue.

Del floated through the Kyle. It swirled into curves and hollows as if he drifted through a landscape of blue fog.

Prince Del-Kurj? That thought came from a woman.

My greetings, Panquai, he answered.

And mine to you, she thought. *Can you access the ISC mesh for Delos?*

I don't know. What do I look for?

Many people see it as a grid. We're hidden by a security cloak, so other users won't notice us, but we should be able to detect them. Their thoughts may look like sparks.

Del concentrated, striving to create a grid out of the mist. None appeared, though the landscape did become more detailed, with orb trees, blue cloud-grass, and sparkles like shimmerflies. ***I see blue. Hills, sky, trees, orbs. No grid.***

I mostly know how military types see it, Panquai said. *Maybe you perceive it differently. But my sensors say we're definitely in the military grid.*

A shimmerfly drifted toward Del. It wasn't a gauzy insect, but a winged woman. ***Hey, I see you! You look like an angel, Panquai.*** It reminded him of a song on his first music anthology: *Angel, be my Diamond Star, before my darkness goes too far.*

Amusement came from Panquai. *I've never been sung to on a mission before.*

Del grinned at her. ***A Jagernaut angel.***

My halo is crooked, she thought. *What else can you find here? Any problems?*

He drifted in a circle, surveying the blue universe. ***Everything looks fine. I don't know how I would see otherwise, though.***

Essentially, you're looking for yourself.

He considered the idea. ***On Earth, my music is available as something called a virt. It's a virtual reality simulation of the songs. It includes an avatar of me that acts as a host. If I go into the virt, I can meet "myself." It's bizarre. Even when it looks and acts just like me, I know it's not.***

That's a good description, Panquai thought. *If you concentrate on that idea, the forgery of your neural patterns might manifest as your virtual self.*

Del closed his eyes and imagined himself in a virt. He picked the song "Rubies," a ballad he had written about his family. The bittersweet music played around him:

Living bound by your empathy
Shelter found in your trinity
Love imprisoning hope for all days
Rubies must give their souls in all ways.

Del opened his eyes. He was standing knee-deep in the grasses of the Dalvador Plains on his home world Lyshriol. Stalks rippled around him, each tipped with an iridescent bubble. The plains stretched out to the horizon in most directions, and to the Stained Glass Forest in the west. Beyond the forest, the Backbone Mountains rose starkly into the sky. The landscape all had a blue tinge, as if he were seeing it through a diaphanous mist.

"This is beautiful," a woman said.

Del turned with a start. Secondary Panquai was a few paces away, looking around, lean and tall in her black leathers.

"Hey," Del said. "Welcome to my world."

She smiled. "Is that you singing?"

"Yeah, that's me." It was hard to say more; the song "Rubies" held a lot of pain.

"It's lovely," she said. "It sounds almost classical. I had thought you sang rock."

"Mostly. I like all kinds of music, though."

"You have an incredible voice."

Feeling awkward, he said, "Thanks." He could see past her, in the distance, to where a figure was approaching them. "Panquai, look. Do you see that?"

Turning, she peered across the field. "A man, I think. It's not you, though."

"Come on." Del headed for the figure. In one of the surreal jumps common in a virt, he and Panquai were suddenly only meters away from the figure. It was a man, a huge one, built like Kelric, but with violet eyes instead of gold. He wore Jagernaut blacks like Panquai.

Startled, Del stopped. "Althor?" Vertigo swept over him; his brother Althor was *dead.*

"My greetings, Del," Althor said, smiling.

Del just frowned. The Traders dishonored his brother's memory with this forgery.

Panquai studied the avatar. "Are you Secondary Althor Valdoria Skolia?"

"A virtual simulation of him, yes," Althor said.

"No, you aren't," Del said. "You're a fake. We're going to erase you." He gave the forgery a hard mental shove, letting his anger push it away. To Panquai, he said, "The Traders have Althor's neural signature, too, from when he was a prisoner of war."

Althor faded, his body becoming translucent, like blue mist. **Del, wait, I'm not a forgerrrry. . . .** The words dissipated as he disappeared.

"We should let Kelric know," Del said. What bothered him wasn't that the forgery existed, but that it seemed so *real.* If he hadn't known Althor was dead, he would have believed it was actually his brother in Kyle space.

Panquai worked on her gauntlet. "I'm notifying the telops. They'll take care of it."

"Why forge Althor? We know he's dead."

"It could be an echo from something else ESComm

is doing. They're so raw with all this, I doubt they realize we can find their neural forgeries."

The sunlight no longer streamed so fully. In fact, the day was turning dark.

"Something is wrong," Del said.

"What do you see?" Panquai asked.

"It's getting dark! Can't you tell?"

She shook her head, the motion difficult to discern in the dusk. "It looks the same to me."

Concentrate, Del told himself. ***Center yourself with songs.*** He thought of "Sapphire Clouds," a song he had written about the loss of childhood innocence:

Running through the sphere-tipped reeds
The suns like gold and amber beads
Jumpin' over blue-winged bees
Don't catch me please
Running, running, running.

The dark became complete and he lost all sense of mooring; only the song kept him anchored. He needed to orient on something definite. Kelric had sent him in here to check for problems with security, which had started with a rip in the Kyle mesh.

Show me the rip, he thought.

A voice answered, deep and inhuman. SPECIFICATION INCOMPLETE.

Del froze. ***What the hell?***

Gods almighty! That came from the usually unflappable Panquai. *Del, you just accessed Comtrace. That's impossible. No way do you have clearance for that.*

QUANTIFY "RIP," the inhuman voice said.

I don't understand, Del said. ***What is Comtrace?***

It's one of our most highly secured intelligence nodes. You shouldn't be able to do this. I certainly can't.

Should I say anything? he asked.

Wait—I'm getting authorization. Brant Tapperhaven is monitoring security for your brother. Then she thought, *All right. Tell it what you mean.*

Del marshaled his thoughts. ***Comtrace, take me to the place in the web where ISC security was compromised, the hole ESComm used to infiltrate our mesh and make it look as if I released "Carnelians Finale."***

DONE, Comtrace answered.

Del was suddenly in a deep grotto. Water swirled around him, green-blue, and gold fronds waved around the ruins of a submerged building with a cracked roof. Brightly colored fish, gold and blue, swam through the broken windows. He floated to the structure and peered inside. Old equipment lay scattered about in there, most of it pitted and corroding past recognition.

THIS SITE WAS CLOSED ONE HUNDRED AND SEVEN YEARS AGO, Comtrace told him. ITS AGED SYSTEMS WERE IMPROPERLY SECURED. WE HAVE REPAIRED IT.

Comtrace, why are you telling me this? Del asked.

YOU ARE CLEARED THROUGH IMPERATOR SKOLIA.

I don't think he intended that, Del thought.

ACCESS IS REQUIRED TO COMPLETE YOUR MISSION.

Primary Tapperhaven says you weren't cleared, Panquai thought. *He thinks you reached Comtrace because of your close relationship to the Imperator and the job he asked you to do here.*

But our relationship isn't close, Del answered.

Kelric and I argue all the time. Wryly he added, ***Maybe his forgery gets along with mine, but in real life***—Del froze. ***Panquai, I know what's going on!*** He kicked hard, arrowing for the surface. ***We have to warn Kelric!***

Telop station fourteen, Panquai said into her gauntlet. *Bring us out of the mesh now!*

Vertigo swept over Del as he was dragged upward. His clothes, boots, everything pulled at him, weighing him down, as if the Kyle itself were refusing to let him go. He fought through the darkening waters, aware of Panquai at his side.

He had found the forgery. But it wasn't him.

It was Comtrace.

XXVII
Gods of Chaos

When the doorway unexpectedly appeared in Aliana's suite, she hoped it was Tide. She should have known better; even before the archway finished opening, she felt the pressure of a Highton mind. A man stalked into her living room without asking permission, a powerful figure with a squarer face than most. Instead of black diamond clothes, he had on a uniform with no trace of anything that might be mistaken for ornamentation except red braid on the shoulders and cuffs. The lack of decoration made him no less imposing; if anything, its severity underscored the force of his presence.

Aliana recognized him, she wasn't certain from where, but she knew he was high even among Hightons. She dropped to one knee and stared at the floor, hoping she hadn't done anything stupid. She and Red were so *close* to freedom, less than an hour away from the exchange. She could no longer deny what she felt, that she would rather be with Skolians than her own people.

The man walked forward with a measured tread. The toes of his black boots came within her field of view. He walked around her, his boots going out of sight on one side and coming back into sight on the other. She wanted to ask why he had come, but she kept her mouth shut. His mind was even more suffocating than what she had felt from Admiral Muze.

"So you're the other slave," the Highton said. "You're nowhere near as unattractive as they claimed. You might bring a good price. I can't feel crap from your mind, though."

Aliana gritted her teeth. She knew Aristos talked to slaves differently than to each other, but still. He sounded more like Harindor than a Highton.

"Get up," he said.

She rose to her feet and looked up at him. No, not "up"; she must have grown again, because she was as tall as this Highton commander.

The moment her gaze met his, he swore and slapped her across the face. Aliana reeled backward, stumbling, but she caught her balance before she fell; all those training sessions with Tide had paid off. Then she just stood, staring at the Highton. Why the blazes had he hit her?

"I didn't give you permission to look at me," he said.

Aliana dropped her gaze. "I'm sorry, Your Glory," she lied. She had no idea what she was supposed to call him, but that seemed safer than, *Tough, you bastard.*

"You should be." He continued walking around her. "Put you in something better than this silly jumpsuit and you might look half decent. Maybe bring in a good price as a pleasure girl."

Aliana froze. *No.* He couldn't do that!

He came around in front of her again. "You a virgin, girl?"

Aliana was smoldering. He wasn't asking because he actually thought he could sell her. It aroused him to talk to her that way, just like it excited him to hit her.

She raised her gaze and met his squarely. "It's none of your damn business."

He showed almost no reaction, just the barest raising of one eyebrow. But the explosion of rage within him was so violent, it hit Aliana even through her mental fortress. She tensed for another blow, but instead he spoke in a deceptively mild tone. "You do realize, you'll be held accountable for everything you say here." His voice hardened. "I will see to it."

Aliana hardly heard him, she was so stunned by what she saw when she looked at his chest. The military ID read Barthol Iquar. Gods almighty. He was the other Joint Commander.

She kept quiet. He could send her to prison or worse for disrespecting him. But she couldn't turn off her loathing; the ugliness in him went deep. He was *angry*, not just about her defiance, but at the emperor, the empress, and the Skolians, and she was the one who would bear the brunt of that anger, because he could take out on her what he couldn't do to them.

He had plans, Aliana realized, something to do with her. She couldn't pick up much from his mind, but she caught enough; whatever he intended wouldn't leave her with the Skolians.

"Turn around," he told her.

Aliana turned so she was facing away from him. His uniform crackled, and in a mirror across the foyer, she saw him remove a syringe from a black pouch on his belt. It had some sort of metallic device on its end. He pressed panels on the syringe, studied them, and made more adjustments. Then he set its tip against the base of her neck, pushing up her collar. She stiffened, intending to jerk away, but it was already too late. A sharp pain exploded in her neck.

"What did you do?" she asked.

"Turn around," he said coldly.

She turned, her neck aching.

"We're preparing you for the trade with the Skolians," he said.

He was lying. He had done something to hurt her. "What did you put in me?"

"I didn't give you permission to speak," he said. But then he relented and added, "Listen, girl, don't worry. It's just an immunization, so you don't get sick from Skolian diseases."

Aliana blinked. She hadn't expected the kindness of a real response. "Thank you," she said, even though she wasn't grateful.

"You will come with me now," he said. "For the exchange."

The warning came in to Kelric while he and Dehya were on the dais in the amphitheatre. The summit had been going for several hours, an intricate dance of diplomacy while the Skolian and Eubian staffs introduced the members of various committees, which would consider the thousand and one details necessary to establish trade relations between their civilizations. After the pharaoh and emperor had appeared this morning on the balconies, they had withdrawn into private, their staffs organizing their first meeting for later this afternoon in one of the tower conference rooms. Their first topic of discussion: how to set up trade that explicitly excluded the sale of human beings.

Kelric had been down in the lobby where the exchange of Aliana and Red for the Eubian agents would take place. Now everyone was returning to the amphitheatre for one final opening ceremony before the negotiations began in earnest. The hall was packed, every Skolian and Eubian delegate present as well as many representatives from their Allied hosts. Jaibriol and his retinue had just walked out onto their balcony above the amphitheatre. His robot arm was docked there, waiting to bring his party here to the dais. This next meeting would be purely symbolic. The delegates had quieted, their rumbles replaced by silence as they waited for the historic moment they were about to witness. It would be the first time in the history of their civilizations that the Eubian emperor and Skolian pharaoh stood together, side by side, in peace.

The message from Security came into Kelric's gauntlet comm, which sent it through his biomech system to Bolt, the node in his spine. Bolt fired his neurons, translating the message into what Kelric interpreted as thought. It was as close as humans had ever come to technology-induced telepathy.

Your brother says it's Comtrace, Brant Tapperhaven told him. *He and Secondary Panquai think ESComm forged your signature so they could mimic Comtrace.*

Damn. Kelric had hoped the ESComm infiltration wouldn't reach so far. They weren't really forging Comtrace, they were forging his own impression of the node, but it could still cause problems. **Transfer**

Comtrace's functions to the backup nodes we set up and send a system-wide alert.

Above them, the giant bronzed hand of the emperor's robot arm was unfolding, leaving the palm open to the ceiling. The Eubians walked across the fingers: Jaibriol, Tarquine, Corbal, Barthol. Four Razers accompanied them, including one that looked eerily like Hidaka, the bodyguard who had died to save Jaibriol's life on Earth.

Dehya, Kelric thought. **Comtrace is compromised.**

Although she kept watching the Traders, her awareness shifted to him. *How bad is it?*

We caught it early. We've switched to our back-ups.

Above them, the giant hand curled around its passengers, forming a secure cup, and descended toward the dais.

Roca's thought came to them. ***What about the exchange for Aliana? Is that compromised?*** She was also watching the Traders, for all appearances focused on them.

Kelric sent a thought to another channel on his comm. **Major Qahot, what is the status of the exchange?** The trade was timed to coincide with the meeting of Dehya and Jaibriol on the dais, the two sovereigns showing goodwill in an exchange of prisoners. Kelric didn't care about the newsworthy symbolism; he wanted the trade to happen when he could monitor it, which meant when he wasn't in the midst of a sensitive negotiation. All he had to do now was stand here and look dignified. ESComm liked the arrangement because Kelric had just finished checking the lobby where the trade would take place, so he and Dehya had re-entered the amphitheatre on its ground level and mounted the dais there. It was rising now, but it still meant the emperor was coming *down* to them, which ESComm undoubtedly felt made Jaibriol look superior. Kelric didn't give a damn; he just wanted Aliana away from the Traders before someone figured out who they were about to lose.

We're in the lobby, Qahot thought, her mood calm and assured. *The Eubians just notified us that they've finished the immunizations and are bringing down the boy and the girl.*

Get the trade done fast, Kelric thought. **No matter what, get Aliana.**

Copy that, sir, Qahot said.

The robot arm with the Eubians was almost level to the dais. As its descent slowed, its bronzed fingers uncurled like a Titan opening his palm to the skies. Jaibriol and his retinue stood on the palm like a set of black diamond Quis dice.

Sir, the Trader group is here for the exchange, Major Qahot thought. She sent a recording to his mind. He was suddenly "in" Qahot's viewpoint, watching the elevator in the lobby, a tall set of reflective doors. They slid open, revealing four Razers, exactly the number of Jagernauts that Qahot had brought with her to guard the ESComm agents. He glimpsed the girl and the boy behind the two front Razers, but he couldn't see them clearly. As the group walked into the lobby, however, the duo came into better view, two beautiful and poignantly *young* people.

Decades of using a mindscape created by his neural implants made it possible for Kelric to simultaneously process what was happening on the dais and in the lobby. With his outer gaze, he watched the bronzed hand dock at the edge of the dais. Bolt controlled Kelric's facial muscles to ensure he revealed nothing of what he was viewing through Qahot's eyes. He saw Aliana and Red join Qahot's group. Aliana was *safe*—

That was when the girl dropped her mental defenses.

Her thought rang through their minds, an inexperienced shout, raw and desperate. ***He put something in my neck! General Iquar! He shot my neck. It's a trick!***

It was as if she had released a sun. She *blazed* with Ruby strength. Roca's eyes widened and Dehya jerked, barely controlling her shock. Jaibriol lifted his hand, then caught himself and lowered it.

Kelric thought, **Aliana, show me in your mind how General Iquar injected you.**

They all felt the girl's mental gasp. ***Freaking gods, who ARE you, blasting my head?***

Oblivious to the mental exchange among the telepaths present, the Eubians with Jaibriol continued their choreographed approach to the dais, the Razers stepping onto the circular platform, including the man who looked like Hidaka. Jaibriol stood on the giant hand, watching the proceedings with an aloof gaze that gave no hint of whatever he picked up from Aliana. Kelric shoved his awareness of Jaibriol deep in his mind, where neither Roca nor any of the four Jagernauts on the dais would sense his reaction and wonder why he thought the Highton emperor might respond to a psion.

Kelric had no time to explain, so he just said, **Aliana, I'm heading the Skolian team for the exchange. You must show me, in your mind, how he injected you.**

This is him, Aliana thought. A picture formed, wavering, her memory of the incident with Barthol. It was an eerie parallel to what Kelric saw now as he faced the general, who was standing on the giant hand. Barthol regarded him with a neutral expression, but the crushing pressure of his Highton mind weighed on Kelric. The main difference in what Kelric saw here and Aliana's mental image was that in her memory, Barthol was holding an air syringe-gun.

That's an immunization syringe, Dehya thought.

Jaibriol walked across the bronzed fingers and stepped onto the dais. He looked more like a sculpture than a man; in Highton terms, he was perfection. He and Dehya inclined their heads to each other. All the Skolians on the dais, except Dehya, bowed to Jaibriol in the same moment that all the Eubians, except Jaibriol, bowed to Dehya.

Kelric thought, **Aliana, he gave you a shot to protect you from Skolian sicknesses. You need those immunities.**

Why is Barthol Iquar giving it to her? Roca asked. ***That's an odd task for the General of the Eubian Army.***

It's not immunities, Aliana thought. ***It's a trick.***

Now Tarquine was stepping from the hand to the dais. She glanced at Kelric, her gaze shrouded, but nothing could disguise the recognition in her eyes. An unbidden memory jumped in his mind, *Tarquine in his arms, her body under his—*

Kelric thrust down the memory, but he was too late; Jaibriol's gaze snapped to him. The emperor immediately intensified his barriers, but not before his surge of rage blasted Kelric.

Concentrate, Kelric told himself, trying to regain his equilibrium. **Aliana, I need to see the syringe better. Show me every detail you can recall.**

Her image became clearer. The syringe looked ordinary, except for its tip. He had seen that configuration before . . .

He shot a timer in her neck, Kelric suddenly thought.

A timer for what? Aliana asked.

We'll find out. To Qahot, he thought, **How the hell did that get past security?**

We're checking, sir, she answered. *Something to do with the Comtrace forgery.*

Jaibriol was speaking to Dehya in Highton, with the minimalist greeting that the highest Aristos reserved for one another. "Pharaoh Dyhianna."

Dehya responded in kind. "Emperor Jaibriol."

We need to take it out of Aliana, Kelric thought. To finally have the girl, and then lose her to some godforsaken intrigue, maybe a time-released poison, would be a crime.

I can check her right now, Qahot thought. *Probably even cut it out of her neck. But the Traders are here. They might see. I've no idea if that matters to them.*

Move away and hide what you're doing, Kelric told her. **But get it done.**

The scene in his mind changed, shifting to Qahot's viewpoint. Aliana was sitting on the marble ledge of a fountain with people all around, shielding her from view. Major Qahot murmured to the girl, and Aliana acted as if she felt sick. The major leaned over, for all appearances being solicitous of a scared child as she brushed the hair off Aliana's neck. The girl looked up, her eyes wide, and in that instant, she looked so much like his brother Althor that Kelric's heart lurched.

Aliana, we'll fix it, he thought. **I promise.**

Here on the dais, Jaibriol was speaking to Dehya. "Pharaoh Dyhianna, my people have a custom. When an event of great import takes place, we observe a silence in its honor."

What the hell? Kelric had never heard of the custom. Flashes of puzzlement came from Jaibriol's retinue; apparently neither had any of them. Barthol thought it was amusing, Corbal considered it odd but acceptable, and Tarquine wondered what her husband was up to.

Dehya spoke to Jaibriol. "Of course, Your Highness."

Then Kelric understood. Jaibriol was giving them time to check Aliana.

Roca stood tensed at Kelric's side, facing the Aristos, and he felt her struggling with her memories of the Hightons who had imprisoned her. To Roca, Jaibriol and his retinue were no different. But he also felt her surprise. She had expected the pressure of all their minds to be overwhelming, not only the Hightons, but also their guards, who were often part Aristo. Yet she felt only Barthol.

In his mind, Kelric saw Qahot take out a med stylus and numb Aliana's neck, then gently slice the skin. Here on the dais, Barthol Iquar's gauntlet hummed. Jaibriol glanced at him with the barest hint of a frown and then looked away, but that one sign spoke volumes; if Barthol interrupted the proceedings, it had better be for a damn good reason. A muscle in Barthol's face twitched.

In Kelric's mindscape, Qahot uncovered a tiny

sphere in Aliana's neck just under the skin. It looked familiar...he had seen something like that—

Qahot, wait! Kelric thought. **That's a damn bomb!**

Ah gods, no. Aliana's thought ricocheted in their minds. *Please, I don't want to die.*

We won't let you, Kelric told her. **Qahot, that sphere uses the release of gamma radiation from nuclear isomers to trigger the creation of nanobots at an explosively fast rate. They immediately become inert because they don't have a continuing energy source, but by then, they've destroyed any solid they've touched, using it to make more of themselves. It happens so fast, it's like an explosion. You have to get that thing out of Aliana.**

That's it, Dehya thought. *We need to evacuate the amphitheatre. Now!*

Stop! A new, unexpected thought burst into Kelric's mind. *Don't touch the bomb! It'll explode if you remove it. If ESComm realizes you know it's there, they'll detonate it.*

Del? Kelric asked. **Good gods, how did you get into this mental link?**

That girl—she's Althor's daughter, isn't she? Del asked.

How the blazes did you find that out?

From your minds, now! Del's mind jumped into an accelerated mode where their thoughts went like sparks of light. *I saw Althor in the Kyle. His forgery. It was my way of seeing his link to this. It's her! The girl. That Comtrace forgery is too clumsy; ESComm KNEW we would find it. Its only purpose was to make*

us doubt the real Comtrace long enough to weaken our security so they could get the bomb through. They knew even that might not work, so the bomb is rigged to blow if you disturb it. The moment you take it out of her neck, it will explode.

Qahot, hold! Kelric thought. **Can you verify that?**

The bomb's nano-mesh is encrypted, sir, Qahot answered. *We're trying to crack it.*

Del's thought came again. ***Kelric, if you leave it in her neck, it will go off as soon as you're close enough that her mind picks up your brain waves. That's what it's for, to kill you and whoever is with you.***

Kelric looked at Barthol, and the general met his gaze with an icy Highton stare. In an almost imperceptible motion, Barthol touched a panel on his gauntlet. In that instant, his intention flared with such power, it broke past Kelric's barriers and flooded his mind. He was giving an order to detonate the bomb.

Kelric shouted into the mental link. **Qahot, get it out of her NOW!**

With enhanced speed, Qahot flipped out the tiny sphere—

An explosion thundered through the building.

XXVIII
The Fist of Eube

Aliana had only a second to hear the huge, thundering thought in her mind, as the man shouted, **Qahot, get it out of her NOW!** The major flicked the point of her blade into Aliana's neck, then threw them both to the ground, Qahot shielding Aliana with her own body.

The world exploded.

Aliana gasped as the ground heaved, flinging her through the air. Her mental tie to the Skolian man snapped off as if someone had slashed it with a blade. She landed on a hard surface and chunks of debris rained down, pummeling her body. People were shouting, alarms screamed, and dust filled the air. She heaved in a breath, then choked as her throat clogged.

Scrambling to her feet, she looked around wildly. It was chaos. The Razers and the five ESComm agents from the exchange were thrown haphazardly against the closed doors of the lift. One of the Razers was struggling to his feet, but everyone else lay still. Qahot was nearby, her body twisted.

"No!" Aliana stumbled through the swirling dust and dropped next to Qahot. The major had suffered because she protected Aliana, leaving herself exposed. Aliana laid her hands against Qahot's neck and gave a relieved cry when she realized the officer was still breathing.

"Red!" she called. "Where are you?" In her mind, she shouted, ***Red! Answer, please!***

People in uniforms were climbing through the debris. Someone called out, "We've got at least two people alive over here." Someone else shouted, "They're evacuating the amphitheatre."

Aliana looked up and saw a ragged hole blown in the ceiling, not above her, but to her left. All the swirling dust hazed her view of the hole, but she glimpsed enough to see that the ceiling here, for the lobby, was the floor of the amphitheatre above them.

One of the rescuers suddenly spasmed, then cried out and crumpled to the ground. Rainbow lights rippled over his body. With a start, Aliana realized that veils of light surrounded the area where the prisoner exchange had taken place, extending from the ground up through the ceiling, adding their translucent colors to the swirling dust.

"Stay back from the lights!" someone called. "Those are cyberlock fields, set to kill."

Psiber what? Aliana froze, afraid to move.

"Zina?" a voice said at her side.

With a choked sob, she swung around. It was Red. She threw her arms around him, holding him close.

His voice came out muffled against her hair. "Am glad to see you, too. But Zina, you crack my spine."

"Oh!" With a shaky laugh, she released her hold. "Sorry."

Aliana. The familiar voice of the Skolian man rumbled in her mind like an anchor in the midst of a storm. **Are you still with us?**

Relief poured over her. ***I'm in the lobby. It blew up! It's terrible. No one can get to us. A locked psiber is killing them.***

Cyberlock, the man told her. **They were installed by both royal parties to protect them in the case of an attack. You're on the inside of the field. As long as you don't try to cross the curtains of light, you'll be fine.**

Is Emperor Jaibriol all right? He was supposed to be a god, and gods couldn't die, but she didn't believe it. What she did believe was that he was different from other Hightons, truly great, and if any of them should live, it was him. ***Are you all right? Major Qahot and her Jagernauts are hurt. They need help.***

We're fine up here, he said. **The safety precautions worked. We're sending people down to help your group.**

Look, Red said, pointing to the ceiling. *Is him, I think.*

She peered where he indicated. A man was kneeling at the edge of the jagged hole in the ceiling. She couldn't see him clearly, other than his huge silhouette in the harsh light from amphitheatre above and behind him.

Is that you kneeling at the hole? she asked.

Yes, he thought. **Can you come here?**

She glanced at Red, and he nodded. Taking his hand, she thought, ***I think so.***

They picked their way over the shattered fountain. The buckled floor made it hard to walk, and the air smelled like graves and electrical discharges. The blast had been centered where the bomblet hit the ground; what had been a row of indoor trees was now a crater with billows of dust.

To reach the hole in the ceiling, they climbed up slanting marble columns that had been shoved away from the vertical, their surfaces cracked and jagged. At the top, they were almost close enough to touch the man. Dust grimed his hair and face.

"Here." He extended his large hand. "Come up, both of you. The amphitheatre is intact, and its supports were built to withstand worse than this."

Aliana wasn't sure how he knew so much about the building, but it made sense that this meeting place would be well built. She wanted Red safe, so she pushed him forward. "You go."

Red grasped the man's hand and the Skolian heaved upward, easily lifting as Red scrambled up next to him. While Red stepped back from the edge, the man reached for Aliana, and with his help, she climbed up. Alarms were still blaring, more distant now. People were calling somewhere, but no one seemed nearby except this man.

Red was staring around at the amphitheatre. It was mostly open air; it didn't have much to collapse other than the seats ringing the area. They looked all right except for a few rows that had cracked and buckled. The evacuation was almost done, with a few people still leaving. No one had come close to this place, the middle of the amphitheatre floor.

As Aliana stepped back from the hole, the Skolian man stood up. He was *huge*. She had never seen someone so big.

"Who are you?" she asked.

"My name is Kelric."

His kind voice reassured her. "What are we going to do?"

"You need to stay with me." He motioned at a group of people across the amphitheatre, gathered near a pile of rubble that looked like a broken disk. "We don't have much time."

As they headed across the amphitheatre, Aliana asked, "Is this place going to collapse?" Parts of the building were crumbling, causing minor showers of broken composite.

"Not the walls." Kelric motioned upward, where large robot arms were docked at balconies. "But the blast may have damaged some of those."

They soon reached the group—and Aliana gave a choked cry. She didn't see everyone, only the man and woman with glittering black hair. She dropped to her knees, hit with a relief so intense, it hurt. Red knelt beside her, his head bowed.

The emperor spoke, his voice still resonant, but also ragged. "Both of you, rise."

As she stood up, she became aware of the other people. It was two groups, each facing the other. On one side, she saw the emperor, the empress, General Iquar, Lord Corbal Xir, and the four Razers—including Tide! On her side, she saw Kelric, four Jagernauts,—

And a woman with gold hair, gold eyes, and gold skin. Metallic gold.

The world seemed to stop for Aliana. Only the two of them were there, her and this golden being in some reality where no explosions could interfere. The woman stared at Aliana, her eyes filling with moisture. A voice came clearly in Aliana's mind, like the rising of a sun, full of warmth and the grief for loved ones lost.

You look so much like him, the woman thought. ***So much like Althor.***

Who . . . who are you? Tears welled in Aliana's eyes. ***You look like me.***

"We have to leave," a harsh voice said in Highton. "This amphitheatre isn't safe."

Aliana's thoughts jerked unceremoniously back to reality. She knew that ugly voice. She hated it. That was General Iquar speaking to the emperor.

"You did this," she said to the general, her voice low and furious. "You tried to blow me up!"

General Iquar gave her a bored look. "Is this child insane or just a fool?"

"I'm not crazy." Aliana looked around at the rest of them. "He did it."

Before anyone could respond, a rumbling started above them. With a start, she looked up. A gigantic bronzed arm with a fisted hand was vibrating at its dock against one wall.

"We should move," Kelric said.

As they retreated across the floor, which was covered with dust and grit, Corbal Xir said, "We can't go far. The cyberlock fields tuned to Emperor Jaibriol and Pharaoh Dyhianna are both set on fatal, and we're inside of them."

Kelric glanced at one of the Jagernauts. "Turn off the lock."

The Jagernaut worked at his gauntlet, making lights flash and noises beep. After a moment, he said, "We can't, sir. It's not working."

Major Qahot? Kelric's thoughts hummed past Aliana's mind. **Can you read me?**

A man answered, sounding very young. *Commander Skolia, this is Lieutenant Kelpner. The rest of the team is injured.*

Then you're in charge, Kelpner. Get these damn cyberlocks off.

We're working on it, sir. Their mesh-systems are jammed. It's a side effect from the clumsy tampering with Comtrace. It won't process their release codes.

One of the Razers was reading a screen on his gauntlet comm as he spoke to Barthol Iquar. "General, the cyberlock frequencies are jammed, some sort of mesh interference."

A Jagernaut said, "Imperator Skolia, you, the Pharaoh, and Councilor Roca can go through the Skolian field. But if you cross the Emperor Jaibriol's field, it will kill you."

Tide spoke in his deep voice. "The same is true for Emperor Jaibriol and Empress Tarquine. They can pass through their field, but not yours."

Kelric scowled at Barthol. "Damn it, Iquar, your clumsy Kyle meddling could get all of us killed."

"I have no idea what you're talking about," the general said coldly.

Above them, the growl of engines was growing louder as the bronzed robot arm with the fisted hand swung slowly above the amphitheatre. Ahead of them, the cyberlock field rippled in a curtain of rainbows. Two Razers and two Jagernauts reached the field at the same time. They turned around, looking upward, and everyone halted to follow their gaze. Above them, the fisted hand also stopped and hung suspended, high in the air.

"Our motion seems to draw it," Empress Tarquine said. "When we stop, it does, too."

Lieutenant Kelpner, check with my brother Del about the Comtrace forgery, Kelric thought. **He may know how it's interfering with the cyberlocks.**

A new thought came into Aliana's mind from another man, an incredible voice, so distinctive she would have recognized it anywhere. It was the Ruby prince who had sung "Carnelians Finale."

Panquai and I think we can untangle it here, Del said. ***We need to clear out the seaweed around the ruins.***

I'm not sure what you mean by seaweed or ruins, Kelric answered. **But if you can help deactivate the locks, then yes, do it.**

The mental chatter was giving Aliana vertigo. They were calling Kelric "sir," and he was giving orders, even to a prince. He was, she realized, probably captain of the pharaoh's bodyguard. The Eubians were drawing away from the Skolians, separating themselves while their Razers worked at their gauntlets. The bronzed fist hung motionless, far above them.

Kelpner, can't security fix that robot arm? Kelric asked. **What's wrong with it?**

It was damaged in the explosion, Kelpner answered. *It's keyed to the emperor's cyberlock, so that when the arm carries him through the amphitheatre, his field always surrounds it. But apparently its coding is corrupted, so it's following everyone within the field.*

Actually, it stopped, Kelric thought.

Eubian Security is trying to link to the nanobots in its structure so they can direct its repair remotely. Maybe it's working.

A low thunder rumbled below them in the lobby. Dust billowed through the hole in the amphitheatre floor.

"We need to get out of here," the golden Skolian woman said.

"The supports should hold up the floor," a melodic voice replied.

Aliana knew that voice. With a start, she turned around. She had been so shocked by seeing the emperor and the golden woman that she hadn't realized who else was here. The Ruby Pharaoh! Two looming Jagernauts flanked her small form.

The pharaoh's thought came like a phantom song on a lost sea. ***Aliana, welcome.***

Aliana was too mesmerized to answer. She felt motion from the pharaoh, yet the woman hadn't moved. It was the pharaoh's mind that was journeying, traveling unseen waters. Standing still, appearing to do nothing at all, Dyhianna Selei was working in ways no one else could, her mind untangling their brains from the cyberlocks.

A growl came from the engines of the robot arm, and Aliana looked up. The bronzed arm was rising higher and swinging toward a docking crane at one of the balconies.

She hoped it stayed there.

The Hand of the God Emperor. Despite its overblown name, Jaibriol had always liked the bizarre robot arm. He watched it move away from them, returning to its hangar at the balcony. Then he glanced around, instinctively checking that Tarquine was safe. She was walking toward Barthol, who was speaking in a low voice to someone on his gauntlet comm. Uneasy,

Jaibriol went over to them. Corbal stayed with the Razers, still trying to deactivate the cyberlock.

Barthol looked up at Jaibriol. "It seems the holocams recording today's session were damaged in the explosion. They aren't working."

Jaibriol didn't particularly care. "What I find odd," he said, "is that the locks meant to protect our lives are working too well."

"I doubt the Skolians find it odd," Barthol said with a twitch of his finger than indicated disgust. "Tampering with our security seems to be one of their favorite pasttimes."

"The Skolians," Tarquine murmured. "You think it's all their fault, dear Barthol?"

Above them, the growl of engines changed pitch. Looking up, Jaibriol saw that the bronzed arm had stopped trying to dock itself.

"It is amazing how people show their true selves in a crisis, don't you think?" Barthol told the empress. "Even the most outwardly accomplished Highton might revert to less exalted speech when she is, shall we say, stressed."

"Oh, but Barthol, you are my kin." She activated her comm and spoke on a private channel only she and Barthol could use. "Direct speech is allowed for such." Her voice came out of Barthol's comm, giving an odd stereo effect, since she was standing right in front of him.

"Something is wrong with that arm," Jaibriol said, peering at the bronzed fist. It was poised near the high balcony.

"Yes, I am your kin," Barthol told Tarquine, his Highton inflections like ice. "Your *heir.*"

Startled, Jaibriol turned back at them.

"My blood." Tarquine's voice was too quiet. For some reason, she was talking on her comm, though Barthol was right here. "For that tie and that tie only, I give you honor this day instead of infamy."

Barthol switched off his comm. "You give me nothing."

"Look up, nephew," she murmured. "See my gift."

Jaibriol followed her gaze. High in the amphitheatre, the bronzed fist was jerking under the force of its great weight. Its engines grated, straining to prevent it from descending.

"What the hell?" Barthol tensed as if he intended to stride away, but he didn't move. His comm was flashing, open to Tarquine even though he had just shut it off.

"Oh dear, I forgot to tell you something," Tarquine said.

Barthol stared at her. "What the blazes are you talking about?"

"Tarquine, move!" Jaibriol backed up, pulling her with him. The bronzed arm was so high, it was hard to tell where it would hit if it dropped. He wanted her well away from there. But as soon as they moved, the arm followed them. When Jaibriol backed up faster, the arm increased its speed, staying with him. He stopped and the arm stopped, but its engines continued to grind, as it strained to stay in place. The entire time, Barthol remained stock still, watching them.

"Don't worry," Tarquine told him. "Barthol is going to be a hero."

"*No.*" Barthol sounded as if he were clenching his teeth, forcing out the word. He stared at Tarquine, his face contorted. If Jaibriol hadn't known him so well, he would have thought Barthol was worried for her safety. But he felt the general's mind; Barthol was trying *not* to run. His body strained as if he were fighting a compulsion to make him move. He suddenly broke into a sprint, running in the direction opposite of Jaibriol and Tarquine. The robot hand immediately swung toward the general, barely holding its altitude as its engines fought its erratic motions.

Tarquine spoke into her comm on the secured channel that only her nephew could receive. "Did you know, Barthol, that the surgery to implant a node in a person's brain is a complex and delicate process, even if that node has only one purpose, to control a person's movements at a crucial time—like making him run when he doesn't want to." Softly she added, "Of course, if the patient is in a coma, that offers the surgeon plenty of time to do the work."

Jaibriol spoke in a low voice. "My God, Tarquine, what did you do?" It suddenly made sense, why he had picked up Barthol's thoughts more strongly than usual. The general hadn't implanted any neural tech in his brain, *Tarquine* had done it, nothing too complex, just enough for her to control his movements this one time. It was unlikely anything she had done could be permanent or stable. It would probably soon disintegrate. But she hadn't needed it to last for long, just until an opportunity presented itself for her to use.

Tarquine watched her nephew, her red gaze cold. He ran as if he were deliberately drawing the broken fist away from them. Its engines ground with the shriek of breaking composites—and suddenly the arm was in free fall, dropping like a gigantic hammer straight at

Barthol. As Jaibriol watched in disbelief, the general looked back at them, his face contorted in fury.

Tarquine spoke one last time into her comm, her voice rough with a bitter anger. "When you tried to kill me, Barthol, I was pregnant. You murdered my son."

The fist finished its fall then, smashing into the ground with the force of its immense weight. Debris leapt into the air and the walls of the amphitheatre shook. The tiers in one section crumbled as the vibrations from the blow spread throughout the hall. The floor under the robot sagged, and cracks shot out in many directions, like lightning running through the stone.

With it, the fist took a man who would be lauded as the hero of the Delos Summit, the general who sacrificed his life to save his emperor and empress.

XXIX
Triad

Kelric felt Barthol die. It exploded in his mind, that shattering moment that ended in abrupt darkness. Kelric's mind reeled and for an instant he could see nothing, only blackness.

The amphitheatre reappeared and Kelric gulped in a ragged breath.

"Gods almighty," Roca whispered next to him.

"Imperator Skolia, are you all right?"

Kelric turned to see the captain of their bodyguards coming toward him. All four Jagernauts were pale. They would have also felt the general die, not with the force it would hit a Ruby psion, but still strong. If Barthol had been a psion, it would have hit them even harder, but any death was a shock, including that of an Aristo, even when it came with a release from the pressure of Barthol's Highton mind. They had all felt it. Looking at the Jagernauts—all of them telepaths—Kelric knew what he had to do. He couldn't operate with them here.

"I'm all right," Kelric said. He brushed a panel on his gauntlet that deactivated his links to his security teams. "I need for you to go down to the lobby. The people below us can't get out of the cyberlock field, either. They need your help."

The captain spoke. "With respect, sir, we're needed here, with your family."

"You have my orders," Kelric said. "Go."

Kelric, for flaming sake, what are you doing? Roca thought.

Dehya's voice came into their link. **Roca, trust him.**

Roca glanced at Dehya, her forehead furrowed, but she said nothing more. The Jagernauts saluted Kelric, stiff with their misgivings, and took off, jogging toward the broken portion of the floor. As they disappeared over its edge, climbing down to the lobby, their minds receded.

Now, Kelric thought to Dehya.

Taking a breath, he headed across the amphitheatre. Dehya joined him, and he slowed his pace, moderating his speed, though his instincts urged him to run, for he knew they had only moments before the cyberlocks released. Right now, no one could reach them. They were isolated. The holocams weren't working. They would probably never have a chance like this again.

Kelric kept walking.

Jaibriol watched them approach, his face impossible to read, his mind saturated with shock. The bitter, astringent smell of broken composite permeated the air. Sounds were muted except for the tread of Kelric's boots on the floor. He and Dehya kept walking, and he was aware of Roca, Aliana, and the boy following, their thoughts uncertain, puzzled.

Jaibriol headed toward him.

The four Razers immediately fell into step with the emperor, their hands dropping to the guns holstered on their hips. Tarquine frowned at her husband, but she walked at his side, and Corbal Xir accompanied them as well.

Kelric. Roca's thought came into his mind. ***They outnumber us. Why did you send away our guards?***

Mother, I want you to wait on the other side of the amphitheatre. Take Aliana and the boy with you.

No. She continued on with him.

Go. Take them.

No.

Dehya glanced at Kelric. When he gave her a questioning look, asking what she wanted to do, she nodded.

So they continued their walk.

They met Jaibriol in the center of the amphitheatre. Their two groups stood there, no one making any move, however slight, that might be interpreted as threatening. Kelric set his mental shields to cut out Roca and the two children. Whether or not he could block a psion as experienced as his mother when she was so close, he didn't know, but he doubted anyone else could pick them up.

It was time. This was the moment.

Kelric thought, **Jaibriol.**

Dehya's thought came like clear water. *Jaibriol.*

The emperor didn't move. He showed no response.

This may be our only chance ever, Kelric thought to him.

Jaibriol stared at them, his face perfectly composed,

no trace of acknowledgement in his manner, and Kelric feared the emperor could never break free of his mental prison.

Then a thought came to Kelric, one like nothing he had ever before felt, vibrant and alive, luminous and deep and full of resonant power. Jaibriol Qox thought, **The Carnelian Throne acknowledges the Mind and the Fist of the Web.**

Dehya exhaled as if she had just heard a singer hit an exquisitely high note. *The Ruby Throne acknowledges the Heart of the Web.*

No. Roca's stunned protest whispered in their minds. ***No, it cannot be.***

Roca, you must not react, Dehya said. *Aliana and Red, if you can hear this, the same is true for you. Even with the holocams off, systems may record us. You must show* NO *sign that anything is going on beyond what people see. You cannot reveal what you hear, not now, not ever.*

Tarquine and Corbal were watching them, Corbal's white hair glittering. The Razers towered in their severe uniforms. One of them, the man who looked exactly like Hidaka, glanced beyond Kelric as if searching for someone. Kelric felt an oddly metallic sense from the Razer. Something he saw in their group moved him greatly. Something—or someone.

Tarquine's gaze flicked from Dehya to Jaibriol. Then she discreetly cleared her throat.

Jaibriol took a breath. "Pharaoh Dyhianna, our summit appears to have a glitch."

Dehya spoke wryly. "It would seem so, Your Highness." Quietly she added, "Our sympathies for your loss."

Jaibriol's voice was so perfect, it sounded ready to break. "Thank you."

Jaibriol, Kelric thought. **We need to ask you a question.**

The emperor regarded him. **Go ahead.**

Did something happen to you on this date? Kelric projected an image of the date when he and Dehya had suffered the attack in Kyle space.

Jaibriol's posture tightened. **Yes.**

Can you tell us what? Dehya asked.

Jaibriol spoke aloud. "We extend our regrets for the deaths of your people in this crisis."

Dehya inclined her head. "We thank you, Your Highness." She thought, *Please, Jaibriol. We need to know.*

What do you believe happened on that date? he asked.

Kelric's thought rumbled. **Someone tried to assassinate you.**

Jaibriol showed no outward response—and that composure was an immense tribute to his control, for inside of his mind, his pain swept through their link. **They failed to kill myself or my wife**. Bitterly he added, **My son was less fortunate.**

Tarquine's black diamond tunic rustled as she shifted her weight. Kelric was too focused on Jaibriol to pick up the minds of anyone outside their loop, but he suspected Corbal and Tarquine had a good idea what was happening. The Razers were impossible to read, other than their readiness to defend the emperor.

Aloud, Dehya said, "Emperor Jaibriol, we hope you have suffered no ill effects as a result of this attack." In her mind, she thought, *My sorrow for your son. We mourn the passing of our kin.*

Jaibriol gave her a formal nod. "We are fine, Your Highness. We hope that you have not suffered from this violence." His thought came as well: **I deeply regret if the attack against my life led to similar against yours.**

The Triad is linked, Kelric thought. **What happens to one, happens to all.**

I cannot do it. Jaibriol's mind ached with his struggle. **To operate as a member of the Triad—I have no way to do this, no understanding, nothing. It's killing me.**

Then he dropped his barriers.

His mind opened like rays of light slanting through a storm, and the parting of those clouds revealed a vulnerability as deep as an ocean. Kelric felt it all, Jaibriol's fight to hide the truth every second, every hour, every day, for years on end, until it left him ravaged with mental scar tissue. Yet through it all shone a mind beyond any other Kelric knew. Jaibriol had inherited the best from all of them: his mother's strength of character, his father's purity, Dehya's brilliance, Kelric's strength, Roca's luminosity, Del's creativity, all that made each of them unique. Within his tortured mind, he was a miracle beyond imagining.

Ah gods, Roca thought. She was no longer the Assembly Councilor meeting her enemy; she had become the mother Kelric had known all his life, the nurturer who loved her children with nothing held back. Jaibriol's face showed no hint of his emotions; outwardly, in every detail, he was the ideal remote Highton. But in his mind, he reached for her golden warmth like a man freezing to death.

In real time, barely seconds had passed. Dehya

was speaking quietly. "Let us not allow these acts of violence to stop the summit."

"We are agreed," Jaibriol said, his voice so distant and cool, he barely seemed human.

Come with us, Roca thought to Jaibriol. ***This is Delos, the world of sanctuary, the place where Skolians, Eubians, and Allieds may walk together. Step across the line. Ask us for asylum. We will take you in.***

I cannot, Jaibriol answered. **I have sworn to find the peace my parents dreamed of. If I stop now, all will have been in vain. They would have died for nothing.**

Your parents? Roca asked. She showed him an image of Soz, her daughter, a woman in a Jagernaut's uniform, standing with her booted feet planted, a laser carbine in her hands, her chin lifted, the wind blowing her hair around her head, black hair that shaded into wine-red and then into metallic gold at the tips.

Yes. My mother. Jaibriol showed them a man, the living image of previous Qox emperors, except that instead of a chilly Aristo in black diamond, this man wore patched trousers and a faded shirt with frayed hems. He was standing on a boulder in an alien forest, laughing, his eyes filled with kindness and love.

My father, Jaibriol thought.

A song swirled in their minds, a Lyshrioli tune Roca had often sung to her children. An image of Soz crooning to her babies formed in Jaibriol's mind. She sang slightly off tune in an untrained voice, yet somehow that only made it more beautiful.

The gauntlets worn by Jaibriol's bodyguards began to flash. At the same time, the pager on Kelric's gauntlet hummed with a high-priority signal. As Kelric lifted his arm, Jaibriol glanced at the Razer to his right, the twin of Hidaka.

"What is it?" Jaibriol asked the Razer.

A message scrolled across the comm in Kelric's gauntlet: *We fixed the cyberlock keys. We're turning off the locks.*

At the same time, the Razer said, "Sire, they've released the cyberlocks. We're free to go."

Jaibriol, listen! Kelric had no more time and so much more to say. He accelerated his thoughts. **That dice game Quis is more than you know. On the world where I learned it, everyone plays it all their lives. They tell stories, mold lives, change their culture. The best players rule the planet. It's more than a predictive device, more than a means to protect your mind. It may be the most powerful social means of change ever invented.**

Kelric, no, Dehya said. *Stop.*

We have to give it to him, Kelric thought.

For what? she asked. *The downfall of humanity under Aristo dominance?*

No. The peace we all seek. The end of Aristo inhumanity.

Every Aristo will learn the game, Dehya said. *Scholars, advisors, commanders, everyone. They will see its potential.*

And we will outplay them, Kelric answered.

Tell me, Jaibriol thought. **We have only an instant left.**

Everyone seemed to move in slow motion. As Kelric's finger descended to reactivate his gauntlet, he thought, **We must teach Quis to everyone. Let it spread**

across Skolia, Eube, the Allied Worlds. We will put our dream of peace into the dice on an interstellar scale. Use it, Jaibriol! Use it wisely and we can change empires.

I will try, Jaibriol said. **If you make me a promise.**

Kelric's finger hovered over his comm. **What do you ask?**

The empress carries my son. The Highton Heir. If ever in his life he needs sanctuary, swear that you will take him in, as I have given you the girl, Aliana.

We swear, Dehya said.

And if ever it is of use, there is this, Jaibriol said. **The Razer you recognize—he is from the same clone group as Hidaka, my bodyguard whose loyalty went beyond all conditioning.** With difficulty, he added, **Hidaka died for that loyalty.**

I remember. Kelric also understood; Hidaka had known the emperor was a member of the Ruby Dynasty and yet remained loyal.

This version of Hidaka is also my bodyguard, Jaibriol said. **But he did not pattern on me. He is in love with Aliana. It is for her that he would give that boundless, unlimited loyalty.** Without pause, he thought. **I must go now.** More softly, he added, **Thank you. For one moment, I have known family.**

The link dissolved.

So it was that the first summit of the new Skolian Triad—perhaps the only one that would ever occur—was completed.

XXX
Kinship

Chaos and people crowded the hotel suite. Aliana held onto Red's hand as if he were a lifeline in the confusion. The Skolians strode through the rooms while people talked, doctors hovered, Jagernauts guarded, and aides aided, so many people jabbing consoles, gauntlets, and other devices. She couldn't understand a word anyone was saying. She stayed close to Kelric, her only anchor here, mainly because he reminded her of Tide. She didn't know what had just happened with the emperor and the pharaoh; even though they had only stood there, speaking like robots, something else had gone on, something big, something beyond her hearing or sight.

The gold woman came with them. She was so beautiful, even covered in dust, with her hair and clothes disarrayed, that it hurt to look at her. Had she been a provider, to have the gold skin? But then why was she with the royal party of the pharaoh?

She look like you, Red thought.

She can't. Aliana felt as if she were going to burst. ***I don't have a family.***

Skolian family, maybe.

It can't be! Too much was happening, too fast, too many people, too much tumult.

Too much death.

The explosion had killed people. The cyberlock field had killed people. She had witnessed ESComm's commander give his life to save his emperor. She had *felt* them die, their minds going from life to blackness in one crushing instant.

Kelric put his large hand against her back, his touch like a calming balm as he guided her through an archway. A doctor went with them, but they were shedding the other people. Aliana's thoughts began to slow down. She took a deep breath, then let it out again.

Zina, Red thought.

Yes?

You crush my fingers.

Oh! Embarrassed, she released his hand. ***I'm sorry.***

A sense of amusement came from him as he gently took her hand again. *Is all right.*

They entered a quiet room. A Jagernaut closed the door, a wooden portal that swung shut under his push. The doctor, a small woman with yellow hair, was passing a gadget back and forth over Kelric's body. She said something to him and he growled his response. The doctor waved her small hand, dismissing whatever protest he had given. Aliana would have thought Kelric would intimidate her, but it seemed the opposite.

With no warning, the doctor turned to Aliana and said something indecipherable.

Aliana squinted at her. "What was that?"

Kelric spoke to her in Highton. "She asked for your name."

"Oh." She spoke awkwardly in Eubic. "I'm Aliana Miller Azina."

The woman answered in heavily accented Highton. "My greetings, Aliana. I am Doctor Sashia, Imperator Skolia's physician. Do you mind if I take a look at you?"

"Imperator Skolia?" Aliana's pulse leapt as she looked around. She saw no one who resembled an Imperator, but then, she had no idea what one looked like. "Where?"

"Here." Kelric's voice rumbled.

She turned back to him. "Are you his bodyguard, too?"

Sashia's mouth opened. Aliana flushed, wondering what she had said wrong.

"I'm not a bodyguard," Kelric said.

"Oh, I'm sorry." Aliana's face heated more. "I thought you were a Jagernaut."

"I am, actually," he said. "Or I was when I was on active duty. Now I command ISC."

"But I thought the Imperator did that," Aliana said.

"That's right," he answered, his voice gentle.

Aliana couldn't absorb his meaning. Her mind was too saturated with shocks. But it gradually soaked in. Gods, she had followed him, hung on him. Miserable at her foolish behavior, she dropped to one knee, aware of Red doing it as well.

"Aliana, Red, no," the golden woman said, her voice warm like a sun. "You never need to kneel again."

Aliana stood, her gaze downcast. She wasn't sure why she would never have to kneel again, unless they planned to put her some place with no one to kneel to. That did make sense, but the idea disappointed her more than it should have. She had no right to expect more.

A different woman spoke, a soft voice she recognized. "Aliana," the Ruby Pharaoh said. "Look at me."

Aliana raised her gaze. The pharaoh was standing in front of her, next to Kelric and the golden woman. The pharaoh took her hands. *Can you hear me, child?*

Yes. I can, Aliana thought. ***I'm sorry if I've caused offense.***

Never. Her smile softened her face. *Do you recognize any of us?*

Aliana glanced at the golden woman. ***You look like me, only pretty instead of ugly. I mean, you look the way I do when my hair and skin and eyes are normal.***

Normal how? the golden woman asked.

Aliana hesitated, afraid they would assume she was a provider. ***Gold. Like metal.***

Yes, she does look like you, the pharaoh said. *And you are beautiful.*

Aliana felt the betraying moisture gathering in her eyes. All her life, she had been alone and unwanted. She had never expected any different. ***Am I . . . is she part of my family?***

Yes. That came from Kelric. He was holding a smart-cloth someone had given him during their harried, hurried journey to this room. As he wiped his face and hair, the cloth cleaned him up, whisking away the dust and grime. Gradually his skin and hair became clear.

Gold skin. Gold hair. Gold eyes.

With a kindness as great in his mind as his physical presence, Kelric thought, **You are my brother's daughter, Aliana. Your father was a prince of the Ruby Dynasty.**

The golden woman thought. ***My name is Roca Skolia. You are my granddaughter.***

And I am your aunt, the Ruby Pharaoh thought.

It was too much. Aliana couldn't take any more. She looked around, shutting out everyone until she could see only what she needed, a chair against the wall, three steps away, an endless distance. Somehow she walked over and sat down. She felt as if she were going to break into a million pieces.

Someone sat next to her and pulled her into his arms. *Don't cry, Zina.*

Ai, Red, I've gone insane. She laid her head against his, and the forbidden tears poured down her face. All her life she had never acknowledged they were inside of her, but now she couldn't stop them. Red held her, rocking her, murmuring nonsense words while she wept.

No one disturbed them. People moved around the room and spoke to one another, but she retreated from it all. They left her with Red and he held her. For so long, she had been his protector, but here in this strange place, he was protecting her heart.

Gradually Aliana became aware of the room again. Kelric, the pharaoh, and the woman named Roca were a few paces away, talking to a man with grey-streaked hair. Although they weren't overtly watching her or otherwise intruding, she felt their awareness of her in their minds.

Aliana spoke up in a ragged voice. "If you're my family, why did you leave me in that *scum hole* with no one but a half-Aristo bastard to take care of me?"

They turned to her then, the pharaoh, imperator, and golden queen. Aliana felt as if she would burn up with the fierce anger that swept across her. "You aren't my family." She got up and went over to them, these great people of Skolia. "My family would never have left me stranded in that garbage heap. My family would never have let my stepfather beat the crap out of me every time he felt like it. My family would never have let my mother take her own life because it had become such *hell.*"

"Aliana—" Roca's voice caught. "I'm sorry."

Aliana dropped out of Highton into the dialect of Eubic that she knew best. "Yeah, cry. Weep for your misfortune, that you're stuck with me."

Kelric answered her—in Eubic. It wasn't the dialect she spoke, but it was close enough that she understood. "We didn't know about you. ESComm broke your father's cover. He had to leave before they captured him. If he had gone back for your mother, they would have captured her, too."

"You're lying." Aliana felt how much Red wanted her to stop. But she couldn't. The words poured out. "You say my father was a *prince?* That's so full of—of—of drilling *dross.*" Her voice broke as she backed away from them. "So, what are you going to do? Make me a princess? Even if I wanted—even if I—if I could—I *can't*—you would never acknowledge dreck like me."

She felt how the words shot into them like barbed weapons. Part of her wanted to take them back, but another part knew she spoke the truth.

"What dreck mean?" Red asked.

She swung around to him, incredulous, and he blinked at her, looking innocent, which he wasn't, because he knew perfectly well what it meant. And then she couldn't help but laugh, shaky and uneven, because it was such an absurd question. Her voice caught with tears.

Kelric spoke. "I'm more sorry than I can ever say for what you've been through. I'm sorry we weren't there when you needed us."

She wiped the tears off her cheeks with the heel of her hand. "It's not—I didn't mean..."

"Give us time." Roca's voice filled with warmth. "Give yourself time."

"Time to do what?" Aliana meant to sound strong, but her voice trembled.

"Time to know us," the pharaoh said.

"Why would you want to know me?"

Red made an exasperated noise. "Zina, do you need someone to hit you on the head to put some sense in there?"

She glared at him. "Stop interfering with my emotional moment here."

"The only emotion is you growling at everyone," he told her.

She wanted to growl at *him,* but her anger was trickling away. He stood there, so handsome and appealing, with those arms that held her so close, saying such random things, that she couldn't stay upset. It ran out of her like sand between her fingers.

She glanced back at Kelric. "I just—I don't know how to act."

"It's all right," he said. "Half the time I don't know how to act around them, either. But they put up with me anyway."

Now he was doing it as well, being absurd. Her smile curved.

"It will get better," Roca said in a voice that reminded Aliana of her mother. "You can live with one of our families while you adjust. Go to school. Figure out what you would like to do with your life."

"Can Red come, too?" Aliana asked.

"Yes, of course," Roca said. To Red, she added, "We can help you . . . heal."

"I'm not provider anymore," he said.

Aliana wondered if any of them realized how huge that was, what he had just said. *I'm not a provider anymore.* With that one sentence, he defied a lifetime of conditioning.

"Neither of you are slaves," the pharaoh said. "Never again."

Aliana didn't know where to put that knowledge. Their lives made so little sense to her. She couldn't imagine these people as her family. They were too removed from any reality she understood.

But maybe, just maybe, she and Red could find a life here better than what they left behind.

When Kelric walked into the Observation Bay on the *Pharaoh's Shield,* he found his mother standing at the view-wall gazing at Delos, which hung in space before them, swirled with clouds, a world of beauty and pain and hope.

He joined her at the curving window. "Soz met him there. On Delos."

"It so hard to believe." She turned ot him. ***How long have you known about Jaibriol?***

For certain? Since he and I met on Earth and signed the treaty.

That was why you met with him. Why you risked being convicted of treason.

Kelric nodded, the memories still painfully fresh

less than a year later. **He wouldn't mindspeak with me then. He couldn't. He had protected himself for so long, he couldn't stop.**

Roca shuddered. ***His life must be misery.***

He has Tarquine. And Corbal. They don't transcend.

And Tarquine Iquar will be the mother of my great-grandson.

There was that. They had found a way, with Jaibriol's help, to free Aliana, but the Highton Heir would always be bound by his legacy. **You can never reveal what you know,** Kelric thought. **Never. Protect him.**

I will, always. Her thought caught with a sense of tears. ***Jaibriol is a miracle.***

And he has no idea. Kelric gazed out at Delos. "We have to make this summit work."

Roca turned around, leaning with her back against the rail. "It won't be easy, not after this. Everyone insists we leave Delos."

"You, Dehya, Tikal, me, yes, we'll have to leave." Kelric regarded her steadily. "But the delegates can stay and continue their work. We'll meet with the emperor's party in virtual simulations, the way we had originally planned."

"Yes." She lifted her chin. "We won't let those who would destroy the treaty succeed."

"That includes our own people." When she gave him a questioning look, he said, "Those commandos who attacked the Eubian merchants weren't Traders. They were Skolian." Kelric hadn't expected what the ISC investigation found, that a Skolian vigilante group had carried out the attack. In the past, the group had retaliated against the Traders for kidnapping Skolian citizens, but they had escalated to first strike attacks this time.

"Have you any leads on finding them?" Roca asked.

"Not yet," Kelric said. "But we will." When he did, their sentence would be stiff. Executing them would be political suicide; he had given that vow to convince ESComm that ISC hadn't authorized the attack. Now, Jaibriol had given him an out: Eube didn't expect an execution. That had been an unexpected and inspired move from the emperor. Jaibriol had given away nothing, yet he made an offer that Kelric valued because it protected the Imperator politically. Clever.

"Is it true," Roca asked, "that two of the agents we turned over to the Eubians were actually Allied citizens who agreed to work with ESComm because they opposed the treaty?"

Kelric grimaced. "Unfortunately, yes."

She shook her head. "What a species we humans are. I wonder how we survive at all."

He rested his hands on the rail and looked out at the nebulae glittering beyond Delos. "Yet somehow we do. We renew ourselves."

"As with Aliana."

Kelric glanced at her. "Yes, I suppose in a way, she is our renewal."

Roca smiled. "She reminds me of you. Except she has Soz's sass."

"What," he laughed, "I have no sass?"

"You're much too stoic to be sassy." Her face gentled. "Her mind is like a sun. Like you."

Untrained, though, Kelric thought. **She didn't catch what went on between Jaibriol and the three of us.**

Someday, Roca thought, ***we must find a way to bring Jaibriol home to us.***

"Aye," he murmured. "Someday." He doubted it would ever happen, but it was a hope they could hold on to, like a treasure locked within a puzzle box that perhaps someday they could learn to open.

Kelric met Del at the docking bay.

"You're sure?" Kelric asked. They were standing next to the military transport that would soon take Del back to Earth. "You could stay for a while and visit."

"I need to get back to Ricki," Del said. "She's worried crazy." He spoke awkwardly. "My life is on Earth now."

"I understand." Kelric hesitated. "It's just that we've hardly had any time together."

Del gave him a wry smile. "Well, you know, it's not like we ever hung out."

Kelric wasn't exactly sure what Del had just said, but he got the idea. "We can change that."

Del looked startled, then pleased. "I'd like to."

"I also." Kelric had never really thought Del *wanted* to spend any time with his militaristic brother. "And, Del."

His brother cocked his head. "Yes?"

"What you did, in the Kyle." He searched for the right words. "I am in your debt. All of us are. If not for you, Security might not have found those leaks, certainly not as fast, maybe not until it was too late. If you hadn't figured out what was going on with Aliana, she would have died. You saved her life." He nodded to his brother. "You did well."

"Hey." Del reddened. "Thanks."

"You're welcome."

Del suddenly grinned. "Look at us! We've talked for five minutes, we've stayed civil, and you told me I did well, on a *military* operation, no less. Peace summits should be easy after this."

Kelric laughed. "I guess so." He pulled off the pouch he had tied to his belt earlier. "I have something for you." He offered Del the bag, which was stuffed full and bulky.

"Hey, ultra." Del took the pouch curiously. "What is it?"

"They're dice," Kelric said.

Del unfastened the bag and rolled out several lustrous pieces, a blue heptahedron, a crystal orb, and a red triangle. "Pretty." He looked up at Kelric. "What do you do with them?"

"Play Quis. It's a strategy game." Kelric hoped Del liked it; he was never sure with his brother, but it seemed the sort of thing that might amuse him. "Or you can gamble with it. At the highest levels, you can use it to make predictions." He indicated the bag. "I put a chip in there with the rules and scoring explanations."

"Cool." Del tucked the dice back into the bag and fastened its string, then tossed it into the air and caught it. He smiled at Kelric, that disarming look that had always come so easily to him. "Thanks. I appreciate it."

"Teach it to Ricki." He thought of Del's blond bombshell of a wife. "She'd be a killer at it."

Del gave him a dry look. "Ricki is a killer at everything. She's terrifying." He looked more satisfied than terrified, though.

After an awkward pause, Kelric said, "It was good to see you."

"Yeah. It really was." Del gave him a mock salute. "I'd better get going before this détente is over and we start arguing again."

Laughing, Kelric said, "Take care of yourself."

"You, too." Del swung up into the open hatchway and waved, then disappeared inside.

Within moments, his brother was on his way to Earth with a military escort. Kelric stood in the docking bay, watching the ships on a view screen as they dwindled in size, until they were gone.

City was like a cloud come to the ground. Aliana couldn't believe people actually lived here. The buildings were luminous in pale colors: blue, white, lavender, and silver-grey. She didn't understand why Kelric said they were inside a space station. It was a world. A strange one, though, where the land curved up like a bowl on all sides until it met the distant sky, which formed a huge blue dome with a sun in the middle. City's ethereal towers rose in the center of rolling parklands with cloud grasses rippling in a breeze.

Aliana wasn't sure if the sunlight was real or not, but it felt wonderful. It shone on Kelric's golden skin, so like hers now that they had undone her disguise.

"Do you live here?" she asked as they followed a path tiled in blue stones. "It's pretty."

"Not in the city." Kelric motioned toward the mountains. "My home is in a valley up there. A big stone house."

Ahead of them, Red was kneeling on the ledge that circled a fountain sculpted like a graceful woman holding an orb. He glanced back at them, his handsome face suffused with happiness. Then he went back to exploring, wandering through the city. Watching him, Aliana felt good. Until they had come here, she had rarely seen Red smile. She hadn't realized he could do it so easily. The traumatized, desperate boy she had met on Muze's Helios was changing, becoming a man.

"Will Red and I live here?" she asked.

Kelric cleared his throat. "About that."

She slanted him a wary look. "What?"

"If you mean, 'live together here,'" he said. "Then no."

"Why?" She instinctively tensed to fight. "Are you taking him away?"

"Aliana, no, we won't split the two of you up." His expression became stern. "But you can't live together. Legally, you're children. And children don't act like they're married."

"Oh." *Married?* She couldn't imagine such a thing. "Red can't marry. He's a provider." Except they weren't Eubian anymore. "Are you saying neither of us can marry here?"

"No, not at all." He motioned to a bench under the overhang of trees with white trunks and translucent green leaves. As they sat together, Kelric said, "You're both free citizens. You can be whatever you each want." He smiled, his strong features relaxing. "As long as you don't break laws."

This was confusing. "I don't know the laws."

"Don't worry. You'll learn them in school. And you'll have guardians to take care of you."

She scowled at him. "I don't want to go to 'school.' It sounds horrible."

"It's not so bad. You might like some of the subjects."

She wanted to glare and stalk away, but that never got her anywhere with Kelric, especially if she forgot herself and cursed, too. So instead she said, "Oh, all right. I'll try."

Her uncle laughed softly. "I seem to recall saying that a few times when I was young."

"It's hard to imagine you ever being young."

"It's been a while."

"Did you grow up here?"

"Not here. On a planet called Lyshriol. It's much more rural." He looked around the city. "I've always liked it here. It's so peaceful. So unlike what I deal with every day."

She couldn't begin to picture his life. "It must be hard being an Imperator."

"I suppose. But I trained for it since childhood." He had a distant look, as if he were seeing memories. "If I'd had a choice, I would have liked to be a mathematician. But this will do."

This will do. What a thing to say about his title. "Do you have any kids?"

He nodded, his smile fading. "Two. But I hardly know them."

"Why not?" A terrible thought came to her, what she had seen on Muze's Helios when an Aristo wanted part of a family, but not all of them. "Did someone take them away?" But no, that wasn't right. He was the one who would do the taking, and he wasn't like that.

And yet, incredibly, he said, "Yes, they did." He spoke slowly, as if the words were hard. "I was a prisoner for nearly twenty years on a planet called Coba. I wasn't allowed to see my children."

She stared at him, dismayed. "I'm sorry."

"Ai," he murmured. "So was I."

"But you could see them now."

"Yes, I can." His expression warmed. "And I have. They came here."

A strange emotion hit her, the painful tug of envy. "Do they live with you?"

"By the time I was free and established as Imperator, they had their own lives. They visited. But then they went home." With difficulty, he said, "For them, this will never be home."

"Oh." Personally Aliana thought they were crazy, to leave a place like this.

They sat for a while, watching Red appear and disappear among statues while he explored. Beyond him, a pale walkway arched between two towers. It detached from one and floated to the ground, carrying several people. After they stepped off its end, the walkway rose like a cloud back to its original position.

"I like this place." Aliana tried to find the courage to ask what was inside her, but the words wouldn't come.

"Are you hungry?" Kelric stretched his arms. "We can collect Red and go to one of the cafés." With an apologetic look, he added, "Then I have to go back to work. But Doctor Sashia is putting together a team of people to help settle you here. I'll leave you and Red with her."

"That sounds good." Ask, she told herself, but the words stayed hidden in her mind.

"Aliana?" Kelric asked. "What's wrong?"

"I want to ask you something. But I'm afraid."

"Don't be afraid."

She wondered how a man who terrified so many

people, who looked so imposing, could have such kind expressions. It was time to ask. If she didn't do it now, later would be too late. Maybe he would say no. Probably he would. But if she never asked, it was a definite no. At least this way, she would find out for certain.

"Would you be my guardian?" she asked.

Kelric blinked, and confusion came from his mind. "You want me to take care of you?"

"I mean, I know you're busy, ruling the universe and all. But, I—I—" She stuttered to a stop, at a loss for where to go from there.

"No one has ever asked me such a thing before."

Her face heated. "I'm sorry. That was silly of me. Never mind."

He spoke softly. "I would be honored to be your guardian."

"Really?" She gaped at him. "*Really?*"

"Yes." He smiled. "Really."

A realization hit her then. *He* was lonely. He had everything any human being could have, but he was lonely. He wanted a family, too.

Red was coming back to them, ambling along, more relaxed than she had ever seen him, dressed in neither the rags they had worn in the slums nor in the lushly expensive clothes of a provider, just simple blue trousers and white shirt. He seemed taller, though she wasn't sure if he had really grown or just stood straighter.

As she and Kelric rose to their feet, Aliana thought that maybe Skolians were all right.

She felt safe.

And happy.

✧ ✧ ✧

Jaibriol stood on a balcony above the Amphitheatre of Providence. The hall was empty tonight except for a few robots cleaning the tiers. Those, and the mech-techs examining the largest robot arm, the giant hand. Unlike the arm on Delos, this one had never malfunctioned. But they were checking it anyway, verifying that whatever had happened on Delos wasn't inherent to the device.

Steps sounded behind him, not his guards, but a smoother tread. He turned as Tarquine joined him at the railing. She watched the techs working on the robot hand. "It looks so innocuous when it's docked."

"I suppose." He knew they would find nothing wrong. "Your nephew died with honor."

She didn't look at him. "So he did."

Jaibriol knew the truth now; Tarquine had never betrayed him. Whatever had motivated Barthol to treason, it didn't manifest in the empress. God only knew, Barthol had been a fool to think he could betray her.

"I would not see my Line dishonored." She seemed subdued. "Neither for my kin nor my heirs."

"There is Barthol's son." If the general had lived a long, full life, some hope might have existed that his son Hazar would someday pull out of his debauched hedonism and be ready to take the helm of the Iquar dynasty. Instead, the title had come to him decades too early.

"Hazar and I have enjoyed a little chat," Tarquine said.

Jaibriol spoke dryly. "My sympathies to Hazar."

"It seems that he has grave doubts about assuming the Iquar title." She regarded him with her calm red gaze. "He has asked that I assume the Iquar

Title once more. To ease his mind, I found it within myself to agree."

"Ah." Jaibriol could just imagine Hazar "agreeing." By the time Tarquine finished with him, he probably hadn't known up from down.

So they had come full circle. Tarquine again ruled her House. Jaibriol knew he would never fathom her mind, how she decided on right and wrong. She lived by a fierce and uncompromising code that benefited even as it chilled him. He didn't know if he would ever reconcile the love he felt for her with his dismay at her actions, but he could no longer imagine his life without her.

She gazed at the techs working on the bronzed hand. "Barthol was my nephew. For all his crimes, his treachery, his cruelty, despite all that, he was my kin."

"I know," he said softly.

They stood for a time, watching the amphitheatre. It would see no assembly of Aristos for some time. Most of Jaibriol's top people were still on Delos, putting the summit back together. He and Tarquine, as well as Corbal and Admiral Erix Muze, would participate from here, on Glory, via virtual reality simulations of the conferences with the Skolians.

He had brought Tide back with him, to remain on his personal guard. So much of what he had valued in Hidaka he had also found in Tide, the intelligence, loyalty, sense of honor. He couldn't give Tide what the Razer most wanted, to marry Aliana, but he would do everything within his power to provide Tide with the best possible life. The Razer had protected Aliana, making it possible for Jaibriol to free his young cousin, and for that Tide would always have his gratitude.

Eventually Tarquine said, "Was it worth it, Jai? So many plans and intrigues, so much grief, so much anguish, all so we and the Skolians could meet in the same place. To what purpose? We are back where we started."

Jaibriol doubted he could ever tell her what it had meant to him. The scene burned into the collective consciousness of humanity was that instant when his party and the Skolians had stood together on the dais: he and the Ruby Pharaoh, Kelric and Barthol, Tikal and Tarquine, Roca Skolia and Corbal Xir. The historians were already writing about that meeting, the chaos that followed it, and the determination of both sides to continue with the peace summit despite everything. They were calling it the moment that changed the history of the human race. But for Jaibriol the greatest moment had been far different, that achingly brief time when he had stood in the shattered amphitheatre having what looked to the rest of humanity like a stilted exchange with the Ruby Pharaoh. Did Tarquine know what else had happened? Did Corbal suspect? If they did, they would never know the full truth. It was locked within Jaibriol, a gift beyond any he had expected.

His kin had begun to heal him. The mental scar tissue that ravaged his mind had melted under the Ruby touch of his family. He had always known a longing, but until they had flooded him with their warmth, he had never understood what he needed. Those moments couldn't fully heal him; that would take years with them that he could never have. He might never see them in person again. But those moments had begun the process, and he would keep the result with him forever. Even if that had been all that he took from his meeting with the Ruby Dynasty, it would have been enough.

But in those few seconds, Kelric had given him something far greater.

Jaibriol had never truly understood Quis. Kelric had shown him Coba, the world where Quis originated, an entire civilization playing Quis, one huge, never-ending game played by tens of thousands of people, so much a part of their culture that they did it from the day they were old enough to pick up the dice until they were too old to hold the pieces in their hands. Those who dominated the Quis shaped their world. It was subtle, gradual, and pervasive, a social phenomenon that stopped at no walls, that could be played at any level, from simple gambling games to a predictive process so complex it verged on precognition.

Jaibriol would give Quis to Eube, to the taskmakers, over two trillion of them. Kelric would give it to Skolia. As it spread, encompassing their peoples, so would the subliminal messages its adepts wove into their game. More than the memes that spread throughout a culture, more than the trends that saturated the multitude of human lifestyles, more even than a song like "Carnelians Finale," the game would spread. Who would care? It wasn't inflammatory, political, or subversive. It was simply a game. And if Jaibriol poured his hopes and dreams of peace into the dice, who would know? If he used Quis to tell the story of a universe without slavery—a place where all humans had the rights of their humanity—the identity of whoever seeded the dice with those ideas would be lost in the ever-evolving process as all humanity played the game.

Eventually, in the decades to come, scholars would analyze Quis. Some people would play it terribly, others with inspiration; some would never play at all, others would become adepts. Societies would become dedicated to developing Quis. Competitors would learn its intricacies. And the Aristos would play. They would realize its power, learn to use it for themselves, and probably believe that in their exalted state of being, they had created that advanced aspect of Quis.

By then, it would be too late.

Several thousand Aristos couldn't stand against trillions of taskmakers if their subjects refused to remain slaves. With the Quis, Jaibriol might achieve what he could never do overtly. He would free his people by changing their culture at its very roots, until they were spinning stories of freedom without realizing it. It was an audacious plan, maybe an impossible one. Whether he and Kelric could actually succeed, he had no idea.

But they would give it one hell of a try.

"Yes," Jaibriol said. "It was worth it."

Epilogue

It was one of the most effective weapons known.

It didn't explode. It shot no projectiles. It didn't spread chemical, biological, or physical poison. It created no flames or shrapnel.

It knew no boundaries.

It was no more than a game.

It could bring down empires.

It was Quis.

Characters & Family History

Boldface names refer to Ruby psions, also known as the "Rhon." All Rhon psions who are also members of the Ruby Dynasty use **Skolia** as their last name (the Skolian Imperialate was named after their family). The **Selei** name indicates the direct line of the Ruby Pharaoh. Children of **Roca** and **Eldrinson** take Valdoria as a surname. The del prefix means "in honor of," and is capitalized if the person honored was a Triad member. Most names are based on world-building systems drawn from Mayan, North African, and Indian cultures.

= marriage

~

Lahaylia Selei	=	**Jarac**
(Ruby Pharaoh: deceased)		(Imperator: deceased)

Lahaylia and **Jarac** founded the modern-day Ruby Dynasty. **Lahaylia** was created in an Aristo offshoot of the Rhon genetic project. Her lineage traced back to the ancient Ruby Dynasty that founded the Ruby Empire. **Lahaylia** and **Jarac** had two daughters, **Dyhianna Selei** and **Roca.**

~

Dyhianna (Dehya) Selei	=	(1) William Seth Rockworth III (separated)
	=	(2) **Eldrin Jarac Valdoria**

Dehya is the Ruby Pharaoh. She married William Seth Rockworth III as part of the Iceland Treaty between the Skolian Imperialate and Allied Worlds of Earth. They had no children and later divorced. The dissolution of their marriage would have negated the treaty, so neither the Allieds nor Imperialate recognize the divorce. *Spherical Harmonic* tells the story of what happened to **Dehya** after the Radiance War. She also appears in almost all of the Ruby Dynasty novels.

Dehya and **Eldrin** have two children, **Taquinil Selei** and **Althor Vyan Selei. Taquinil** is an extraordinary genius and untenably sensitive empath. He appears in *The Radiant Seas, Spherical Harmonic,* and *Carnelians.*

~

Althor Vyan Selei	=	**Akushtina (Tina) Santis Pulivok**

The story of **Althor** and **Tina** appears in *Catch the Lightning.* **Althor Vyan Selei** was named after his uncle, **Althor Izam-Na Valdoria.** The short story "Avo de Paso" in the anthologies *Redshift,* edited by Al Sarrantino, and *Fantasy: The Year's Best, 2001,* edited by Robert Silverberg and

Karen Haber, tells the story of how **Tina** and her cousin Manuel deal with Mayan spirits in the New Mexico desert.

~

Roca = (1) Tokaba Ryestar (deceased)
= (2) Darr Hammerjackson (divorced)
= (3) **Eldrinson Althor Valdoria**

Roca is the sister of the Ruby Pharoah and in the direct line of succession to the Ruby Throne and all three titles of the Triad. She is also the Foreign Affairs Councilor of the Assembly, a seat she won through election rather than as an inherited title. A ballet dancer turned diplomat, she is considered one of the most beautiful women alive. She appears in almost all of the Ruby Dynasty novels.

Roca and Tokaba Ryestar had one child, **Kurj** (Imperator and Jagernaut). Genetically, **Kurj** is the son of his grandfather. **Kurj** married Ami when he was a century old, and they had one son named Kurjson. **Kurj** apears in *Skyfall, Primary Inversion,* and *The Radiant Seas.*

Although no records exist of **Eldrinson's** lineage, it is believed he descends from the ancient Ruby Dynasty. He is a bard, farmer, and judge on the planet Lyshriol (also known as Skyfall). His spectacular voice is legendary among his people, a gift he bequeathed to his sons Eldrin and Del-Kurj. The novel *Skyfall* tells the story of how **Eldrinson** and **Roca** meet. They have ten children:

Eldrin (Dryni) Jarac (bard, consort to Ruby Pharaoh, warrior)

Althor Izam-Na (engineer, Jagernaut, Imperial Heir)

Del-Kurj (Del) (singer, warrior, twin to **Chaniece**)
Chaniece Roca (runs Valdoria family household, twin to **Del-Kurj**)
Havyrl (Vyrl) Torcellei (farmer, doctorate in agriculture)
Sauscony (Soz) Lahaylia (military scientist, Jagernaut, Imperator)
Denric Windward (teacher, doctorate in literature)
Shannon Eirlei (Blue Dale archer)
Aniece Dyhianna (accountant, Rillian queen)
Kelricson (Kelric) Garlin (mathematician, Jagernaut, Imperator)

All ten offspring briefly appear as teens or younger children in the novella, "Stained Glass Heart" (*Irresistible Forces,* ed. Catherine Asaro).

~

Eldrin appears in *The Final Key, Triad, Spherical Harmonic, The Radiant Seas, The Ruby Dice, Diamond Star, Carnelians,* and *Catch the Lightning.*. See also **Dehya**.

~

Althor Izam-Na = (1) Coop and Vaz
= (2) Cirrus (former provider to Ur Qox)

Althor has a daughter, Eristia Leirol Valdoria, with Syreen Leirol, an actress turned linguist. Coop and Vaz have a son, Ryder Jalam Majda Valdoria, with **Althor** as cofather. **Althor** appears in his youth as a fighter pilot in *Schism* and *The Final Key.* **Althor** and Coop appear in *The Radiant Seas.* Vaz and Coop appear in *Spherical Harmonic.* **Althor** and Cirrus also have a son.

~

Del-Kurj, often considered the renegade of the Ruby Dynasty, is a rock singer who made his fame on Earth. His twin sister is **Chaniece**. His story is told in *Diamond Star,* which is accompanied by a soundtrack of the same name cut by the rock band Point Valid with Catherine Asaro. The songs on the CD all appear in the book. Ther are available at www.cdbaby.com/cd/pointvalidca, on iTunes and other online vendors, and from Starflight Music at PO Box 4, Simpsonville, MD 21150. **Del** also appears in *The Quantum Rose, Schism,* and the novella "Stained Glass Heart."

~

Havyrl (Vyrl) Torcellei = (1) Liliara (Lily) (deceased)
= (2) Kamoj Quanta Argali

The story of **Havyrl** and Lily appears in "Stained Glass Heart," in the anthology *Irresistible Forces,* edited by Catherine Asaro. The story of **Havyrl** and Kamoj appears in *The Quantum Rose,* which won the 2001 Nebula Award. An early version of the first half was serialized in *Analog,* May 1999–July/August 1999.

~

Sauscony (Soz) Lahaylia = (1) Jato Stormson (divorced)
= (2) Hypron Luminar (deceased)
= (3) **Jaibriol Qox** (aka **Jaibriol II**)

Schism tells the story of **Soz** at seventeen, when she enters the Dieshan Military Academy. *The Final Key,* which is the sequel to *Schism,* tells of the first war between the Skolians and the Traders. **Soz**'s rescue efforts on the world New Day appear in the novelette "The Lost Dawn" (*The Mammoth Book of SF Wars*, ed. Ian Whates and Ian Watson), which includes the story of how she met Hypron. The story of **Soz** and Jato appears in the novella, "Aurora in Four Voices" (*Analog*, December 1998). **Soz** and **Jaibriol**'s stories appear in *Primary Inversion* and *The Radiant Seas.* They have four children: **Jaibriol III, Rocalisa, Vitar,** and **del-Kelric.**

Jaibriol Qox Skolia (aka **Jaibriol III**)	=	Tarquine Iquar (Finance Minister and Iquar queen)

The story of how **Jaibriol III** became the Emperor of Eube at seventeen appears in *The Moon's Shadow.* The story of how Jaibriol and Kelric deal with each other appears in *The Ruby Dice* and *Carnelians.* **Jaibriol** also appears in *The Radiant Seas* as a teenager.

~

Denric takes a position as a teacher on the world Sandstorm. His harrowing introduction to his new home appears in the short story, "The Edges of Never-Haven" (*Flights of Fantasy,* ed. Al Sarrantino). He also appears in *The Quantum Rose.*

~

Shannon is the most otherworldly of the Ruby Dynasty. He inherited the rare genetics of a Blue Dale Archer from his father. He leaves home at sixteen and seeks out the legendary Archers so he can live with them. He appears in *Schism, The Final Key,* and *The Quantum Rose.*

~

Aniece = Lord Rillia

Aniece is the most business-minded of the Valdoria children. Although she never left Lyshriol, she earned an MBA and became an accountant. Lord Rillia rules a province on the world Lyshriol, which includes the Rillian Vales, Dalvador Plains, Backbone Mountains, and Stained Glass Forest. **Aniece** decided at age twelve she would marry him, though he was much older and already a king, and she kept at her plan until eventually she achieved her purpose. **Aniece** and Rillia appear in *The Quantum Rose.*

~

Kelricson (Kelric) Garlin	=	(1) Corey Majda (deceased)
	=	(2) Deha Dahl (deceased)
	=	(3) Rashiva Haka (Calani trade)
	=	(4) Savina Miesa (deceased)
	=	(5) Avtac Varz (Calani trade)
	=	(6) Ixpar Karn (closure)
	=	(7) Jeejon

Kelric appears in *Carnelians, Diamond Star, The Ruby Dice* (novel, 2007), "The Ruby Dice" (novella, *Baen's Universe 2006*), *The Last Hawk, Ascendant Sun, The Moon's Shadow,* the novella "A Roll of the Dice" (*Analog,* July/August 2000), and the novelette "Light and Shadow" (*Analog,* April 1994). **Kelric** and Rashiva have one son, Jimorla Haka, who becomes a renowned Calani. **Kelric** and Savina have one daughter, **Rohka Miesa Varz,** who becomes the Ministry Successor in line to rule the Estates of Coba.

~

The novella "Walk in Silence" (*Analog*, April 2003) tells the story of Jess Fernandez, an Allied Starship Captain from Earth, who deals with the genetically engineered humans on the Skolian colony of Icelos.

The novella "The City of Cries" (*Down These Dark Spaceways,* ed. Mike Resnick) tells the story of Major Bhaaj, a private investigator hired by the House of Majda to find Prince Dayj Majda after he disappears.

The novella "The Shadowed Heart" (*Year's Best Paranormal,* ed. Paula Guran, and *The Journey Home,* ed. Mary Kirk) is the story of Jason Harrick, a Jagernaut who just barely survives the Radiance War.

Time Line

Circa 4000 BC	Group of humans moved from Earth to Raylicon
Circa 3600 BC	Ruby Dynasty begins
Circa 3100 BC	Raylicans launch first interstellar flights; rise of Ruby Empire
Circa 2900 BC	Ruby Empire begins decline
Circa 2800 BC	Last interstellar flights; Ruby Empire collapses
Circa AD 1300	Raylicans begin to regain lost knowledge
1843	Raylicans regain interstellar flight
1866	Rhon genetic project begins
1871	Aristos found Eubian Concord (aka Trader Empire)
1881	Lahaylia Selei born
1904	Lahaylia Selei founds Skolian Imperialate

2005	Jarac born
2111	Lahaylia Selei marries Jarac
2119	Dyhianna Selei born
2122	Earth achieves interstellar flight
2132	Allied Worlds of Earth formed
2144	Roca born
2169	Kurj born
2203	Roca marries Eldrinson Althor Valdoria (*Skyfall*)
2204	Eldrin Jarac Valdoria born; Jarac dies; Kurj becomes Imperator; Lahaylia dies
2205	Major Bhaaj hired by Majdas to find Prince Dayj ("The City of Cries")
2206	Althor Izam-Na Valdoria born
2209	Havyrl (Vyrl) Torcellei Valdoria born
2210	Sauscony (Soz) Lahaylia Valdoria born
2219	Kelricson (Kelric) Garlin Valdoria born
2223	Vyrl and Lily elope and cause a political crisis ("Stained Glass Heart")
2227	Soz starts at Dieshan Military Academy (*Schism*)
2228	First war between Skolia and Traders (*The Final Key*)
2237	Jaibriol II born
2240	Soz meets Jato Stormson ("Aurora in Four Voices")
2241	Kelric marries Admiral Corey Majda
2243	Corey assassinated ("Light and Shadow")
2258	Kelric crashes on Coba (*The Last Hawk*)

2255	Soz goes on rescue mission to New Day and meets Hypron ("Pyre for a New Day")
early 2259	Soz meets Jaibriol (*Primary Inversion*)
late 2259	Soz and Jaibriol go into exile (*The Radiant Seas*)
2260	Jaibriol III born (aka Jaibriol Qox Skolia)
2263	Rocalisa Qox Skolia born; Althor Izam-Na meets Coop ("Soul of Light")
2268	Vitar Qox Skolia born
2273	del-Kelric Qox Skolia born
2274	Radiance War begins (also called Domino War)
2276	Traders capture Eldrin. Radiance War ends; Jason Harrick crashes on the planet Thrice Named ("The Shadowed Heart")
2277–8	Kelric returns home (*Ascendant Sun*); Dehya coalesces (*Spherical Harmonic*); Kamoj and Havyrl meet (*The Quantum Rose*); Jaibriol III becomes emperor of Eube (*The Moon's Shadow*)
2279	Althor Vyan Selei born
2287	Jeremiah Coltman trapped on Coba ("A Roll of the Dice"); Jeejon dies (*The Ruby Dice*)
2288	Kelric and Jaibriol Qox sign peace treaty (*The Ruby Dice*)
2298	Jess Fernandez goes to Icelos ("Walk in Silence")
2328	Althor Vyan Selei meets Tina Santis Pulivok (*Catch the Lightning*)

The following is an excerpt from:

DARKSHIP RENEGADES

SARAH A. HOYT

Out of the Frying Pan

I was a princess from Earth and he was a rogue spaceman from a mythical world. He saved my life three times. I rescued him from a fate worse than death. We fell madly in love.

We married and lived happily ever after.

Ever after comes with an expiration date these days. We'd been married less than year when Kit got shot in the head.

It started with our return from Earth. No. Wait, what it really started with was my meeting Kit, in the powertrees which are biological solar collectors in Earth orbit. They were put up way back when bioengineered rulers governed the Earth. And ever since the turmoils sent the bioengineered rulers—you probably know them as Mules so called because, of course, they couldn't reproduce—fleeing the Earth in a ship called Je Reviens, the powertrees have been haunted by legends of darkship thieves.

Which is all anyone ever thought the darkship thieves were. After all, even if the mules really had left in an interstellar ship, and of course, there are doubts that the ship ever existed, why would they come back to harvest powerpods from the powertrees—the biological solar energy collectors in Earth orbit? And why would no one else see them but powerpod collectors?

I found out the legend was less legendary than advertised when a mutiny aboard Daddy Dearest's space cruiser sent me fleeing in a lifeboat into the powertrees. Where I met Kit who rescued me and took me to his homeworld, Eden.

Eden is where all the bioed servants of the mules stayed behind, instead of going to the stars with their masters. They had perhaps had enough of being ruled by Mules, which considering what the mules did to the Earth I couldn't really blame them for, but they also couldn't live on Earth, since this was the time of the turmoils and anyone with even a hint of bio-improvement would get killed in a horrible way.

So, they'd stayed behind in Eden, which is an asteroid they hollowed inside. Its naturally erratic orbit hides it from Earth detection. But it still needs power. And for its power it depends on darkships, which are ships built to be non reflective and pretty much undetectable, provided they harvest while the powertrees are in Earth shadow.

Each of the darkships is piloted by a Cat—no, they are wholly human, but they are bioengineered so their eyes resemble those of cats, and also so that they had very fast reflexes—and a Navigator whose memory, mechanical skill and sense of direction were bio-enhanced to make him or her ideal to help steer darkships which cannot have any of its data in a form Earth might capture if it captures a darkship.

Which until recently was very much an unfounded fear. No darkship had ever been captured... Until the Good Men of Earth realized that I must have been taken up by a darkship and started an all out search for me.

By then I was Kit's Navigator, and married to him, a combination that's not mandatory but has grown to be expected. His catlike eyes, his reflexes, had ceased to seem alien. And when I was radiation burned in an attempt to capture me, he chose to surrender to Earth to save me, instead of following procedure and killing both of us, and destroying the ship, leaving Earth nothing but a burned out hull.

It had paid off for us, we'd come back out of Earth alive and I'd been healed of the radiation burn.

The problem was the return to Eden. I had no idea how Eden would react to news that not only had we failed to self-destruct, but we'd chosen to land on Earth and seek treatment. It was probably useless to try to get forgiveness for this by explaining we'd left a good portion of the Earth in flames behind us, and probably a revolution brewing.

Eden had been colonized by refugees of a persecuted people, by people who never, ever ever again would trust any authority. I'm not saying that Eden was paranoid, because worlds can't be paranoid. But if Eden had been an individual, he'd live in a compound with motion-sensor-triggered burners at every entrance and would fingerprint his own children twice a day to make sure no one had slipped ringers in on him.

So, three months after we left Earth, we hailed Eden on approach.

Kit has said you could land on the surface of the

asteroid that contained Eden and never guess that there was a thriving civilization inside. I don't know if that's true. Never tried it. I don't like to take his word for it. He could be wrong. But I did know we could not land IN Eden unless they let us. Well, not intact. Kit had once threatened to ram his ship into the asteroid, and from the reaction, this was possible even if it would kill us. It was impossible to get into the landing tunnels—whose covers didn't even show to radar—without someone inside letting us in. Whoever said *knock and it shall be opened* had Eden in mind.

We called on the link. Kit reached for my hand and squeezed it, hard, while his other hand pressed the com link button. "Cat Christopher Bartolomeu Sinistra and Nav Athena Hera Sinistra, piloting the *Cathouse* on behalf of the Energy Board. I request permission to land."

My heart beat somewhere between my esophagus and my mouth. And don't tell me that's a physiological impossibility. I know what I felt. Given just a little more nervousness, my heart would have jumped out of my mouth and flopped around the instrument panel like a landed fish.

There was a silence from the other side, long enough for my heart to almost stop. I took a deep breath, two and told myself that if Eden didn't want us, we'd go back to Earth, or perhaps to Ultima or Proxima Thule, Eden's two water-mining colonies.

Not only was I bluffing, I knew I was bluffing. To make it elsewhere we'd need food and fuel and a world that rejected us wouldn't be likely to hand over rations and powerpods. All that kept me from shaking was the impression of Kit's mind, warm and amused.

We could mind-talk, an ability bio engineered into pilot and navigator couples in his world and engineered into me for a completely different purpose. Most often it was much like talking in voice, only we could do it privately or over a great distance. In extreme circumstances, we could connect at a deep deep level, but that wasn't sustainable. It didn't help preserve sanity not knowing which body went with your mind. But sometimes, like now, there was just the impression of feelings. And the feelings Kit was giving off were reassurance and amusement. Which meant he was lying.

But it would be a pity to waste his effort, so I managed a half smile in his general direction, as the voice of Eden's Dock Control crackled over the link: "The *Cathouse* is more than six weeks late. It has been entered in the roll of losses. Cat Christopher Sinistra and Nav Athena Sinistra are dead."

I registered the little shock I always felt at hearing Kit called by my surname. It was Eden's custom, though not mandatory, to have the husband take the wife's name.

"Not really," I cut in. I felt almost boneless with relief. I hate bureaucracy as much as anyone else, but not nearly as much as I hate exploding. That they were talking instead of burning us out of the sky was a very good sign. "Only late."

"You cannot be late. You only had fuel for a four month trip. Three weeks later you'd be out of reserves and dead. You--"

"We were down on Earth," I said.

The silence didn't last long, but it gave the impression of being a very large silence. The type of silence that could envelop and swallow a whole fleet of darkships. Then the answer came, sounding like a clap of thunder announcing the beginning of a storm. "What?" the Controller asked. "You were where?"

Kit cleared his throat. I could see him reflected in the almost completely dark screens in front of him: his eyes bioengineered for piloting in total darkness looked like cat eyes, glimmering green and very wide open, in worry. His calico-colored hair seemed vivid and garish against his suddenly colorless skin. It was an accidental mutation caused by the same virus that had given him the catlike eyes, super-human coordination and speed of movement. Without the modifications to his eyes and hair, Kit would have been a redhead, so his skin was normally that shade of pale that can turn unhealthy-looking at the slightest disturbance. Now he looked white and grey, like spoiled milk. Even if he continued to lie at me with an amused and calm mind-projection and his voice sounded firm and clear, his face gave him away, "Nav Sinistra had radiation poisoning and we stopped on Earth for regen treatment."

"You *stopped* on Earth for *treatment*?"

I swallowed hard, to prevent having to grope for my heart somewhere on the control board. "Well, it wasn't that simple, but yes," Kit said. "I'll be glad to tell you the whole story after we land."

"You'd better, *Cat*." He pronounced Kit's professional title as an insult. The term "pilot" had long since become "cat" in Eden. "And you'd better make it convincing. This is most irregular."

"Controller," I said, thinking it was time to add another consideration to his decision. "We must land. Kit's family is expecting us." Kit's birth family, the DeNovos, were socially powerful in Eden. His sister Kath would have been a force to be reckoned with in any size society. It was a good thing she'd been born in Eden. If she had been on Earth, she'd probably now be sole supreme ruler of the whole world, a feat slightly more difficult to achieve on Eden which had no rulers of any sort, much less supreme ones.

Another silence and the Dock Controller's voice sounded dour as it came back, "Navigator Sinistra, if you delayed your collection run for personal reasons, you have to know that the Energy Board will fine you for the delay in supply, and all the boards will want to interview you for potential breaches of security. Also--"

"I *know*, Controller. Now, could you give us a dock number, please? Before I go crazy and just give my Cat instructions to dash at Eden in the area of the landing control station. We earthworms are *so* temperamental"

Kit chuckled aloud, then stopped with an intake of breath. His mental impression wavered a little allowing me to see some fear beneath the amusement.

"Dock fifty five, but I want you to know that I shall have armed hushers ready and that you will be examined for any evidence of undue influence and that--"

I flicked the comlink off. A sleevelike structure extruded from Eden and Kit piloted us into it, then leaned back as dock remote controls took over the navigation. His foot skimmed along the floor next to him, flicking up the lever that turned off our artificial gravity now that we were covered by Eden's. Not that keeping it on would give us double the gs, but one could interfere with the other and cause some really interesting localized gravity effects.

It wasn't until our ship settled into one of the landing bays, that Kit released the seatbelt that criss-crossed his chest, and, without letting go of my hand, got up and said, "You know, you really shouldn't have taunted the controller."

I got up in turn. I knew. One of the first rules I'd been taught was never to pick on people. The second was probably to always be gracious.

I'd been born the only daughter Good Man Milton Alexander Sinistra, one of fifty men who controlled the near-endless land and resources of Earth. My parents, my nannies, the heads of various boarding schools, the commanders of various military academies, and the psychological medtechs that ran several rest homes, sanatoriums and mental institutions upon which Daddy Dearest had wished me, had all told me I had an aggression problem and must control my impulses.

If I had followed their instructions I wouldn't be alive now. And neither would Kit. Something Kit knew very well, which was why he put his arm around me and smiled as he shook his head.

We walked like that through two air locks, then waited while the last door cycled open, letting us see that we were in one of the cavernous, circular bays that admitted ships to Eden. An out of use bay, because there were no power pod unloading machines nearby. Instead, a large group of young men, all armed, stood in front of our ship's door all aiming their burners directly at us.

To the left side and a little behind the young men stood two older men, a dark haired one and a blond one.

The dark haired one was the dock controller. He wore the grey uniform of the position, and he had that harassed, frustrated look of someone who was sure he'd been born to better things, but who found himself confined to an inglorious desk job.

The blond was something else altogether different. To begin with he didn't wear any uniform, but a well cut black suit consisting of something much like an Elizabethan doublet and leg-outlining pants, tailored to make the wearer look good, whether he did so when naked or not. The fabric shimmered with the dull shine of real silk and conveyed an unavoidable sense of wealth and sensuousness. The face, above the suit, was sharp and vaguely threatening. He looked like a young Julius Caesar or at least a Julius Caesar from a world where people didn't lose their hair unless they chose to.

It was the blond man who spoke. His words had far more force than if they'd been spoken by a mere bureaucrat. "Cat Christopher Bartolomeu Sinistra," he said, each syllable dropped in place like an essential part of exacting machinery. "You are under arrest for treason against Eden."

—end excerpt—

PRAISE FOR LOIS McMASTER BUJOLD

What the critics say:

The Warrior's Apprentice: "Now here's a fun romp through the spaceways—not so much a space opera as space ballet… It has all the 'right stuff.' A lot of thought and thoughtfulness stand behind the all-too-human characters. Enjoy this one, and look forward to the next."
—Dean Lambe, *SF Reviews*

"The pace is breathless, the characterization thoughtful and emotionally powerful, and the author's narrative technique and command of language compelling. Highly recommended." —*Booklist*

Brothers in Arms: "…she gives it a genuine depth of character, while reveling in the wild turnings of her tale… Bujold is as audacious as her favorite hero, and as brilliantly (if sneakily) successful."
—*Locus*

"Miles Vorkosigan is such a great character that I'll read anything Lois wants to write about him… a book to re-read on cold rainy days." —Robert Coulson, *Comics Buyers Guide*

Borders of Infinity: "Bujold's series hero Miles Vokosigan may be a lord by birth and an admiral by rank, but a bone disease that has left him hobbled and in frequent pain has sensitized him to the suffering of outcasts in her very hierarchical era…. Playing off of Miles's reserve and cleverness, Bujold draws outrageous and outlandish foils to color her high-minded adventures." —*Publishers Weekly*

Falling Free: "In *Falling Free* Lois McMaster Bujold has written her fourth straight superb novel…. How to break down a talent like Bujold's into analyzable components? Best not to try. Best to say: 'Read, or you will be missing something extraordinary.'"
—Roland Green, *Chicago Sun-Times*

The Vor Game: "The chronicles of Miles Vokosigan are far too witty to be literary junk food, but they rouse the kind of craving that makes popcorn magically vanish during a double feature."
—Faren Miller, *Locus*

MORE PRAISE FOR LOIS McMASTER BUJOLD

What the readers say:

"My copy of *Shards of Honor* is falling apart I've reread it so often.... I'll read whatever you write. You've certainly proved yourself a grand storyteller.

—Lisa Kolbe, Colorado Springs, CO

"I experience the stories of Miles Vorkosigan as almost viscerally uplifting... But certainly, even the weightiest theme would have less impact than a cinder on snow were it not for a rousing good story, and good story-telling with it. This is the second thing I want to thank you for... I suppose if you boiled down all I've said to its simplest expression, it would be that I immensely enjoy and admire your work. I submit that, as literature, your work raises the overall level of the science fiction genre, and spiritually, you work cannot avoid positively influencing all who read it."

—Glen Stonebreaker, Gaithersburg, MD

"'The Mountains of Mourning' [in *Borders of Infinity*] was one of the best-crafted, and simply best, works I'd ever read. When I finished it, I immediately turned back to the beginning and read it again, and I can't remember the last time I did that."

—Betsy Bizot, Lisle, IL

"I can only hope that you will continue to write, so that I can continue to read (and of course buy) your books, for they make me laugh and cry and think ... rare indeed."

—Steven Knott, Major, USAF

What do you say?

Cordelia's Honor
pb • 0-671-57828-6 • $7.99
Contains *Shards of Honor* and Hugo-award winner *Barrayar* in one volume.

Young Miles
trade pb • 0-671-87782-8 • $17.00
pb • 0-7434-3616-4 • $7.99
Contains *The Warrior's Apprentice*, Hugo-award winner *The Vor Game*, and Hugo-award winner "The Mountains of Mourning" in one volume.

Cetaganda
0-671-87744-5 • $7.99

Miles, Mystery and Mayhem
pb • 0-7434-3618-0 • $7.99
Contains *Cetaganda, Ethan of Athos* and "Labyrinth" in one volume.

Brothers in Arms
pb • 1-4165-5544-7 • $7.99

Miles Errant
trade pb • 0-7434-3558-3 • $15.00
Contains "The Borders of Infinity," *Brothers in Arms* and *Mirror Dance* in one volume.

Mirror Dance
pb • 0-671-87646-5 • $7.99

Memory
pb • 0-671-87845-X • $7.99

Miles in Love

hc • 1-4165-5522-6 • $19.00
trade pb • 1-4165-5547-1 • $14.00
Contains *Komarr, A Civil Campaign* and "A Winterfair Gift" in one volume.

Komarr

hc • 0-671-87877-8 • $22.00
pb • 0-671-57808-1 • $7.99

A Civil Campaign

hc • 0-671-57827-8 • $24.00
pb • 0-671-57885-5 • $7.99

Miles, Mutants & Microbes

hc • 1-4165-2141-0 • $18.00
pb • 1-4165-5600-1 • $7.99
Contains *Falling Free* "Labyrinth", and *Diplomatic Immunity* in one volume.

Diplomatic Immunity

hc • 0-7434-3533-8 • $25.00
pb • 0-7434-3612-1 • $7.99

Cryoburn

hc • 978-1-4391-3394-1 • $25.00

Falling Free

pb • 1-4165-5546-3 • $7.99